STARCHILD

THE LONG WAY HOME

Author with Space Shuttle Enterprise

STARCHILD

The Long Way Home

by Marvin Arnold

COLLECTORS EDITION

There were giants in those days, when the sons of God came unto the daughters of men and they bore them children. These were the mighty men of old, the men of renown and legend . . . Genesis 6:4

The Military Industrial Complex

STARCHILD
   A novel by Marvin Arnold

Samco Publishing
www. Storydomain .com

© 2003, 2012...all rights reserved
Published in the United States of America

Based on an original screenplay
"Starchild II" by Marvin Arnold
WGA 1026927

No part of this book may be reproduced, stored in
a retrieval system or transmitted by any means
without the written permission of the author.

First draft - 09/01/2012
First printing - 12/03/18
ISBN-13:978-0615711362
ISBN-10:0615711367

Samco Publishing   CreateSpace   Amazon Books

Flying Saucers Are Real

**Starchild the novel is
Dedicated to the memory of**

Thomas Wolfe
1900-1938 You Can't Go Home Again

Ray Bradbury
1920-2012 The Martian Chronicles

Philip K Dick
1928-1982 Blade Runner

***

In a desert land far away lived a young prince. One morning he went to the café in the market for food and drink.

To his surprise, he saw Death seated at one of the tables across the room.

When Death looked up at him, the young prince knew that Death must surely have come for him.

The young prince bounded out the door, mounted his white stallion and rode as fast as he could out into the desert… he road all morning, all afternoon and most of the night.

Finally exhausted, the young prince dismounted, dropped the reins of his steed and stumbled on into the night.

He came upon an oasis and there, by the moonlight, he saw Death waiting for him.

The young prince called out to Death, "But I saw you in the market place only this morning."

"Yes." Death replied, "Imagine my surprise! For, I have always known that I would come for you here." Author Unknown

Quantum Mathematics

STARCHILD THE NOVEL

XFV-12A Tethered Test

Chapter One – Dietrich Space Center

It is always darkest before the dawn was never truer than on this damp and dreary early morning. A chorus of croaking frogs and chirping crickets break the otherwise eerie silence.

Nearby, a large open marshland extends to the shoreline of an inland waterway a half a kilometer away. At the water's edge, the ocean waves break against a white sandy beach and the phosphorous in the water creates a dull glow on the horizon.

A massive rocket in the foreground stands on a gantry ready for launch. A thick mist from the evaporating frost of its fuel tanks rises like heavier things do not. The glow of a hundred floodlights illuminate the towering rocket as the mist drifts away in the darkness blocking out any visible stars in the sky above.

Suddenly, the launch pad is engulfed in a ball of flames as though the rocket had exploded. Instead of breaking into its million component parts, it rises like a phoenix from the flames.

The giant rocket ascends slowly skyward accelerating geometrically and lighting the marshland with the glow of mid-day. The thundering thump of the powerful booster engines pound the air.

The dark sky quickly swallows up the rocket and only the bright white ball of the engine's flame can be seen as it climbs steadily into the stratosphere.

The second stage booster flashes briefly against the dark sky and fades. The final stage of the rocket fires and separates. Now only a speck in the sky and disappears out of site. On the far horizon, the coming dawn is slowly turning the sky a lighter shade of gray.

An hour or so passes and the native sounds of the marshland have returned. A concrete bunker is now visible in the morning light. A steel door at the side of the bunker opens with a clank exposing the brightly lit control room inside.

The figure of a tall, slender, middle-aged man exits the bunker allowing the door to close slowly behind him and shuts with a clank. The man fumbles in his jacket pocket for something as he walks slowly across the small unlit parking area to where a half dozen or so vehicles are parked.

Noah Langston, scientist and lead researcher on a hyper-light development project, has just observed the first rocket launch with the prototype of the newly completed hyper-light Cyclatron device onboard.

Noah's wide, slightly graying mustache and wrinkled sport jacket, along with his demeanor, are reminiscent of a quintessential college professor. This and the fact that years ago he used to teach physics at a nearby university lead to the nickname "Professor" for the distinguished Doctor Noah Langston. The Professor was the name by which almost everyone called him behind his back, but Noah preferred not to be addressed as that in person.

Noah approaches a silver ultra-modern, sports coupe on the right-hand driver's side and pushes the button on the door. The door opens vertically and the vehicle starts with a low humming sound.

His lean stature does not allow him any extra room to fit in the small coupe, but he manages to close the door. Noah's car pulls away onto a narrow blacktop road that runs along the coastline. The daylight brightens the morning sky and the low lying ground fog begins to burn off as his car progresses up the coastal highway.

***

It is going to be another sweltering hot day here at the space research facility.

A gun-metal-gray hovercraft circles not too high overhead along the shoreline and turns to follow Noah's car as it speeds along.

Inside the hovercraft are two crewmen in black uniforms with reverse-swastika insignias on their high-neck collar blouses. Their shiny black flight helmets with heavily tinted visors obscure their faces. They are talking over the intercom.

"Is that him?" the pilot asks.

"Affirmative, I have a positive ID on the infrared scanner," replies the electronic systems operator."

The pilot keys his mike to transmit, "Control, this is H-one-nine. We have positive contact and are tracking the Professor's car at this time. He appears to be proceeding directly to headquarters at the main space center complex."

"Maintain surveillance," is the mundane reply that comes back to the pilot over his radio receiver.

The systems operator comments to the pilot, "Why do you think they want us to shadow the Professor?"

"Beats me," the pilot replies, "We're paid to fly this thing. They don't pay us to think."

***

Approaching the main space center complex, Noah's car passes several direction signs that contain backward and indistinguishable lettering.

The characters bear some similarity to the Russian alphabet, but they are actually the characters of the thirty-two-letter Tropian alphabet.

Tropia's life forms and technology have developed nearly identical to that of present day Earth except they are slightly more advanced.

Tropia is an Earth-like planet in a distant arm of the Milky Way galaxy millions of light-years from Earth's solar system. The major difference being the planet Tropia is eons out of sync with Earth on the universal space-time continuum.

***

Noah's car approaches a security gate. A space center security guard, in a dungaree uniform made of black Kevlar with an automatic rifle on his shoulder, recognizes Noah and waves him through.

Surprisingly, the space center facility resembles a modern-day NASA facility on the planet Earth,

Noah pulls his car into a reserve parking space out front of the ultra-modern silver and glass office structure. The large silver letters over the front entrance identifies it as the Dietrich Air and Space Research Center.

Several television station remote microwave broadcast trucks are assembled in front of the building. It is now clear to Noah the he will not be presenting the results of this morning's test to a small group of fellow scientists and staff as he had expected.

Apparently, the Director of the space center has called a press conference and invited dignitaries to attend; most likely all now assembled in the center's lecture hall.

Noah exits his car and glances skyward to watch the hovercraft, that has been following him, peel off and takes up a heading back towards the nearby military air base that adjoins the space center complex.

Noah enters the main entrance of the building through the large glass double-doors and is met by a crowd of reporters and cameramen.

"Professor, Professor Langston! Can you answer a few questions for us?" a lady reporter hollers trying to get Noah's attention.

Noah smiles politely as he makes his way through the crush of media people.

"Professor Langston is it true that the rocket just launched contains one of the new Cyclatron devices?" another reporter asks.

Noah ignores the reporters and ducks once to keep from getting hit in the head by one of the cameras pushed in his face.

A middle-aged, slightly overweight, but very attractive, dark-haired lady meets Noah at the door of the large lecture hall. She smiles as she hands him a folded-up piece of paper.

Noah knows by the smile on the face of his long-time friend and associate, Doctor Aramora, that the results of the test report are good.

"Three microseconds, ten light years!" she says to him.

"Thanks, Dusty," Noah replies and takes the folded flight test report paper she has handed him and stuffs it in his jacket pocket.

Desdemona Aramora, called Dusty by all who know her, is a medical doctor and research biologist at the space center.

Dusty falls in behind Noah as he enters the crowded lecture hall and takes a seat in the front row marked off with a 'Staff-Only' sign.

The room quiets as reporters and guests take a seat. Camera operators and sound technicians man their equipment.

Noah steps onto a platform stage where a podium and half dozen microphones have been set up and takes one of the seats arranged in a semi-circle behind the podium. Seated behind the podium with Noah are four men and one woman.

The woman and two of the men are wearing the black uniforms of the Reichs Guard. One is a high-ranking officer. On their collars are the same reverse swastika insignias as were on the uniforms of the pilot and crewman in the hovercraft.

The other two men seated behind the podium are civilians. The man wearing a sky-blue jumpsuit is Captain Jack Harkins. Jack is a well-known astronaut who made early space fights to both of Tropia's moons and explored Tropia's nearest small planet; the barren and desolate red planet DioGurr.

The other man wearing a white shirt, tie and dark trousers is Ph.D. physicist, Samuel Conner, a brilliant middle-age designer and the lead engineer on several Low Orbiter Craft project, LOC for short. The newest LOC craft was recently named the Starchild and designated the SC-1. Both Jack and Sam are close friends and associates of Noah.

The space center director, Doctor Alfred Dietrich, steps to the podium. Director Dietrich's father was one of the founders of the Space Research Center. He is an esteemed scientist in his own right and well-liked by all who know and work with him.

"Ladies and gentlemen, members of the press and distinguished guests," Dietrich says, turning slightly to acknowledge the military officers seated behind him, you have been invited here today to hear an announcement of a breakthrough in space exploration. So may I introduce Doctor Noah Langston, theoretical physicist and developer of the Cyclatron hyper-light device… Doctor Langston."

Noah approaches the podium and looks over the large group of attendees. He removes the folded-up flight test report from his jacket pocket and slowly puts on a pair of reading glasses. This is his thinking time.

He leans forward to speak into the covey of microphones mounted on the podium and says, "I don't really need these, but I've been told they make me look distinguished."

Subdued, light-hearted laughter drifts across the large conference room.

Noah reads from the paper, "Two point eight-five minus zero, constant to the sixth power and accelerating geometrically."

Noah pauses, removes his reading glasses and places them in his shirt pocket.

He speaks slowly and deliberately, "I know this data readout does not mean much to most of you here, but simply stated it means that a paradigm shift occurred early this morning in the world of science. At zero-six-hundred hours this morning, we were able to successfully achieve space flight at speeds in excess of the universal constant; the speed-of-light… And I believe it is the long sought after solution to intragalactic space travel."

Gasps from those in the audience who understand the announcement and its significance, plus muffled questioning from the many that do not, are heard throughout the room.

Several photographers and cameramen move to take close-up photographs of Noah at the podium.

He ignores the photographers and news people attempting to ask questions.

Noah continues, "On top of the rocket launched earlier this morning was a nosecone which housed the first operational Cyclatron device. The rocket's nosecone was inserted into a geosynchronous orbit from where the test was initiated. When the Cyclatron was activated, the nosecone vanished from orbit for six-microseconds or about the time it takes light to travel two kilometers."

Undiscernible exclamations are heard across the room. Noah glances up momentarily, but continues, "For the nosecone to travel to the celestial point in space preset in the device, it would have had to have done so at a speed equal-to-or- greater-than three times the speed-of-light."

"Why must it be launch from space?" a reporter in the front of the room rises to his feet hollers out without being called on.

With elfish sarcasm in the tone of his voice, Noah says, "I didn't know we had already moved to the question and answer phase of our announcement, but then again why not... The Cyclatron has a nuclear core and we actually did not know what might go wrong if it were launched in Tropia's industrially polluted atmosphere. It is possible the device might very well have burned up during initial acceleration."

"It all sounds like science fiction to me!" the somewhat embarrassed reporter says as he sits back down.

Noah continues, "Yes it does. Science fiction writers have long theorized the possibility of space travel in excess of the speed-of-light. It has been referred to as folding space, warp speed, holes in space, stargates and many other names. I prefer the term hyper-light speed. Based on the Laws of Relativity, most scientists have never actually believed it to be achievable."

Someone yells out from the back of the room. "Some little green spacemen land here and whisper the secret formula to light-speed in your ear, Professor?"

Several in the room laugh and Noah smiles.

"Not that I know of," Noah says, reaching for the flight test report from his jacket pocket, "However, the figures in this report, which I read from, are the actual telemetry from the accelerated nosecone. It shows that the device did momentarily exceed the speed-of-light."

Noah places the printout face down on the podium, takes out his writing pen to jot down a couple of notes as a dozen reporters jump to their feet simultaneously yelling out questions.

"Please, one at a time!" Noah says pointing to one of the reporters, "You, you there, go ahead."

The reporter Noah pointed to asks, "How is it that this device is able to defy the E equals M times C squared equation that physicists have always held to be so valid?"

Noah replies, "Approaching or exceeding the speed-of-light or the maximum known velocity, as it is sometimes referred to, seemed to be most restricted by the mass factor. That is to say that once an object begins to increase in mass it can no longer accelerate. We therefore began by addressing how best to overcome that part of the equation… and I believe we've succeeded."

"Follow up question, Professor," the reporter asks over several other reporters trying to ask their questions.

"Yes, go ahead."

"How exactly is it that the device can overcome the mass of a spacecraft?"

"Through a process we refer to as angular momentum and quantum coupling the device re-establishes an object's location in time and space back to zero velocity relative to the object's current position in the universal space-time continuum each time it accelerates and is its own singularity, so to speak."

Someone yells out, "Thought you said, 'simply' Professor!" and light hearted laughter fills the room.

Noah says, "I did say that, didn't I? Again, the Cyclatron simply cycles. Think of it as railway cars that jerk on each other in a chain reaction to the locomotive as the train first pulls away from a standing stop; except in this case, it's the same railway car every time."

"With all due respect, Professor," the reporter critiques as he takes his seat, "That sounds like scientific double-speak."

"It probably is," Noah replies, "The breakthrough came when we first began to understand quantum particles and that they were both a particle and a wave at the same time. Our research then pointed to quantum mechanics and the manipulation of quantum particles as the solution."

A distinguished gray-haired reporter holding a note pad rises to his feet and says, "Quantum mechanics relies heavily upon randomness and chaos in the manipulation of quantum particles does it not? The reporter looks down to read from his notes and says, "I believe you have stated on several occasions that, 'The creator god does not shoot craps with the universe' isn't that correct?"

"That's correct and yes, I have said that on several occasions," Noah replies.

"Then are these not irreconcilable contradictions?" the reporter asks.

"For our purposes they are not," Noah says, "Quantum entanglement plays a critical role in the ability of the Cyclatron to function. However, quantum particles act very much like bits in the machine language of a computer, that is to say that they are either on or off. In the case of quarks they either spin left or spin right, which is as easily recognizable as on or off. We simply designed a control system to cascade in response to one or the other of those two states."

"So how do you stop the damn thing?" someone yells out from the back of the room and the crowd laughs.

"Actually, the answer to this one is actually very simple," and to make light of the way the person had asked his question, Noah raises his voice slightly and says, "You turn the damn thing off!"

Once again, laughter echoes across the room.

Noah points to the lady reporter who attempted to stop him in the hallway, "You had a question earlier?"

"Yes, but I have a different one now. It occurs to me that you had no way of knowing this morning where or what speed the device had traveled once it was several light years away. Wouldn't it take several years for the data transmission to return here?

"Very astute of you to pick up on that… Actually, the Cyclatron itself returned with the data. It took a star fix at the point where it reversed course and returned to its point of origin. Based on the M-map of the universe, we were able to compare that fix to our own currently known position in the universe and very accurately determine the distance traveled."

The lady reporter seems surprised by Noah's quick answer and stammers to ask her next question. Noah takes the opportunity to point to a young man who has been waiting patiently and says, "Yes, go ahead."

The young man asks, "How soon will a spacecraft utilizing the Cyclatron be operational and what problems do you expect to encounter with hyper-light travel?"

"As always the pace of any development project depends on the funding available," Noah explains, "Regarding problems yet to be overcome, there are some navigational and control issues we haven't yet solved, but they're mostly minor and I anticipate will overcome them in short order."

The remaining reporters and interested researchers have gathered now at the front of the conference room directly in front of the podium, even filling the empty seats marked for staff. Other invited guests have either left or broken into small groups at the back of the room and are discussing what has just been announced.

A reporter, a nice looking young man who had previously been unable to ask his question, asks, "If time slows approaching the speed-of-light, does it stop at the light-speed and if so then by exceeding the speed-of-light, why wouldn't we then expect time to go backwards from that point in time?"

Noah recognizes the young man asking the questions and says, "I believe you were in one of my physics classes a few years ago."

"Yes Sir," the young reporter replies smiling."

Noah says jokingly, "Based on what I remember of your grades, I am glad to see you've found work as a journalist."

The others grouped around laugh goodheartedly at the young man's expense.

Noah says thoughtfully, "No, I think not. It doesn't seem conceivable to me that one would be able to return to the past and murder their own grandfather before they were born. Whoever or whatever created this universe seems to have designed it so that backward travel through time would not be possible."

The young man moves quickly to ask a follow-up question and says, "I recall in astrophysics that the lesson stated at the edge of the universe seems to be moving away at speeds in excess of the universal constant, the speed-of-light. Is that still the currently held belief?"

Noah replies, "Yes, and if you all have been playing 'let's stump the professor' you win on that one because I don't understand it any more than the rest of the experts."

Noah takes a deep breath and says wearily, "Okay, last question."

The lady reporter who had forgotten her question earlier asks, "What affect do you anticipate hyper-light speeds having on the space travelers themselves?"

"We don't anticipate seeing anything different from what we have already experienced at partial light-speeds. Time throughout the universe is relative to speed and direction. A person departing our planet at hyper-light-speeds will age only a few years while here on the planet thousands of years or even millenniums will pass. A preeminent novelist once wrote a story entitled, 'You can't go home...' and that seems to be no truer than in this case. What is one man's future is another man's past in the universe, but that's philosophy, not science!"

Noah stuffs the now wrinkled flight-test report in his jacket pocket and says, "Thank you all for coming. You've been a wonderful audience,"

He steps back from the podium to return to the group seated in the semi-circle of chairs.

"What did you mean when…" a reporter yells as other reporters yell questions from the back of the room.

The reporters' questions go unanswered by Noah who takes his seat back behind the podium.

The space center director returns to the podium, "This will conclude our press conference. Copies of a printed press release will be available at the public relations office within the hour. You're welcome to pick one up. Thank you for coming."

The noise level in the room rises as conversations begin. Several reporters address questions to the director, but are ignored.

"Again, thank you for coming," the director says speaking into the microphones.

The director turns to Noah and the two civilians, Sam Conner and Jack Harkins, behind him and says, "Noah, you Jack and Sam, I need to see you in my office right now! Oh and Noah, ask Dusty to join us."

"Yes, Sir," Noah says, "We're coming."

Noah motions for Dusty to come with them and she joins Noah and the others as they exit a door behind the stage into a private corridor.

In the corridor, Noah asks Jack, "Who were those military officers seated with you? I don't think I've ever seen those three here before."

Jack replies with a somewhat disgusted tone in his voice saying, "A request or should I say orders came down directly from the Triad for me to show them around the facility. I'll fill you in later."

***

Chapter Two – The Triad

The planet Tropia is slightly larger in mass than Earth making its gravity about 1.05 that of Earth's gravity field. The oceans on Tropia are about the same size as Earth's oceans, but Tropia has slightly more land mass.

There are three major continents on Tropia with three separate governments. They are referred to simply as the Eastern, Western and Southern powers. Until most of the territorial disputes were finally settled, the three powers had been at war for the better part of two centuries. Currently, the territories remain deadlocked in a cold war.

Each government has its own senate, its own political structure, army and police. All decisions arriving from disputes, between the three powers, rest within the preview of the Triad. The Triad is a body of nine men and women. Three each are elected or appointed for life from each of three continental governments.

The powers of the Triad are limited mainly to arbitration, but it also oversees several intercontinental projects; one being environmental control which has failed miserably. However, there has not been a war on Tropia since the Triad was created six decades ago.

For the most part, the Triad's rulings are honored and respected by the three continental governments. At best, it barely works most of the time and right now the Triad is facing a major crisis on how to deal with the several doomsday satellites presently in geosynchronous orbit around the planet.

The Space Research Center is supported and contributed to by all three governments. As a result, all the technology developed at the Center must be shared equally among the three governments.

The militaries of all three governments have vied for some time to get control of the Space Center and its projects. So far, all attempts to do so have been held off and this is largely due to the firm-handed control of the center's director, Doctor Alfred Dietrich.

***

At a secure door in the hall, with the four in toe, the director places his hand on an ID pad. The door to a large, brightly lit office opens where a half-dozen clerical personnel are seated at widely separated desks.

The room is plushly carpeted and the desks and furnishings are of a very expensive quality. One or two workers glance up, but most pay no attention to the four following the director as he crosses the room to his private office.

"We're not to be disturbed," the director says to an attractive middle-aged secretary as he passes her desk and enters his expansive private office.

The thick glass door to the outer office closes automatically and the routine office noise is muffled.

The entire wall of one side of the office is clear glass facing onto a large plaza.

The panoramic view out the large office window looks onto a massive well-manicured lawn. On the grounds of the plaza are numerous chrome and marble structures. The largest of these is a sculpture of a chrome winged lady mounted atop a gigantic marble pedestal.

The director is always pleased to explain to anyone who asks that the structures are a modern Stonehenge from which various celestial predictions can be obtained; that is if you know or can figure out the key.

He is also quick to add that the winged lady statute is only there because he just likes her. She has nothing to do with the key to the celestial sightings.

The director takes a seat behind his desk and pushes a button on his desk causing the light-sensitive transparent glass wall to turn opaque.

The small gathering, accustomed to being called to meetings in this room, take their customary seats in the director's office.

"What the heck was all that stuff back there about 'you can't go home again,' anyway?" the director asks Noah who is slouched down in a chair and was gazing out the window until the director closed it, "Giving up science to become a philosopher are you?"

Dusty giggles. Jack and Sam both laugh out loud.

Noah just smiles good-naturedly as he straightens up in his chair to take an old wooden pipe from his jacket pocket and packs it with fresh tobacco.

"No smoking in here! You know the rules, Noah." Noah ignores the director's comment and lights his pipe.

Noah lays the burned out wooden match in nearby antique china dish, for lack of an ashtray and says, "Go on, Al, what's on your mind? You have our undivided attention."

Alfred Dietrich and Noah had been on a first name basis since graduate school and again working together as young engineers at the Tiarell Corporation. Few, but Noah, ever dared to address the director as Al or for that matter by his first name.

The director says, "Jack and Sam had the pleasure of meeting our three visiting military officers earlier this morning. Noah, you and Dusty will have the pleasure tomorrow evening. I'm having a fancy dress celebration tomorrow evening at my estate. I'm calling it a Cyclatron Gala. It will in honor of you, Noah and your recent successes with the hyper-light theory. So please try to be there on time and have all your guys there."

"I'm not a guy!" Dusty quips in her low sultry voice, "Just in case you haven't noticed lately, Sir."

Letting Dusty's comment pass, the director says, "The senior officer is General Hinkle and the other two are his administrative assistants, a Commander Von Dormer and the female is Lieutenant Marilyn something-or-other."

"Probably the general's bimbo," Jack remarks sarcastically.

"I don't know she strikes me as more the AC DC type," Dusty comments.

"I think you're probably both right," Noah interjects.

Sam asks, "Why is the military interested in us all of a sudden? Most of the stuff we're doing is pure research. Except for Noah's recent success, ninety percent of our projects don't even have a practical application."

The director touches his index finger momentarily to his lips and cuts his eyes slightly. Nothing further needed to be indicated, as his three guests pick up on the fact the director is indicating he suspects his office is being bugged and small talk is okay, but politics are off limits.

***

Indeed, not far away in the back of a large military tractor-trailer truck, two technicians in Reichs Guard uniforms sit in front of an array of audio and video monitoring devices recording conversations taking place in several locations throughout the complex. The director's office has been added to those being monitored.

"Got a feeling those people know that room is bugged," one monitoring technicians says to the other.

"You think we ought to tell the general they suspect they are being bugged?" the other technician asks.

"Naw, the higher-ups will have to figure it out for themselves. Our job is just to record all this bullshit."

***

Back in the director's office, the director goes on to explain, "Actually, the military officers are not here because of the Cyclatron project, although I suspect they will have a strong interest after today's announcement. As you know, Jack will be flight-testing the new SC-1 sometime in the next few days and that's primarily the reason for their visit."

Noah asks, "Is this civil version of Starfighter going to perform as well as all the hype I've been hearing?"

Sam replies, "Yes, in fact, all of the preliminary test data indicate that the SC-1will be capable of achieving orbital altitudes from a runway takeoff. The craft has two pairs of engines, conventional and the newly developed scram engines and yes, they really are that powerful."

"All this at a tenth of the cost of a rocket launched high orbital spacecraft," the director adds and then asks, "Are we on schedule for actual flight?"

"We're A-Okay for first flight," Jack replies. "The military version of our craft can deliver a unit of Space Marines or EVA a crew of technicians to a satellite and then stand guard to defend the satellite or space station. The way Sam and I have it figured, the SC-1 will outperform any shuttle craft in service today."

This brief exchange between Noah, Sam and Jack is solely for the benefit of the director. Noah had been involved in the project since its inception and followed the project almost daily through to its completion.

Dusty asks the director, "Sir, what's the story on this actress rumored to be coming to dedicate the SC-1?"

"Yes, who exactly is she, Sir?" Sam says echoing Dusty's question.

The director answers, "She's the granddaughter of old man Fairchild, the founder of the aircraft company that built some of the world's most notable aircraft."

Dusty says, "Okay, I know who she is now. Her name is Gloria Fairchild. She fancies herself a movie star, but she's only a minor actor. I'll bet her agent sees this as an opportunity for some free publicity."

"Yes, Gloria Fairchild, that's her name," the director says, "I understand she has thought up some name for the SC-1 and plans to christen the craft with that name. It really doesn't make any difference to me what she calls it. How about you, Jack, what would you name the craft?"

Jack replies, "Don't matter much to me either. Most of the time the pilots give the craft a nickname and for better or worse, that's the name that usually sticks, not the one the manufacture hangs on it. For what it's worth, I learned to fly in an early Fairchild trainer and the Fairchild engineering department was one of the first to propose a Starfighter that could reach orbit."

Sam asks the director, "Sir, what are all these rumors the press has picked up on about a decaying doomsday satellite? Do you have any information you can share on the subject?"

By the expression on the director's face, it appears he would rather not have to discuss the matter, but after some hesitation he replies, "There's very little unclassified information available, but I believe they are referring to the nuclear device on several, so called, doomsday satellites that were placed in orbit towards the end of the last world war, which was before the Western and Eastern powers signed the current peace treaty."

"Yeah, signed the damn treaty after a half million good soldiers and airmen lost their lives," Jack mumbles.

Sam says, "I haven't heard anything about this before now," and then Sam asks, "So why don't they just shoot the damn thing down with a missile and be done with the problem all together?"

"Not that simple," the director replies, "The thing has an automatic self-defense mechanism built-in. It can shoot down a missile or a manned craft. If anything succeeds in getting too close, as a final defense it will detonate with unknown consequences."

"How do we even know this is valid information and it's not just a rumor?" Jack questions.

The director confides, "I had one of our departments track the satellite for a few days and it appears that its orbit is decaying. My guess is that someone fears it could accidently detonate re-entering Tropia's atmosphere."

Sam seems overly concerned and says, "With all the pollution in our atmosphere, a nuclear air burst... well I'd rather not say until I've done some more checking."

"Sounds like somebody's got a real problem on their hands," Noah says rising to his feet.

Sam says, "Yeah, maybe that somebody is all of us."

Noah has remained silent during most of the conversation on the doomsday device primarily because he and several scientists from the other two Triads have been in communication regarding the problem. They have not been able to come up with a workable solution yet.

Dusty says, "Noah, you got a full agenda of meetings tomorrow and remember you and your staff are all invited to the director's wing-ding tomorrow evening."

The director says, "Yes and it's in your honor, Noah! I know it's a lot to ask, but please be on your best behavior and try to piss-off as few people as possible."

Noah says, "Okay, see you tomorrow evening, Al. What time?"

The director replies, "Around seventeen hundred hours and don't eat before you all come. I'm spending a big chunk of our entertainment budget on catering and an open bar. I really want everyone to have a good time."

The director, Sam, Jack and Dusty all offer their personal congratulations to Noah for his recent achievement before leaving the director's office.

***

In the hallway leaving the director's office, Noah asks Dusty, "Where you parked?"

"In the back parking lot," Dusty replies. "You do want to avoid that bunch of reporters, don't you?"

"You bet. I'll leave my car out front and maybe they'll think I'm still here. You don't mind dropping me at my apartment, do you? If you want to come in, I'll fix you breakfast."

"Knowing you, you sly old fox, you've got more on your mind than breakfast," Dusty says and laughs throwing her head back and shaking her long, dark brunette hair, "Why don't we just go to my place? It's closer."

Noah smiles and says, "Thought you'd never ask.

Dusty smiles back as she leans against him and takes his arm as they walk.

They disappeared down the long dark hallway. Daylight illuminates the hallway for a moment as they go out the exit and the heavy metal door slams shut behind them.

***

Chapter Three – Cyclatron Gala

The following evening, at the reception to celebrate Professor Langston's recent success, forty or so guests arrive at the director's estate. The ladies are adorned in the latest fashion hairstyles and evening dresses, the gentlemen are in tuxedos or formal military uniforms.

A large den opens onto a cabaña and pool at the rear of the estate. Several small groups of guests mill around the pool and equal numbers languish in the large, lavishly furnished den.

Waiters in white jackets move among the guests serving an assortment of mixed drinks from trays.

As Dusty and Noah enter the den area, Jack hollers and waves from across the room, "Over here."

Dusty lifts a mixed drink from one of the waiters' trays as she and Noah work their way across the room pausing briefly several times to speak with an acquaintance or well-wisher.

Jack, Sam and Sam's wife Janet are seated on a brown leather couch in a conversation-pit in front of a massive stone fireplace with a low flickering fire. Janet Conner, a tall slender woman, is dressed in a black off-the-shoulder gown. She sits quietly seemingly preoccupied.

Dusty greets her, "Good evening, Janet."

Janet nods politely and forces a smile.

Sam rises for Dusty and says to Noah, "We were just discussing that decaying satellite situation."

Noah and Dusty take a seat on an adjoining couch behind the large coffee table in front of the fireplace.

"Yes, we listened to a panel discussion about it on one of the national radio broadcasts driving over here," Noah replies. "Have you checked any of this out, Sam?"

"Sorry you asked," Sam says glancing around where they are seated checking to see who might overhear what he was about to say, "Yes, this afternoon I accessed some of our old classified data files and discovered…"

Janet, obviously bored with the conversation, catches sight of someone she had been watching for and says, "If you all will excuse me," as she rises to leave the company of the small group.

"Well go on, Sam, spit it out!" Dusty says. "What did you find out?"

Sam leans forward to the edge of the couch and says, "It's not good! In fact, the media is soft-pedaling the whole thing, more than likely to keep it from being censored. It seems the device is much worse than Dietrich suspected. It was designed to create a nuclear chain reaction and now they're faced with the real possibility that the thing might go off on re-entry."

Noah glances over at Jack's concerned expression as he says, "So? A nuclear burn is only proportional to the amount of fuel onboard. How big can the thing be?"

Jack had heard the results of Sam's investigation earlier that day and directs his comment to Sam saying, "I think Noah wasn't paying close attention. Try him again."

Sam speaks slowly, "I said chain reaction, Noah, not just a reaction."

"You're not talking about an inert gas reaction are you?" Noah asks sarcastically. "That's just a theory. The only person I've ever known to suggest the possibility of that even working was 'ol Bernstein, a kooky physics instructor Alfred and I had back in graduate school!"

"Yes and I also recall you telling me he claimed to have figured it out," Sam replies.

"Next, you're going to tell me that Bernstein's name was on some of the documentation you researched today?"

"That's exactly what I'm telling you!"

Noah was notorious among his close associates for his dry sense of humor, which often manifested itself in scientific double-speak. He once filled out a supply requisition for a powered milling machine to grind quarter inch wood shafts to a conical point. When asked by the supply clerk what it looked like, he replied, "Kind of like an electric pencil sharpener."

But at this moment, Noah's quick mind had gone completely blank. He looks over at Dusty expecting her to have some sort of a knee-jerk comment.

Dusty says nothing. She leans forward and sets the drink she was holding on the coffee table in front of her. Her hand is shaking.

The two visiting military officers had been working their way across the room towards Noah.

As they approach, Noah pretends not to notice them and says to Sam and Jack, "Seems to me that the bio-linier modulator on the secondary power supply unit warrants rechecking before the test flight. What do you all think?"

Sam and Jack, knowing there was no such component on the SC-1, pick up on the fact that Noah is suggesting their ad hoc meeting be concluded.

"I'll have it checked first thing," Sam says ending his sentence as the two of the military officers approach.

"Good evening, Sir," Jack says standing to greet General Hinkle. "You've both met Sam Conner here, but I don't believe you've been introduced to Doctor Aramora and the infamous Noah Langston."

"Understand you're planning to be here for the SC-1 test flight later this week," Noah says cheerfully.

"Yes, we're looking forward to observing the test," General Hinkle replies. "May I introduce my senior staff officer, Commander Von Dormer?"

Dusty shakes hands with the two officers. "Pleased to meet you," she says politely and steps back.

The general looks over his shoulder for the female lieutenant who had accompanied them and says, "I don't see Marilyn. Oh, she's over there talking to some lady."

"That's my wife Janet, I believe," Sam comments.

Across the room Marilyn and Janet Conner appear, to any observer, a bit too familiar as they touch and laugh.

"Well, I was going to introduce you to my assistant, but I see she is occupied at the moment."

The clanging of a fork against a crystal glass interrupts the conversations around the room and Director Dietrich speaks, "If I can please have your attention. Honored guests, General Hinkle and fellow workers at the research center, I would like to make a toast to one we refer to around here affectionately as the Professor. Doctor Langston and his research team yesterday proved the feasibility of travel through space in excess of any heretofore known limits." The director raises his wine glass and says, "To Noah Langston, congratulations and continued success in your scientific quests!"

Many in the room cheer and several yell, "Congratulations!"

Noah stands and waves his hand politely accepting there congratulations and applause.

Dusty beams with a wide smile.

Jack raises his glass of ice water and Sam raises his tumbler of cognac as they chorus, "Here, here!"

Former combat pilot and astronaut, Captain Jack Harkins, has been a recovered alcoholic and teetotaler for only the last few years. After his estranged wife, whom he loved very much, died of cancer, Jack was well on his way to drinking himself to death; if it hadn't been for Noah's and Sam's friendship and caring, he would have.

Jack's teenage son still blames his father for the separation. However, the marriage ended mostly because Jack's wife was emotionally unable to handle the stress of Jack's aerospace ventures. His son, John Harkins Junior, has recently become rebellious and a problem for Jack to handle or to communicate with.

***

The guests return to the conversations they were having before the director's announcement and a music trio begins a medley of songs out by the cabana near the psychedelically lite swimming pool.

One of the executive from the aerospace center administration approaches where Noah and the general are talking and says, "Excuse me. General, I have some people I'd like you to meet" and ushers General Hinkle off to meet them.

Commander Von Dormer takes a seat on the couch with the small group and says, "I'm a military man, Professor Langston. Not much of a scientist, but could you explain to me in a little more detail what you meant this morning in the press conference when you referred to the M-factor and overcoming it?"

Noah obliges, "Certainly Commander. Are you familiar with electrical equations like those used to determine voltage and amperage, that sort of thing?"

"Like E over I times R. Sure I took a basic electronics class at the military academy years ago."

"It's that simple, except the formula for relativity is E for energy, equals M for mass times C for the constant velocity, squared. Thus, as an object's speed increases so does its mass or weight. This continues until the object's mass becomes infinitely heavy and then it is just not going to move anymore."

"Yes, yes I got that part!" The commander says.

"That is except…" Noah interjects.

"I thought maybe there might be an 'except' in there somewhere," the commander replies with a half-smile.

Noah says, "Everyone has always assumed that the C or the constant in our time honored equation was the speed-of-light.

Why is that?" The commander asks.

"Because it's the fastest thing we've been able to measure and is consistent throughout the known universe," Noah explains, "That was until now, now that we've proved otherwise with the Cyclatron device."

"Does this mean that the old formula is no longer valid?" the commander asks.

"In my opinion, there is no formula more valid for the dimensions of space and time in a three dimensional universe, but it is possible that the universe actually exists in only two dimensions and the third dimension is derived from a projection."

"You mean a hologram, right? So you really weren't able to exceed the speed-of-light. You just took a short-cut."

"There is also the possibility were dealing with a fourth or possibly even eleven dimensions. The fact still remains we succeeded in placing an object on the other side of the speed-of-light and several times over. However, I am personally beginning to suspect that we may not have actually traveled through space in excess of the speed-of-light, but rather somehow jump there!"

"Now you've really have me confused, Professor!"

"Ah, my inquisitive Commander, It took me twenty years to even begin to understand the concept. You should not feel bad you're failing to understand the entire course of study in just one evening."

Jack and Sam chuckled subtly.

Dusty smiles and gets up, "I'm going to go check out the buffet table. Can I get anyone anything?"

Noah holds up his empty drink glass indicating he would like another bourbon and water.

Sam has looked around the room several times trying to locate his wife who has disappeared somewhere.

Jack and Sam take turns telling long-winded stories about recent rocket tests to deflect additional questioning of Noah by the commander.

Finally, the commander becomes bored with the small talk and says, "If you all will excuse me, I'll go and catch up with the general. Captain, I guess we'll see you in the morning."

***

The general is standing talking with a small group of VIPs. As the commander approaches the general excuses himself. The general and the commander move away from the others.

"Sir, I am growing increasingly suspicious of that group of scientists we just met," and the commander goes on to explain his thinking to the general.

"Yes, I agree," the general says, "I've had my suspicions about them ever since we first learned of their project."

"Should I assign additional surveillance to them?" the commander asks.

"Yes, it would be a good idea," the general replies.

The two men move out of the large den area and onto the pool area continuing to discuss the matter.

***

A short time later, Jack's son comes over to speak to his father. They step over to the large stone fireplace and only parts of their muffled conversation can be overheard by Sam and Noah.

The gist of the conversation is mostly about money. Apparently his son is asking his father for money to pay some gambling debts. Jack refuses, maintaining that he has already given the boy far too much money, which he has squandered irresponsibly.

Jack's son storms off to join two waiting friends.

Jack apologizes to those nearby saying, "My son has always been a good kid, but he hasn't been himself since his mother passed away."

Dusty returns from her trip to the buffet table and delivers Noah's bourbon and water.

Sam, who has given up trying to locate his absentee wife, gets up disgustedly to go look for her mumbling, "Guess I better go look for Janet."

Dusty seeming to have a sixth sense about the situation says, "Forget it, Sam. She'll show up sooner or later," and to change the conversation she adds, "Thought that commander fellow would never leave,"

Sam sits back down on the couch.

Noah says, "Sam, there's no way I can get over to the hangar in the morning. I've got a crew reworking the second prototype of the Cyclatron putting in some advanced capabilities."

Dusty says, "We all really need to talk in private. I can get away from the lab early afternoon, no problem.

Sam suggests, "Evening would really be better. After eighteen-hundred-hours most of the workers will be gone, how about then?"

Jack concurs, "You heard the commander. I'm scheduled to take him and the general on a tour of the launch pad and other facilities tomorrow, but free tomorrow evening, I'm pretty sure.

Sam asks, "Will that work for you, Noah?"

Noah shrugs and replies, "Sure."

Sam shares a passing thought, "That'll be better. It will give me time to bypass the surveillance system in the ready room and we can meet in there."

"You mean that place is bugged, too?" Noah asks.

"Not exactly bugged," Jack interjects smiling, "Let us just say monitored. Sam's got this recording of an empty ready room he can wire into the monitors to entertain them while we use the room."

"You two do wonders for my psyche. Maybe I'm not getting paranoid after all," Noah says jokingly.

***

Jack's son returns a short time later to face his father once again. He has been drinking with friends out by the pool and possibly also doing drugs. Jack stands as he approaches anticipating a problem.

Jack's son screams, "You no good bastard, you caused my mother's death! You broke her heart!" and then takes a wild swing at his father.

Jack easily steps out of the way.

His son loses his balance and falls across the large coffee table knocking drinks out across the floor. Before he can get to his feet, two large male waiters, grab hold of the young man under each arm and lift him up. They walk him to the front door with his feet barely touching the ground and throw him out.

Noah chuckles to himself, because he recognizes the two men in waiter's attire, escorting Jack's son out. They are both secret service agents assigned to protect the director.

Jack sits down on the edge of the couch and stares at the floor. "Don't know where I went wrong with that kid."

Noah goes over and places his hand on Jack's shoulder, "Don't take it so hard, pal. The kid just had too much to drink."

"Maybe you're right," Jack says to Noah, "Think I'll go and sit by the pool a while, little early to call it a night."

Noah says to Dusty, "Go on with Jack and keep him company. I need to make a run down the hall."

***

On his way to find the bathroom, Noah turns down a wide marble floored hallway into the living quarters. He thought he remembered the way, but must have made a wrong turn. As he passes one of the bedrooms, he hears voices emanating from behind a partially open door.

Through the opening into the lavishly furnished bedroom, Noah can see the lieutenant he knows only by the name Marilyn, setting on the edge of the large round bed putting on her bra. Her tunic and the rest of her uniform are strung about the floor of the bedroom.

Sam's wife Janet is standing beside the bed and its wrinkled gold silk bedspread with her black evening dress half on. She stands on one foot putting on one of her red patent-leather high-heels and then the other.

It takes a lot to shake Noah's calm, easy going manner, but he is clearly startled. He pauses for a moment, then moves quickly on down the hall.

After Noah leaves the bathroom and starts back down the hall, he passes Sam's wife straightening her hair in a hallway mirror. She pretends not to notice him as he passes behind her.

***

Noah locates Jack and Dusty out by the pool.

"Here we are; saved you a seat," Dusty says as Noah joins them, "Sam came to tell us he was taking his wife home early. She wasn't feeling well."

"I think it's more than that," Noah replies with real concern in the tone of his voice. "I think they may be having some marital problems."

Dusty asks, "I know Sam always wanted children, but he told me one time his wife was dead set against it. Maybe it's something along those lines."

"I'll tell you later," Noah says glancing over at Jack seated comfortably in a lounge chair listening to the music.

"Jack, you okay?" Noah inquires.

"I'm fine," Jack replies, "You two go on if you're ready to leave. I'm going to stay for a while. Don't need to go home to that big empty house just yet."

"Okay, see you tomorrow evening, Jack," Dusty says as she and Noah leave.

"Yeah, see you," Jack says giving a slight wave.

On the way out, Noah stops to speak to his host who is seeing guests out. "Thanks for the good words, Al, but it really wasn't necessary."

"It was necessary. I wish we had ten more just like you, Noah. And Dusty, thanks for coming too."

"Always a pleasure, Sir," Dusty says with a smile, "Try to get the same caterer again next time we do this, the food was great,"

***

As Noah and Dusty exit the front door onto the well-lit circle drive in front of the house, Noah asks, "We in your car or mine?"

"Both, don't you remember we stopped by the center and picked your car up on the way over here."

"That's right… are you coming over?"

"Not tonight, Dearie. You've had a big day. You need a good night's rest and so do I. You know, they might put your name in the physics books or maybe even the history books one of these days.

You think?"

Noah walks Dusty to her car and goes to get his car as she drives off.

Noah stands for the longest time, before opening his car door, staring up at the night sky. There is a smog layer from the industrial complexes rolling in to the lowlands.

Nevertheless, it's a reasonably clear night for the planet Tropia. He can still see a few of the brighter stars in the late night sky. Tropia's smaller moon, Zea, is just coming up over the eastern horizon.

Noah recalls as a young boy, when he lived in the old country, how many more stars he could see at night.

He stands for the longest time staring skyward before opening the door to his car and getting in to drive home to his empty apartment.

***

Chapter Four – Starchild SC-1

Noah's car speeds toward the perimeter of the airbase that adjoins the space center. Approaching the gate, Noah slows, but does not stop as his ID badge will be read electronically. A computer screen in the gatehouse displays who he is and a guard waves him on past.

Looming up ahead in the evening dusk is the large hangar where the Starchild is being readied for its first test flight. Off in the distance, beyond the hangar and ramp, is a large airfield complex with a mile long concrete runway.

The work shift is about over and the workers' shuttle bus is waiting in the adjoining gravel parking lot to take them back to the main space center parking area. Only upper echelon personnel are permitted to drive private vehicles on the airbase.

Noah pulls up to the hangar and parks next to Dusty's car. Jack's car is already parked on the edge of the tarmac next to the hangar. Sam has most likely been there all day hard at work since the early morning hours.

***

Noah enters the hangar through the large, partially open hangar door passing by a dozen or so workers who are leaving for the day. Sam is over in a well-lit shop area at the opposite corner of the hangar from the sleek ultramodern Starchild aircraft. He is talking with two technicians, a young man and young woman both in their late twenties.

As Noah approaches, he overhears Sam say to the two workers, "I need you to stay and work this evening. I'll see that you get back over to the space center employee's parking lot when we're through work tonight. Is that okay?" and both workers readily agree.

The female technician is Leica Braun and the young man technician is Hans Dieter. Both are graduates of the National Technical Institute of Engineering where they attended lectures by Noah. It is only natural for them to refer to Noah as Professor."

Leica and Hans have worked for Sam ever since graduating from the University. They are loyal to Sam and his projects to a fault.

Leica says, "Good evening, Professor."

Noah replies, "Good evening. Sounds like another long evening for you two."

Hans says, "Sure does, Sir."

***

In the far, dimly lit corner of the hangar, near a large workbench stacked high with test equipment, stands the largest version of a Starfighter ever built; the passenger-cargo version, the SC-1 Starchild.

The Starchild is the lone aircraft in the hangar and Noah walks over to the large craft and slowly circles it as though mentally reviewing each feature of the craft.

The craft looks very much like a larger version of the UTAF's most modern Starfighter except that it has certain features like oval windows and a plush cabin built into the cargo bay and, of course, the readily apparent four massive engines instead of the usual two as on the fighters.

The craft has a solid white polymer coating. The underside of the belly and wings are coated with a dull-black corning material. The word Starchild in gold script letters is painted on the nose. A small space center insignia and the designation SC-1 are painted in black on the tail. There are no other markings.

Jack is inside the craft where he has been checking out the instrumentation in the cockpit. He will be the pilot in command on the Starchild's maiden flight.

Noah turns as Jack exits the craft from the rear airstair door and greets Noah saying, "There you are. Dusty got here earlier. She is waiting for you over in the ready room where I guess we're going to meet."

Noah and Jack walk to the front of the craft and stand under the high spire nose of the craft where a single spotlight illuminates the area. Jack is sweating from working in a tight space in the craft and is drinking from a water bottle.

Noah engages Jack in idle conversation by asking questions, "This craft has vertical takeoff and landing capabilities what they call VTOL. Isn't that right?"

"To be more specific it would be classified as an STOL, a short takeoff and landing aircraft. In other words, it takes much less distance to takeoff and land than other aircraft its size."

Noah asks, "Really fast too, I guess?"

"For reaching ultra-high altitudes and quickly punching through the sound barrier it has two small auxiliary Scram engines." Jack explains, "The higher you go, the faster it flies." Jack turns and points to one of the rear engines and says, "There you can see one of the Scram engines faired-in just under the main engine. It's the same on the other side. This bird is a one-of-a-kind and flies with ease at the threshold of space. The pressurization system and hull design are so over-designed, I think it would even operate fine in outer space.

Noah is impressed and says, "A really super high performance craft, indeed! We didn't build it from scratch though. I remember when it arrived it was mostly complete. I watched it being modified day by day; with the cabin and all. I should've paid more attention, but my attention was occupied with problems developing the Cyclotron during most of that time."

Jack clarifies by saying, "This particular craft was originally being built as an ultra-high altitude orbital platform with all kinds of spy gear onboard, but the Triad ordered its development stopped. How we came to inherit the bird was by suggesting that it would make a really fine high altitude research lab."

Noah remarks, "But in its present configuration, it is more or less a nondescript passenger aircraft."

Jack agrees saying, "More or less. That was done intentionally to declassify and DEMIL the aircraft."

"By DEMIL, you mean demilitarize," Noah says.

"The craft has seats for eight souls, a pilot, copilot and six crew or in this case six passengers," Jack says.

Sam approaches Jack and Noah and picks up on their conversation saying, "Not anymore. I just finished instructing Hans to remove the far aft passenger seat. We'll have to mount the Cyclatron unit to the floor there."

Sam lowers his voice and says to Noah, "Walk with me to the rear of the craft I want to show you something."

Jack turns to go back up the airstair into the Starchild. He says, "Got a couple of loose avionics harness bundles I need to finish tying up. You two go on to the ready room, I'll catch up in a few minutes."

Sam takes Noah around to the back of the craft behind the engine exhausts and explains, "It's safe to talk here. I've checked the area out. The surveillance system's video and audio doesn't cover this corner of the hangar. The ready room where we're going to meet is a hot area so what I've done is tapped into the system and set up a recording that shows an empty silent room while we are meeting in there. If the roving patrol comes by, we need to quickly come back out here in the hangar."

Noah asks, "How will we know when a patrol does come by?"

Sam explains, "There is an infrared warning system around the hangar perimeter, concealed of course. The two technicians working late will monitor the system and alert us if and when anyone approaches the hangar."

"We come back out here so that what the guards find is in agreement with what their surveillance cameras were showing. Ingenious, Sam, once again you have outdone yourself," Noah says with a smile.

"That is correct," Sam replies.

"I assume Jack is already aware of these weaknesses in the security system?"

"Yes, he helped me map them out."

"I didn't realize it until tonight when I came through the gate that the air base parameter security had been turned over to the Reichs Guard."

"Yes, they laid-off all the civilian contract guards several days ago," Sam explains. "I think the territorial government has designs on taking over this whole facility here at their first opportunity."

Noah shakes his head in disgust, "That's not good!"

***

Noah, Sam and Jack enter the ready room and are greeted by Dusty who is seated at the large conference table in the center of the room. Sam and Jack take seats across the table from each other and Noah takes a seat at one end of the table.

"I guess the first item on the agenda is the status of the doomsday satellite," Noah says turning to Sam.

Sam says, "We have our own tracking system now and can get real time data on the satellite. We kludged it together out of some satellite array equipment. You saw the receiver units stacked on the workbench with our other test equipment. The best place to hide a needle is not in a haystack, but in a stack of needles."

Noah inquires of Sam, "Those two young technicians obviously had a hand in building up the equipment. Do you feel like you can trust them?"

"Yes implicitly," Sam replies, "In fact, I believe they would join us in this endeavor if we invited them. Trust me on that."

Noah says, "Anyway, back to the subject at hand..."

Jack says, "bottom line is that the satellite's orbit is continuing to decay and possibly the rate of decay is increasing slightly."

Sam says, "We have also been monitoring some of the military radio traffic and the chatter is not good. It seems there is a layer in Tropia's upper atmosphere that is highly saturated with some unstable, radioactive form of hydrogen."

Noah comments, "I'm unfamiliar with that. That's certainly not a natural state for hydrogen."

Sam continues, "Yes, I know. Apparently, it occurred as a result of some industrial processes in use years ago. Anyway, if the nuclear device onboard the satellite goes off in that layer, the result will be a chain reaction that will circle the globe. What life forms are not killed off immediately by the radiation will eventually die in the resulting nuclear winter."

Noah groans, "Thus, it seems, this is what we must now contend with at the end results of hundreds of years of carelessness by our military industrial complex!"

"I just don't know where it all started to go wrong," Sam says despondently.

Dusty asks Sam, "What is your personal evaluation of what the falling satellite will actually do?"

"I've analyzed the hell out of the data. My best guess is that it depends on the angle of impact with the atmosphere," Sam replies.

Dusty says, "Please explain a little more."

Sam obliges and says, "If the angle is shallow enough, it could skip a couple of times and most likely wander off into space, eventually, harmlessly falling into the Tropia's solar star."

Dusty gives a sigh of relief and says. "Now that sounds much better."

Noah adds, "However, an air burst is the most likely scenarios and of course the most lethal."

"Right," Sam replies agreeing with Noah, "And it would most likely take millions of years for any kind of life to re-establish itself on Tropia."

Dusty asks, "What if the nuclear device makes it through the hydrogen layer and comes straight in for a ground impact, couldn't we just come back in and land on the other side of the planet? Surely the impact area would be contained within a few hundred kilometers."

Jack comments, "Good thinking Dusty, but we would still have to be above the hydrogen layer during the satellites re-entry to have that option."

Noah pauses for a moment, "Okay, we'll consider that to be our primary option. I'd just like to make sure everyone understands that not only our lives are on the line here, but a whole lot more. If we are wrong or if we proceed and fail our careers are over. We will be disgraced and most probably charged with treason."

"In light of the alternative," Jack says, "the total annihilation of everything we know, it seems to me to be a moot point."

"However…" Sam adds, "We should be able to calculate something pretty definitive on the angle the satellite will approach the upper atmosphere within the next twelve to fourteen hours… but right now it's not looking real good!"

"Now there's the key to our problem, Noah," Jack, kind of thinking out loud, says. "If the satellite starts to look like it is going to skip off into space, like Sam says it might, we can cover our asses by saying it was just a test flight. However, if we don't move right now to get the Cyclatron installed, we really don't have any options at all; nada, nothing!"

Noah asks Sam in his most serious tone of voice, "You're that sure the most likely scenario is going to be the chain reaction, is that right?"

"I'm not at a hundred percent yet, but I'm approaching it rapidly," Sam replies.

***

Chapter Five – Doomsday Satellite

The subject matter of the conversations had been getting a little heavy and the group had decided to take a break. Everyone grabbed a soft drink from the cooler and walked out into the hangar to get a little fresh air.

Standing around in the hangar, as usual Jack began telling old flying stories of situations he and his crews had gotten into. In no time he had everyone laughing. They have returned now to the ready room, hopefully in a slightly better mood, to deal with the serious issue at hand.

Noah places his folded hands on the table. He looks seriously at his three closest friends and says, "As you know we planned to install one of the Cyclatron devices in the Starchild after it became operational anyway for testing, so the installation design work is all completed and ready to go. Thus, in preparation for what I will call our doomsday option plan' do you all agree that we proceed?"

The three nod their heads yes.

"Me too," Noah says. "So what do we have to do to get it installed?"

Sam says, "Actually, we've already started. The two technicians working out there now will pre-wire the installation where the ninth seat was removed. Most of that will be completed before we quit for the night. As soon as you can get the device over here in the morning we'll begin the installation. So as not to unduly alarm any of the regular crew, I will tell all of the workers we're only doing a test prototype installation."

"We're down to seven seats," Jack says. "This means we need to talk about who is going, if we go."

"There are the four of us here to begin with," Dusty says. "So who else do we need or might want to go?"

Jack says, "I've been giving this some thought. We need an astronomer and I know just the fellow for the job. Tom Bradley, all of you will remember him. He went on the Arres mission with me. He's a qualified spacecraft pilot and one of the best celestial navigators I know. He's still single and he's quite an adventurer at heart. I think I can convince him to come along."

"Great idea," Noah says. "We definitely need some redundancy in the pilot area. I don't think I could land one of those crafts safely, if my life depended on it."

Sam speaks up, "My wife of course. I assume she will be going when I explain it all to her."

"Of course," Noah says. "Okay that leaves one open seat, any other suggestions?"

Jack speaks up, "I'm a little hesitant to bring this up, but with a seat open anyway, I've been thinking that maybe I should try to take my son along. Don't think he has much of the future here."

"Okay that's seven," Dusty says. "To sum up where we are so far, we have agreed only to proceed with giving ourselves an option and what the details of those options are. The execution of any of these options is to be determined based on upcoming data."

Noah glances at each of the others and they seem to concur. "It appears so. Moving on, who has comments and questions? Let's get whatever concerns we have out on the table and off our chests right now so we don't have to deal with them later.

After a short period of silence Dusty speaks up, "I'm sure going to miss my red sports car. Jack, don't you think you could rig something out of the Starchild so we could take it along with us?"

This lightens the mood in the room a little and all smile goodheartedly.

"Hard to think in terms of an apocalypse," Noah says. "I often think back to when I was a young boy in the old country across the sea. After my father died in the Eastern wars, my mother and I went to live with my grandfather. I recall how clear the nights were and the first time I ever saw the glow of the Zoatropeia.

Noah pauses then says, "My granddad was an amateur astronomer and he explained things to me. That was where my first interest in stars and physics began. I can still recall how bright and brilliant blue the day time skies were there in that peaceful little town of Innisfree."

There is quiet in the room for a bit and then Jack says, "I have a question for you, Noah. I've traveled at about one third the speed-of-light and felt no noticeable effect from it at all, but what can we expect to experience when traveling at hyper-light speeds?"

Noah replies, "I believe the actual jumps will only take micro-seconds, likely occurring too fast for sensory perception. However, during acceleration and deceleration into hyper-light speeds you will experience a red-blue color spectrum shift when looking outside the craft. This may cause some disorientation until you adjust. Ahead, you will only see a field of black, but approaching a star or planet, it will glow with a bluish tint."

Jack comments, "Yes, I'm familiar with the light-doppler effect. We saw just the very beginnings of that on the vogue to Arres."

Noah continues, "And you may actually be able to see part of the way around to the far side of an approaching object. Light curves near objects in space, called gravitational lensing, but this is not the reason, it is only because of moving forward in time. Objects passing to the side will also appear curved or distorted and objects to the rear moving away, will glow with a reddish tint."

Jack asks Noah, "Are you still convinced that this mass thing won't have any effect on our weight inside the spacecraft?"

"It is true that passing from light speeds to hyper-light speeds the craft should become infinitely heavy based on the laws of relativity, but apparently it doesn't work that way. Whatever the Cyclatron does, E equals MC squared doesn't seem to have any effect on it."

Noah continues, "Let me give you an example. Our planet, Tropia, rotates at a little over 1700 kph while also orbiting its solar star once every three-hundred and seventy-one days. It also circles the spiral galaxy we call the Zoatropeia once every two million Tropia years. The Zoatropeia is only one of many million galaxies drifting through space in a universe and we have observed the edge of the universe is expanding faster than the speed-of-light.

"And so…" Jack says.

"And so, all of this combines into some quite fantastic speeds. Are we any heavier because of this?"

"Well no. it's just that I can't seem to get my head around the concept," Jack replies.

Okay, let's try this… most people don't seem to understand the operation of a simple thermostat…"

Jack interrupts and in a monotone says, "You're going to explain that turning the tempter dial up on a thermostat only lengthens the time the unit runs while attempting to obtain the requested tempter and does not cause the unit to output any higher tempter than before.

"Very good, you paid attention in thermal dynamics class," Noah says with a smile. "Using that as an example I'll give you an over simplified clarification of how the Cyclatron works that I do not exactly understand myself.

The others in the room wait quietly for Noah to make his point because they've heard it all before.

Noah explains, "As simply as I can explain it is that the Cyclatron creates a Stasis Field in some kind of fifth dimension and goes there. Even though I have used the term 'exceeding the speed-of-light' numerous times in explaining my work, I have come to believe that the Cyclatron, and anything attached to it in free space, may not actually travel through space at all. Again, like the lowly thermostat, setting the dial on the Cyclatron to go faster only makes it run longer and thus it arrives at a more distant point and time in the space-time continuum."

Jack has been listening more intently then his usual half paying attention and seems to have had an epiphany. He says, Then that's the reason you often use the term jump when referring to the Cyclatron. It's more like jumping through space and time than actually flying through it at speeds greater than the speed-of-light. That's what is happening, isn't it?"

"It's the only explanation for mass not being a factor in the equation I can think of." Noah says agreeing,

Sam speaks up, "Before we get off on a lengthy discussion on black holes or some other such thing, there's something that has been bothering me. Here on Tropia we've been in the space age for well over two hundred years, have we ever once made contact or found any sign of intelligent alien life in the universe?"

Noah, Jack and Dusty all shake their head no.

"Okay then where in hell are we going if and when we leave here?" Sam asks.

Jack replies, "Any one of several hundred solar systems that have habitable planets in their Goldilocks zone. That's why we need an experienced astronomer along with us. Tom has all that data on these exoplanets."

Dusty asks, "That's where the dials all read right for supporting life. Is that what you're referring to?"

"That's right," Jack replies, "We can weed out the no good ones with a flyby. Once we find a good candidate, we'll have enough fuel onboard to make at least three maybe four entries onto the best possible candidate planet with a habitable atmosphere. That's it!"

Sam says "You're saying we don't have much of a chance of finding intelligent life, so we are on our own. We are going to be making astronomical history and there will be no one to share our discovery with?"

"Like Jack said, that's it!" Noah says.

Jack adds, "Tom Bradley has developed some really good theories based on the probabilities of intelligent life. It seems that it's more a timing problem than anything else, relative to the age of the universe, any given civilization only lasts for a very short period of time, so you see when they exist, we don't and vice versa."

Dusty speaks up, "Noah, I think I know what your two friends are really trying to ask and are beating around the bush about. So I'll ask it as simply as I can. Is the damn thing safe?"

Noah looks at each of them questioningly and then asks "Is that the underlying issue here?"

"Kind of," Sam replies.

Jack says. "You see Noah, one time you say we travel faster than the speed-of-light and another time you say we jump in space and time. Witch is it?"

"I'm sure I do, so let me try to explain," Noah replies, "Suppose you're watching a movie with others in real time and for some reason you see the whole movie, but you are at a point later in the movie than everyone else watching. The question then becomes, did you watch the movie faster or did you jump forward in the movie?"

"Think I'm beginning to catch on a little, but only a little." Jack concedes.

Sam is half serious and half joking when he quips, "How do we really know when we make a space jump and pass to the other side of light speed that our body mass won't become infinite heavy and we collapse into a micro-mini black hole?"

Dusty chuckles at Sam's choice of the term 'micro-mini black hole. Noah and Jack laugh out loud.

Noah says, "You got me on that one, Sam. I can only tell you what I know. The Cyclatron device has mass, and there was no damage to the Cyclatron unit itself when it came back."

"Yeah, I guess that's right," Sam says. "I hadn't bothered to think that part through. "

Noah picks up a writing pen from the table and drops it on the table. "We've all discussed many times the probability of an object falling up instead of down when dropped. I understand that several hundred years ago, when we first set off a uranium bomb, one of the scientists calculated the odds of it blowing up the entire planet. I don't know what the odds were, but I'm equally certain there are also odds against us surviving this endeavor."

Dusty changes the subject, "Should we attempt to take a lot of scientific data with us in order to preserve it for posterity?"

"As far as I'm concerned, only what's required to operate the craft and to navigate," Jack says.

"I'm kind of against taking any technology that we can get along without," Sam explains. "A lot of it is in our heads anyway. Certainly, not take anything that can be easily weaponized."

At that instant, the intercom on the desk in the ready room buzzes rapidly three times. Sam jumps to his feet, "That's the signal the roving patrol guards have pulled up out front. Let's go, everyone out in the hangar!"

The four position themselves at the predetermined spot in the hangar and engage in small talk as two large men in Reichs Guard uniforms with heavy duty weapons on their hip come through the hangar door.

Sam speaks up, "Good evening, may I help you?"

The guard with sergeant stripes on his uniform, obviously the senior of the two officers, replies, "Good evening Mister Connor."

Sam walks over to engage the two guards in the center of the hangar, "Oh, you know my name."

"Part of the job, but you do look very much like your ID photo on file," the guard says and leans over to look past Sam at the other three, "Good evening Doctor Langston, Doctor Aramora and Captain Harkins."

Each of the three nod politely as they are addressed by the guard.

The guard says to Sam, "We saw the cars here earlier when we passed by. You people are working kind of late, aren't you?"

"Behind schedule and trying to catch up," Sam says.

The senior guard walks over to the ready room door followed by Sam and the other guard. He opens the door and looks in. Sam holds the door for the guard as he goes in and over to the table where Noah's pipe is laying on the table. He feels the bowl of the pipe and glances around.

Sam swallows as the guard exits the ready room. As luck would have it, Noah had let his pipe go out earlier in the meeting and had not bothered to relight it. The bowl was cool to the touch.

The guard pauses outside the ready room. "We received a memo to get ready for some kind of VIP dedication ceremony. I assume it's for that aircraft parked over there in the corner. Some movie star is supposed to be coming here, I understand."

"Yes, that's another reason we are working late tonight," Sam replies.

The guard asks, "Who is this movie star?"

Sam explains, "It's a woman. Actually, she is more of a celebrity than a star. She is the granddaughter of Clarence Fairchild the founder of the Starchild Aircraft Company. I think the event is more of a publicity stunt than anything else."

The senior guard removes a pair of black leather gloves from his jacket pocket and puts them on slowly. He says, "We won't keep you from your work any longer. Have a good evening."

Sam walks the two guards to the small hangar exit door and they depart.

Sam over hears the senior guard say to his assistant, "See where they were standing, over there in that corner, I suspect that's a dead spot in the surveillance system. Write that up in your next report. That needs to be corrected."

Sam goes back to where the other three are waiting, "Tell me something, Noah, had you lit your pipe in the last half hour or so?"

Noah shrugs his shoulders questioningly, "No, I think it went out when we first started the meeting and I never re-lit it. Why do you ask?"

Sam sighs, "Not important, forget I asked. Listen you all, I'll call you in the morning as soon as I'm sure of a trajectory on the satellite."

"Please do," Dusty says, "and try to get some sleep tonight, if you can, Sam."

Sam smiles politely. "Thanks, Dusty, I'll try."

Jack says, "I'm going to stay a little longer and finish checking out some of the avionics systems in the Starchild's cockpit. I'll get with Tom Bradley in the morning and get his answer."

The four say goodnight and Jack goes to climb aboard the Starchild followed by Sam who is going into the cabin to check on his two worker's progress.

As Noah and Dusty go out the hangar side exit door Noah says, "Don't think I've had anything to eat all day."

"Okay," Dusty replies. "Come on over to my place and I'll fix you something. After all the stuff we've discussed tonight, I won't be able to sleep anyway. By the way, you never did tell me about you know who. Remember you said you'd tell me later."

***

Chapter Six – Leaving Tropia

The following morning at Dusty's ultra-modern apartment, Noah is asleep in the bedroom. Dusty is in the small kitchen pouring two cups of coffee. She enters the bedroom, places one of the cups on the end table. The digital clock on the table reads o-nine-hundred.

Dusty, holding her coffee with both hands, sits down on the side of the bed as Noah starts to wake up.

"Going to sack out all day sleepyhead?" Dusty asks.

Noah sits up in bed, drags a couple of pillows over and leans back against the headboard.

He says, "Guess not, guess I better get going."

"No you don't, not till you tell me about Janet like you promised. Remember, you got a little distracted last night and then fell asleep so let's have it."

Noah reaches for the cup of coffee and takes a sip and says, "Not all that much to tell so I'll just tell you what I saw and you can judge for yourself."

Noah goes on to explain in detail exactly what he had seen the other night at Dietrich's house on his way down the hall to the restroom.

Dusty listens patiently until he is through and then says, "That's about what I had figured, but good to have confirmation. I feel sorry for Sam, but it is what is!"

Dusty's phone, laying on the end table, rings and she answers it, "Hello… Yes, he's right here." She hands the phone to Noah and says, "It's Sam. He tried your number, but it's turned off, but figured you were here."

Noah answers and listens for a moment then says, "Great, it did get there okay then. I had left instructions late last night with my foreman to get the Cyclatron over to the hangar first thing this morning. How's it going?"

As Noah listens to Sam his face shows more and more concern. "We're on our way!" He hangs up.

Dusty says, "Not good, huh?"

"Not good at all. We'll go straight to the hangar. Grab anything small of value you might want to take with you. Odds are we won't be back here."

Dusty is already dressed for work. She goes over to the closet, kicks off her high heel shoes and steps into a comfortable pair of loafers. She goes to a jewelry box on top of her dresser and grabs a double handful of jewelry and crams it in her large purse.

She pauses for a moment, opens one of the dresser drawers and takes out a small automatic pistol, wraps in a pair of Bermuda shorts and drops it in her purse with the jewelry.

Dusty glances over at Noah who is getting dressed. He is staring at her and she says, "What?"

"You sure you want to take that thing?"

"You never know," Dusty replies and slams the dresser drawer shut… "I'm ready," she says placing one hand on her hip.

As they are leaving Dusty's apartment, she asks, "What did Sam actually say?"

"Worst possible scenario, the satellite is headed straight in at exactly the angle and velocity that nearly guarantees its detonation."

"How much time do we have?"

"About twelve hours max!"

***

A few kilometers away, at the highway intersection out front of the main Space Center entrance, a car weaving in and out of traffic at high speed enters the intersection as another car turns in front of it. The high-speed car crashes into the turning car and is catapulted into the air.

The car does a half spiral in midair crashing to the ground and careening into the oncoming traffic. The car comes to a stop on its roof and catches fire. There is one person trapped in the car, the driver. He is a bloody mess, but still conscious and is struggling to get out of the upside down car.

Like in most major traffic incidents, mass confusion ensues and traffic comes to a halt. Several individuals run to the turned over car. They pull the badly injured driver from the car and lay him on the ground.

Those assisting the driver step back as Space Center security pulls up and a uniformed security guard comes over. The guard kneels down to check on the man. The man is trying to say something and the guard leans over to listen, trying to hear what the young man is saying.

***

At the hangar, most of the workers that did show up for work are gathered in the ready room watching a news broadcast on television.

As Noah and Dusty enter the hangar and are met by Sam. "Is the Cyclatron installed and tested?" Noah asks.

Sam says, "Yes and she's almost ready to go.

"Excellent!" Noah replies, "Where is Janet and is Jack's son already here?"

"Haven't seen or heard from the boy," Sam says, "That being said, Janet is refusing to come. We had a fight over her coming early this morning and I've been on the phone with her several times since. Someone seems to have convinced her there is no imminent danger."

Noah asks, "How are you about still going, if she doesn't come?"

"To tell you the truth, I don't think I even care. That woman has changed since we were married. She's gotten really strange and distant the last couple of years."

Noah and Dusty walk with Sam over to the ready room where several of the workers are preparing to leave.

Noah comments to Sam, "There must have been a bad wreck at that busy intersection over near the Space Center entrance. Traffic was backed up for several kilometers in both directions."

"We came on the back road," Dusty adds, "So we missed most of it, but several emergency vehicles went past us on the way to the accident sight."

Sam pauses outside the ready room door and takes his car key card out of his wallet. "I'm going to send the rest of the workers home. Give me your car key cards. They are going to have to get back over to the Space Center parking lot to get their own cars."

"Noah hands Sam his keycard and says, "Good thinking, extra people around questioning could be a real problem when we roll the Starchild out."

Dusty says, "I didn't drive. I rode with Noah."

Sam turns to go into the ready room. "That's okay, I've got Jack's card and that'll be enough. This will only take a few minutes."

Noah and Dusty enter the ready room behind Sam and stand in the back of the room. Sam goes to the front of the room where the TV is playing. On the TV, a news person is explaining that people are being advised to remain in their homes or indoors in the event of a possible minor nuclear flash high up in the atmosphere.

Sam turns the TV off in order to addresses the small group and says, "I'd like to have your attention, please. I know most of you are worried about what you're hearing on the news. Some of your fellow workers didn't even show up for work this morning, which is understandable. It will be best for all of you to go on home and be with your families. Take the rest of the day off."

One of the workers speaks up, "There is no bus to shuttle us back to our cars."

"I'm aware of that." Sam says holding up the three keycards, "Here are the cards to the cars parked out front. You all double up and use those cars. I need three drivers."

Three workers come forward and take the keycards from Sam, "Just leave the cars in the parking lot. If any of you need transportation further, use the cars and leave them at your destination. We'll worry about getting them returned later."

The workers file out of the ready room into the hangar talking about what they should do next. Noah, Dusty and Sam follow them out and walk across the hangar floor to the Starchild.

***

It is now early evening. The only workers now remaining at the hangar are Leica, Hans and an older fellow by the name of Harold, a senior engine mechanic working with Jack on a glitch in one of the engine fuel flow indicators.

A uniformed police officer from the Space Center enters the hangar side door and asks, "Is there a Captain Harkins here?"

Sam goes to confront the officer and says, "Captain Harkins is busy checking out an aircraft right now. Can I help you?"

The officer replies, "I better talk to him personally. It's in regard to his son."

"Okay, come with me," Sam says and shows the officer to the other side of the hangar where Jack and Harold are working. Jack is holding a test probe on some contacts inside the right engine nacelle with his back to the approaching officer and Sam.

Sam points and says, "That's him there."

"Captain Harkins?" the guard inquires.

Jack turns around and replies, "Yes, I'm Captain Harkins. What can I do for you?"

"It's about your son, Sir," the officer hesitates for a moment as though collecting his thoughts.

"Go on! What kind of trouble has my son gotten into this time?" Jack inquires.

"It's a little more serious than that, Sir." The officer says respectfully, "Earlier today, your son, John Harkins, Jr. was involved in a major traffic accident."

"Is he all right?" Jack asks.

The officer says, "I'm sorry to inform you that your son did not survive the crash."

"Had he been drinking?" Jack asks crustily.

"I arrived on the scene shortly after it happened and yes that was readily apparent," the officer explains, "There is one other thing I need to tell you. He was still alive when I first arrived. Although badly injured he kept trying to speak. The only words I could make out were, 'Tell my dad' and then he slipped into unconsciousness."

"That's it?" Jack pleads.

The officer nodes and says, "Yes."

"Thank you for coming in person, Officer." Jack says, "Tell the authorities I will be in touch, but I need to remain here right now to finish my work?"

"I understand," the officer says. As he turns to leave he comments, "It's been a rough day, especially for you, Sir, but from what I hear on the news it may turn out to be a rougher day tomorrow for all of us"

Sam is standing nearby and has been quietly listening to the officer and Jack. Sam steps forward. He reaches out to put his hand on Jacks shoulder, but does not know what to say.

Jack turns away and goes back to work.

Sam, who is also hurting, steps back a ways. He pauses thoughtfully and then mumbles to himself, "I guess one man can only stand so much hurt."

***

At the Reichs Guard security monitoring center, the junior guard that had inspected the hangar with the sergeant the night before is reviewing some of the digital files from the hangar monitoring system.

He pauses one of the images of the hangar ready room on the monitor and hollers, "Hey Sarg, come in here and take a look at this."

The sergeant enters the room and asks, "What is it, what you got?"

The junior guard backs up the image and runs it again saying, "Take a look at this. Watch as the camera scans across the conference table in the center of the room and tell me what you see."

The sergeant watches impatiently and then says, "An empty table, so what?"

"Last night when we were at the hangar, did you not go back and feel the bowl of a pipe lying on the table before we left?"

"Damned, if you're not right," the Sergeant says angrily, "Just as I suspected, they've rigged the security system. Something is going on over there. Get a squad together we're going over to that hangar!"

***

Back at the hangar, four are gathered by the Starchild's airstair. Tom Bradley arrives carrying a briefcase full of star charts.

Jack introduces Tom to Noah and Dusty. Sam and Tom had worked together in the past, so they already knew one another. Jack yells out to Hans and Leica, "We're running out of time, let's go!"

Jack climbs the airstair to board the aircraft. Tom and Dusty follow him up the stairs and enters the cabin.

Harold is standing by the nose of the Starchild where the APU is plugged in. Jack gives him a thumbs-up and he starts the unit. The hangar fills with a high pitch whine from the power coming on in the aircraft.

Harold goes over to where Sam and Noah are talking with Hans and Leica at the foot of the airstair.

Noah asks, "Why didn't you three go with the others when they left? Surely, you are aware of the impending catastrophe."

Hans replies, "Oh yes, we are very aware of the situation. The three of us discussed it and we were needed here to help you get the Starchild ready."

Sam explains to Noah, "I've known of their plan for some time. You may not be aware that there are extensive concrete tunnels throughout the airbase for the air conditioning and power lines. Part of it runs right under this hangar. Some of these tunnels were even approved as air raid shelters during the last war."

Hans say, "Yes, that is our plan."

Leica nods in agreement.

Noah says to Sam, "We have two empty seats. It's worth asking."

Sam understands what Noah means and turns to the three workers to ask, "Due to extenuating circumstances there are two empty seats on the Starchild and…"

Leica exclaims, "I was afraid you weren't going to offer. Yes, yes I want to go!"

Sam says to Leica, "Then you better get on board."

Leica who is still in her work jumpsuit asks, "Can I go to my locker and get some other clothes?"

"Don't have time," Sam replies.

Leica says, "Right," and scrambles up the airstair.

Noah says to Harold and Hans, "There's still one empty seat. Do you two want to flip a coin for it or do you both want to stay here and take your chances?"

Harold says. "No need to toss for it. I'm sure Hans wants to go. Besides, I'm way too old and I'm just plain not interested in knocking around up there in space in that kludged-up contraption I helped you all put together."

Sam says, "Okay on board, Boy Wonder. Let's go."

Hans boards the Starchild, laptop computer underarm and small toolbox in hand.

Sam and Noah shake their heads and chuckle.

Noah jokes, "Hope he doesn't have his data stored in a cloud. He's going to have a hard time connecting to the Internet out there."

Harold grins showing his worn and tarnished teeth and says to Noah, "Good luck to you, Professor." He wipes his hands with a shop towel and shakes hands with Sam. "It's been an honor working with you."

Sam stammers, "I'm sorry I…"

"No need to apologize, Sir. My boy was killed in the last war and my wife died of cancer a few years ago. I was born here on this planet and if it's time to die, then right here's the place I want to be."

Off in the far distance the sound of sirens from several security vehicles can be heard approaching the hangar at high speeds.

"From the sound of what's coming," Noah says, "We better get going."

"I'll get the APU out of the way as soon as Jack fires one engine," Harold assures them, "I'll open the hangar doors when you're ready to roll. You two better get on board."

Sam and Noah run up the airstair. Sam pulls the airstair door shut and latches it.

Sam yells out, "Seven souls on board, Captain."

Five men and two woman are now onboard the Starchild, off on the adventure of a lifetime or their certain demise.

Harold is positioned out front of the Starchild where the APU is plugged in and running. He watches Jack in the cockpit. When Jack looks at him, he waves his hand in the air with a circling motion. From the cockpit, Jack gives him a thumbs-up. Harold increases the power on the APU and stands by as Jack cranks the first engine.

With the first engine running, Harold unplugs the APU and pushes it out of the Starchild's way. Jack cranks the second engine and Harold runs to open the hangar doors. Harold pulls the hydraulic lever to open the large doors and the warning horn sounds as the doors roll back.

The sound of sirens from the approaching vehicles grows louder, which Jack cannot hear inside the cockpit. Harold points with both hands indicating to Jack to expedite his exit from the hangar.

The Starchild rolls onto the tarmac out front of the hangar as the lead police car crashes through the gate and into the gravel parking lot beside the tarmac. Jack applies full power to swing the Starchild around and the engines pallet the arriving vehicle with dirt and gravel.

Several large gravel rocks are picked up by the jet blast which shatters the police vehicle's windshield. Two officers attempt to exit the car, but are forced back in for shelter from the flying gravel.

Two additional police cars arrive as the Starchild pulls away. The junior officer jumps out of the second car, draws his automatic weapon and points it at the rapidly moving away Starchild.

The yells at the junior officer, "Don't fire! That aircraft is loaded with fuel and it could blow up.

The junior officer lowers his weapon.

The sergeant breathes a siy of relief and says, We'd both be courts marshaled for destroying a piece of equipment that expensive."

More composed now, the sergeant stats yelling out orders again, "Get on the radio to the tower, tell them to deny takeoff to that aircraft and block the runway with fire trucks if necessary."

***

In the Starchild's cockpit, Jack is in the left pilot's seat and Tom is in the right copilot's seat. Noah is seated behind Jack and Sam is seated behind Tom.

Dusty and Leica are in the next row of seats. Dusty is behind Noah and Leica behind Sam.

Hans is seated in the right rear seat behind Leica and across the aisle from the airstair. The Cyclatron is on the floor behind his seat.

The Starchild approaches the end of the taxiway and is ready to roll onto the runway for takeoff.

The control tower calls on the radio, "Starchild S-1, if you're on this frequency, you are ordered to return to the hangar area immediately."

Jack keys the mic button on the yoke for his headset and replies, "Tower, if you got any traffic in the area, clear it out of the way, we're rolling."

The Starchild swings onto the runway.

Tower calls again, "Jack is that you?"

Jack ignores the call as he makes his final pre-takeoff scan of the panel and asks, "Tom, you ready?"

Tom gives a thumbs-up and nods his head yes.

Jack: "We ought to be able to lift off at about one-twenty so give me a read out at every ten after ninety.

Tom: "Got it, coming up with full power now."

The Starchild starts its takeoff roll down the runway; at first very slowly, but accelerating geometrically.

Jack gets a good grip on the yoke and hollers back into the cabin, "If anyone's not buckled up yet, now would be a good time to do so."

Dusty is looking back out of the side window and says excitedly, "There are a couple of cop cars with their lights flashing coming up fast behind us!"

The tower calls, "I know that's you, Jack. I recognized your voice. This is Phil, your old flyin buddy."

Jack to tower, "I know, Phil, I also recognized your voice. How you been?"

Tower: "Jack, who gave you permission to fly the Starchild today?"

Jack to tower, "God almighty, I guess, Phil."

Laughter comes over the tower radio.

Then Phil asks, "Exactly what frequency was it he called you on?"

"You always were kind of a wise ass, Phil. Have a nice day, whatever is left of it. We're rolling!"

Tower, "I can see that. Okay, Jack, have it your way, but officially, I have to say that takeoff permission is denied. Oh, for what it's worth, all air traffic in the vicinity is cleared out of your way at all altitudes."

Jack to tower, "You're a good man, Phil. Why don't you get the hell out of that tower, go home to your family. Find a safe good shelter or a good deep hole in the ground and stay there for the next twenty-four hours."

Tower, "I'll consider it. By the way, Jack, there's a large reception party down at the far end of the runway waiting on you. Correction, I think they're starting to roll towards you now."

Tom calls out, "Ninety," and then says, "Those fire trucks are heading right for us."

Large airport crash trucks are coming three abreast straight for the Starchild down the center of the runway. Jack holds the runway heading.

Tom reads aloud, "One-hundred."

Jack calls out, "Full flaps, now!"

Tom lowers the flaps and Jack pulls back hard on the control yoke. The Starchild leaps into the air clearing the oncoming lead fire truck by only a meter or two as it went over the cab.

It all happens so fast, the truck driver probably thinks the Starchild vanishes into thin air right before his very eyes.

Jack levels out for a moment to gain airspeed and calls, "Flaps up. Stand by to engage scramjets."

Tom responds, milking the flaps up slowly and says, "Flaps full up standing by scramjets."

"To save fuel," Jack replies, "we'll wait till we get to thinner air to engage them."

Jack hauls back on the controls and points the Starchild skyward pulling a constant two Gs.

Tom exclaims, "I had no idea this bird would perform like this on one set of engines…"

***

In the control tower, Phil and a couple of controllers watch as the Starchild climb out at a seventy degree angle accelerating steadily.

At that instant, the Starchild punches through the sound barrier and goes supersonic.

The windows of the tower rattle twice with the signature sound of the Starchild passing the sound barrier.

The one controllers in the control tower with Phil exclaims, "Wow, look at that puppy go!"

"Take a good look," Phil replies. For better or worse you'll never see that starfighter again.

The Starchild glistens in the morning sun and disappears from site passing through flight level one hundred and doing about Mach three.

Phil, back in the tower, watches as the Starchild goes out of sight. He removes his controller's headset, pitches it on the radio control console and says, "Good afternoon gentlemen. I'm going home to be with my family."

***

Chapter Seven – Another Dimension

At flight level one-ten, the Starchild's engines, starving for intake air, begin to stall. Tom engages the scramjet engines and shuts down the turbojets.

Jack noses the Starchild over into level flight, but with the excessive power from the scramjets, the Starchild continues to climb to flight level one-twenty and to accelerate through Mach four.

Dusty glues her nose to the oval window by her seat. "What a view," she exclaims and then jokes, "So the place really was round and not flat after all."

Jack leans back to inform Sam and Noah. "I've taken up a heading for the north polar regions. We're doing about Mach five now. I can easily give you more speed, but I don't think we can get a whole lot more altitude."

"Why's that?" Noah asks.

"Coefficient of lift; air is too thin up here for the high speed wings on this aircraft. I can continue to accelerate and trade the speed for some more altitude, but we're sure going to burn up a lot of fuel we may need later."

"That's fine as long as you can maintain this altitude for a few minutes, we don't need to go any higher and we certainly don't need any more speed."

Jack says to Tom, "Okay, shut it all down and take the controls. The autopilot is not going to work up here in this thin air either, so just keep her level for a while. We can coast up here for at least twenty minutes or so while Noah shows how this Cyclatron thingy works."

The roar from the engines stop abruptly and it's suddenly so quiet a whisper can easily be heard.

Leica excitedly says to Dusty, "I feel almost weightless. I feel like if I unbuckle my seat belt I will float right out of my seat."

"Me too," Dusty replies.

Jack hears their comments and says, "You might feel lighter. I'm not sure I'd call it weightless though. That feeling will increase as we begin to slow and basically start to fall out of this low orbit. So everyone stay buckled in."

Tom says, "Okay, we're all shut down and our speed is slowly starting to taper off no problem holding our altitude,"

Noah leans forward to talk with Jack and Tom. "Then we better get a move on. You will be operating the Cyclatron from your center panel. Hans is also trained in operating the unit. It can be engaged and disengaged at the unit itself if that becomes necessary."

Sam asks, "Are we going to do that short burst test so we'll know if we have a return option?"

"I first thought so, but now I've ruled it out. We need more altitude for thinner air and we've no way to obtain it right now. We can accomplish both with this first jump." Noah explains, "Okay, Tom, that rather simple remote control device there on the console is the Cyclatron remote control. You can see I've preset the indicator dial to one microsecond. All you need to do this first time is to press the engage button and that will initiate our first very short jump. The device will then shut down automatically."

"That's it?" Tom asks.

"That's it..." Noah replies, "According to a couple of thousand computer simulated computations that one microsecond should move us well to the other side of the geosynchronous orbital belt where most of the satellites are in orbit.

Jack says, If it fails, our only option will be re-entry back into the atmosphere. Then assuming we don't burn up on reentry and the doomsday satellite doesn't explode and we can successfully glide to some landing sight back on Tropia, and…"

Tom interrupts, "I get the picture. My mom would have said sounds like jumping out of the frying pan into the fire."

Jack says, "Were ready. Does it make any difference which direction the aircraft is headed when we engage the device?"

"Not in this instance," Noah replies. "We'll discuss attitude and direction later and I'll also explain the timing a little further."

Tom comments, "Great, I'm going to need all of that to attempt any kind of reasonably accurate guesstimation in our navigation."

"I'll do my best to assist you with the calculations, Tom. So whenever you're ready…" Noah says, "Go ahead and push the button."

***

When the Cyclatron was engaged, a light wave, passing through the full light spectrum, went through the cockpit and cabin of the craft at about the speed and intensity of the flash on a camera.

The jump was over in less than an instant. In addition to testing the Cyclatron, the jump had positioned the Starchild in a much higher orbit.

With the exception of one or two gasps heard in the cabin, there was total silence.

That was until Leica shouts, "Wow! I will float right out of my seat if I release my seatbelt. We really are weightless now, aren't we?"

Several in the cabin laugh.

"Look!" Hans exclaims. "The planet is much smaller now. We must have moved a great distance away."

"If our calculations were correct," Noah says, "we should be positioned several thousand kilometers above the planet's surface now and well above the geosynchronous orbit of the satellites."

Sam looks at his watch. "Speaking of calculations and orbits, according to my chronometer, the doomsday satellite should be starting to fall out of orbit just about now."

Tom says to Jack, "We haven't tried the positioning jet packs yet. Now would be a good time."

Jack returns his seat forward and swings the craft around with the jet packs which work fine.

Hans leans forward in his seat looking out the window towards the back of the craft. "I think I see it. Back behind us to the far left there's something beginning to streak across the dark sky above the planet. It looks like a comet or maybe even a large meteor. It must be the satellite!"

The Starchild is now positioned so that Tropia is in easy view of the cabin windows and so everyone onboard can see the planet far below them.

"Are we going to be able to see the satellite when it impacts the planet?" Dusty asks.

"What do you think, Tom?" Sam asks. "You're the astronomer here."

Tom says, "Hans has already caught a glimpse of it impacting the upper atmosphere. It will fall rapidly now. Only a matter of minutes, I'm sure we will be able to see it. The impact was forecast to be along the western continent's coast line. We're not in synch with the planet's rotation, but it is coming into view just now."

"Oh great gods, look!" Dusty exclaims.

Far below the Starchild, the Doomsday Satellite falls out of orbit and plummets towards Tropia's thermosphere trailing a thin white tail. The tail turns a bright yellow as the satellite enters the upper edge of the atmosphere. It impacts the trapped unstable hydrogen layer and a brilliant red burst is sent out a thousand kilometers in every direction; forming a ring around the satellite.

The remaining section of the giant satellite impacts Tropia's surface. A giant mushroom cloud of gray-white ice crystals forms. The flame red ring continues to move outward in every direction like an airborne tsunami. The shock wave moves faster and faster.

A quarter of the way around the planet, a second satellite begins its descent. This process will duplicate itself time and time again completely covering the upper altitudes of Tropia's sky from horizon to horizon.

Sam gasps, "One fourth of the planet is already covered! That means the shock wave has gone supersonic. Exactly what I was afraid would happen all the time. This means nuclear winter will inevitably set-in. Not even taking into consideration the fallout from the radiation, I fear nothing presently alive on the planet will be able to survive."

"A Ring of Fire…" Jack exclaims softly under his breath. "Wasn't there something in the ancient writings about a ring of fire that would end a cycle on our planet?"

"Yes, I read about it in a very old quatrain, but I always assumed it was referring to a tectonic plate shift and volcanic action. Not this!"

Several of the Starchild's occupants turn away from the horrific sight and settle back into their seats. They sit now with blank expressions on their faces. After a bit, Noah turns away from the window he has been watching from and positions himself between Jack and Tom.

"Okay, Tom," Noah says, "Here's what you need to know about the computations. The acceleration induced by the Cyclatron is not linear. It increases in accordance with the Abaci sequence."

"Interesting…" Tom says, "Each subsequent unit is the sum of the previous two. What is the smallest unit?"

"As best we can calculate, about one microsecond." Noah replies, "The control for the Cyclatron is more akin to a thermostat than a cruise control. As in thermodynamics, when you set a thermostat, it doesn't get any hotter it simply runs until it obtains the temperature set. The same is true with the Cyclatron controller."

"Okay, got it," Tom says clarifying his understanding of what Noah has just explained. "The counter on the dial sets how long in microseconds the device is going to run."

"Isn't that simple enough?" Noah says, "Here are several X-Y graphs I made up to help you until you get used to the settings. X is run-time and Y is distance in lightyears."

"Please tell me we're going to stay in our own galaxy." Tom asks smiling. "I mean this place is a hundred-thousand light years across and the next nearest galaxy is three-million light years away."

Noah, "I know you're kidding, but yes. To do otherwise would be far too risky. In fact, let's start our exoplanet search in our own local star neighborhood and work our way out from there. Another thing, your logs on the bearing and duration of each jump are essential to our being able to back-track if necessary."

"My thinking exactly," Tom says reaching for his pack of star charts.

Tom spreads out his master M-map that indexes each of his sub-region charts.

Sam, Dusty, Leica and Hans divide their attention between watching out the window as the planet Tropia continues to be engulfed and listening as Noah instructs Jack and Tom on setting up for their first operational jump.

"There is one thing you all can help with," Noah says addressing the group. "We'll avoid sudden insertions into jumps. We need everyone alert and looking around. Situational awareness! That is to say, let's not fly blind during entry and coming out of hyper-light. Everyone be observant and sound off with anything you think might be helpful."

A half-dozen or so minutes pass and Jack says, "We're starting to lose a little altitude."

Noah asks Tom, "Have you got the bearing and azimuth for our jump to the first candidate star?"

"Yes, indeed I do." Tom says, "Relative to our present position, we need an azimuth of eighty degrees and a heading of two-eight-zero."

Noah says to Jack, "On that first jump I said that our heading wasn't important, but now it is because the Cyclatron is now aligned with the center line of the Starchild."

"I'm on it," Jack says, as he uses the jet packs to turn the craft to the requested heading. "The destination star will become our new magnetic north pole for every jump. Got it!"

Tom says, "Now position the craft at an inclination of forty-one degrees and that will agree with my star fix."

Jack raises the Starchild's nose slowly holding the previously set directional heading.

Tom instructs Jack, "You're almost there. Easy does it. That's it, hold what you got."

Jack asks, "So now with the Starchild in this attitude and heading, this is the direction we're going. Right?"

"Right," Noah says. "Now Tom, give me your best guess on the distance to your first candidate star."

"That would be the Sentrie12 solar system at six point nine-five light years away," Tom replies.

Noah says, "To get the runtime the Cyclatron will convert that to microseconds."

Tom stares up at the cabin ceiling mumbling for a moment and then says, "In the interest of checking it, I did it in my head. That should be about two-hours and fifteen minutes."

Tom leans forward and enters the light-year numbers into the Cyclatron remote dial on the panel. The indicator's digital dial spins for a moment; then displays one-hundred and thirty-five point three minutes.

Tom says with a smile, "Close enough, I guess."

Noah says, "You did that calculation in your head?"

Tom jokes, "Actually, it was the decimal that slowed me up a bit."

Sam comments, "I've seen him do harder problems than that in his head."

Jack says, "I hate to break up this little chat fest , but our heading and attitude are getting more and more difficult to hold."

Noah sits back down in his seat and buckles up. "Engage, when you're ready."

***

The Starchild initiates insertion into hyper-light. It is not really hyper-light as in the science fiction implications of the word. Noah often explains it as 'More akin to hitching a ride on one of two entangled quantum particles who suddenly decides to join up. This is the reason it is referred to, more simply, as a jump.'

The now gray planet Tropia begins to glow blue and the light from the stars up ahead have a reddish tint.

This is known as the red-blue light spectrum shift or color light-doppler effect. It is a common, but effective tool used by astronomers to tell if an object is moving towards them or away from them.

The Starchild's accelerating course takes it rapidly past Tropia's two moons. Zea, the small silver-white moon shifts from red to blue in color and drops away. On the left of the craft the larger moon, Zeo, comes into view and also drops away.

Now even Tropia's bright yellow solar system star takes on a bluish tent and fades to a small dot in the distance behind them.

As suddenly as the time before, a light wave passes through the full light spectrum and moves through the cabin.

The star field disappears. Outside of the craft was the absence of all light; the blackest of blacks. The Starchild was now in full jump mode.

Several attempt to speak and their voices are distorted. It seems like each knows what the other is going to say before they says it and so there seems to be no need to say it.

The same thing is true of seeing. One can see what they turning to look at before they turn to look at it.

At first, it is very confusing. However, it is only a temporary inconvenience as they will grow uses to it over the next few jumps.

Noah watches over Jack's shoulder as the Cyclatron's amber digital readout dial starts to tick down.

The digital readout on the console spins faster and faster. He knows, from prior test-runs, that the real time in the cabin will not agree with the preset time calculation, but he does not know exactly what the delta between the two will be.

In less than ten minutes of real time on the cabin clock the Cyclatron dial reads all zeros.

Tom exclaims sarcastically, "I'm guessing we've dropped out of hyper-light."

The star field reappeared as suddenly as it disappeared and visibility became as clear as the best summer night for seeing.

Whatever happened to the two and a quarter hours is simply unknown.

Noah jokes, "We must have left some of the jump time in the space-time continuum."

The usually quiet Leica asks, "Professor, what do you really think happened to the missing time."

Noah replies, "I know every place in the universe is in its own time zone, but maybe we passed through something like a space savings time zone and forgot to set our clocks back," and Noah smiles."

Leica asks again, "No, seriously now, tell me what you really think may have happened to the missing time."

Noah says, "A multiverse."

Leica pursues Noah's answer further, "I think I know what you mean, but please explain it to me."

"Okay," Noah concedes, "I don't like taking positions on unproven theories, but if there are parallel universes or there are other dimensions unknown to us, I think maybe the Starchild must have taken a shortcut through one of them. That's my best guess, anyway."

Leica starts to ask something more and Noah says, "I know this is a field of interest for you, Leica, but we'll have to discuss this in more detail later. Right now, Tom and Jack need my assistance as we make this planetary evaluation pass."

Jack says, "Based on our closing rate on that star up ahead, we're moving pretty fast, but we're also slowing."

"If we're lucky," Tom says, "That star should be Sentrie12 and the planet we are looking for should be the second or third one orbiting it."

Noah suggests, "Go ahead and turn on the side scan radar and the spectral analysis equipment."

"Coming on now," Jack replies.

Tom says, "We need to make the best of one flyby. A turnaround would be difficult and a waste a lot of time if the planet is unsatisfactory."

Jack agrees, "We also don't want to get too close to the planet because of gravitational pull and atmospheric drag, assuming there is an atmosphere."

Noah is up out of his seat peering out of the windscreen between Jack and Tom. Noah says, "Good plan, but we can always use the Cyclatron to make short jumps in an emergency. That is, so long as you stay in rarefied air. It's powered by radioactive plutonium so it shouldn't run out of fuel like the Starchild could."

Sam is watching out the cabin window. He points cabin left and says, "There! I saw something sparkle just coming out from behind the star."

"I see it now too," Hans calls out.

Tom is using the radar to scan with and says, "That's it, that's about the right size and distance from its star. The radar returns confirm that it is a solid planet, not a gas planet."

"Great! Sam says excitedly. "So far, so good,"

"We're slowing more now." Jack says, "I think we're going to be able to coast right up to the planet. In fact, we're moving almost perfectly into position for us to make the flyby."

***

An hour or so passes as Tom and Jack continue to collect and process data from the planet orbiting Sentrie12.

Tom is not smiling. "It doesn't look very good," he says. "The spectral analyses show no signs of surface water. The radar returns indicate the planet is a little small, meaning the gravity would be only about four-fifths of that on Tropia."

Tom continues, "The planet does have an atmosphere, but it contains very little oxygen by percentage and there are some airborne methane gases. The really bad news is the temperature on the planet is close to the boiling point of water, about ninety degrees centigrade, in the daytime and below freezing at night."

Noah says to Tom, "First of all, I congratulate you for your navigation skills. Secondly, I would never have guessed we could be this accurate in finding a single planet in the vastness of space on our first try."

"The truth is that it was probably beginners luck. I don't see how we can hope to always be this accurate," Tom says.

He takes a marking pen and strikes through the star name Sentrie12 on his list.

***

Chapter Eight – Goldilocks Zone

Noah says, "With your math and my luck at guessing distances, how could we miss?"

"You two guys don't get too big-headed yet." Jack interjects jokingly, "Where do we go next, Tom?"

Tom reaches for another set of charts. "That would be Tansedi58. I'll get started calculating the coordinates."

"You are keeping a good log of each of our jump settings, aren't you, Tom?" Sam asks.

"I'm logging them manually right here on these charts."

Tom adds, "Oh yes, plus the Nav computer is recording them and I plan to download a copy of that data when we're done."

"That's great!" Sam says. "I guess you know the only way we could ever find Tropia again, assuming we wanted to, is by reversing that data. Or for that matter just reversing course,"

Tom concurs, "We have a really good celestial navigational computer onboard this craft and I believe I can use it for star fixes. Which means I can almost dial in the coordinates for a star position and reverse calculate it back to our position. What do you think of that?"

Sam says, "Kind of like the star locator on an amateur astronomy telescope, right?"

Tom replies, "Right. I'll get to work on our new course calculations."

Jack says, "Sam this will be a good time to check out your idea about artificial gravity. As I understand we're going to put the Starchild into a large sideways loop, not nose to tail, but sideways, making it an extended leg of a giant imaginary space station wheel. Is that correct?"

Sam leans forward, "Yes, you're going to use only a very small blast from two of your jet packs to start the Starchild moving sideways and up. The computer program I wrote will memorize this curve and the Starchild will make a complete loop. After that the Starchild should continue to coast through the arc completing the loop. It won't feel like gravity but it should give about a half G pull toward the floor and I suspect it may make one list slightly to the side kind of like walking in the fun house.

Jack says, "Okay you all get buckled up while we try out this idea Sam has of an imaginary space wheel."

The Starchild completes the lazy sideways loop and all are amazed as they feel the centrifugal force.

Sam laughed, "Well, at least when you drop something it will kind of try to fall to the floor."

Dusty says, "I think it's great, better than floating around in the cabin like we've been doing."

Noah says, "Good ideas Sam!"

Sam stands up to stretch by placing his hands on the cabin ceiling and alternately the back of his seat as he straightens his shirt and pants. "Take all the time you want. I for one thought the blackout period was a little spooky."

To the rest of those in the cabin Sam says, "If you all will excuse me I need to use the facilities. For everyone's information, it's a vacuum operated system and you probably ought to read the instruction plaque on the wall before using it."

Sam makes his way to the back of the craft to where the small but plush toilet compartment is located just behind the Cyclatron hard mounted to the cabin floor.

Dusty says to Sam, "I checked it out earlier. How'd you get the Finance people to pay for something as lavish and expensive as that on an experimental craft? Why it's got mahogany inlayed trim and a mosaic vanity."

"They didn't. You know that big old four-engine executive jet parked out behind our hangar?"

"Yes, I think it belonged to the State Department. It hasn't moved in years. Don't tell me…"

"You bet we did. We pulled the whole thing out of that old behemoth and installed it here in the Starchild. I figured no one would ever miss it."

Noah, who has been listening to Sam and Dusty, asks, "You're right about that, particularly in light of recent events. What I am really curious about is where did you get that state-of-the-art water recycler? I hadn't seen that little gem before."

Sam smiles, "You can't guess? Well, you can thank Hans' for that one. The other night, he went out to one of those space shuttles that was grounded due to a recent treaty and let's just say borrowed it for our trip."

Noah replies, "I guess there are advantages to working the night-shift after all."

Sam announces, "Oh yeah gang, there is a small case of bottled water back here. Mark your name on the bottles because we'll have to refill them from the recycler. I suggest you try not to get dehydrated as that will increase your chances of hypoxia in this thinner pressurization air. There are also some cases of nutrition bars, all I could scrounge up on short notice; help yourselves."

Noah turns around in his seat and pats Dusty on the leg, "You've been awful quiet, Gal, how you doing?"

"Scared as hell most of the time!"

"If it's any consolation to you, so am I."

"Not much help, but thanks for sharing. What do I do now? I mean what should I worry about most?"

"Based on the limiting factors, the first being our oxygen supply, the Oxygenator. It, however, seems to be working okay. Hans has been checking it regularly."

Dusty glances aft as though looking for the unit.

Noah adds, "Isn't that right, Hans?"

"Yes Sir that's correct. The cabin pressurization is holding better than we expected. However, the lead casing on the Cyclatron seems to be a little warm to the touch."

"Please continue to monitor it and let me know if it starts to get a lot warmer."

"Yes Sir, I will."

Noah turns back to Dusty. "There you have it. So at some point we will find a suitable planet to land on…"

Dusty says, "Or we will run out of water and nourishment or some major part will fry or we will burn up all our fuel making low passes on possible habitable planets till we're out of options!"

Noah pauses then shrugs and says, "More or less."

Dusty says with sarcasm, "I know I asked and thank you for explaining. I feel so much better now!"

Most in the cabin have been listening to Noah and Dusty's conversation and they laugh along with Noah at Dusty's recitation. It is a nervous laugh, but a light-hearted moment never-the-less."

"On the other hand," Noah says as an afterthought, "All of that could take several weeks so you see we have a good chance of success in our search before anything bad happens," and he smiles.

***

The flight deck on the Starchild is slightly elevated from the passenger compartment. It is a step and a half up.

The sweep-back wings are far aft and the panoramic windshield in the cockpit provides for a wide field of view.

What is now the passenger compartment (the cabin) was previously a large bomb bay designed to house a multi-missile launcher that could be lowered into position or retracted back into the bomb bay for super sonic flight.

These features came about because the Starchild's design, for the new space passenger craft, was originally based on the popular FXC-122 star wars fighter bomber currently in service with the UTAF.

****

Leica goes forward with two bottles of water. She stands on the cockpit entry step and offers them to Jack and Tom. She says, "Sam says for us not to forget to drink water."

Jack takes both bottles from Leica. He sets them down beside the seats and says, "Thanks."

"Would either of you like a nutrition bar?

Tom shakes his head no.

Jack says, "No, thanks, not right now. Tell me something Leica, is there a coffee maker on board this homemade rocket ship."

"No. I'm sorry there isn't. I could sure use a good cup of java right now myself."

Jack mumbles, "Damn," under his breath.

Tom finishes his calculations and reads them to Jack who inputs them as Tom reads them.

Tom makes a pointing gesture out the windshield and says, "That's the best I can do. Let's haul ass."

Jack says to Leica, "Better take your seat now, Honey. We're fixin' to jump again."

In a louder voice Jack says, "Welcome aboard Starchild Airline. You'll buckle up now, you hear. We'll be arriving at a planet in the Tansedi58 solar system or somewhere in the universe in about forty-five minutes, give or take a half hour," thus continuing to making fun of the delta in the unknown two times.

The cabin clock is showing twenty-four-hundred hours, the beginning and end of their first day's journey across the known universe to find a new home.

It is now mid-day of their second real time day in space. Sam and Hans are in the back by the Cyclatron discussing the devices condition.

Sam says, "I don't think the overheating is severe enough to worry about."

Hans concurs, "I also have a new blower fan in my spare parts; if we get a chance I could replace it."

Sam says, "Only if we had we had to!"

Hans asks, "I have a question on another subject if you wouldn't mind my asking."

"Sure go ahead."

"When we first come out of hyper-light, the Starchild seems to slow more rapidly at the higher speeds than later on? It feels to me like something is putting on the brakes hard and then letting up after we slow."

"We are riding in a laboratory experiment for an unknown field of astrophysics, so anything is possible. I'm assuming you have some kind of theory about this."

"I first believed there might be some sort of force like gravitational fields affecting the craft from distant celestial bodies. Then I considered widely spaced molecules."

Sam agrees, "Yes, even in space there are gases like hydrogen and helium, and particles like carbon and nitrogen."

"I'd like your opinion. Could dark matter or dark energy drag be the cause? Could they have some effect on an object at or near light speeds; like the sound barrier had a limiting effect on early jet aircraft speeds?"

Sam is impressed at Hans' perception of the events and says, "Possibly, in fact that's an astute observation on your part. Bottom line is we haven't made much scientific progress in those areas. Noah may have an opinion on this. Ask him when you get a chance."

Noah has nodded off to sleep in his seat. Leica moves up to sit in Sam's seat across the aisle from Noah so as to position herself to ask questions of Noah when he wakes.

Which he does shortly and Leica pounces, "Professor, I was wondering if…"

Noah straighten up in his seat and says, "A lot of people back at the space center called me that, but I have a feeling the seven of us are going to be together for a long time so just call me Noah. Now what's your question?"

Hans moves into Leica's seat. He may not get a chance to ask his questions, but at least he will be close enough to listen to whatever Noah explains to Leica.

Leica explains her question, "Right now we are floating in space somewhere in the Tansedi58's solar system, but where are we when we are being hurled across space-time by the Cyclatron at speeds greater than the speed-of-light? Are we actually passing through space? If we are, what keeps us from crashing into some giant red star like Beetlejuice or burning up in the white hot nebula of a newly forming star as we travel through?"

Noah says, "Sadly, I have no really good answer for what you have obviously thought through so very carefully and I suspect that my attempt to answer will only create many more questions I also do not have the answers for."

"Please try me. I'm not a scientist, but astrophysics is kind of a hobby for me." Leica pleads.

"Okay, what is the smallest unit of motion; a microsecond or one thousandth of a microsecond or what?" Noah asks, "We don't really know, do we?"

Leica shakes her head no.

"However, like a single bit on a digital recording, it must exist. This begs the question." Noah says, "What is in between those two lowest denominators?"

Leica takes a deep breath, shrugs her shoulders and says, "I don't guess I really know."

Noah answers for her, "I chose to call it the non-continuum of space-time."

"Oh." Leica says.

Noah explains, "I think the most likely scenario is that when we are traveling faster than the speed-of-light we are temporally suspended in non-space-time or to over simplify we are in another dimension. As of yet, what or where that is we don't really know."

"How will we find out?" Leica asks.

"The best clue we have is when we are connected to the Cyclatron, inside the Starchild, we are like single quantum particle. We can know where we are, but not how fast we are going or vise-versa, but not both. I assume you have studied quantum entanglement, haven't you?"

Leica and Hans both nod their heads yes,

Dusty has been thumbing through a wrinkled movie magazine some worker left and everyone has read several times out of boredom, but mostly lessening to Noah.

"Now you're confusing the girl, Noah." Dusty says.

"No, really he's not," Leica insists.

Tom motions for Noah t come forward.

Noah says to Leica ad Hans, "That will have to end the lesson for now. I need to help Tom with some calculations. Remind me and we'll discuss it some more later. That is, if you're interested."

"Oh yes, I'm very interested in this sort of thing." Leica assures Noah.

"You'll have to remind him, Leica," Dusty says. "I assure you he'll forget."

Tom asks Noah to check his figures for the next hyper-light jump. Noah goes forward and reviews Tom's calculations on his pad. "It all looks correct to me."

Jack announces, "Buckle up! Even though it won't do much good if we fly into a giant asteroid at sub-light speeds."

Tom adds, "But it might keep you from bumping your head on something when we enter and exit jumps."

Tom reads Jack the attitude and heading needed to position the Starchild for their next jump.

Jack motions for Tom to press the button on the Cyclatron, which he does and the Starchild begins its insertion into hyper-light.

***

Hours later the yellowish, obviously desert, planet they had arrived at and surveyed begins to glow blue and the stars up ahead shift their glow from white to red as they give up on Tansedi58 and depart for Centuri5.

Noah watches, once again, over Jack's shoulder as the Cyclatron digital counter dial starts its ticks down.

Behind them, an entire solar system fades into the distance and the craft enters the realm of hyper-light.

As suddenly and as mysteriously as each time before, a light-wave passes through the entire spectrum of light and moves through the cabin.

The star field outside the craft disappears and everything outside the cabin goes completely black.

The digital readout on the console spins increasingly faster downward from its original numeric setting. In about twelve minutes, real time, the dial reads all zeros.

The star field comes into view once again, but through the front windscreen the Starchild is not closing on any observable star.

Jack exclaims, "Clearly, we have dropped out of hyper-light, but where is Centuri5?"

Tom questions, "It is possible that we could we have overshot?"

Hans turns in his seat to look behind them. "I can't see anything aft."

Noah, from the opposite side of the cabin, turns in his seat to look back behind them for a star or planet.

Noah says, "Nothing on this side either."

Jack uses the jet packs to slowly roll the craft so as to look under them. Then he makes a three-hundred-sixty degree swing back to their original heading and attitude with no visual contact.

Noah concludes, "That's it then. The best candidate star has to be that distant one directly up ahead of us. It's on basically the same heading as our original course."

Tom shrugs and says, "The distance was at best a guess. I don't think there is an error in my calculations. I just missed it. I agree. That star ahead has to be at least a half-a-light year away."

Jack says, "Even at the speed we are coasting, it would take us a couple of years to get to that star. We'll have to go hyper-light again."

"What do you think, Tom, you want to use a half-a-light year?" Noah asks,

"Let's use point forty-five of a light year. I think that would be much closer. I'd rather undershoot than overshoot."

Noah scribbles a number on Tom's pad. "Here," and he passes the pad back to Tom.

"Let me know when you're ready," Jack says, "but there is one thing I want to start doing different. I'm going to turn the long range radar on as we drop out of hyper-light from now on."

"Sam says, "Good idea! Odds are, we can go hurdling through space at sub-light all day long and not run into anything. We sure don't want to emerge headed right for a Kuiper belt or fly into an Oort cloud."

Jack says, "The radar can see a lot further ahead and I'll be able to take evasive action quicker. We don't have to worry about that massive black hole, Tom says we are not going anywhere near the center of the galaxy"

"Tell me something, Jack," Sam asks jokingly. "Is it true that the first thing a pilot does in an emergency is turn off the autopilot?"

Jack laughs. "Truer words were never spoken."

"I don't get the joke," Dusty says to Sam. "Explain it to me?"

"It's about pilots and their egos. They always think they can fly a craft better than any device no matter how smart it is."

"Oh," Dusty says, like she would have preferred not to have shown her ignorance on the subject by asking.

"You all can relax for a bit," Tom says. "I'm going to recheck all my calculations one more time."

Leica asks, "I wonder if any of the rest of you have been feeling some of the things I have?"

"Like what, for example?" Dusty asks.

"When we are in hyperspace, it seems as though the past, present and future of the moment are all being experienced simultaneously."

Several of the others in the cabin readily agree.

"Exactly," Dusty says, "and it seems to be much more pronounced as we enter hyper-light and again when we drop back out. Noah, what's your take on this?"

"I've been experiencing it, too. I do know that it has always been theorized that at speeds approaching the speed-of-light, one would be able to see around corners."

Noah continues, "There's one other that is supposed to occur and that's time relative to the point of origin seems to slow until it almost stops. That's in theory, so it is likely you are experiencing what you say you are."

"Oh," Noah adds, "I don't think it's harmful. Think of it as a real version of those fictional Stasis Fields so popularly used in those sci-fi novels you like to read."

"Sam, you have any suggestions," Dusty asks.

"It seems to me to be more of a mental state than a physical state." Noah says.

Sam says. "My suggestion is to do what pilots often do when they are flying on instruments and experience vertigo. Fix your attention on something in the cabin or on one idea and don't let your thoughts drift into a confused state. Mostly, these jumps are only for a short period of time and I think you can overcome it that way."

Tom is ready and Jack hollers back, "Buckle up we're going to make another short jump."

***

The exoplanet orbiting the star Tansedi58 turned out to be a frozen ice planet and did not take long to check out.

Tom crossed it off of his list.

The next two planets Tom had lined up were around the stars Gliese14 and Cancria23. They also proved to be uninhabitable.

So time after time Tom calculated the settings, dialed in the numbers, aligned the Starchild and they jumped at hyper-light speeds across the Zoatropia to star after star. Again and again they failed to find a habitable planet.

True to the ancient nursery rhyme, each planet was either too hot or too cold, too big or too small, too toxic or no atmosphere at all... and so it went.

***

Chapter Nine – Lost In Space

By the mission lapsed-time clock on bulkhead, the Starchild's passengers are now beginning their fifth, real time, day in space. Over a hundred and twenty hours by the cabin clock. Not only have they been traveling through space, but the accumulation of the total hyper-light jump distances has advanced them millions of years forward in the space-time continuum.

At this point, they are all mentally and physically exhausted. Plus, the disorientations during jumps has also added to their fatigue. More than anything else, their failure to find a suitable planet is psychologically wearing on each of them.

The group is now dressed alike in red white and blue Starchild T-shirts. How this came about was when the Cyclatron began overheating and the environmental system began having trouble keeping the cabin cool. Street clothes and jump suits became uncomfortably warm. Maintaining modesty had become a real problem.

Hans remembered a box of commemorative T-shirts in the cargo compartment that were never given out due to the fact that the Starchild christening ceremony never took place. Hans passed them out to everyone and all appreciated the new cooler attire.

The white T-shirts read 'Starchild Aircraft Corporation' in red and blue letters across the front. The colorful T-shirts also perked everyone up for a bit.

Leica had long since shed her work coveralls under which she had a pair of gym shorts.

Dusty had fortunately stuffed a pair of Bermuda shorts in her large handbag when she rush to leave her house with only what she had on at the time.

The Starchild is still adrift near large nebula cloud. Jack is taking a nap in his seat and Tom is frantically recalculating all of you be equations; mostly to no avail because he checked was correct.

Sam says to Dusty, "You seemed deep in thought. What seems to be bothering you? "

Dusty sighs, "Mostly what I was thinking about, at least for the last hour or so, is about those poor people back on Tropia, if anyone survived the initial blast and what they must be going through right now."

"This may sound crude, but…" Sam hesitates to go on with what he was about to say.

"But what?" Dusty asks.

Noah, who had turned around to listen, looks away because he knows what Sam is about to try to explain.

Sam continues, "As difficult as it might be to think in these terms, those we knew back on Tropia have been deceased now for thousands of years."

Dusty asks, "What are you talking about, Sam?"

Sam looks at Noah pleadingly for assistance but none is forthcoming so Sam says, "I've been too busy with all that's going on to think about all of that or maybe I am just in denial."

"Okay, explain it to me," Dusty says.

Everyone onboard except Tom who is busy, has now turned to listen to what Sam has to say.

Sam starts again to explain, but chokes and says, "Go on, Noah. Please, you expllain it to her."

"You see," Noah says, "While it has only been a matter of a couple days since we left Tropia, each time we've made a hyper-light jump, onboard the Starchild only a few minutes passed for us in real time, but millenniums passed back on Tropia. Those people you are remembering on Tropia, are no longer there."

Dusty says, "I remember now about the time and distance thing. So even if they survived the nuclear winter, it all happened a long time ago. That's correct isn't it?"

Sam explains further, "Actually, it happened a 'long time ago in a galaxy far, far away...' so to speak."

Noah adds, "With the exception of that first jump, when we were in orbit above Tropia, the Abaci sequencing of the Cyclatron has accelerated us multiple times the speed-of-light into the future."

Dusty asks, "Could we ever go back?"

Sam answers, "Possibly if we needed to or wanted to, but millenniums would have passed on Tropia. That's the reason Tom is keeping such a detailed and accurate log of our jump times. You wouldn't be able to go home to what you remember. It just wouldn't be there. The planet might still be there but it may not yet be habitable."

With Dusty's concerns and questions put to rest, Hans and Leica once again corner Noah.

Noah says, "Before we get back to playing twenty questions about basic physics, it might be worth our time to look more closely at the point Sam made."

Leica asks, "What is that, Sir?"

Noah explains, "Many theoretical scientists believe the reason there are no super advanced, highly intelligent civilizations in the universe is because when each reaches a point in technology where they can destroy itself, they usually do!"

Hans and Leica pause for a few thoughtful moment and then begin taking turns bomb-barding him with one astrophysics question after another."

Leica asks, "Could there be short-cuts through space and what about wormholes in space?"

"Short-cuts in space maybe, but wormholes are pure science fiction," Noah replies.

Hans asks, "What do you base that on, Sir?"

Noah anticipated the question and quickly answered, "If they do exist, you couldn't use them for travel because the instant you approached one, because of the extremely high energy levels it would take to keep a wormhole open, you and your spacecraft would be instantly reduced to atomic and subatomic particles ."

Leica says, "Then you categorically rule out the use of worm holes as a means of space travel?"

Noah reassures Leica, "Yes, even if they were found to exist, I still do!"

Hans says, "Tell us about black holes, what they are and why they exist?"

"Ah, now there's a good subject." Noah says, "I often open my lectures with 'Black holes are not black and not holes at all!' and then I go on to explain."

Hans asks, "Which is it, they are not black or they are not holes?"

"Both, you see the gravitational pull, caused by the great mass of the black hole, is so strong that neither light nor reflected light can escape. Thus, invisible or stealth might be better a nomenclature. Black is classified as a color and the color black is defined as the absence of all color. So maybe the name is appropriate after all."

"Now the part about them being holes is altogether another thing. Some people seem to think that black holes are donut shaped or shaped like a horn-of-plenty. Science fiction writers make this mistaken identity even more absurd by flying space ships into or through them."

Hans and Leica both chuckle.

"What's worse," Noah continues, "Is that they even fly their fictional space ships into the black hole or through the black hole and come out unscathed into some mysterious new world."

Leica says, "So nothing falls into the black hole?"

Noah says, "Let me tell you a story. When I was a young man I traveled to see for myself what was left of the vast rain forests and meet the jungle people who lived there. The natives mined the sand in the nearby river bed for gold dust and traded it for whatever goods and supplies they could. Occasionally, they would pound small nuggets into paper thin sheets called gold leaf. On religious holidays they would take the gold leaf to a nearby temple and gild it onto a giant wooden altar. Over the years, the golden altar grew larger and larger."

"Got it!" Leica says, "Stuff simply goes splat, planets stars and all, onto its surface forming a paper thin coating of collapsed atoms to build up and build up. Is that correct?"

"Sure, it's not a hole it's a solid mass." Noah says with an elfish grin on his face.

Hans says, "I get it, too. I understand now, too! If we are through with the subject of black holes, may I tell you about a theory I have. I discussed it with Sam the other day and he recommended I ask you about it."

Hans goes on to tell Noah about what he observed when the Starchild slows, coming out of hyper-light, and its possible connection to dark matter and dark energy."

Noah, like Sam, is impressed with Han's analysis and says, "Those are very astute observations on your part, Hans. You are to be commended on your observations and original thinking."

Hans smiles and says, "Thank you, Sir."

Noah goes on to say, "As I am sure you are aware, we haven't made significant progress in the understanding of dark energy, or dark matter. Here is what we know and don't know about dark matter is that it does not interact with light and that it does feel the force of gravity."

Noah pauses to think for a moment and then says, "Depending on where we end up, civilization wise, in the future I will make every effort to help you setup a research project on the subject. However, for now, you two will have to excuse me. It looks like Tom has finished his calculations."

Tom swings around in his seat and says to the group, "We've worked our way across most of the open area between two of the outer arms of the Zoatropeia. Now we are moving into a much more star-rich environment."

"You mean stars with exoplanets?" Dusty asks.

Tom replies, "Yes and also the right age of stars. This area was well charted by many astronomers back on Tropia, but by now that was millenniums ago. So here's the problem, we have now moved so far forward in time it is becoming increasingly more difficult to extrapolate our exact position in the vast star field."

"So how bad off are we?" Sam inquires.

"Short version… we're lost," Tom replies.

Noah listens with the rest of the group, then says, "I kind of figured that out on my own, however, giving up is not an option! Tell us what you do know and don't know."

"Okay!" Tom begins, "We know from experience that the stars with exoplanets seem to be within a belt about twenty-six thousand light years from the center of the Zoatropeia where the super massive black hole is located. We need to stay within that radius."

Noah asks, "If we can't get a star fix, how do we maintain that radius? With the result we have had so far, we are not likely to just stumble onto a candidate planet."

"Actually, I have a plan," Tom replies smiling, "There is a very good candidate star only eight point six light years from the star Sirius. On my chart the star is identified as Terrain and the canidate planet is Terra3."

"So how do we get to Terrain Star?" Noah asks, "No wait, where having this discussion because it's not that easy. Am I right?"

"Yes, right as usual. We can't there from here." Tom explains, "To find it we're going we have to first locate the star system Sirius and that's the problem. You remember my saying that if I could locate three really good pulsars, I could use triangulation to locate our position. They're as good as GPS beacons out here."

"Doesn't he mean quasar?" Hans whispers to Sam.

Sam whispers, "A quasar is a radio signal beamed from the center of a galaxy. He means pulsar the X-Ray flash from a collapsed neutron star."

Jack speaks up, "And guess what folks, the Starchild has an X-Nav unit installed and it works. I haven't seen one of these units in years; didn't even know the military used them anymore."

Sam says, "They don't, but we had a brand new X-Nav unit in stock. So I had it installed; thought we might need one out here."

"So now what's the problem?" Noah asks.

Jack answers Noah, "We can't get a fix on the one or more of the three pulsars we need. That's the problem!"

"That's right," Tom says, "I think the problem is that massive nebulae. That newly forming star off of our right-wing has a lot of density and there's also a large amount of what is referred to as the local fluff in this area."

Noah asks, "So you're saying we can't get there through these local fluff, nebulas cloud and stuff."

"No, I'm not saying that at all," Tom says, "I am relatively certain we have passed through or over this area more than once in our previous jumps, but once on the other side the X-Nav well work and we can locate Sirius."

"So again, why is Sirius important?" Sam asks.

"The star consists of a one large star, a smaller star and a dead star all orbiting each other." Tom says, "That way we can make a positive identification of our location."

Sam asks, "Are there no prospective planets orbiting Sirius?"

"My guess is no." Tom says, "Even if there are, it is a trinary star and any planets would most likely have very erratic orbits."

Tom scans the cabin looking for any disagreement or comments.

There are none. In fact, no one says anything.

Tom turns his seat back forward into the cockpit.

Jack says, "Hay, you all back there in the cabin, buckle up and sound off when you're all ready to go."

***

Chapter Ten – Small Blue Planet

After having cleared the nebulous cloud and making a slow confirmation pass by Sirius' triple star, the Starchild drops out of the third jump with the Starchild positioned at the apex of the Terrain solar system.

Still coasting at near light-speed, the craft is floating millions of kilometers above Jupiter. Five of the nine planets are readily visible as points-of-light in the distance plus the brilliant Terrain's star, the Earth's Sun.

The planets are aligned like ducks in a row. This occurs about every twenty years in multi-planet solar systems. The planet's distance from their solar star has more to do with their mass, size and composition than anything else. For example, the rocky planets seem to stay in close to their solar star while the gas giants are grouped further out.

It is interesting to note that planets orbiting a solar star, within the galaxy, orbit at different speeds based on their distance from the star. Inversely, stars orbiting in a galaxy all travel at the same speed regardless from their distance from the center of the galaxy.

Jack and Tom descend the Starchild into the orbital plane of the planets and turn inbound towards the sun. This apex down approach was conceived by Jack and Tom as being the best way to insert the craft into a solar system at sub-light-speeds. This allows the craft to avoid the denser parts of the Kuiper belt, usually dense past the orbital plain, and the vast outer Oort area filled with small ice planets or planetoids.

The space travelers are treated to spectacular scenic views of the two gas giants as they fly by Jupiter with its ranging red storm and Saturn with its many rings.

The Starchild is slowing geometrically now. Jack is keeping the Starchild a little above the orbital plane as they descend towards the sun. This has he would be quick to say, he figures there are fewer rocks in the road just above the orbital plane.

They pass the asteroid belt never seeing so much as one meteor and continue their descent on to the planet Mars.

Jack has been narrating what he sees from the cockpit over the intercom to those in the cabin who do not have as good a forward view.

As they approach Mars, Jack says, "There are four rock planets between here and the sun and are usually good candidates for having an atmosphere. The one up ahead is clearly a desert planet and probably has a very thin atmosphere if any at all. We'll pass it up for now. The best candidate is that distant blue planet coming up next. Blue is a good indication it may have an abundance of water and where there is water there is usually life."

Dusty can no longer stand the suspense. Even though the artificial gravity is off, she unbuckles her seatbelt and makes her way handover seatback up to the cockpit between Jack and Tom.

Jack glances around to see Dusty hanging onto the side of his seat and says, "Curiosity finally got the best of you, huh?"

Dusty, a little out of breath replies, "Are you kidding! Please, please let this next one be a habitable planet. Oh please!"

Tom says to Dusty, "We'll know in just a little while."

Tom says, "We better start slowing now or we'll rip past that blue planet or worse, fly into its atmosphere and burn up like a marshmallow in a roaring campfire."

"Firing retro thrusters now," Jack says and then turns to Dusty, who is still hanging on the side of his seat to say, "You better go back and get buckled in. The rest of this ride is going to get a little rough.

Tom says to Dusty as she turns to leave, "If it's any encouragement to you, judging from the massive halo glow of sunlight around the blue planet, it's going to have a more than adequate atmosphere."

Dusty says, "Oh I do so hope!"

Jack picks up his narration to those in the cabin by continuing to describe what he sees and says, "We're passing the only moon the blue planet appears to have."

Jack comments to Tom, "An advanced civilization would likely have a space station on its moon."

Tom says, "The dark side of the moon, the one that always faces away from the planet, is coming up on our left now. If there was an advanced civilization on the blue planet, it would be more logical to put a space station or communication station on the side facing the planet, unless they wish to hide the space base."

Noah is looking out his cabin window and raises his voice to be heard, "I'm viewing the moon's surface now. Pretty dark everywhere, don't see anything like a lit up space station. I'll look back as we pass the face of the moon and see if I can see anything."

As the Starchild passes the moon, Noah says, "Nothing on the face anywhere either. Looks like a giant barren rock with lots of meteor craters."

As the Starchild draws near the third rock from the sun, Tom exclaims, "Well, would you look at that!"

"I'm looking," Jack yells out, "Large bodies of water, oceans in fact, and great big continents. I don't want to jump to conclusions, but I think we may be home."

Everyone onboard the Starchild cheers.

Now the challenge becomes how to safely descend into the planet earth's atmosphere without burning up the Starchild in the process.

Jack and Tom spend the next couple hours carefully skipping the Starchild off of the denser and denser atmosphere layers as they descend towards terra firma. As they descend, they check oxygen and poisonous gases.

The Starchild circles the earth at high orbital altitudes several times and then descends to the lowest possible orbital altitude. Jack has rolled the Starchild several times facilitating views for the cabin passengers, but no one has seen any signs of civilization yet.

Tom says, "If there were any cities of any size of consequence, we should have seen them by now. We're moving around now to the night side of the planet where we surely will be able to see any non-natural lights."

On the night side of the planet, Sam calls out, "I've been watching very carefully. I've seen several massive forest fires, obviously been burning for a long time, and a half-dozen active volcanoes, but no cities."

Jack says, "We're reaching a flight level where the Starchild can fly so I'm going to engage the engines. We'll go down and take a good look with a low pass. You all should be feeling that natural gravity now. "

Leica says, "Boy are we, feels great!"

The Starchild descends over the Mediterranean valley which is now hundreds of miles of beautiful green pastures with animals grazing on it. The land barrier at Gibraltar has not yet broken through to allow the Mediterranean Sea to be created.

Dusty exclaims, "Great gods! Those are dinosaurs!"

Noah, who is also watching out the cabin window says, "Looks like it to me, too. Who would have ever thought that something like that still existed?"

Dusty adds, "Yeah, it's a virtual Jurassic zoo."

Jack has slowed the Starchild to speed slightly above stalling in order to allow a good long look at what they are flying over.

Dusty begins rattling off the names of dinosaurs she can recognize. "Look, there is a herd of Stegosaurs and over there's a group of Raptors hunting. Oh and look, we're coming up on a large herd of Brachiosaurus and those over there, I don't even know what they are."

Jack says, "It's for damn sure we don't need to land here. What do you say we go explore that other continent over across the smaller ocean?"

Tom, Noah and Sam are all in agreement. Jack goes supersonic to cross the Atlantic and as the airspeed drops off the Starchild descends over the area that, millenniums later, will become known as the Bermuda triangle.

There is a large island about 100 km long and 50 km wide in the shallow waters about 200 km off the coast of the new continent; the uninhabited island of Atlantis.

In the western regions of the northern continent there are a lot more active volcanoes, but no sign of man.

Noah suggests, "Why don't we park the Starchild in a low orbit and save what fuel we have left. This will give us a chance to organize our thoughts and decide if we are going to stay here or not."

By mutual agreement, they abandon their tour of the planet and the Starchild climbs out into a low orbit.

***

With the Starchild floating in orbit and artificial gravity restored, the group discusses their options or as Noah would put it, what they know and don't know.

Tom says to Dusty, "Let's start with the assumption that our Terra3 candidate planet is developing along the same lines as Tropia."

Dusty replies, "A fair assumption."

Tom asks, "Roughly what time period are we looking at for the development of modern civilization."

Dusty gathers her thoughts and says, "It's hard for an untrained observer like me to be able to tell if the dinosaurs we saw in the field were from the late Triassic or mid Jurassic period. So, I am just going to guess that the planet is in about the middle of the Mesozoic era."

Tom says, "And so?"

Dusty shrugs her shoulders, replies, "And so, that would be about 145 million years before modern man will be the dominant species on this planet."

Sam comments, "We certainly know now why civilizations never make contact with each other. When somebody calls there is nobody home at the time."

Tom looks over at Noah and says, "I know you've got some thoughts on the subject. I can see the wheels turning in your mind from here. What you got?"

Noah begins, "Reminds me of a story. An astronaut, before leaving on a long trip, takes all his money and invests it at compound interest. When he returns years later, he calls his bank to hear of the millions he has made. An operator answers and says please deposit $10,000 for the first three minutes of your call."

Tom says to Sam, "I understand the joke, but explain it to me. What is he really saying?"

Sam replies with a smile, "Noah just means things change."

Tom says, "That's it?"

Noah laughs.

Sam is about ready to laugh as he says, "No Tom, just having a little fun at your expense. What Noah is referring to is the old wives tale about the astronaut who leaves in a spaceship traveling at the speed of light.

Tom says, "I need more."

Sam continues, "That's where E equals MC squared kicks in. Time slows or even stops at the speed of light. The astronaut ages hardly any while everyone back on his home planet grows old and die. It's never been tested because no one has ever lived long enough to greet the astronaut on his return."

Tom says, "Thank you, Sam, for explaining. So, Noah, you think we need to test the theory?"

Noah replies, "More or less. The way I see it, we have two choices based on one unknown. We have no idea at this point whether aging, to any extent, has affected us when we jump. So first, we could try an extended jump for several hours to gauge the results. If that doesn't work, we can always use the backup plan."

Tom asks, "And that is?"

Noah replies, "To travel a U-turn in space for several years in duration and see if that brings us back to an acceptable time era on the planet."

Tom again, "That's it. That's our plan?"

Sam says, "What choice do we have? If we have to go to the backup plan, possibly traveling at the speed-of-light, we would neither age nor starve to death."

Dusty says, "Oh, I so hope the first plan works."

Tom asks, "Is that okay with everyone?"

Sam speaks up, "I've heard it said that there are only four chromosomes difference between a chimpanzee and our species. I don't want to go stumbling into an advanced civilization that is four chromosomes smarter than we are and end up being treated like a damn chimpanzee. If we're going to do this, let's make our time estimates on the conservative side."

Tom agrees, "You got it Sam."

Tom asks again, "Is that okay with everyone?"

Jack says, "There's a better way to put that, Tom. Does anyone want off the bus here with the dinosaurs? "

No one answers, but several chuckle.

Tom is clearly through talking and Noah says, "Let's do the math and see what it looks like."

Tom retires to the cockpit to begin his tedious calculations on how to return them to the planet at a time millions of years in the future. He consults with Noah several times over the next few hours working until they are both convinced of their best guess to use for the longest jump insertion they will ever undertake.

Awhile later Tom announces, "Looks like about two hours and forty-five minutes real time."

Sam asks, "That's for plan one, right?

Tom replies, "Affirmative."

Noah says, "Sounds about right to me!"

Jack calls out, "Good night, sweet dreams. It's time for the big sleep. You all holler out when you're ready."

High above the planet earth, labeled on Tom's star chart as Terra3, their cumulative hopes are that they can return to earth and make it their home.

The Starchild is inserted into the long jump designed to return them to the same point in space except millenniums later.

***

Chapter Eleven – Ancient Egypt

The notes on this page are from a screenplay treatment and have not been written into the unfinished novel yet. The story will change considerably.

Forty-five real-time minutes later the Starchild materializes in orbit above planet Earth like a fictional Klingon spaceship uncloaking.

"Where is the moon," Sam asks.

Tom replies, "It appears to be on the far side of the planet. Don't think will have a chance to review it on our way in and I don't want to burn the fuel to go over there just to have a looksee. We're down to forty percent on our fuel right now. If we have to make it go-around or a takeoff on the planet we'll burn another fourteen percent."

Sam says, "So much over looking for a moon base on our way in. Sure hope it's not as super advanced civilization or even worse still dinosaurville!"

Dusty asks Tom, "How many millenniums do you think may have passed?"

"Based on the way that Cyclatron increases geometrically with time, I would say it's going to be more like eons instead of millenniums. We won't be able to tell for sure until we get lower to the planet."

Jack says, "I'm going to begin our skip descent into the planet. It will probably be about two hours before we can make visual contact with the surface. That is except for major metropolitan areas and we should have been able to make them out by now; even from this altitude."

The Starchild begins its slow descent into Earth's atmosphere. The planet marked on Tom's charts as Terra3.

Tom asks, "Does anyone smell smoke except me?"

Hans replies, "Yes it's the wiring on the Cyclatron!"

Sam adds, "it's the insulation on the wiring that was overheating when we shut the unit down. The Cyclatron really took a beating on that last long jump."

Hans comments, "I was a little bit afraid of that military surplus wire we had to use, but it was the only thing available without having to account for. I took the liberty to take the role of high dollar water from supply and threw it in with my toolbox. It can be repaired, but it will take a day or two. Hope we don't need it right away."

Sam says, "It's a tedious job of soldering, but it's mostly the external wiring that's fried. I'm sure none of the internal parts to the unit were damaged as it is mostly made of titanium inside."

Jack says, "in that case all we can hope for is a good landing spot to park this bird and give you a couple days to work on it. In the meantime if the slope gets worse let me know and I'll deploy the oxygen masks."

***

An hour or so later the Starchild passes over the Eastern Hemisphere and into the night side of the planet.

Noah remarks, "I've been watching and I haven't seen anything that looks like a large cities lit up at night."

Sam adds, "Me neither from this side of the ship. I also haven't seen anything that looks like an active volcano as I did before. That's good, I guess."

The Starchild crosses into daylight as it passes through the day/night terminator. They are descending over the Mediterranean Valley where they had observed the dinosaurs grazing in the field.

Dusty exclaims, "Look the Valley where we saw the dinosaurs is now a gigantic sea. I wonder what happens to the dinosaurs."

The Atlantic Ocean had broken through at Gibraltar and allowed the formation of the Mediterranean Sea and, of course, the dinosaurs had been extinct for a very long time now. They died off in a nuclear winter caused by the giant meteor that hit Earth forming the Gulf of Mexico.

Jack says, "We're basically in a glide right now so I'm going to make a wide circling turn out over water and come back to the mouth to go up that large river coming out of the desert."

Tom says, "Good thinking. If there is any civilization growth it will generally develop around fresh water sources.   Island villages xx

Jack fires the Starchild of the mouth of the river Nile with Giza in view of the left-wing.

They arrive on Earth at a point in time BC in Egypt. The Starchild lands in Giza in ancient Egypt and are witnessing early construction on the Sphinx.

During the decent, they observe people working on a construction site of a huge stone structure; the early Sphinx.

There is only a limited amount of conventional fuel remaining on board the Starchild, just enough for one more flight.

The craft immediately on the flat surface marble surface of a desert, which appears on the horizon. The Starchild lands and comes. Several Travelers walk toward a small tent village of locals who are the workers at the construction of the Sphinx.

After landing, several leave the craft and walk toward the construction site, mingling in with some of the workers a couple remain to repair the Cyclatron

Which pre-dates the Pyramids by thousands of years as some archeologists believe.

.

They have intentions of remaining at this location, at least for a while. They meet a small group of friendly workers.

They move toward a tent encampment of nomads and are greeted suspiciously by the elders of the tribe, but are eventually accepted by the group.

At first, language is a problem, but through hand gestures and learning some of the local phrases. With the help of a hand held voice translator they are soon able to communicate.

It is here that the jewelry and handgun that Dusty brought will be used in the story here.

They show the Pharaoh how to position the pyramids with the stars and will help the Egyptians as to align the pyramids with Orion's belt and show them the slight offset of the center star.

On the second night of their stay, a young Egyptian girl, Efra, decides to dance before the group after the evening meal.

Efra was the daughter of a minor ruler in the area who lost a border war. He and his wife, the Efra's parents, were executed in front of her when she was six years old. \

One of the elders working on the Sphinx took her into his household. She understands that the visitors are not gods and equates them to other royalty that she knew as a child.

Efra is fascinated with the visitors and dances provocatively in front of them.

Hans is mesmerized with her beauty and dancing and finds her later and takes her to bed.

The young warrior, who the dancer is betrothed to attacks Hans in a fit of jealous rage and Tom is stabbed in the ensuing fight.

Later around an evening campfire the Judeans sing and dance.

Tom says if he were to die "the things I've seen" like in Blade Runner, but not in this version; he is only wounded here. Just a minor Dusty tell him he is not going to die; comedy relief.

Dusty uses her jewelry to trade with Egypt tribes. She also carries a small handgun in her purse may and she shoots one of the Egyptians.

Tropians prepare to leave Efra wants on go with him. It is explained that if she leaves she will never see her people again.

She insists on going anyway and leaves with the group in the Starchild.

Where will Efra set… temp with Hans

Presently of no value to the Tropians, the Sam thinks the gold might be good metal for making replacement electrical contacts for the
Starchild's magnetic oscillator system. They take what they can carr.

They decide they must leave Egypt. They calculate that they have one more chance to move forward in time to a more modern technological era.

This next flight will require only a fraction of a second at hyper-light speed, but they will have expended all of their conventional fuel. They prepare to leave.

Starchild is jump away from earth and back. Relativity has moved them many billions of miles from their home planet arriving in Earth during a period of the early pharaohs. A relatively good guess for the factors involved.

Coming out of the insertion, they once again descend in the Starchild to the earth's surface to discover that they have landed at a time of ancient Egypt shortly after the building of the Sphinx. The landing is made in the desert near tribesmen

Time span only a few days.The Starchild circles the Sphinx looking for a landing spot in the Geza desert.They are greeted by some local tribes people. Through a series of hand jesters and picking up some of the native phrases, they explain that theyare travelers just passing through.

The Starchild is parked some distance away, hidden from the local peoples sight. elelers stay for two night with the locals observing the construction on the Sphinx.

She visits Hans brings him food and water as he works. The girl is an orphaned. The daughter of an asinated ruler.

She tells his of the dream she had of him coming for her She live in the family of the local tribal leader
.
At a dinner in a large tent, on the third evening, had a little too much local wine and ends up in bed with one of the local women, a dancer. They look just like us!

That night four of the Travelers are asleep together, except the Engineer who is sleeping in the Dancers tents.

It is the girls gilted lover who steps out of the darkness and stabs tom in the stomach with a knife.

Dusty uses her jewelry to trade with Egypt tribes people. Dusty carries a small handgun in her purse may she shoots the Egyptian That stabbed Tom.

Tom is wounded in the fight. (OMIT part about body is placed in an Egyptian tomb or British Museum) Need Tom and Efra to return to Tropia)

After a lengthy discussion, Travelers decide to make one more jump in time Always forward, relativity does not permit backward travel in time) to see if they can arrive at a period of time modern technology is being developed.

During preparation for departure, young Girl Efra (Effie) is going with them boards the Starchild upon departure.

***

Chapter Twelve – 20th Century Earth

The notes on this page are from a screenplay treatment and have not been written into the unfinished novel yet. The story will change considerably.

This is the beginning of their thirty year stay on earth; 1939 to 1969. They will leave earth after moon landing July 20, 1969 in Chapter 19.

With seven souls on board, four men and three women, the Starchild lands on earth.

Having made several hyper-light jumps, they now feel that they can more closely control the time lapse.

A short hyper-light flight, remaining in Earth orbit, is made into the future.

Descending on the Tropians land the Starchild on a small grass airstrip.

The Starchild is once again drops out of the hyper-light speed and find themselves in orbit above1939 Earth.

Low on JP and nuke core, they will have to make their own in miss more modern times again.

The Starchild is very low on fuel and some of the electronic circuitry is beginning to fail.

They estimate that the technology they need to repair the Starchild should be available by that time.

Entering the atmosphere and descending somewhere over the eastern United State of America, the craft glides easily, while Jack searches for a remote area to land.

They are flying the Starchild like a space shuttle now, passing through the sound barrier creating a sonic boom occurs.

The sonic boom is heard across the New England countryside.

At this particular time on Earth, many people were reporting sightings of flying saucers, so the boom and the sighting of a unique metal object were attributed to this phenomenon.

Jack is on a committed final approach when he sees a small grass strip in White Rock Lake a suburb of Dallas Texas.

The Starchild is damaged on landing as it runs into trees at the end of the runway.

They are unharmed in the crash landing and pull the Starchild into an old empty hangar on the run down airport.

They walk in the dark to abandon house joining the airstrip, an old county estate For Sale sign on the property. The property is owned by the old man who also owns the airport.

The old WW I Flyer, Gus Branson who lives alone and befriends them.

The estate includes an abandoned airstrip with an old hangar on it (where they hid the Starchild). They would like to purchase the property.

They tell Gus they are a group of foreigners who have arrived in this country to work in the scientific community.

Problems with a local Sheriff and Sam say to Noah "I've always wanted to say this… "Take me to your leader' which only confuses the Sheriff."

Dusty opens the doors of the old garage and finds an old, dust covered, Duesenberg Phaeton. Fondly remembering her sexy red sports car, she decides wants this classic automobile.

She is told that the Duesenberg goes with the estate. Dusty fully restores the old Duesenberg and drives it everywhere (Dusty rides again).

They settle in the estate. Each has their own room and pursues separate interests. Before the old Flyer retires, he stays in story.

Gus and Jack become good friends and the Flyer teaches Jack how to fly his old biplane.

The country manor restored. Noah and Dusty take up residence. The others remain as house guests on the estate. Noah and Dusty occupy the master bedroom.

They are accepted as Europeans because of their thick accents and broken English, but quickly learn speak American English.

One morning, she asks him when he intends to make an honest woman out of her and he replies, maybe when we go home.

This is the first that she realizes that Noah might be seriously considering returning to Tropia.

Everyone and everything they had ever known on Tropia vanished millenniums ago and it is very likely that the environment has not fully recovered.

The Tropians are without any currency with which to purchase everyday necessities.

Leica takes the gold medallions and jewelry he acquired in Egypt and sells them to a dealer for enough money to assimilate the group into the local society.

Hangar rented on Redbird Airport to store Starchild .

While moving into the manor house, neighbors arrive to welcome them (on horseback, dressed in fox hunting attire). They dismount and introduce themselves.

Dusty introduces herself as an exiled countess from a European royal family, and Noah as her husband.

When the guests depart and Noah quips, "What does that make me, some kind of a Duke?"

Jack manages the air field (grass strip) where they had landed. This allows him to keep watch.

Jack sometimes gives flying lessons in a WWI biplane. One day while teaching a young student pilot, they run off the end of the runway and crash nose down.

As a small crowd runs towards the crash, the student and Jack emerge unscathed. "Laughing'" Jack says", don't worry about it kid, I always say any landing you can walk away from is a good one.

Besides, I've wanted a new plane anyway". The next day his new Waco biplane is delivered.

Noah takes a position lecturing at a nearby university.

While teaching a physics class on electrodynamics bodies in motion, if the speed-of-light in truly the ultimate speed in the universe.

Noah replies that it was an interesting question and that he understands that Albert Einstein, who developed the Principle of Relativity, had also been working on what he called the Special Law of Relativity.

Someday in the future, the answer may be known for sure.

One night Noah and Dusty are lying in bed in the manor house's stately master bedroom. Noah asks her, "Do you love me?" She answers, "What do you mean, do I love you?" He asks again, "Do you?"

She replies, "I have worked beside you for twenty years, I have been your mistress for almost that long, I follow you half way across a universe, and you ask me if I love you?" He asks again, "Well, do you?" She answers, "I'll think about it, go to sleep."

Dusty really gets into the spirit of the times. She volunteers at a local hospital, helping them set up a new research center that is named after her.

She accepts the Duesenberg roadster from Gus as a gift.

Large garden parties (Great Gatsby style) are given at the country manor hosted by the Judean girl (who is now married to Jack).

She likes to dress up in costumes which are variations on her own tribal dress. Her attire is a cross between flapper and a Middle Eastern dancing girl.

Realizing that in order to survive, they need the currency used during this time period.

Hans uses a laser device out of the Starchild to make a set of printing plates and proceeds to make counterfeit money.

After a period of time, two government Investigators come to the small nearby town to talk to the Sheriff about the counterfeit bills that seem to be originating from the area.

The problem, the investigators explain, is that the bills are not poor quality, but are as good as or better than those produced at the Treasury.

When Noah gets wind of this from the sheriff, he has the stop counterfeiting money printing stopped and destroys the printing plates.

Sam and Hans start an electrical engineering company which produces technological advanced components for radios.

The company begins to show a profit. The corporation is named SAC for Starchild Corporation of America.

The Starchild is repaired patchwork and it might now be used for a short hyper-light flight.

However, it is not likely that in its present condition it could be used for an extended period.

Efra is fascinated with all the new things like the electric stove and television and takes care of the household.

Hans tinkers at the airport hangar with parts from the Starchild and is building an electronic music synthesizer in his spare time.

Dusty goes to work at a small medical clinic and does gene research in her spare time.

Noah takes a lecture position at a nearby university where he mentors students. He also sets Hans up with his own research center.

There has been a continual investigation into UFO sightings in the area for the past two years.

Agents of an unnamed government entity (men in black types) begin to investigate the reports that were generated from the Starchild's decent.

Jack operates the old airport, selling gas, giving flight instructions and sightseeing rides in an old Steersman biplane.

He encounters a young female attorney who works for the government agency. They become involved and he takes her flying in the biplane.

The next morning, after they have spent the night together, she leaves before he wakes, leaving him a good-bye note.

She reports back to her supervisors that the suspicions of UFO activities in the airport area are a hoax.

She believes that the reports were a hoax, in spite of the fact that the Starchild was in the hangar only forty feet from where she had been standing the day before.

Crash landing in the small airport, the old ww one pilot, they hide the damage charge, Starchild

There is only a moment or two of time that passes and the Astronaut is at the controls of the Starchild as it breaks out of time and space into orbit above earth.

The aircraft wings are overheating and the dissent angle is greater than needed. Several systems fail during descent.

The east coast of the U.S. looms on the horizon. The glide angle is set for what would turn out to be the countryside near a small town and there appears to be a small airstrip nestled in a wooded area.

As the Starchild touches down, it has too much speed and runs off the end of the runway into the trees. Aircraft is damaged, but no one on board is injured as it comes to a stop.

There is now only the stillness of the countryside with birds chirping.

They exit the aircraft and walk back toward an old metal hangar,

There are several bi-planes parked around the grass strip airport.

The Oldtimer is watching WWI pilot lives in the hangar becomes a friend Travelers rent his house a biplane and a flost-plane

Jack jokes…. you got us we're Martian Take me to your leader… always wanted to say that

Aboard the Starchild between 6000 BC and 1939 AD orbiting earth. the Girl takes the empty sixth seat.

Diode is vacuum tube type prior to transistorized etc, the Island of Atlantis has sunk with no trace.

***

Chapter Thirteen – The Metroplex

The notes on this page are from a screenplay treatment and have not been written into the unfinished novel yet. The story will change considerably.

In the community where they establish a local identify.

Noah becomes involved at a local university, Dusty eventually goes on staff at the hospital, Jack and tom will take over the small airport.

Hans becomes involved with electronic music.

The problem that current technology does not allow for the development of the type of systems needed for the Starchild repairs. This is as close to modern times as their best guess a relativity navigation is able to bring them to.

These guesses being based on calculations in micro-seconds.

To attempt to jump again, even though the Starchild might be able to be repaired at some furture date, could cause them to miss a future date by thousands of years rather than a few decades.

This bad of a miss could bring them into a planetary environment having just undergone a nuclear holocaust or a poisoned environment. If that happened, their chances of moving forward (they cannot go back).

Finding a suitable environment would be much less practical than taking their chances on survival where they are now.

The Starchild is stored in one of the old metal hangars under lock and key. It is damaged beyond repair based on current technology.

After learning to fly the old biplanes, Jack gives rides and has a few students he is teaching to learn to fly in the old biplane.

Noah devises a plan for developing mico circuitry which can be sold via a cover corporation that he has created.

They lease the old rundown large home from Gus on an estate where they reside as a group. Dusty restores it to its original glory

At the Starchild hangar, Jack is supervising the design for a new SC-2.

Sam, Hans, Leica and Efra are working on Noah's ideas for the latest advanced technology and also building a new Cyclatron.

Hans is also building a music synthizor as music is his hobby and her want to be a rock star.

Dusty has found an old Duesenberg which she has restored and drives to work every day at the clinic where she works. She delights in taking it out on the backroads of the countryside.

Noah and Dusty have developed the beginnings of a relationship and she wants him to marry her. He tells her his reason for waiting and kids her about it.

Relationships develops between Hans and Efra (who is eighteen now); Jack and Liz Abrams the FBI agent; Tom and Leica; Sam and Barbra an earth Christian woman.

They try to stay uninvolved, but now several government agencies have begun to investigate foreigners and she thinks they may be communist sympathizers.

At the small airport, Jack is preparing to go flying in a restored Stearman biplane.

Jack encounters Liz (the female Government investigator) who has snooping around the airport and investigation as to who they are.

She leaves convinced that he is not suspicious, but with some lingering doubts.

Jack takes Liz to go flying in the 310 later. There is an attraction here, but it is not pursued.

Noah makes the decision to abandon their quiet country life and set up a major corporation in Dallas with a subsidiary in Austin.

Several years pass and technology is on the threshold of breaking through to the advances needed by in order to rebuild the Starchild.

WWII begins

The mansion is sold and the airport shutdown. Dusty insists on keeping her Duesenberg roadster and has it shipped where they are going.

***

Chapter Fourteen – Tiarell Corporation

The notes on this page are from a screenplay treatment and have not been written into the unfinished novel yet. The story will change considerably.

A new Tiarell Corp named after the old one on Tropia. Like Ling Electric, batteries and Texas Gage (TI), diods, etc.

Noah lectures at various universities on astrophysics.

Jack and Dusty serve as consultants and members of the board of directors.

Hans forms a rock group that perform in makeup like kiss called Smack.

Need more accurate data for star positions needs to be recovered, so Jack plans to take a seaplane to Aerocebo and visit an astronomer acquaintance who is working there.

Hopefully, during this visit, they can record some of the data that is needed to more accurately recalculate the time and distances for a return to Tropia

Should they be successful in eventually reproducing the original Cyclatron technology.

As work progresses on the Starchild in the Dallas Love Field hangar, a meeting they hold to discuss more accurate celestial navigation if they were to attempt a return to Tropia.

It is estimated that millions of years have passed since they had left the planet and that there is a possibility that a total ecological recovery of the planet could have taken place.

***

Chapter Fifteen – Dark Side Of The Moon

The notes on this page are from a screenplay treatment and have not been written into the unfinished novel yet. The story will change considerably.

Covers Area 51 (by Tom) and Religion (by Sam)

Smack (by Hans) Smack performing at a rock concert in Star Plex at Fair Park Dallas. .

Running things about Jack asking people about the space station on the dark side of the. No one knows anything about it

The Starchild II is nearing completion and they meet to discuss their departure from earth in hopefully successful return to Tropia.

There is a lengthy discussion about what they are to expect when they get home to Tropia. The group goes into the hangar where the Starchild II is.

The next evening, Noah is lecturing at a nearby university and Dusty is attending with him.

Jack is working in the hangar when Liz arrives trying to argue her way past one of the security guards. Jack hears the commotion and goes to lets her in the hangar.She explains that the government agents are planning a raid on the hangar to discover its contents sometime in the middle of the night.

Jack contacts on beeper (not used at this time).

Noah, leaving the lecture is followed by a young student who asks for a further explanation on some points in his lecture.

Opening his briefcase, Noah extracts a fistful of notes, handing them to the student. He says that some of the calculations may not be correct, but all of what you ask about is here.

Noah and Dusty run for her Duesenberg in the parking lot and race through Highland Park to Love Field.

It is late evening now and a slow drizzling rain had started; at the civilian aircraft ramp on the north part of Love Field.

In the ATC an operator is looking at a radar screen. He remarks to his co-worker, what the hell was that taking off.

The other controller replies, oh, probably one of those things that the government is experimenting with out there at Dry Lake, some people refer to it as Aera-51.

***

Chapter Sixteen – Lear Jet SC-2

The notes on this page are from a screenplay treatment and have not been written into the unfinished novel yet. The story will change considerably.

Once again, their actions have aroused the suspicions of several government agencies and they are now being actively pursued by Agent Liz Abrams, the female that had encountered Jack earlier is once again part of the investigation.

Liz meets with her subordinates in the government agency and it is decided that while the motives the are unknown that they should be hauled in for extensive questioning.

Liz is now beginning to ask lots of questions, some of which will soon be answered.

That night at a local restaurant/bar, Jack recognizes Liz who is a government investigator on his trail. He invites her to have dinner with him as she is obviously following him anyway.

Jacks apartment bedroom (obviously, Jack and Liz spent the night together). Liz wakes and asks, how commit is that we always seem to end up in bed with each other.

Jack is in the bathroom shaving and he tells her to get up and get ready that he is going to take her somewhere.

He drags her off still as she is trying to get her clothes and makeup on

They arrive at the airport where they fly depart in a Cessna 310 for Wichita, Kansas. Arriving at Wichita Municipal Airport, they meet with the CEO of the aircraft factory in his plush offices windows overlooking the ramp.

In Mr. Lear's office, they discuss the work that Noah has been providing them for the development for new electronic technology, the 8-track stereo tape and solid state inverters.

Jack hands Mr. Lear a cashier's check for payment in full and takes delivery on one of the first Learjets ever built. The FAA has not yet certified the aircraft.

Jack goes to the ramp where the jet is parked and begins to preflight it. Liz is tagging along behind him. The chief flight test engineer is standing near the airplane with a clipboard.

He tells Jack he cannot fly the plane as it is only being used for test flights. Taking the clipboard out of the engineer's hand, Jack signs it as the test pilot and he and the Liz board the aircraft and crank the engine.

Jack is working very closely with William P. Lear following the development of his new Learjet.

Jack and Liz fly to Wichita to get the new jet which as yet has not been flight tested.

They meet and befriend some smugglers and spend the night with them.

They visit the radio observatory and meet with a student of Noah's. New charts of the sky are made and taken with them.

At the Dallas Love Field, a hangar is leased and placed under heavy security guard. The first delivery of a commercial air jet is purchased and placed in the hangar.

The wrecked remains of the original Starchild is recovered from the old airport hangar in New England and trucked secretly by night to the new Love Field hangar.

This project is being funded by the stocks in which Noah has invested in several electronics companies.

Arrive at the airport where they fly depart in a Cessna 310 for Wichita, Kansas. Arriving at Wichita Municipal Airport, they meet with the CEO of the aircraft factory in plush offices with windows overlooking the ramp.

In Mr. Lear's office, they discuss the work that the Professor has been providing them for the development for new electronic technology; 8-track stereo tape and solid state inverters. Jack hands Mr. Lear a cashier's check for payment in full and takes delivery on one of the first Lear Jets built. The FAA has not yet certified the aircraft.

Jack goes to the ramp where the jet is parked and begins to preflight it. Liz is tagging along behind him. The chief flight test engineer is standing near the airplane with a clipboard. He tells Jack he cannot fly the plane as it is only being used for test flights. Taking the clipboard out of the engineer's hand, the Jack signs it as test pilot. He and the Lady board the aircraft an

d crank the engine. Group discusses the possibility of returning to Tropia.

***

Chapter Seventeen – Trip To Arecibo

The notes on this page are from a screenplay treatment and have not been written into the unfinished novel yet. The story will change considerably.

Dallas, Texas in the 1950s Noah, Sam and Hans are working as consultants and serving on the board of directors of several electronic companies. One of which will develop advanced computer chip technology.

Liz meets Gus the old Flyer in the keys. Jack and Gus fly to Arecibo, Porta Rico.

Jack flies to the Caribbean and lands at a small airport near Miami, Florida. There is an old Catalina flying boat parked on the beach nearby.

Sam arrives by airline and rents a car.

They board the flying boat and takeoff and fly under the ADAZ of radar to a small coaster town in Puerto Rico.

At Arecibo, where the radar observatory is located, they proceed up the mountains to meet with an Astronomer who is an acquaintance of Noah's.

In the early days in Dallas, Noah founds Texas Gauge (TI) developing new electronic systems.

Noah and Sam help the company design and develop miniaturized solid state devices.

Sam, joking privately with Noah, reaches in his pocket and opens a small of what appear to be grains of sand (parts from the Starchild), placing his finger in the box several adhere.

SAM remarks, he wonders what the company would say if they knew what the circuitry in one of these little babies?

Noah acknowledges this with a smile.

The sun is setting over the water to the west of the island as the seaplane materializes on the horizon and lands on the water near the beach.

As the plane taxis on the beach, a bullet passes through the cockpit window, narrowly missing both pilots. Jack and Gus jump from the plane and run into the bushes while bullets are kicking up the sand at their feet.

They have no idea who is shooting at them. Except for Sam, who will meet them in the morning at a prearranged place up the road, no one should know that they are here.

Liz swears she has told no one. Jack and Gus circle around behind were the rifle fire is coming from. They jump two grungy looking men in dirty khakis. The men are rum runners waiting on a boat.

They smuggle duty free, boot leg rum in knock-off Bacardi bottles to customers in the States. It is a case of mistaken identity.

The rum Runners thought that the Travelers were either the Feds or a competitor coming to raid them.

Things settle down and the Travelers join the two rum runners at their campfire that evening for dinner and pineapple juice with rum.

The two black men helpers entertain with some Reggae style music until the early morning hours when everyone passes out and falls asleep.

The morning sunlight coming through the palm trees awakens them.

A van up the road is honking. It is the Astronomer who has come to pick them up.

The old Flyer says he will stay with the seaplane that is parked on the beach.

They make their way through the tropical bushes and to a clearing beside the road where the Astronomer is waiting. Greeting exchanged and they get in the van.

They drive up the mountains to the Arecibo Radio Observatory where they park the van and enter the facility.

They go to a recording center under the antenna to take the required readings.

These new and more accurate readings will be run through a computer to determine the precise future location of Tropia a need to realign the cone as the Earth is about to pass through the portion of the solar system is located.

***

Chapter Eighteen – Halcyon Days

The notes on this page are from a screenplay treatment and have not been written into the unfinished novel yet. The story will change considerably.

Time to leave … Apollo 11 is the spacecraft that landed the first two modern men on the earth moon. Mission Commander Neil Armstrong and pilot Buzz Aldrin both Americans landed the lunar modules Eagle on July 20, 1969.

At a meeting, the people in the room are being viewed on a monitor screen from an unknown office some distance away. The people watching the monitor from this unknown office are themselves being watched through a window in the space needle style building.

Another monitor screen, viewing those in the office building is onboard a space station. The people watching the monitor on the space station are viewed through the window of the space station from a point in space. Others are watching, i.e. a triple pullback.

The Travelers begin making preparations for their departure to Tropia. The Starchild II is being fitted with everything except the Cyclatron, which is coming from Anaconda.

So as not to arouse suspicion, the Cyclatron has been shipped FedEx routinely. The following evening, the Professor is speaking at SMU and lecturing to a group of young scientists and students.

The Technician, who has completed all the work except installing the Cyclatron, is at a rock concert where he has promoted his way into performing with the rock group.

***

Chapter Nineteen – Good Day To Die

The notes on this page are from a screenplay treatment and have not been written into the unfinished novel yet. The story will change considerably.

Dusty get new 69 Mark III Phaeton from Eagle Shortly before departing to return to Tropia.

The travelers have each become very succesful during their time on earth and have individually and corporately acquired much wealth. They cannot just disappear. So a plan is devised to cover their escape back to Tropia.

Their corporate plane is equipped with a radio control device that will allow it to apply to the middle of the Pacific Ocean and crash over the Mariana straight according to press releases all on board will perish.

Their personal and corporate wealth will be donated to worthy charities and their dangerous interventions will be destroyed so as to deny them to posterity.

Their departure from love field is very dramatic.

Hans and Efra arrive in a limo just as Noah and Dusty round the corner and skid onto the tarmac.

The four run for the open hangar door. Sirens in the background indicate that the men in black, with help, are on their way.

Liz is standing on the tarmac talking on her hand-held radio as the engines on the Learjet are fired up by Jack.

Starchild II starts to taxi toward the four that are running for the aircraft. The airstair door is down as they board the aircraft, the airstair is being pulled up by Jack see dialog for here.

Liz hesitates then runs to the open airstair. She has decided to go with them and run to get on board..

She announces that she doesn't know where they are going, but she intends to go with them.

The airstair door is shut as the jet taxi onto the runway and the tower gives clearance for takeoff.

The Learjet rolls down the runway and lifts off into the darkness with its beacon light flashing climbing skyward.

***

Chapter Twenty – Can't Go Home Again

The notes on this page are from a screenplay treatment and have not been written into the unfinished novel yet. The story will change considerably.

The notes on this page are from a screenplay treatment and have not been written into the unfinished novel yet. The story will change considerably.

On board the Starchild and the return to the planet Tropia. Lands on the planet Tropia they discover that it now has a beautiful evolved environment with no industrial pollution whatsoever.

What has taken place on Tropia, is that the satellite did not actually destroy the entire planet as the Travelers had first believed. The environment was seriously damaged and there was much suffering. As the planet began to recover, there were major leap in technology.

Unfortunately, there were two major powers which evolved to control the planet's countries. These two powers met in an allout nuclear war a few hundred years after the Travelers had left and for all practical purposes most of civilization was lost.

The survivors became little more than prehistoric cave men and had never reached any significant level of technology. All of this is of little importance to our story because millions of years after the Travelers had originally departed. Everything they knew had been lost in antiquity.

The Cyclatron is engaged as they climb for the highest obtainable altitude of earth. The Starchild is transitioning into light speed with the six xx Travelers on board.

Aboard the Starchild, the crew is experiencing the effects of light speed they are desperately trying to calculate the time and distance back to Tropia as accurately as possible.

Liz is very excited about what she is experiencing and expresses unbelievable amazement. The Cyclatron is disengaged and all waits anxiously to see where they have arrived in space.

The Starchild is coasting just inside the orbit of Tropia's largest of two moons with the earth-like plant in the distance. It is obviously different than earth because although it is the same blue and white planet, the continents are shaped different than the world of Earth.

As the Starchild enters atmosphere, the airframe is overheating and it is questionable as to whether or not the aircraft will hold together during the descent.

As soon as some atmosphere is encountered, the pilot (Jack) engages the jet engines to decrease the descent angle.

The Starchild circles over a rolling hillside and turns to make a final approach in an open meadow not too far from the village. The spot they will land at resembles a small village in southern Ireland with thatched roofed houses and stone fences.

In the distance, there are some people who are looking up to watch the Starchild land and a small crowd of a couple of dozen gather near the village.

The Starchild comes to rest with some dust flying in the wind and the airstair door opens and the Travelers depart.

Jack, Tom and Hans are unloading some equipment from the aircraft. Mostly personal items and souviers from Earth. Without explanation,

Hans appears to be monkeying a device wired to the Cyclatron. He hands small handheld remote control to Jack and walk up the dirt road towards the village people.

The Leica and Efra are dancing in a circle for joy, if for no other reason than that they are still alive.

Several of the Travelers throw packs over their shoulders. The group walks on ahead toward the village except for Jack and Noah. Both are smiling and Jack says, "Who was that author that we read about on Earth?" Noah, "I think his name was Thomas Wolfe."

As they continue to walk, Jack has a small backpack over his left shoulder. He raises his right hand containing the small remote control when they are about two hundred yards from the Starchild which is behind them in the background and pushes the button.

The Starchild explodes in a gigantic mushroom ball of fire filmed in slow motion. Pieces are falling to the ground like feathers from the sky.

Neither man looks back, only ahead at the villages who are now greeting the Travelers who went on ahead. Jack says, "Who says you can't go home again."

***

Chapter 30 - Particle physics

Particle physics is a branch of physics that studies the nature of particles that constitute matter and radiation. Although the word particle can refer to various types of very small objects (e.g. protons, gas particles, or even household dust), particle physics usually investigates the irreducibly smallest detectable particles.

The fundamental interactions necessary to explain their behavior. By our current understanding, these elementary particles are excitations of the quantum fields that also govern their interactions.

The currently dominant theory explaining these fundamental particles and fields, along with their dynamics, is called the Standard Model. Thus, modern particle physics generally investigates the Standard Model and its various possible extensions, e.g. to the newest "known" particle, the Higgs boson, or even to the oldest known force field, gravity.

All particles and their interactions observed to date can be described almost entirely by a quantum field theory called the Standard Model.

The Standard Model, as currently formulated, has 61 elementary particles. Those elementary particles can combine to form composite particles, accounting for the hundreds of other species of particles that have been discovered since the 1960s.

The Standard Model has been found to agree with almost all the experimental tests conducted to date. However, most particle physicists believe that it is an incomplete description of nature and that a more fundamental theory awaits discovery.

Theory of Everything - In recent years, measurements of neutrino mass have provided the first experimental deviations from the Standard Model.

All matter is composed of elementary particles dates from at least the 6th century BC.]In the 19th century, John Dalton, through his work on stoichiometry, concluded that each element of nature was composed of a single, unique type of particle.

The word atom, after the Greek word atomos meaning "indivisible", has since then denoted the smallest particle of a chemical element, but physicists soon discovered that atoms are not, in fact, the fundamental particles of nature, but are conglomerates of even smaller particles, such as the electron.

The early 20th century explorations of nuclear physics and quantum physics led to proofs of nuclear fission in 1939 by Lise Meitner (based on experiments by Otto Hahn), and nuclear fusion by Hans Bethe in that same year; both discoveries also led to the development of nuclear weapons.

Throughout the 1950s and 1960s, a bewildering variety of particles were found in collisions of particles from increasingly high-energy beams. It was referred to informally as the "particle zoo".

That term was deprecated after the formulation of the Standard Model during the 1970s, in which the large number of particles was explained as combinations of a (relatively) small number of more fundamental particles.

Standard Model -The current state of the classification of all elementary particles is explained by the Standard Model.

It describes the strong, weak, and electromagnetic fundamental interactions, using mediating gauge bosons. The species of gauge bosons are eight gluons and the photon.

The Standard Model contains and their associated anti-particles), which are the constituents of all matter.

Finally, the Standard Model also predicted the existence of a type of boson known as the Higgs boson. Early in the morning on 4 July 2012, physicists with the Large Hadron Collider at CERN announced they had found a new particle that behaves similarly to what is expected from the Higgs boson.

Theoretical particle physics attempts to develop the models, theoretical framework, and mathematical tools to understand current experiments and make predictions for future experiments.

There are several major interrelated efforts being made in theoretical particle physics today. One important branch attempts to better understand the Standard Model and its tests.

By extracting the parameters of the Standard Model, from experiments with less uncertainty, this work probes the limits of the Standard Model and therefore expands our understanding of nature's building blocks. Those efforts are made challenging by the difficulty of calculating quantities in quantum chromodynamics.

Some theorists in this area refer to themselves as phenomenologists and they may use the tools of quantum field theory effective field theory. Others make use of lattice field theory and call themselves lattice theorists.

Another major effort is in model building where model builders develop ideas for what physics may lie beyond the Standard Model (at higher energies or smaller distances). This work is often motivated by the hierarchy problem and is constrained by existing experimental data.

It may involve work on supersymmetry, alternatives to the Higgs mechanism, extra spatial dimensions (such as the Randall-Sundrum models). Preon theory, combinations of these or other ideas.

A third major effort in theoretical particle physics is string theory. String theorists attempt to construct a unified description of quantum mechanics and general relativity by building a theory based on small strings, and branes rather than particles. If the theory is successful, it may be considered a "Theory of Everything", or "TOE".

There are also other areas of work in theoretical particle physics ranging from particle cosmology to loop quantum gravity.

Practical applications - In principle, all physics (and practical applications developed therefrom) can be derived from the study of fundamental particles. In practice, even if "particle physics" is taken to mean only "high-energy atom smashers", many technologies have been developed during these pioneering investigations.

Particle accelerators are used to produce medical isotopes for research and treatment (for example, isotopes used in PET imaging), or used directly in external beam radiotherapy. The development of superconductors has been pushed forward by their use in particle physics. The World Wide Web and touchscreen technology were initially developed at CERN.

Additional applications are found in medicine, national security, industry, computing, science, and workforce development, illustrating a long and growing list of beneficial practical applications with contributions from particle physics.

The primary goal, which is pursued in several distinct ways, is to find and understand what physics may lie beyond the standard model. There are several powerful experimental reasons to expect new physics, including dark matter and neutrino mass. There are also theoretical hints that this new physics should be found at accessible energy scales.

Much of the effort to find this new physics are focused on new collider experiments. The Large Hadron Collider (LHC) was completed in 2008 to help continue the search for the Higgs boson, supersymmetric particles, and other new physics.

An intermediate goal is the construction of the International Linear Collider (ILC), which will complement the LHC by allowing more precise measurements of the properties of newly found particles. In August 2004, a decision for the technology of the ILC was taken but the site has still to be agreed upon.

In addition, there are important non-collider experiments that also attempt to find and understand physics beyond the Standard Model.

One important non-collider effort is the determination of the neutrino masses, since these masses may arise from neutrinos mixing with very heavy particles.

In addition, cosmological observations provide many useful constraints on the dark matter, although it may be impossible to determine the exact nature of the dark matter without the colliders.

Lower bounds on the very long lifetime of the proton put constraints on Grand Unified Theories at energy scales much higher than collider experiments will be able to probe any time soon.

In May 2014, the Particle Physics Project Prioritization Panel released its report on particle physics funding priorities for the United States over the next decade.

This report emphasized continued U.S. participation in the LHC and ILC, and expansion of the Deep Underground Neutrino Experiment, among other recommendations.

High energy physics compared to low energy physics. The term high energy physics requires elaboration. Intuitively, it might seem incorrect to associate "high energy" with the physics of very small, low mass objects, like subatomic particles.

By comparison, an example of a macroscopic system, one gram of hydrogen, has ~ 6×1023 times the mass of a single proton.

Even an entire beam of protons circulated in the LHC contains ~ 3.23×1014 protons, lower than the mass-energy of a single gram of hydrogen. Yet, the macroscopic realm is "low energy physics" that of quantum particles is "high energy physics".

The interactions studied in other fields of physics and science have comparatively very low energy. For example, the photon energy of visible light is about 1.8 to 3.1 eV. Similarly, the bond-dissociation energy of a carbon–carbon bond is about 3.6 eV.

Photons with far higher energy, gamma rays of the kind produced in radioactive decay, mostly have photon energy between 105 eV and 107 eV – still two orders of magnitude lower than the mass of a single proton. Radioactive decay gamma rays are considered as part of nuclear physics, rather than high energy physics.

The proton has a mass of around 9.4×108 eV; some other massive quantum particles, both elementary and hadronic, have yet higher masses. Due to these very high energies the single particle level, particle physics is, in fact, high-energy physics.

Experimental laboratories -The world's major particle physics laboratories are:

Brookhaven National Laboratory (Long Island, United States). Its main facility is the Relativistic Heavy Ion Collider (RHIC), which collides heavy ions such as gold ions and polarized protons. It is the world's first heavy ion collider, and the world's only polarized proton collider.

Budker Institute of Nuclear physics, Novosibirsk, Russia. Its main projects are now the electron-positron colliders VEPP-2000, operated since 2006, and VEPP-4, started experiments in 1994.

Earlier facilities include the first electron-electron beam collider VEP-1, which conducted experiments from 1964 to 1968; the electron-positron colliders VEPP-2, operated from 1965 to 1974; and, its successor VEPP-2M, performed experiments from 1974 to 2000.

CERN (European Organization for Nuclear Research) (Franco-Swiss border, near Geneva). Its main project is now the Large Hadron Collider (LHC), which had its first beam circulation on 10 September 2008, and is now the world's most energetic collider of protons.

It also became the most energetic collider of heavy ions after it began colliding lead ions. Earlier facilities include the Large Electron–Positron Collider(LEP) It was stopped on 2 November 2000 and then dismantled to give way for LHC; and the Super Proton Synchrotron, which is being reused as a pre-accelerator for the LHC.

DESY (Deutsches Elektronen-Synchrotron) (Hamburg, Germany). Its main facility is the Hadron Elektron Ring Anlage (HERA), which collides electrons and positrons with protons.

Fermi National Accelerator Laboratory (Fermilab) (Batavia, United States). Its main facility until 2011 was the Tevatron, which collided protons and antiprotons and was the highest-energy particle collider on earth until the Large Hadron Collider surpassed it on 29 November 2009.

Institute of High Energy Physics (IHEP) (Beijing, China). IHEP manages a number of China's major particle physics facilities, including the Beijing Electron Positron Collider (BEPC), the Beijing Spectrometer (BES), the Beijing Synchrotron Radiation Facility (BSRF), the International Cosmic-Ray Observatory at Yangbajing in Tibet

The Daya Bay Reactor Neutrino Experiment, the China Spallation Neutron Source, the Hard X-ray Modulation Telescope (HXMT), and the Accelerator-driven Sub-critical System (ADS) as well as the Jiangmen Underground Neutrino Observatory.

KEK (Tsukuba, Japan). It is the home of a number of experiments such as the K2K experiment, a neutrino oscillation experiment and Belle, an experiment measuring the CP violation of B mesons.

The Linac Coherent Light Source X-ray laser as well as advanced accelerator design research. SLAC staff continue to participate in developing and building many particle detectors around the world.

SLAC National Accelerator Laboratory (Menlo Park, United States) has a 2-mile-long linear particle accelerator began operating in 1962 and was the basis for numerous electron and positron collision experiments until 2008. Since then the linear accelerator is being used.

Many other particle accelerators also exist. The techniques required for modern experimental particle physics are quite varied and complex, constituting a sub-specialty nearly completely distinct from the theoretical side of the field.

***

Chapter 31 - Fibonacci Numbers

In mathematics the Fibonacci numbers (named after mathematician Fibonacci are the numbers in the following integer sequence, called the Fibonacci sequence, and characterized by the fact that every number after the first two is the sum of the two preceding ones.

Often, especially in modern usage, the sequence is extended by one more initial term….
1,\;1,\;2,\;3,\;5,\;8,\;13,\;21,\;34,\;55,\;89,\;144, etc.
The Fibonacci spiral: an approximation of the golden spiral is created by drawing circular arcs connecting the opposite corners of squares in the Fibonacci tiling; this one uses squares of sizes 1, 1, 2, 3, 5, 8, 13 and 21.

By definition, the first two numbers in the Fibonacci sequence are either 1 and 1, or 0 and 1, depending on the chosen starting point of the sequence, and each subsequent number is the sum of the previous two.

The sequence Fn of Fibonacci numbers is defined by the recurrence. Fibonacci numbers appear to have first arisen in perhaps 200 BC in work by Pingala on enumerating possible patterns of poetry formed from syllables of two lengths.

The Fibonacci sequence is named after Italian mathematician Leonardo of Pisa, known as Fibonacci. His 1202 book Liber Abaci introduced the sequence to Western European mathematics, although the sequence had been described earlier in Indian mathematics.

The sequence described in Liber Abaci began with F1=1. Fibonacci numbers were later independently discussed by Johannes Kepler in 1611 in connection with approximations to the pentagon.

Their recurrence relation appears to have been understood from the early 1600s, but it has only been in the past very few decades that they have in general become widely discussed.

Fibonacci numbers are closely related to the Lucas sequence. They are intimately connected with the golden ratio; for example, the closest rational approximations to the ratio are 2/1, 3/2, 5/3, 8/5.

Fibonacci numbers appear unexpectedly often in mathematics, so much so that there is an entire journal dedicated to their study.

The Fibonacci Quarterly - Applications of Fibonacci numbers include computer algorithms such as the technique and the Fibonacci heap data structure, and graphs called Fibonacci cubes used for interconnecting parallel and distributed systems.

They also appear in biological settings such as branching in trees, phyllotax is the arrangement of leaves on a stem; the fruit sprouts of a pineapple the flowering of an artichoke, an uncurling fern and the arrangement of a pine cone's bracts.

Thirteen ways of arranging long and short syllables in a cadence of length six. Five end with a long syllable and eight end with a short syllable.

A page of Fibonacci's Liber Abaci from the Biblioteca Nazionale di Firenze showing (in box on right) the Fibonacci sequence with the position in the sequence labeled in Latin and Roman numerals and the value in Hindu-Arabic numerals.

The Fibonacci sequence appears in Indian mathematics, in connection with Sanskrit prosody. In the Sanskrit poetic tradition, there was interest in enumerating all patterns of long (L) syllables of 2 units duration, juxtaposed with short (S) syllables of 1 unit duration.

Counting the different patterns of successive with a given total duration results in the Fibonacci numbers: the number of patterns of duration m units isF_{m+1}.

Susantha Goonatilake writes that the development of the Fibonacci sequence is attributed in part to Pingala (200 BC), later being associated with Virahanka (c.700 AD), Gopala (c.1135) and Hemachandra (c.1150).

Parmanand Singh cites Pingala's cryptic formula ("the two are mixed") and cites scholars who interpret it in context as saying that the number of patterns.

For (F_{m+1}) is obtained by adding one (S) to the F_m and one (L) to the F_{m-1} cases. He dates Pingala before 450 BC.

However, the clearest exposition of the sequence arises in the work of Virahanka, whose own work is lost, but is available in a quotation by Gopala (c.1135):

Variations of two earlier meters is the variation... For example, for (a meter of length] four, variations of meters of two and three being mixed) five happens; works out examples 8, 13, 21... In this way, the process should be followed in all prosodic combinations.

$$***$$

Chapter 32 - Occam's Razor

Ockham's razor or Okham's razor in Latin is lex parsimonies or law of parsimony is the problem-solving principle that the simplest solution tends to be the correct one. When presented with competing hypotheses to solve a problem, one should select the solution with the fewest assumptions.

The idea is attributed to English Franciscan William of Ockham (c. 1287–1347) a scholastic philosopher and theologian.

In science, Occam's razor is used as an abductive heuristic in the development of theoretical models, rather than as a rigorous arbiter between candidate models. In the scientific method, Occam's razor is not considered an irrefutable principle of logic or a scientific result of the preference for simplicity in the scientific method is based on the criterion.

For each accepted explanation of a phenomenon, there may be an extremely large, perhaps even incomprehensible, number of possible and more complex alternatives. Since one can always burden failing explanations with ad hoc hypotheses to prevent them from being falsified, simpler theories.

The term Occam's razor did not appear until a few centuries after William of Ockham's death in 1347. Christian Philosophy of the Soul, takes credit for the phrase, speaking of navicular Occam.

Ockham did not invent this principle, but the razor and its association with him may be due to the frequency and effectiveness with which he used it. Ockham stated the principle in various ways, but the most popular version,

Entities are not to be multiplied without necessity. Non sunt multiplicanda entia sine necessitate was formulated by the Irish Franciscan philosopher John in his 1639 commentary on the works of Duns Scotus.

Formulations before William of Ockham - The origins of what has come to be known as Occam's razor are traceable to the works of earlier philosophers such as John Duns Scotus (1265–1308), Robert Grosse teste (1175–1253), Maimonides (Moses ben-Maim, 1138–1204), and even Aristotle (384–322 BC) as Aristotle writes in his Posterior Analytics,

Phrases such as It is vain to do with more what can be done with fewer and A plurality is not to be posited without necessity were commonplace in the 13th century scholastic writing. Robert Grosse teste, in Commentary on Aristotle's Posterior Analytics Books. Commentaries in Posterior Analytic Libras (c. 1217–1220)

The Summa Theological of Thomas Aquinas (1225–1274) states that it is superfluous to suppose that what can be accounted for by a few principles has been produced by many.

Aquinas uses this principle to construct an objection to God's existence, an objection that he in turn answers and refutes generally and specifically, through an argument based on causality.

Hence, Aquinas acknowledges the principle that today is known as Occam's razor, but prefers causal explanations to other simple explanations (cf. also Correlation does not imply causation).

William of Ockham (circa 1287–1347) was an English Franciscan friar and theologian, an influential medieval philosopher and a nominalist. His popular fame as a great logician rests chiefly on the maxim attributed to him and known as Occam's razor.

The term razor refers to distinguishing between two hypotheses either by shaving away unnecessary assumptions or cutting apart two similar conclusions.

While it has been claimed that Occam's razor is not found in any of William's writings, one can cite statements such as Numquam ponenda est pluralitas sine necessitat must never be posited without necessity which occurs in his theological work on the Sentences.

Peter Lombard Questions et decisions in quitter labors Sententiarum Petri Lombardi (1495, I, dist. 27, qu. 2, K).

Nevertheless, the precise words sometimes attributed to William of Ockham, Entia non sunt multiplicanda praeter necessitatem. Entities must not be multiplied beyond necessity are absent.

William of Ockham's contribution seems to restrict the operation of this principle in matters pertaining to miracles and God's power; so, in the Eucharist, a plurality of miracles is possible, simply because it pleases God

This principle is sometimes phrased as Pluralitas non est ponenda sine necessitate Plurality should not be posited without necessity.

In his Summa Totties Logical, William of Ockham cites the principle of economy, Frustra fit per plura quod potest fieri per pauciora. It is futile to do with more things that which can be done with fewer.

To quote Isaac Newton, "We are to admit no more causes of natural things than such as are both true and sufficient to explain their appearances. Therefore, to the same natural effects we must, as far as possible, assign the same causes."

Bertrand Russell offers a particular version of Occam's razor: Whenever possible, substitute constructions out of known entities for inferences to unknown entities.

Around 1960, Ray Solomon off founded the theory of universal inductive inference, the theory of prediction based on observations; for example, predicting the next symbol based upon a given series of symbols.

The only assumption is that the environment follows some unknown but computable probability distribution. This theory is a mathematical formalization of Occam's razor.

Another technical approach to Occam's razor is onto logical parsimony. Parsimony means sparseness and is also referred to as the Rule of Simplicity.

This is considered a strong version of Occam's razor. A variation used in medicine is called the Zebra : a doctor should reject an exotic medical diagnosis when a more commonplace explanation is more likely, derived from Theodore Woodward's dictum When you hear hoof beats, think of horses not zebras .

Ernst Mach formulated the stronger version of Occam's razor into physics which he called the Principle of Economy stating: Scientists must use the simplest means of arriving at their results and exclude everything not perceived by the senses.

This principle goes back at least as far as Aristotle, who wrote Nature operates in the shortest way possible. The idea of parsimony or simplicity in deciding between theories, though not the intent of the original expression of Occam's razor, has been assimilated into our culture as the widespread layman's formulation that the simplest explanation is usually the correct one.

Aesthete - Prior to the 20th century, it was a commonly held belief that nature itself was simple and that simpler hypotheses about nature were thus more likely to be true. This notion was deeply rooted in the aesthetic value that simplicity holds for human thought and the justifications presented for it often drew from theology.

Thomas Aquinas made this argument in the 13th century, writing, If a thing can be done adequately by means of one, it is superfluous to do it by means of several; for we observe that nature does not employ two instruments one suffices.

Beginning in the 20th century, epistemological justifications based on induction, logic, pragmatism, and especially probability theory have become more popular among philosophers.

Empirical - Occam's razor has gained strong empirical support in helping to converge on better theory applications.

In the related concept of overfitting, excessively complex models are affected by statistical noise (a problem also known as the bias-variance trade-off simpler models may capture the underlying structure better and may thus have better predictive performance.

It is, however, difficult to deduce which part of the data is noise and thus the selection test should be applied i.e, minimum description length as in the Bayesian inference

***

Chapter 33 - Möbius

The Möbius Strip/Coil or Möbius or in the German møːbiʊs, also spelled Mobius or Moebius, is a surface with only one side, when embedded in three-dimensional Euclidean space, and only one boundary. The Möbius strip has the mathematical property of being un-orientable. It can be realized as a ruled surface.

Its discovery is attributed to the German mathematicians August Ferdinand Möbius and Johann Benedict Listing in 1858, though a structure similar to the Möbius strip can be seen in Roman mosaics dated circa 200–250 AD.

An example of a Möbius strip can be created by taking a paper strip and giving it a half-twist, and then joining the ends of the strip to form a loop. However, the Möbius strip is not a surface of only one exact size and shape, half-twisted paper strip depicted in the illustration.

Rather, mathematicians refer to the closed Möbius band as any surface that is homeomorphic to this strip. Its boundary is a simple closed curve, i.e., homeomorphic to a circle. This allows for a very wide variety of geometric versions of the Möbius band as surfaces each having a definite size and shape.

For example, any rectangle can be glued to itself (by identifying one edge with the opposite edge after a reversal of orientation) to make a Möbius band. Some of these can be smoothly modeled in Euclidean space, and others cannot.

A half-twist clockwise gives an embedding of the Möbius strip different from that of a half-twist counterclockwise – that is, as an embedded object in Euclidean space, the Möbius strip is a chiral object with right- or left-handedness.

However, the underlying topological spaces within the Möbius strip are homeomorphic in each case. An infinite number of topologically different embedding of the same topological space into three-dimensional space exist, as the Möbius strip can also be formed by twisting the strip an odd number of times greater than one, or by knotting and twisting the strip, before joining its ends. The complete open Möbius band is an example of a topological surface that is closely related to the standard Möbius strip, but that is not homeomorphic to it.

Finding algebraic equations, the solutions of which have the topology of a Möbius strip, is straightforward, but, in general, these equations do not describe the same geometric shape that one gets from the twisted paper model described above. In particular, the twisted paper model is a developable surface, having zero Gaussian curvature. A system of differential-algebraic equations that describes models of this type was published in 2007 together with its numerical solution.[6]

The Möbius strip has several curious properties. A line drawn starting from the seam down the middle meets back at the seam, but at the other side. If continued, the line meets the starting point, and is double the length of the original strip. This single continuous curve demonstrates that the Möbius strip has only one boundary.

Cutting a Möbius strip along the center line with a pair of scissors yields one long strip with two full twists in it, rather than two separate strips; the result is not a Möbius strip. This happens because the original strip only has one edge that is twice as long as the original strip. Cutting creates a second independent edge, half of which was on each side of the scissors. Cutting this new, longer, strip down the middle creates two strips wound around each other, each with two full twists.

If the strip is cut along about a third of the way in from the edge, it creates two strips: One is a thinner Möbius strip. It is the center third of the original strip, comprising one-third of the width and the same length as the original strip. The other is a longer but thin strip with two full twists in it. This is a neighborhood of the edge of the original strip, and it comprises one-third of the width and twice the length of the original strip.

Other analogous strips can be obtained by similarly joining strips with two or more half-twists in them instead of one. A strip with three half-twists, when divided lengthwise, becomes a twisted strip tied in a un-ravelled, the strip has eight half-twists.) A strip with N half-twists, when bisected, becomes a strip with N + 1 full twists. Giving it extra twists and reconnecting the ends produces figures called paradromic rings.

Geometry and topology - An object that existed in a mobius-strip-shaped universe would be indistinguishable from its own mirror image - this fiddler crab's larger claw switches between left to right with every circulation. It is not impossible that the universe may have this property, see Non-orientable wormhole.

To turn a rectangle into a Möbius strip, join the edges labelled A so that the directions of the arrows match. One way to represent the Möbius strip as a subset of three-dimensional Euclidean space is using the parametrization:

Widest isometric embedding in 3-space - If a smooth Möbius strip in three-space is a rectangular one – that is, created from identifying two opposite sides of a geometrical rectangle with bending but not stretching the surface then such an embedding is known to be possible if the aspect ratio of the rectangle is greater than the square root of three.

(Note the shorter sides of the rectangle are identified to obtain the Möbius strip.) For an aspect ratio less than or equal to the square root of three, however, a smooth embedding of a rectangular Möbius strip into three-space may be impossible.

As the aspect ratio approaches the limiting ratio of any such rectangular Möbius strip in three-space seems to approach a shape that in the limit can be thought of as a strip of three equilateral triangles, folded on top of one another so that they occupy just one equilateral triangle in three-space.

If the Möbius strip in three-space is only once continuously differentiable (in symbols: C1), however, then the theorem of Nash-Kuiper shows that no lower bound exists.

A method of making a Möbius strip from a rectangular strip too wide to simply twist and join (e.g., a rectangle

Only one unit long and one unit wide) is to first fold the wide direction back and forth using an even number of folds an "accordion fold" so that the folded strip becomes narrow enough that it can be twisted and joined, much as a single long-enough strip can be joined.

With two folds, for example, a 1 × 1 strip would become a 1 × ⅓ folded strip whose cross section is in the shape of an 'N' and would remain an 'N' after a half-twist. This folded strip, three times as long as it is wide, would be long enough to then join at the ends.

This method works in principle, but becomes impractical after sufficiently many folds, if paper is used. Using normal paper, this construction can be folded flat, with all the layers of the paper in a single plane, but mathematically, whether this is possible without stretching the surface of the rectangle is not clear.

Topology - A Möbius strip can be defined as the square {\displaystyle [0,1]\times [0,1]} with its top and bottom sides identified by the relation {\displaystyle (x,0)\sim (1-x,1)} for {\displaystyle 0\leq x\leq 1} as in the diagram on the right.

A less used presentation of the Möbius strip is as the topological quotient of a torus.

The diagonal of the square (the points (x, x) where both coordinates agree) becomes the boundary of the Möbius strip, and carries an orbifold structure, which geometrically corresponds to "reflection" geodesics (straight lines) in the Möbius strip reflect off the edge back into the strip.

Notationally, this is written as T2/S2 – the 2-torus quotiented by the group action of the symmetric group on two letters (switching coordinates), and it can be thought of as the configuration space of two unordered points on the circle, possibly the same (the edge corresponds to the points being the same), with the torus corresponding to two ordered points on the circle.

The Möbius strip is a two-dimensional compact manifold surface with boundary. It is a standard example of a surface that is not orientable. In fact, the Möbius strip is the epitome of the topological phenomenon of non-orientability.

This is because two-dimensional shapes are the lowest-dimensional shapes for which nonorientability is possible and the Möbius strip is the only surface that is topologically a subspace of every non-orientable surface. As a result, any surface is nonorientable if and only if it contains a Möbius band as a subspace.

The Möbius strip is also a standard example used to illustrate the mathematical concept of a fiber bundle. Specifically, it is a nontrivial bundle over the circle S1 with a fiber the unit interval. Looking only at the edge of the Möbius strip gives a nontrivial two point bundle.

Computer graphics - A simple construction of the Möbius strip that can be used to portray it in computer graphics or modeling packages is:

The group of isometries of this Möbius band is single dimensional and is isomorphic to the special orthogonal group.

Take a rectangular strip. Rotate it around a fixed point not in its plane. At every step, also rotate the strip along a line in its plane (the line that divides the strip in two) and perpendicular to the main orbital radius. The surface generated on one complete revolution is the Möbius strip.

Take a Möbius strip and cut it along the middle of the strip. This forms a new strip, which is a rectangle joined by rotating one end a whole turn. By cutting it down the middle again, forms two interlocking whole-turn strips.

It may be constructed as a surface of constant positive, negative, or zero (Gaussian) curvature. In the cases of negative and zero curvature, the Möbius band can be constructed as a (geodesically) complete surface, which means that all geodesics a straight lines on the surface may be extended indefinitely in either direction.

Constant negative curvature: Like the plane and the open cylinder, the open Möbius band admits not only a complete metric of constant curvature 0, but also a complete metric of constant negative curvature.

One way to see this is to begin with the upper half plane (Poincaré) model of the hyperbolic plane of the action of this group can easily be seen to be topologically a Möbius band and is also easy to verify that it is complete and non-compact, with constant negative curvature.

Constant Positive Curvature: A Möbius band of constant positive curvature cannot be complete, since it is known that the only complete surfaces of constant positive curvature are the sphere and the projective plane.

This may be thought of as the closest that a Möbius band of constant positive curvature can get to being a complete surface: just one point away. The group of isometries of this Möbius band is also single dimensional and isomorphic to the orthogonal group.

The group of bijective linear trans formations of the plane to itself (real 2×2 matrices with non-zero determinant) naturally induces bijections of the space of lines in the plane to itself, which form a group of self-homeomorphisms of the space of lines.

Hence the same group forms a group of self-homeomorphisms of the Möbius band described in the previous paragraph. But there is no metric on the space of lines in the plane that is invariant under the action of this group of homeomorphisms. In this sense, the space of lines in the plane has no natural metric on it.

***

Chapter 34 - Drake Equation

The Drake equation is used to estimate the number of communicating civilizations in the cosmos, or more simply put, the odds of finding intelligent life in the universe.

First proposed by radio astronomer Frank Drake in 1961, the equation calculates the number of communicating civilizations by multiplying several variables. It's usually written, according to the Search for Extraterrestrial Intelligence (SETI)

The Drake Equation:
$N = R^* \cdot fp \cdot ne \cdot fl \cdot fi \cdot fc \cdot L$ Where…

N = The number of civilizations in the Milky Way galaxy whose electromagnetic emissions are detectable.

R^* = The rate of formation of stars suitable for the development of intelligent life.

fp = The fraction of those stars with planetary systems.

ne = The number of planets, per solar system, with an environment suitable for life.

fl = The fraction of suitable planets on which life actually appears.

fi = The fraction of life bearing planets on which intelligent life emerges.

fc = The fraction of civilizations that develop a technology that releases detectable signs of their existence into space.

L = The length of time such civilizations release detectable signals into space.

The challenge (at least for now) is that astronomers don't have firm numbers on any of those variables, so any calculation of the Drake Equation remains a rough estimate for now. There have been, however, discoveries in some of these fields that give astronomers a better chance of finding the answer.

The recent discoveries of rocky worlds near Proxima Centauri (a star of the Alpha Centauri system) and TRAPPIST-1 have increased the public's attention on the search for life. These stars, however, are red dwarfs that might be too volatile for life. More study is needed to understand where life might be possible, and whether it could persist long enough to communicate with other civilizations.

Exoplanet discoveries - Astronomers certainly could imagine the existence of other planets outside the solar system in 1961, but it took until 1995 until the first confirmed exoplanet was found around a main-sequence star Called 51 Pegasi b, the discovery ushered in a new era when astronomers were able to track down many other planets across the universe.

Traditionally, planets have been found through two methods: watching them transit across a star (which causes a dimming that can be measured from Earth) or examining the gravitational wobbles the planets induce as they orbit around their parent star.

More recently, a technique called "verification by multiplicity" allows astronomers to quickly identify multiple-planet systems.

Estimating the total number of planets in the universe is difficult, but one statistical study suggests that in the Milky Way, each star has an average of 1.6 planets – yielding 160 billion alien planets in our home galaxy.

The study used a technique called gravitational lensing that observes changes in light curves when a relatively nearby star passes in front of more distant objects.

As of March 2018, more than 3,708 exoplanets have been confirmed. The vast bulk of them were due to an observatory called the Kepler Space Telescope, which scrutinized a single spot in the Cygnus constellation between 2009 and 2013 before switching to its K2 mission, which rotated between different locations in the sky. Plumbing the data, astronomers continue to make discoveries from the information.

Suitable for life - While Jupiter-sized planets are easier to spot in telescopes due to their large size and effect on their parent star, emerging research from the Kepler Space Telescope suggests that rocky planets are extremely common.

A slew of Kepler discoveries for example, mainly contained super-Earths, or planets that are slightly larger than Earth and are considered by many astronomers to be habitable under the right conditions.

Habitability" is usually defined as the zone around a star in which a rocky planet can maintain liquid water on the surface.

Among the planets discovered by all telescopes, however, only a tiny fraction of them are likely to have an environment suitable for life.

Astronomers can't measure this metric for sure yet, but a few factors likely come into play, such as how close a planet is to its parent star and what its atmosphere contains.

***

Chapter 35 – Galaxies

A galaxy is a gravitationally bound system of stars, stellar remnants, interstellar gas, dust, and dark matter. The word galaxy is derived from the Greek galaxias literally "milky", a reference to the Milky Way. Galaxies range in size from dwarfs with just a few hundred million (108) stars to giants with one hundred trillion (1014) stars, each orbiting its galaxy's center of mass.

Galaxies are categorized according to their visual morphology as elliptical, spiral, orirregular. Many galaxies are thought to have supermassive black holes at their centers. The Milky Way's central black hole, known as has a mass four million times greater than the Sun.

As of March 2016, GN-z11 is the oldest and most distant observed galaxy with a commoving distance of 32 billion light-years from Earth, and observed as it existed just 400 million years after the Big Bang.

Recent estimates of the number of galaxies in the observable universe range from 200 billion (2×1011) to 2 trillion (2×1012) or more, containing more stars than all the grains of sand on planet Earth.

Most of the galaxies are 1,000 to 100,000 parsecsin diameter (approximately 3000 to 300,000 light years) and separated by distances on the order of millions of parsecs (or megaparsecs). For comparison, the Milky Way has a diameter of at least 30,000 parsecs (100,000 LY) and is separated from the Andromeda Galaxy, its nearest large neighbor, by 780,000 parsecs (2.5 million LY).

The space between galaxies is filled with a tenuous gas (the intergalactic medium) having an average density of less than one atom per cubic meter. The majority of galaxies are gravitationally organized into groups, clusters, and superclusters. The Milky Way is part of the Local Group, which is dominated by it and the Andromeda Galaxy and is part of the Virgo Supercluster.

At the largest scale, these associations are generally arranged into sheets and filaments surrounded by immense voids. The largest structure of galaxies yet recognised is a cluster of superclusters that has been named Laniakea, which contains the Virgo supercluster.

Etymology - The origin of the word galaxy derives from the term for the Milky Way, galaxias (γαλαξίας, "milky one"), or kyklos galaktikos ("milky circle") due to its appearance as a "milky" band of light in the sky. In Greek mythology, Zeus places his son born by a mortal woman, the infant Heracles, on Hera's breast while she is asleep so that the baby will drink her divine milk and will thus become immortal. Hera wakes up while breastfeeding and then realizes she is nursing an unknown baby: she pushes the baby away, some of her milk spills, and it produces the faint band of light known as the Milky Way.

In the astronomical literature, the capitalized word "Galaxy" is often used to refer to our galaxy, the Milky Way, to distinguish it from the other galaxies in our universe. The English term Milky Way can be traced back to a story by Chaucer c. 1380:

Galaxies were initially discovered telescopically and were known as spiral nebulae. Most 18th to 19th Century astronomers considered them as either unresolved star clusters or anagalactic nebulae, and were just thought as a part of the Milky Way, but their true composition and natures remained a mystery.

Observations using larger telescopes of a few nearby bright galaxies, like the Andromeda Galaxy, began resolving them into huge conglomerations of stars, but based simply on the apparent faintness and sheer population of stars, the true distances of these objects placed them well beyond the Milky Way.

For this reason they were popularly called island universes, but this term quickly fell into disuse, as the word universe implied the entirety of existence. Instead, they became known simply as galaxies. The realization that we live in a galaxy which is one among man galaxies, parallels major discoveries that were made about the Milky Way

The Greek philosopher Democritus (450–370 BCE) proposed that the bright band on the night sky known as the Milky Way might consist of distant stars. Aristotle (384–322 BCE).

However, believed the Milky Way to be caused by "the ignition of the fiery exhalation of some stars that were large, numerous and close together" and that the "ignition takes place in the upper part of the atmosphere, in the region of the World that is continuous with the heavenly motions.

The Neoplatonist philosopher Olympiodorus the Younger (c. 495–570 CE) was critical of this view, arguing that if the Milky Way is sublunary (situated between Earth and the Moon) it should appear different at different times and places on Earth, have parallax, which it does not. In his view, the Milky Way is celestial.

According to Mohani Mohamed, the Arabian astronomer Alhazen (965–1037) made the first attempt at observing and measuring the Milky Way's parallax, and he thus "determined that because the Milky Way had no parallax, it must be remote from the Earth, not belonging to the atmosphere.

The Persian astronomer al-Bīrūnī (973–1048) proposed the Milky Way galaxy to be "a collection of countless fragments of the nature of nebulous stars.

The Andalusian astronomer Ibn Bâjjah Avempace, d.1138, proposed that the Milky Way is made up of many stars that almost touch one another and appear to be a continuous image due to the effect of refraction from sublunary material, citing his observation of the conjunction of Jupiter and Mars as evidence of this occurring when two objects are near.

In the 14th century, the Syrian-born Ibn Qayyim proposed the Milky Way galaxy to be "a myriad of tiny stars packed together in the sphere of the fixed stars.

The shape of the Milky Way as estimated from star counts by William Herschel in 1785; the Solar System was assumed to be near the center.

Actual proof of the Milky Way consisting of many stars came in 1610 when the Italian astronomer Galileo Galileiused a telescope to study the Milky Way and discovered it is composed of a huge number of faint stars.

In 1700 the English astronomer Thomas Wright, in his original theory or new hypothesis of the Universe, speculated (correctly) that the galaxy might be a rotating body of a huge number of stars held together by gravitational forces, akin to the Solar System but on a much larger scale.

The resulting disk of stars can be seen as a band on the sky from our perspective inside the disk. In a treatise in 1755, Immanuel Kant elaborated on Wright's idea about the structure of the Milky Way.

The first project to describe the shape of the Milky Way and the position of the Sun was undertaken by William Herschel in 1785 by counting the number of stars in different regions of the sky. He produced a diagram of the shape of the galaxy with the Solar System close to the center.

Using a refined approach, Kapteyn in 1920 arrived at the picture of a small (diameter about 15 kiloparsecs) ellipsoid galaxy with the Sun close to the center.

A different method by Harlow Shapley based on the cataloguing of globular clusters led to a radically different picture: a flat disk with diameter approximately 70 kiloparsecs and the Sun far from the center.

Both analyses failed to take into account the absorption of light by interstellar dust present in the galactic plane, but after Robert Julius Trumpler quantified this effect in 1930 by studying open clusters, the present picture of our host galaxy, the Milky Way, emerged.

A fish-eye mosaic of the Milky Way arching at a high inclination across the night sky, shot from a dark-sky location in Chile. The Magellanic Clouds, satellite galaxies of the Milky Way, appear near the left edge.

Galaxies outside the Milky Way are visible on a dark night to the unaided eye, including the Andromeda Galaxy, Large Magellanic Cloud and the Small Magellanic Cloud.

In the 10th century, the Persian astronomer Al-Sufi made the earliest recorded identification of the Andromeda Galaxy, describing it as a "small cloud. In 964, Al-Sufi probably mentioned the Large Magellanic Cloud in his Book of Fixed Stars (referring to "Al Bakr of the southern Arabs since at a declination of about 70° south it was not visible where he lived); it was not well known to Europeans until Magellan's voyage in the 16th century.

The Andromeda Galaxy was later independently noted by Simon Marius in 1612. In 1734, philosopher Emanuel Swedenborg in his Principia speculated that there may be galaxies outside our own that are formed into galactic clusters that are miniscule parts of the universe which extends far beyond what we can see. These views "are remarkably close to the present-day views of the cosmos.

In 1750, Thomas Wright speculated (correctly) that the Milky Way is a flattened disk of stars, and that some of the nebulae visible in the night sky might be separate Milky Ways. In 1755, Immanuel Kant used the term "island Universe" to Photograph of the "Great Andromeda Nebula" from 1899, later identified as the Andromeda Galaxy the end of the 18th century,

Charles Messier compiled a catalog containing the 109 brightest celestial objects having nebulous appearance. Subsequently, William Herschel assembled a catalog of 5,000 nebulae. In 1845, Lord Rosse constructed a new telescope and was able to distinguish between elliptical and spiral nebulae. He also managed to make out individual points in Kant's earlier conjecture.

In 1912, Vesto Slipher made spectrographic studies of the brightest spiral nebulae to determine their composition. Slipher discovered that the spiral nebulae have high Doppler shifts, indicating that they are moving at a rate exceeding the velocity of the stars he had measured. He found that the majority of these nebulae are moving away from us.

In 1917, Heber Curtis observed nova S Andromedae within the "Great Andromeda Nebula" (as the Andromeda Galaxy, Messier object M31, was then known). Searching the photographic record, he found 11 more novae. Curtis noticed that these novae were, on average, 10 magnitudes fainter than those that occurred within our galaxy. As a result, he was able to come up with a distance estimate of 150,000 parsecs. He became a proponent of the so-called "island universes" hypothesis, holds spiral nebulae are actually independent galaxies.

In 1920 a debate took place between Harlow Shapley and Heber Curtis (the Great Debate), concerning the nature of the Milky Way, spiral nebulae, and the dimensions of the Universe. To support his claim that the Great Andromeda Nebula is an external galaxy, Curtis noted the appearance of dark lanes resembling the dust clouds in the Milky Way, as well as the significant Doppler shift.

In 1922, the Estonian astronomer Ernst Öpik gave a distance determination that supported the theory that the Andromeda Nebula is indeed a distant extra-galactic object. Using the new 100 inch Mt. Wilson telescope, Edwin Hubble was able to resolve the outer parts of spiral nebulae as collections of individual stars and identified

Cepheid variables, thus allowing him to estimate the distance to the nebulae: they were far too distant to be part of the Milky Way. In 1936 Hubble produced a classification of galactic morphology that is used to this day.

Modern research - Rotation curve of a typical spiral galaxy: predicted based on the visible matter and observed. The distance is from the galactic core.

In 1944, Hendrik van de Hulst predicted that microwaveradiation with wavelength of 21 cm would be detectable from interstellar atomic hydrogen gas; and in 1951 it was observed. This radiation is not affected by dust absorption, and so its Doppler shift can be used to map the motion of the gas in our galaxy.

These observations led to the hypothesis of a rotating bar structure in the center of our galaxy. With improved radio telescopes, hydrogen gas could also be traced in other galaxies.

In the 1970s, Vera Rubin uncovered a discrepancy between observed galactic rotation speed and that predicted by the visible mass of stars and gas. Today, the galaxy rotation quantities of unseen dark matter.

Scientists used the galaxies visible in the GOODS survey to recalculate the total number of galaxies. Beginning in the 1990s, the Hubble Space Telescope yielded improved observations. Among other things, Hubble data helped establish that the missing dark matter in our galaxy cannot solely consist of inherently faint and small stars.

The Hubble Deep Field, an extremely long exposure of a relatively empty part of the sky, provided evidence that there are about 125 billion (1.25×1011) galaxies in the observable universe.

Improved technology in detecting the spectra invisible to humans (radio telescopes, infrared cameras, and x-ray telescopes) allow detection of other galaxies that are not detected by Hubble.

Particularly, galaxy surveys in the Zone of Avoidance (the region of the sky blocked at visible-light wavelengths by the Milky Way) have revealed a number of new galaxies.

In 2016, a study published in The Astrophysical Journal and led by Christopher Conselice of the University of Nottingham using 3D modeling of images collected over 20 years by the Hubble Space Telescope concluded that there are over 2 trillion (2×1012) galaxies in the observable universe.

***

Chapter 36 - Quantum Mechanics

The discipline quantum mechanics (QM) is also known Squantum physics, quantum theory, the wave mechanical model, or matrix mechanics, including quantum field theory, is a fundamental theory in physics which describes nature at the smallest scales of energy levels of atoms and subatomic particles.

Classical physics, the physics existing before quantum mechanics, describes nature at ordinary (macroscopic) scale. Most theories in classical physics can be derived from quantum mechanics as an approximation valid at large (macroscopic) scale.

Quantum mechanics differs from classical physics in that energy, momentum, angular momentum and other quantities of a bound system are restricted to discrete values (quantization); objects have characteristics of both particles and waves (wave-particle duality); and there are limits to the precision with which quantities can be measured (uncertainty principle).

Quantum mechanics gradually arose from theories to explain observations which could not be reconciled with classical physics, such as Max Planck's solution in 1900 to the black-body radiation problem, and from the correspondence between energy and frequency in Albert Einstein's 1905 paper which explained the photoelectric effect. Early quantum theory was profoundly re-conceived in the mid-1920s by Schrödinger, Werner, Max Born and others.

The modern theory is formulated in various specially developed mathematical formalisms. In one of them, a mathematical function, the wave function, provides information about the probability amplitude of position, momentum, and other physical properties of a particle.

Important applications of quantum theory include quantum chemistry, quantum optics, quantum computing, superconducting magnets, light-emitting diodes, and the laser, the transistor and semiconductors such as the microprocessor, medical and research imaging such as magnetic resonance imaging and electron microscopy.

Explanations for many biological and physical phenomena are rooted in the nature of the chemical bond, most notably the macro-molecule DNA.

Quantum mechanics (QM; also known as quantum physics, quantum theory, the wave mechanical model, or matrix mechanics), including quantum field theory, is a fundamental theory in physics which describes nature at the smallest scales of energy levels of atoms and subatomic particles.

Quantum mechanics gradually arose from theories to explain observations which could not be reconciled with classical physics, such as Max Planck's solution in 1900 to the black-body radiation problem, and from the correspondence between energy and frequency in Albert Einstein's 1905 paper which explained the photoelectric effect. Early quantum theory was profoundly re-conceived in the mid-1920s by Schrödinger, Werner, Max Born and others.

Classical physics, the physics existing before quantum mechanics, describes nature at ordinary (macroscopic) scale. Most theories in classical physics can be derived from quantum mechanics as an approximation valid at large (macroscopic) scale.

Quantum mechanics differs from classical physics in that energy, momentum, angular momentum and other quantities of a bound system are restricted to discrete values (quantization); objects have characteristics of both particles and waves (wave-particle duality); and there are limits to the precision with which quantities can be measured (uncertainty principle).

The modern theory is formulated in various specially developed mathematical formalisms. In one of them, a mathematical function, the wave function, provides information about the probability amplitude of position, momentum, and other physical properties of a particle.

Important applications of quantum theory include quantum chemistry, optics, quantum, superconducting magnets, light-emitting diodes, and the laser, the transistor and semiconductors such as the microprocessor, imaging such as magnetic resonance imaging and electron microscopy. Explanations for many biological and physical phenomena are rooted in the nature of the chemical bond, most notably the macro-molecule

Mathematical formulation of quantum mechanics - In the mathematically rigorous formulation of quantum mechanics developed by Paul Dirac, David Hilbert, John von Neumann, and Hermann Weyl.

The possible states of a quantum mechanical system are symbolized as unit vectors (called state vectors).

Formally, these reside in complex separable Hilbert space variously called the state space or the associated Hilbert space of the system—that is well defined up to a complex number of norm 1 (the phase factor).

In other words, the possible states are points in the projective space of a Hilbert space, usually called the complex projective space. The exact nature of this Hilbert space is dependent on the system.

The state space for position and momentum states is the space of square-integral functions, while the state space for the spin of a single proton is just the product of two complex planes

Each observable is represented by a maximally Hermitian (precisely: by a self-adjoin) linear operator acting on the state space.

Each eigenstate of an observable corresponds to an eigenvector of the operator, and the associated eigenvalue corresponds to the value of the observable in that eigenstate. If the operator's spectrum is discrete, the observable can attain only those discrete eigenvalues.

In the formalism of quantum mechanics, the state of a system at a given time is described by a complex wave function, also referred to as state vector in a complex vector space. This abstract mathematical object allows for the calculation of probabilities.

For example, it allows one to compute the probability of finding an electron in a particular region around the nucleus at a particular time. Contrary to classical mechanics, one can never make simultaneous predictions of conjugate variables, such as position and momentum, to arbitrary precision

For instance, electrons may be considered (to a certain probability) to be located somewhere within a given region of space, but with their exact positions unknown.

Contours of constant probability density, often referred to as "clouds", may be drawn around the nucleus of an atom to conceptualize where the electron might be located with the most probability. Heisenberg's uncertainty quantifies the inability to precisely locate the particle given its conjugate momentum.

According to one interpretation, as the result of a measurement, the wave function containing the probability information for a system collapses from a given initial state to a particular eigenstate. The possible results of a measurement are the eigenvalues of the operator representing the observable—which explains the choice of Hermitian operators, for which all the eigenvalues are real.

The probability distribution of an observable in a given state can be found by computing the spectral decomposition of the corresponding operator. Heisenberg's uncertainty principle is represented by the statement that the operators corresponding to certain observables do not commute.

The probabilistic nature of quantum mechanics thus stems from the act of measurement. This is one of the most difficult aspects of quantum systems to understand. It was the central topic in the famous Bohr–Einstein debates, in which the two scientists attempted to clarify these fundamental principles by way of thought experiments. In the decades after the formulation of quantum mechanics, the question of what constitutes a "measurement" has been extensively studied.

Newer interpretations of quantum mechanics have been formulated that do away with the concept of "wave function collapse" (see, for example, the relative state interpretation). The basic idea is that when a quantum system interacts with a measuring apparatus, their respective wave functions become entangled, so that the original quantum system ceases to exist as an independent entity. For details, see the article on measurement in quantum mechanics.

Generally, quantum mechanics does not assign definite values. Instead, it makes a prediction using a probability distribution; that is, it describes the probability of obtaining the possible outcomes from measuring an observable.

Often these results are skewed by many causes, such as dense probability clouds. Probability clouds are approximate (but better than the Bohr model) whereby electron location is given by a probability function, the wave function eigenvalue, such that the probability is the squared modulus of the complex, or quantum state nuclear attraction.

Naturally, these probabilities will depend on the quantum state at the "instant" of the measurement. Hence, uncertainty is involved in the value. There are, however, certain states that are associated with a definite value of a particular observable. These are known as eigenstates of the observable

"Eigen" can be translated from German as meaning "inherent" or "characteristic".

In the everyday world, it is natural and intuitive to think of everything (every observable) as being in an eigenstate. Everything appears to have a definite position, a definite momentum, a definite energy and a definite time of occurrence.

However, quantum mechanics does not pinpoint the exact values of a particle's position and momentum (since they are conjugate pairs) or its energy and time (since they too are conjugate pairs). Rather, it provides only a range of probabilities in which that particle might be given its momentum and momentum probability. Therefore, it is helpful to use different having uncertain values and states having definite values.

Usually, a system will not be in an eigenstate of the observable (particle) we are interested in. However, if one measures the observable, the wave function will instantaneously be an eigenstate (or "generalized" eigenstate) of that observable. This process is known as wave function collapse, a controversial and much-debated process that involves expanding the system under study to include the measurement device.

If one knows the corresponding wave function at the instant before the measurement, one will be able to compute the probability of the wave function collapsing into each of the possible eigenstates.

For example, the free particle in the previous example will usually have a wave function that is a wave packet centered around some mean position x0 (neither an eigenstate of position nor of momentum). When one measures the position of the particle, it is impossible to predict with certainty the result.

It is probable, but not certain, that it will be near x0, where the amplitude of the wave function is large. After the measurement is performed, having obtained some result x, the wave function collapses into a position eigenstate centered at x.

The time evolution of a quantum state is described by the Schrödinger equation, in which the Hamiltonian (the operator corresponding to the total energy of the system) generates the time evolution.

The time evolution of wave functions is deterministic in the sense that—given a wave function at an initial time—it makes a definite prediction of what the wave function will be at any later time.

During a measurement, on the other hand, the change of the initial wave function into another, later wave function is not deterministic, it is unpredictable (i.e., random). A time-evolution simulation can be seen here.

Wave functions change as time progresses. The Schrödinger equation describes how wave functions change in time, playing a role similar to Newton's second law in classical mechanics.

The Schrödinger equation, applied to the aforementioned example of the free particle, predicts that the center of a wave packet will move through space at a constant velocity (like a classical particle with no forces acting on it).

However, the wave packet will also spread out as time progresses, which means that the position becomes more uncertain with time. This also has the effect of turning a position eigenstate (which can be thought of as an infinitely sharp wave packet) into a broadened wave packet that no longer represents a (definite, certain) position eigenstate.

The corresponding to the wave functions of an electron in a hydrogen atom possessing definite energy levels (increasing from the top of the image to the bottom: n = 1, 2, 3, ...) and angular momenta (increasing across from left to right: s, p, d, ...). Denser areas correspond to higher probability density in a position measurement.

Such wave functions are directly comparable to Chanda's figures of acoustic modes of vibration in classical physics, and are modes of oscillation as well, possessing a sharp energy and, thus, a definite frequency. The angular momentum and energy are quantized, and take only discrete values like those shown (as is the case for resonant frequencies in acoustics).

Some wave functions produce probability distributions that are constant, or independent of time—such as when in a stationary state of constant energy, time vanishes in the absolute square of the wave function. Many systems that are treated dynamically in classical mechanics are described by such "static" wave functions.

For example, a single electron in an unexcited atom is pictured classically as a particle moving in a circular trajectory around the atomic nucleus, whereas in quantum mechanics it is described by wave function surrounding the nucleus. However, that only the lowest angular momentum states, labeled s, are spherically symmetric.

The Schrödinger equation acts on the entire probability amplitude, not merely its absolute value. Whereas the absolute value of the probability amplitude encodes information about probabilities, its phase encodes information about the interference between quantum states. This gives rise to the "wave-like" behavior of quantum states.

As it turns out, analytic solutions of the Schrödinger equation are available for only a very small number of relatively simple model Hamiltonians, of which the quantum harmonic oscillator, the particle in a box, the dihydrogen cation, and the hydrogen atom are the most important representatives.

Even the helium atom—which contains just one more electron than does the hydrogen atom—has defied all attempts at a fully analytic treatment.

There exist several techniques for generating approximate solutions, however. In the important method known as perturbation theory, one uses the analytic result for a simple quantum mechanical model to generate a result for a more complicated model that is related to the simpler model by (for one example) the addition of a weak potential energy.

Another method is the "semi-classical equation of motion" approach, which applies to systems for which quantum mechanics produces only weak (small) deviations from classical behavior. These deviations can then be computed based on the classical motion. This approach is particularly important in the field of quantum chaos.

Cryptography - Researchers are currently seeking robust methods of directly manipulating quantum states. Efforts are being made to more fully develop quantum cryptography, which will theoretically allow guaranteed secure transmission of information.

An inherent advantage yielded by quantum cryptography when compared to classical cryptography is the detection of passive eavesdropping.

This is a natural result of the behavior of quantum bits; due to the observer effect, if a bit in a superposition state were to be observed, the superposition state would collapse into an eigenstate.

Because the intended recipient was expecting to receive the bit in a superposition state, the intended recipient would know there was an attack, because the bit's state would no longer be in a superposition.

Quantum computing - Another goal is the development of quantum computers, which are expected to perform certain computational tasks exponentially faster than classical computers. Instead of using classical bits, quantum computers use qubits.

It can be in super-positions of states. Quantum programmers are able to manipulate the superposition of qubits in order to solve problems that classical computing cannot do effectively, such as searching unsorted databases or integer factorization.

IBM claims that the advent of quantum computing may progress the fields of medicine, logistics, financial services, artificial intelligence and cloud security.

Another active research topic is quantum teleportation, which deals with techniques to transmit quantum information over arbitrary distances.

Macroscale quantum effects - While quantum mechanics primarily applies to the smaller atomic regimes of matter and energy, some systems exhibit quantum mechanical effects on a large scale.

Superfluidity, the frictionless flow of a liquid at temperatures near absolute zero, is one well-known example.

It is the closely related phenomenon of superconductivity, the frictionless flow of an electron gas in a conducting material (an electric current) at sufficiently low temperatures.

The fractional quantum Hall effect is a topological ordered state which corresponds to patterns of long-range quantum entanglement. States with different topological orders (or different patterns of long range entanglements) cannot change into each other without a phase transition.

Quantum theory also provides accurate descriptions for many previously unexplained phenomena, such as black-body radiation and the stability of the orbitals of electrons in atoms. It has also given insight into the workings of many different biological systems, including smell receptors and protein structures.

Recent work on photosynthesis has provided evidence that quantum correlations play an essential role in this fundamental process of plants and many other organisms. Even so, classical physics can often provide good approximations to results otherwise obtained by quantum physics, typically in circumstances with large numbers of particles or large quantum numbers.

Since classical formulas are much simpler and easier to compute than quantum formulas, classical approximations are used and preferred when the system is large enough to render the effects of quantum mechanics insignificant.

Free particles - Consider a free particle. In quantum mechanics, a free matter is described by a wave function. The particle properties of the matter become apparent when we measure its position and velocity. The wave properties of the matter become apparent when we measure its wave properties like interference.

The wave–particle duality feature is incorporated in the relations of coordinates and operators in the formulation of quantum mechanics.

Since the matter is free (not subject to any interactions), its quantum state can be represented as a wave of arbitrary shape and extending over space as a wave function. The position and momentum of the particle are observables.

The Uncertainty Principle states that both the position and the momentum cannot simultaneously be measured with complete precision. However, one can measure the position (alone) of a moving free particle, creating an eigenstate of position with a wave function that is very large (a Dirac delta) at a particular position x, and zero everywhere else.

This is called an eigenstate of position or stated in mathematical terms, a generalized position eigenstate (eigen distribution). If the particle is in an eigenstate of position, then its momentum is completely unknown.

***

Chapter 37 - Big Bang Theory

The Big Bang Theory is the prevailing cosmological model for the observable universe from the earliest known periods through its subsequent large-scale evolution.

The model describes how the universe expanded from a very high-density and high-temperature state, and offers a comprehensive explanation for a broad range of phenomena, including the abundance of light elements, the cosmic microwave background (CMB), large scale structure and Hubble's law the farther galaxies are, the faster they are moving away.

If the observed conditions are extrapolated backwards in time using the known laws of physics, the prediction is that just before a period of high density there was a singularity which is associated with the Big Bang.

Physicists are undecided whether this means the universe began from a singularity, or that current knowledge is insufficient to describe the universe at that time. Detailed measurements of the expansion rate of the universe place the Big Bang at around 13.8 billion years ago, which is thus considered the age of the universe.

After its initial expansion, the universe cooled sufficiently to allow the formation of subatomic particles, and later simple atoms. Giant clouds of these primordial elements (mostly hydrogen, with some helium and lithium) later coalesced through gravity, eventually forming early stars and galaxies, the descendants are visible today.

Astronomers also observe the gravitational effects of dark matter surrounding galaxies. Though most of the mass in the universe seems to be in the form of dark matter, Big Bang theory and various observations seem to indicate that it is not made out of conventional baryonic matter (protons, neutrons, and electrons) but it is unclear exactly what it is made out of.

Since Georges Lemaître first noted in 1927 that an expanding universe could be traced back in time to an originating single point, scientists have built on his idea of cosmic expansion. The scientific community once divided between supporters two different theories the Big Bang and the Steady State theory, but a wide range of empirical evidence has strongly favored the Big Bang which is now universally accepted.

In 1929, from analysis of galactic redshifts, Edwin Hubble concluded that galaxies are drifting apart; this is important observational evidence consistent with the hypothesis of an expanding universe.

In 1964, the cosmic microwave background radiation was discovered, which was crucial evidence in favor of the Big Bang model, since that theory predicted the existence of background radiation the universe before it was discovered.

More recently, measurements of the redshifts of supernovae indicate that the expansion of the universe is accelerating, an observation attributed to dark energy's existence. The known physical laws of nature can be used to calculate the characteristics of the universe in detail in time initial state extreme and temperature.

Belgian astronomer and Catholic priest Georges Lemaître proposed on theoretical grounds that the universe is expanding, which was observationally confirmed soon afterwards by Edwin Hubble. In 1927 in the Annales de la Société Scientifique de Bruxelles (Annals of the Scientific Society of Brussels) under the title "Un Univers homogène de masse constante et de rayon croissant rendant compte de la vitesse radiale des nébuleuses extragalactiques"

A homogeneous Universe of constant mass and growing radius accounting for the radial velocity of extragalactic nebulae"), he presented his new idea that the universe is expanding and provided the first observational estimation of what is known as the Hubble constant. What later will be known as the "Big Bang theory" of the origin of the universe, he called his "hypothesis of the primeval atom" or the "Cosmic Egg".

American astronomer Edwin Hubble observed that the distances to faraway galaxies were strongly correlated with their redshifts. This was interpreted to mean that all distant galaxies and clusters are receding away from our vantage point with an apparent velocity proportional to their distance; the farther they are, the faster they move away from us, regardless of direction.

Assuming the Copernican principle (that the Earth is not the center of the universe), the only remaining interpretation is that all observable regions of the universe are receding from all others. Since we know that the distance between galaxies increases today, it must mean that in the past galaxies were closer together.

The continuous expansion of the universe implies that the universe was denser and hotter in the past. Large particle accelerators can replicate the conditions that prevailed after the early moments of the universe, resulting in confirmation and refinement of the details of the Big Bang model.

However, these accelerators can only probe so far into high energy regimes. Consequently, the state of the universe in the earliest instants of the Big Bang expansion is still poorly understood and an area of open investigation and speculation.

The first subatomic particles to be formed included protons, neutrons, and electrons. Though simple atomic nuclei formed within the first three minutes after the Big Bang, thousands of years passed before the first electrically neutral atoms formed.

The majority of atoms produced by the Big Bang were hydrogen, along with helium through gravity to form stars and galaxies, and the heavier elements were synthesized either within stars or during supernovae.

The Big Bang theory offers a comprehensive explanation for a broad range of observed phenomena, including the abundance of light elements, the CMB, large scale structure, and Hubble's Law.

The framework for the Big Bang model relies on Albert Einstein's theory of general relativity and on simplifying assumptions such as homogeneity and isotropy of space.

The governing equations were formulated by Alexander Friedmann, and similar solutions were worked on by Willem de Sitter. Since then, astrophysicists have incorporated observational and theoretical additions into the Big Bang model, and its parametrization as the Lambda-CDM model serves as the framework for current investigations of theoretical cosmology.

The Lambda-CDM model is the current "standard model" of Big Bang cosmology, consensus is that it is the simplest model

Can account for measurements and observations relevant to cosmology. Extrapolation of the expansion of the universe backwards in time using general relativity yields an infinite density and temperature at a finite time in the past.

This singularity indicates that general relativity is not an adequate description of the laws of physics in this regime. Models based on general relativity alone can not extrapolate toward the singularity beyond the end of the Planck epoch.

This primordial singularity is itself sometimes called "the Big Bang", but the term can also refer to a more generic early hot, dense phase of the universe. In either case, "the Big Bang" as an event is also colloquially referred to as the "birth" of our universe since it represents the point in history where the universe can be verified to have entered into a regime where the laws of physics as we understand them (specifically general relativity and the standard model of particle physics) work.

Based on measurements of the expansion using Type Ia supernovae and measurements of temperature fluctuations in the cosmic microwave background, the time that has passed since that event otherwise known as the "age of the universe" is 13.799 ± 0.021 billion years. The agreement of independent measurements of this age supports the ΛCDM model that describes in detail the characteristics of the universe.

Despite being extremely dense at this time—far denser than is usually required to form a black hole—the universe did not re-collapse into a black hole. This may be explained by considering that commonly-used calculations and limits for gravitational collapse are usually based upon objects of relatively constant size, such as stars, and do not apply to rapidly expanding space such as the Big Bang.

The earliest phases of the Big Bang are subject to much speculation. In the most common models the universe was filled homogeneously and isotropically with a very high energy density and huge temperatures and pressures and was very rapidly expanding and cooling. Temperatures were so high that the random motions of particles were at relativistic speeds, and particle-antiparticle pairs of all kinds were being continuously created.

Approximately 10−37 seconds into the expansion, a phase transition caused a cosmic inflation, during which the universe grew exponentially during which time density fluctuations that occurred because of the uncertainty principle were amplified into the seeds that would later form the large-scale structure of the universe.

After inflation stopped, reheating occurred until the universe obtained the temperatures required for theproduction of a quark–gluon plasma as well as all other elementary particles. This resulted in the predominance of matter oveantimatterthe entire near-infrared sky reveals the distribution of galaxies beyond the Milky Way. Galaxies are color-coded by redshift.

The universe continued to decrease in density and fall in temperature, hence the typical energy of each particle was decreasing. Symmetry breaking phase transitions put the fundamental forces of physics and the parameters of elementary particles into their present form. After about 10−11 seconds, the picture becomes less speculative, since particle energies drop to values that can be attained inparticle accelerators.

At about 10−6 seconds, quarks and gluons combined to formbaryons such as protons and neutrons. The small excess of quarks over antiquarks led to a small excess of baryons over antibaryons. The temperature was now no longer high enough to create new proton–antiproton pairs (similarly for neutrons–antineutrons), so a mass annihilation immediately followed, leaving just one in 1010 of the original protons and neutrons, and none of their antiparticles.

A similar process happened at about 1 second for electrons and positrons. After these annihilations, the remaining protons, neutrons and electrons were no longer moving relativistically and the energy density of the universe was dominated by photons (with a minor contribution from neutrinos).

A few minutes into the expansion, when the temperature was about a billion (one thousand million) kelvin and the density was about that of air, neutrons combined with protons to form the universe's deuterium and helium nuclei in a process called Big Bang nucleosynthesis. Most protons remained uncombined as hydrogen.

As the universe cooled, the rest mass energy density of matter came to gravitationally dominate that of the photon radiation.

After about 379,000 years, the electrons and nuclei combined into atoms (mostly hydrogen); hence the radiation decoupled from matter and continued through space largely unimpeded.

This relic radiation is known as the cosmic microwave background radiation. The chemistry of life may have begun shortly after the Big Bang, 13.8 billion years ago, during a habitable epoch when the universe was only 10–17 million years old.

Over a long period of time, the slightly denser regions of the nearly uniformly distributed matter gravitationally attracted nearby matter and thus grew even denser, forming gas clouds, stars, galaxies, and the other astronomical structures observable today.

The details of this process depend on the amount and type of matter in the universe. The four possible types of matter are known as cold dark matter, warm dark matter, hot dark matter, and baryonic matter.

The best measurements available, from Wilkinson Microwave Anisotropy Probe (WMAP), show that the data is well-fit by a Lambda-CDM model in which dark matter is assumed to be cold (warm dark matter is ruled out by early reionization).

It is estimated to make up about 23% of the matter/energy of the universe, while baryonic matter makes up about 4.6%. In an "extended model" which includes hot dark matter in the form of neutrinos,

Lines of evidence from Type Ia supernovae and the CMB imply that the universe today is dominated by a mysterious form of energy known as dark energy, which apparently permeates all of space. The observations suggest 73% of the total energy density of today's universe is in this form.

When the universe was very young, it was likely infused with dark energy, but with less space and everything closer together, gravity predominated, and it was slowly braking the expansion. But eventually, after numerous billion years of expansion, the growing abundance of dark energy caused the expansion of the universe to slowly begin to accelerate.

Dark energy in its simplest formulation takes the form of the cosmological constant term in Einstein's field equations of general relativity, but its composition and mechanism are unknown and, more generally, the details of its equation of state and relationship with the Standard Model of particle physics continue to be investigated both through observation and theoretically.

All of this cosmic evolution after the inflationary epoch can be rigorously described and modeled by the ΛCDM model of cosmology, which uses the independent frameworks of quantum mechanics and Einstein's General Relativity. There is no well-supported model describing the action prior to $10-15$ seconds or so. Apparently a new unified theory of quantum gravitation is needed to break this barrier. Understanding this earliest of eras in the history of the universe is one of the greatest unsolved problems in physics.

The Big Bang theory depends on two major assumptions: the universality of physical laws and the cosmological principle. The cosmological principle states that on large scales the universe is homogeneous and isotropic.

These ideas were initially taken as postulates, but today there are efforts to test each of them. For example, the first assumption has been tested by observations showing that largest possible deviation of the fine structure constant over much of the age of the universe is of order $10-5$. Also, general relativity has passed stringent tests on the scale of the Solar System and binary stars.

If the large-scale universe appears isotropic as viewed from Earth, the cosmological principle can be derived from the simpler Copernican principle, which states that there is no preferred (or special) observer or vantage point. To this end, the cosmological principle has been confirmed to a level of $10-5$ via observations of the CMB. The universe has been measured to be homogeneous on the largest scales at the 10% level.

General relativity describes spacetime by a metric, which determines the distances that separate nearby points. The points, which can be galaxies, stars, or other objects, are themselves specified using a coordinate chart or "grid" that is laid allspacetime.

The cosmological principle implies that the metric should be homogeneousand isotropic on large scales, which uniquely singles out the Friedmann–Lemaître–Robertson–Walker metric (FLRW metric). This metric contains a scale factor, which describes how the size of the universe changes with time. This enables a convenient choice of a coordinate system to be made, called comoving coordinates.

In this coordinate system, the grid expands along with the universe, and objects that are moving only because of the expansion of the universe, remain at fixed points on the grid. While their coordinate distance (comoving distance) remains constant, the physical distance between two such co-moving points expands proportionally with the scale factor of the universe.39]

The Big Bang is not an explosion of matter moving outward to fill an empty universe. Instead, space itself expands with time everywhere and increases the physical distance between two comoving points. In other words, the Big Bang is not an explosion in space, but rather an expansion of space. Because the FLRW metric assumes a uniform distribution of mass and energy, it applies to our universe only on large scales—local concentrations of matter such as our galaxy are gravitationally bound and as such do not experience the large-scale expansion of space.

Features of the Big Bang spacetime is the presence of particle horizons. Since the universe has a finite age, and light travels at a finite speed, there may be events in the past whose light has not had time to reach us. This places a limit or a past horizon on the most distant objects that can be observed. Conversely, because space is expanding, and more distant objects are receding ever more quickly, light emitted by us today may never "catch up" to very distant objects.

This defines a future horizon, which limits the events in the future that we will be able to influence. The presence of either type of horizon depends on the details of the FLRW model that describes our universe.

Our understanding of the universe back to very early times suggests that there is a past horizon, though in practice our view is also limited by the opacity of the universe at early times. So our view cannot extend further backward in time, though the horizon recedes in space. If the expansion of the universe continues to accelerate, there is a future horizon as well.

During a 1949 BBC radio broadcast, saying: "These theories were based on the hypothesis that all the matter in the universe was created in one big bang at a particular time in the remote past."

It is popularly reported that Hoyle, who favored an alternative "steady state" cosmological model, intended this to be pejorative, but Hoyle explicitly denied this and said it was just a striking image meant to highlight the difference between the two models.

The Big Bang theory developed from observations of the structure of the universe and from theoretical considerations. In 1912 Vesto Slipher measured the first Doppler shift of a "spiral nebula" (spiral nebula is the obsolete term for spiral galaxies).

Soon discovered that almost all such nebulae were receding from Earth. He did not grasp the cosmological implications of this fact, and indeed at the time it was highly controversial whether or not these nebulae were "island universes" outside our Milky Way.

Ten years later, Alexander Friedmann, a Russian cosmologist and mathematician, derived the Friedmann equations from Albert Einstein's equations of general relativity, showing that the universe might be expanding in contrast to the static universe model advocated by Einstein at that time.

In 1924 Edwin Hubble's measurement of the great distance to the nearest spiral nebulae showed that these systems were indeed other galaxies. Independently deriving Friedmann's equations in 1927, Georges Lemaître, a Belgian physicist, proposed that the inferred recession of the nebulae was due to the expansion of the universe.

In 1931 Lemaître went further and suggested that the evident expansion of the universe, if projected back in time, meant that the further in the past the smaller the universe was, until at some finite time in the past all the mass of the universe was concentrated into a single point, a "primeval atom" where and when the fabric of time and space came into existence.

Starting in 1924, Hubble painstakingly developed a series of distance indicators, the forerunner of the cosmic distance ladder, using the 100-inch (2.5 m) Hooker telescope atMount Wilson Observatory. This allowed him to estimate distances to galaxies whose redshifts had already been measured, mostly by Slipher

In 1929 Hubble discovered a correlation between distance and recession velocity now known as Hubble's law. Lemaître had that this was expected, given the cosmological principle

In the 1920s and 1930s almost every major cosmologist preferred an eternal steady stateuniverse, and several complained that the beginning of time implied by the Big Bang imported religious concepts into physics; this objection was later repeated by supporters of the steady state theory.

This perception was enhanced by the fact that the originator of the Big Bang theory, Georges Lemaître, was a Roman Catholic priest. Arthur Eddington agreed with Aristotle that the universe did not have a beginning in time,viz., that matter is eternal. A beginning in time was "repugnant" to him. Lemaître, however, thought that

If the world has begun with a single quantum, the notions of space and time would altogether fail to have any meaning at the beginning; they would only begin to have a sensible meaning when the original quantum had been divided into a sufficient number of quanta. If this suggestion is correct, the beginning of the world happened a little before the beginning of space and time.

During the 1930s proposed as non-standard cosmologies to explain Hubble's observations, including the Milne, the oscillatory universe (originally suggested by Friedmann, but advocated by Albert Einstein and Richard Tolman) and Fritz Zwicky's.

After World War II, two distinct possibilities emerged. One was Fred Hoyle's steady state model, whereby new matter would be created as the universe seemed to expand. In this model the universe is roughly the same at any point in time.

The other was Lemaître's Big Bang theory, advocated and developed by George Gamow, who introduced big bang nucleosynthesis (BBN) and whose associates, Ralph Alpher and Robert Herman, predicted the CMB. Ironically, it was Hoyle who coined the phrase that came to be applied to Lemaître's theory, referring to it as "this big bang idea" during a BBC Radio broadcast in March 1949.

For a while, support was split between these two theories. Eventually, the observational evidence, most notably from radio source counts, began to favor Big Bang over Steady State. The discovery and confirmation of the CMB in 1964 secured the Big Bang as the best theory of the origin and evolution of the universe.

Much of the current work in cosmology includes understanding how galaxies form in the context of the Big Bang, understanding the physics of the universe at earlier and earlier times, and reconciling observations with the basic theory.

In 1968 and 1970 Roger Penrose, Stephen Hawking, and George F. R. Ellis published papers where they showed that mathematical singularities were an inevitable initial condition of general relativistic models of the Big Bang.

Then, from the 1970s to the 1990s, cosmologists worked on characterizing the features of the Big Bang universe and resolving outstanding problems. In 1981, Alan Guth made a breakthrough in theoretical work on resolving certain outstanding theoretical problems in the Big Bang theory with the introduction of an epoch of rapid expansion in the early universe he called "inflation".

Meanwhile, during these decades, two questions in observational cosmology that generated much discussion and disagreement were over the precise values of the Hubble Constant and the matter-density of the universe (before the discovery of dark energy, thought to be the key predictor for the eventual fate of the universe).
In the mid-1990s, observations of certain globular clusters appeared to indicate that they were about 15 billion years old, which conflicted with most then-current estimates of the age of the universe (and indeed with the age measured today).

This issue was later resolved when new computer simulations, which included the effects of mass loss due to stellar winds, indicated a much younger age for globular clusters. While there still remain some questions as to how accurately the ages of the clusters are measured, globular clusters are of interest to cosmology as some of the oldest objects in the universe.

The earliest and most direct observational evidence of the validity of the theory are the expansion of the universe according to Hubble's law (as indicated by the redshifts of galaxies), discovery and measurement of the cosmic microwave background and the relative abundances of light elements produced by Big Bang nucleosynthesis. More recent evidence includes observations of galaxy formation and evolution, and the distribution of large-scale cosmic structures, These are sometimes called the "four pillars" of the Big Bang theory.

Precise modern models of the Big Bang appeal to various exotic physical phenomena that have not been observed in terrestrial laboratory experiments or incorporated into the Standard Model of particle physics. Of these features, dark matter is currently subjected to the most active laboratory investigations. Remaining issues include the cuspy halo problem and the dwarf galaxy problem of cold dark matter.

Dark energy is also an area of intense interest for scientists, but it is not clear whether direct detection of dark energy will be possible. Inflation and baryogenesis remain more speculative features of current Big Bang models. Viable, quantitative explanations for such phenomena are still being sought. These are currently unsolved problems in physics.

Distant galaxies and quasars show that these objects are redshifted the light emitted from them has been shifted to longer wavelengths. By taking a frequency spectrum of an object and matching the spectroscopic pattern of emission lines or absorption lines corresponding to atoms of the chemical elements interacting with the light.

These redshifts are uniformly isotropic, distributed evenly among the observed objects in all directions. If the redshift is interpreted as a Doppler shift, the recessional velocity of the object can be calculated. For some galaxies, it is possible to estimate distances via the cosmic distance ladder. When the recessional velocities are plotted against these distances, a linear relationship known as Hubble's law.

Hubble's law has two possible explanations. Either we are at the center of an explosion of galaxies—which is untenable given the Copernican principle—or the universe is uniformly expanding everywhere. This universal expansion was predicted from general relativity by Alexander Friedmann in 1922 and Georges Lemaître in 1927, well before Hubble made his 1929 analysis and observations, and it remains the cornerstone of the Big Bang theory as developed by Friedmann, Lemaître, Robertson, and Walker.

That space is undergoing metric expansion is shown by direct observational evidence of the Cosmological principle and the Copernican principle, which together with Hubble's law have no other explanation.

Astronomical redshifts are extremely isotropic and homogeneous, supporting the Cosmological principle that the universe looks the same in all directions, along with much other evidence.

If the redshifts were the result of an explosion from a center distant from us, they would not be so similar in different directions.

Measurements of the effects of the cosmic microwave background radiation on the dynamics of distant astrophysical systems in 2000 proved the Copernican principle, that, on a cosmological scale, the Earth is not in a central position.

Radiation from the Big Bang was demonstrably warmer at earlier times throughout the universe. Uniform cooling of the CMB over billions of years is explainable only if the universe is experiencing a metric expansion, and excludes the possibility that we are near the unique center of an explosion.

The cosmic microwave background spectrum measured by the FIRAS instrument on the COBE satellite is the most-precisely measured black body spectrum in nature.

In 1964 Arno Penzias and Robert Wilson serendipitously discovered the cosmic backgrour adiation, an omnidirectional signal in the microwave band. Their discovery provided substantial confirmation of the big-bang predictions by Alpher, Herman and Gamow around 1950.

Through the 1970s the radiation was found to be approximately consistent with a black body spectrum in all directions; this spectrum has been redshifted by the expansion of the universe, and today corresponds to approximately 2.725 K.

This tipped the balance of evidence in favor of the Big Bang model, and Penzias and Wilson were awarded a Nobel Prize in 1978.

The shape of the universe to be spatially almost flat by measuring the typical angular size (the size on the sky) of the anisotropies.In early 2003, the first results of the Wilkinson Microwave Anisotropy Probe (WMAP) were released, yielding what were at the time the most accurate values for some of the cosmological parameters.

The results disproved several specific cosmic inflation models, but are consistent with the inflation theory in general.The Planck space probe was launched in May 2009. Other ground and balloon based cosmic microwave background experiments are ongoing.

The Big Bang model is possible to calculate the concentration of helium-4, helium-3, deuterium, and lithium-7 in the universe as ratios to the amount of ordinary hydrogen.The relative abundances depend on a single parameter, the ratio of photons to baryons. This value can be calculated independently.

In 2011, astronomers found what they believe to be pristine clouds of primordial gas by analyzing absorption lines in the spectra of distant quasars. Before this discovery, all other astronomical objects have been observed to contain heavy elements that are formed in stars.

These two clouds of gas contain no elements heavier than hydrogen and deuterium. Since the clouds of gas have no heavy elements, they likely formed in the first few minutes after the Big Bang, during Big Bang nucleosynthesis.

The age of the universe as estimated from the Hubble expansion and the CMB is now in good agreement with other estimates using the ages of the oldest stars, both as measured by applying the theory of stellar evolution to globular clusters and through radiometric dating of individual Population II stars.

The prediction that the CMB temperature was higher in the past has been experimentally supported by observations of very low temperature absorption lines in gas clouds at high redshift. This prediction also implies that the amplitude of the Sunyaev–Zel'dovich effect in clusters of galaxies does not depend directly on redshift. Observations have found this to be roughly true, but this effect depends on cluster properties that do change with cosmic time, making precise measurements difficult.

Future gravitational waves observatories might be able to detect primordial gravitational waves, relics of the early universe, up to less than a second after the Big Bang.

Mysteries and problems have arisen as a result of the development of the Big Bang theory. Some of these mysteries and problems have been resolved while others are still outstanding. Proposed solutions to some of the problems in the Big Bang model have revealed new mysteries of their own.

For example, the horizon problem, the magnetic monopole problem, and the flatness problem are most commonly resolved with inflationary theory, but the details of the inflationary universe are still left unresolved and many, including some founders of the theory, say it has been disproven.

What follows are a list of the mysterious aspects of the Big Bang theory still under intense investigation by cosmologists and astrophysicists. It is not yet understood why the universe has more matter than antimatter. It is generally assumed that when the universe was young and very hot it was in statistical equilibrium and contained equal numbers of baryons and antibaryons. However, observations suggest that the universe, including its most distant parts, is made almost entirely of matter.

A process called baryogenesis was hypothesized to account for the asymmetry. For baryogenesis to occur, the Sakharov conditions must be satisfied. These require that baryon number is not conserved, that C-symmetry and CP-symmetry are violated and that the universe depart from thermodynamic equilibrium. All these conditions occur in the Standard Model, but the effects are not strong enough to explain the present baryon asymmetry.

***

Part II - STARCHILD THE MOVIE

<u>Misc Data & Definitions:</u>

Terra – home planet of the Terrains
Tropia – home planet of the Tropians
Zoatropeia – galaxy, Milky Way
Vialacta – galaxy, Milky Way
Solar Star – a sun
Zea – the small closer moon
Zeo – the large more distant moon
DioGurr – planet similar to Mars
Exoplanet – planet orbiting an alien solar star
Cyclotron – apparatus for accelerating atomic and subatomic particles
Cyclatron – an art work or misspelling of cyclotron or a fictional device
Cyclatron – in science fiction Fluxgate, Fluxtron, Varatron, Warp-drive
Tierell in Star Wars and similar to Tyrell in Blade Runner
Tierail Corporation – a fictional technology company
Tiarell - In numerology calculates as five
Tyrell or Tiarell - Means autonomous, curious or exploratory
UTAF – United Tropian (or Terrain) Air (or Aero) Force
Stasis Field – fictional suspended state of existence
Quantum Corporation – a fictional technology company
Quantum coupling or entanglement, unexplained communication
Haydian – the blockade of Hydian Way in Star Wars and Hadrian's Wall
Event Horizon – boundary around black hole from which no light escapes
Singularity – a state or quality of being single
Superheterodyne – type of radio receiver
Genesis 6:4 - There were giants in those days, when the sons of God came
unto the daughters of men and they bore them children. These were the
mighty men of old, the men of renown and legend…
Paradigm Shift - a revolution or change in science (Thomas Kuhn's book)
Paradigm - a pattern in the way of doing something or series of events
The width of Milky Way galaxy is about 107,000 light-years across.
The universe is 90 billion light years across and 13 billion years old and
could end in a quantum phase shift
Our sun and planetary belt is 26,000 light years from center of spiral arm.
Sirius is 8.9 l light-years to earth
Local fluff - planetary dust adrift in a galaxy
Pulsars – collapsed star (used as beacons to navigate
Quasar – radio source from the center of a galaxy
X-Nav uses three pulsars as beacons to navigate like a GPS

***

Chapter 21   STARCHILD - **Screenplay Treatment**

*The original screenplay concept
developed in 1978 by Marvin Arnold
WGA #200979 and #601261*

It is night. Across a small inlet of water, a rocket is sitting on a launch pad beside a well-lighted gantry. There are no sounds except the rippling of water on the shoreline and the normal night time sounds. (1) The gantry comes alive with flames from the rocket engines and the missile begins to lift off. The chest pounding noise breaks the soft still night air. The sky glows a bright yellow-gray, then fades as the missile becomes only a speck of light among the stars. It is even darker than before and the soft night sounds return.

Inside the brightly lit Launch Control Center, several dozen scientists and engineers go through normal post-launch procedures and prepare for a work-shift changeover. Singled out among the many in the room are The Professor, a guidance controller, The Engineer, a tracking officer and The Commander, who is a former astronaut.

The Professor is the head of a special research project on hyper-light given the code name, STARCHILD. He was in attendance as an observer at the launch. Mounted on top of the missile that was launched is a special nose cone capable of exceeding the speed-of-light. (2) As the work-shift changes, The Professor, The Engineer and The Commander leave the building together discussing the successful launch. The Professor then invites them to his home the following afternoon for an outdoor party and small celebration. They are to come and bring their wives and girlfriends too.

As they exit, it becomes obvious by observing the surroundings that it is not the 1970s, but more in the time period of 1980 to 1990. The environmental conditions are very poor, the sky is not clear and the air is hazy. The cars are conventional, but more modern. Many things are familiar, but there are minor differences in dress, road signs, etc. (The fact being that we are not on Earth at all, but on the planet Terra.)
 Terra is a planet, which at this point, is only slightly advanced over present day Earth. Terra is suffering from the technological destruction of its atmosphere. (3)

The Professor then drives to the launch gantry where two launch Technicians are supervising the cleanup and shutdown of the operation. As he gets out of the car, the two Technicians walk over to meet him. They discuss the flawless success of the missile launch and The Professor invites them to attend the celebration at his home the next day. They accept.

A patrol helicopter follows The Professor's car as he drives to a large hangar some distance away. The hangar is very isolated and well-guarded. An entry sign indicates that it is a Restricted Area. He is given entry by the guard who recognizes him as he enters. In the very large, dimly lit hangar, a small craft about the size of a jet fighter, sits alone in the center of the hangar. As The Professor walks slowly around the craft, he is engrossed in deep thought. The name on the side of the craft reads STARCHILD. It is a six passenger spacecraft which has been built to test hyper-light. It is currently in phase two of the project. Phase one of the project was the unmanned nose cone atop the missile launched earlier that day. The nose cone from the unmanned missile will go into outer-space, be inserted into hyper-light speed for only a micro-second, then recovered and returned. No one actually knows how far an object will go when traveling at hyper-light speed for even a fraction of a second.

The Professor looks up as he hears footsteps coming across the hangar floor. As the darkened figure approaches, he recognizes The Director of the Space Center. The Director informs The Professor that the nose cone went into hyper-light approximately fifteen minutes earlier. No trace of it has been found as of yet, but he feels that with the sophisticated tracking equipment onboard, there will be no problem in finding and returning the nose cone. At sub-light, depending on the distance, it could take months or years for the nose cone to be recovered.

The Professor seems to be pre-occupied. When The Director asks if anything is wrong, The Professor goes into a rage about not understanding how science can accomplish something as complicated as developing a hyper-light spacecraft and then stand idly by and let nations and corporations destroy the world's environment. The Director is startled at The Professor's hostility, then realizing that is not The Director's fault, but all the world's fault, The Professor apologizes. The two men leave the hangar together and STARCHILD stands alone in the darkened hangar.

At the outdoor party the next afternoon, there are twelve guests present. A Woman Scientist, who is an

astrobiologist, stands near a table spread with hors'deurves and drinks. Several other guests are standing with her as she discusses her latest research project which is cloning. (4) Her research is being conducted at the space center laboratories. Someone suggests that cloning is such a morbid subject and proposes that they toast to yesterday's successful launch. The occasion turns to a happy one, The Professor seems pleased.
The atmosphere is very hazy and someone remarks that the day has turned out nice for a cookout. One assumes then that the environmental conditions are very bad if this is considered a good day.

The Director and his wife leave. The two Technicians have left to take their girlfriends home and have returned. The conversation now comes around to the hyper-light Project. It is jokingly remarked that there is no great secret about what the project is, only in how it is going to be achieved. The conversation then turns to the bad environmental conditions, the armed satellites in space and other current scientific problems of the day.

The Professor goes to freshen his drink, he is followed by The Commander who engages him in a conversation about what would happen if a carbon nuclear bomb were set off in the present unstable carbon monoxide atmosphere. The Professor, who is still in a joking mood, replies that he would not want to be around to test that theory.

The Commander looks very concerned and asks The Professor to come and see him at the space center the next day. They then rejoin the others at the party.

The next day The Commander and Professor meet. The Commander explains that a foreign power had placed several carbon-nuclear warhead satellites into orbit some years ago. That a project, which he is involved in, tracts these satellites. They have discovered that one of the warhead satellites is in a very low orbit that is decaying rapidly. (5)

The Professor calls in The Director and three other scientists to help in calculating the orbital decay and the potential for a nuclear reaction. It is calculated that the satellite will enter the atmosphere within a matter of hours and that a nuclear chain reaction will occur. It is suggested that the satellite be shot down by a missile. However, by the time the missile can be launched, the satellite will already be too close to the atmosphere and a chain reaction cannot be prevented.

The Professor now reveals that the untested spacecraft, STARCHILD is ready for flight. The craft is capable of carrying unlimited weight, but there is only life support systems for six persons. The Girl Scientist arrives to meet The Professor. She enters the room unaware of the grim conclusions which have just been reached. She has in her hand a plastic container, in the container is a small plant which she excitedly explains is a second generation A-Amana, (6) a hybrid plant which has just been developed. She then realizes that something is wrong.

The Director who has observed and remained silent up until now suggests they should try to put three couples into outer space to survive the probable destruction of the world. The Director declines to go as he feels somewhat guilty for the current state of events. The two Technicians agree voluntarily to stay behind. The Engineer's wife is called and told to come to the space center.

In the large hangar, two technicians ready the STARCHILD for the flight. The Director sits alone in the launch control center. There are some emotional moments as The Engineer talks with his wife on the phone, she will not leave her small child based on a scientific theory that the world is coming to an end and risk her life in an untried spacecraft. The Commander's girlfriend is involved in a spectacular car crash on the way to the Space Center. At the last minute, five men and one woman board the STARCHILD. The hangar door rolls open and the craft lifts off (7) into the dark starlit evening sky.

The craft must remain sub-light until it is well clear of the atmosphere. As the six space travelers look back at the world, (8) the atmosphere begins to glow red at one small point, then the blue-white begins to glow red all over. The nuclear chain reaction is no longer a theory but a fact. There is sadness among the six. The world as they knew it, no longer existed.
The Professor assisted by the Commander inserts the STARCHILD into hyper-light and Terra becomes only a small point of light in a vast star field.

Traveling at hyper-light for several weeks, The Commander, who is a celestial navigation expert, calculates that they are nearing a sun approximately the same size as their former sun. The Commander suggests that they should go sub-light and look for a habitable planet.

Looming ahead is the planet Earth. So much like Terra that they are suspect of what they see. Entering Earth orbit, they make a spectra-analysis of the whole planet. The atmosphere is pure. It is too good to be true. They search for an area of medium terrain on which to set the STARCHILD down. An attractive river valley, later to be known as the Mediterranean Valley (9) is selected for landing site.

The space-travelers have not aged during their trip. They later discover that no aging will again occur until the real-time has elapsed. (The period of time which it would take to travel the same distance at the speed-of-light which they have traveled at hyper-light.) It will take 6,000 to 10,000 years for this to occur. Except for bodily damage beyond repair or healing, they are immortal for the time being.

They have in fact, landed on Earth during a period thousands of years BC They have not gone through a time warp. (10) They have not landed on the same planet from which they departed.

The six emerge from the STARCHILD. They marvel at the beautiful Earth, thinking that a long time ago Terra must have been much like this. They begin to take stock and make camp. It will soon be dark.

The next day, The Technician uses a one-man retro- rocket (11) to make an aerial survey of the area. He encounters some nomads. They are homosapiens (12) which are native to Earth, but still not men as we know them today.

The space travelers befriend the natives and for a time they live among them, treating them more like friendly children than equals. They show them how to make fire, purify meat and roll things on wheels.

Years pass and by now it is evident that the six space-travelers are not aging. They move to a mountain top home and install many conveniences which they build from scratch. It seems to the Earth men that they are truly gods. The Commander, one day kills a beast (13) with a laser gun. He becomes known as Thor. The Technician who often flies around on a Mercury powered rocket pack, becomes known as Mercury, the messenger of the gods. (14) The Girl Scientist becomes known as Pallasathena, the name given to her means Protectress of Civilized Life.

A crude form of Latin, the language of Terra, is then taught to the natives. Several of the male space-travelers mate with the humanoid women of Earth, (15) but the offspring are not ageless like their space-traveler parents. In fact, Adam, the first Terra-Earth Man only lives 130 years, but his son, Seth, became a powerful ruler in Mediterranean and lives 912 years. (16)

Although the space-travelers can copulate with the humanoids who cohabit the Earth, it is decided, after several decades, that each man will marry Athena. They will raise a family of a least three female children. She will then formally divorce herself of that man and wed another, repeating this procedure five times. It is found that the offspring are highly evolved like their parents, but are not ageless because they are born within their own time frame. It then becomes necessary for the men from Terra to mate with other than their own offspring for several generations. This is so that the offspring will never marry closer than a third cousin. (17)

The only woman space-traveler becomes the (Eve) mother of the New Earth. The twelve original daughters become the mothers of the twelve major tribes of Earth. Their early offspring have long life spans, but after cross-breeding and in-breeding (18) takes place their life spans shorten. (19)

During the next several thousand years, the space-travelers inhabit various parts of the planet Earth. In their travels, they are able to meet and visit with two other extraterrestrial. The first landed in Tibet. His name is BoDa. (20) He has traveled her sub-light from Himala, and his people are known as Manchu. The planet Himala is about 15 light-years away in the region of the constellation Draco (the Dragon). He has made the trip knowing that he cannot return.

He ascended to Earth in a small shuttle craft. The larger interplanetary vehicle was burned up in the Earth's atmosphere. BoDa can communicate with his home planet by thought wave, but the longer he stays on Earth, the more his power is weakened. The Manchus are a very religious, highly evolved people. It is said by BoDa that he does not believe anyone else will follow him to Earth. He remains in Asia for many years and he and his descendants found most of the worlds great religions.

The other landing by extra-terrestrials is a group of 7-feet tall, thin, dark-skinned people who have traveled here from Sirius E-2, a planet having two suns (21) in the constellation Canis. Their home planet is suffering from a 3000 year drought.

It is doubtful that anyone who remained on Sirius will survive. Their craft too is a sub-light craft and its atomic fuel has been expended on this migration. It is agreed, with their leader NaGa, that his people may remain in Africa. Their descendants along with some of the descendants of the Manchu later unite to form the Egyptian empire.

The space-travelers from Terra establish a great civilization on the island of Atlantis. North America is to remain undeveloped, more of an experimental than anything else. They consider it like an international park or game reservation. It will be preserved until time and population demand that it be used. They are able to travel from continent to continent by means of an anti-gravity device taken from the engines of the STARCHILD. This is attached to simple baskets or carriages for carrying several people. Often, they take friends or offspring aboard these crafts. One who is unfamiliar with a flying craft, which can climb high above the clouds, would describe their encounter as being carried to heaven by the gods. (Legends carried down through various cultures, described heaven as like sitting around on puffs of clouds.)

An understanding of the current (22) flows of the great oceans is taught to the sailor merchants of the time. Trading throughout the world is done on a large scale. They teach these same merchants how to use the sail like the air-foil of an airplane to pull the boat across the water instead of being pushed by the wind.

Two of the original space-travelers are destroyed by a natural disaster. The others build a pyramid, the first pyramid in the Nile River Valley, to focus cosmic energy and help preserve their remains. They have knowledge of cloning and by storing the remains of their two companions, they know that someday it will be possible to reinstate them to life form.

During a major Earth catastrophe, the island of Atlantis sinks and the Mediterranean Valley is destroyed by flood. The main power cell from the STARCHILD is lost at the sinking of Atlantis. (23)

During the time of Moses, three of the space-travelers visit with him and instruct him as to how to build a radio receiver into the temple walls. This would allow them to communicate with him in times of need. They also assist in the destruction of the evil cities of Sodom and Gomorra with an atomic device. Moses was very important to them because he is the leader of the people who are the direct descendants of the survivors of the original Earth base.

The four remaining space-travelers from Terra become involved in a project to civilize the world, the founding of the Athenian empire. (24) This project is interrupted after about 200 years when a foreign space craft arrives from Olmac, in the constellation Ophiuchus (the Snake Bearers). It lands in Peru, South America. The four remaining space-travelers go to meet the new extra-terrestrials who are somewhat humanoid. (25) Stranded here on Earth forever, they are forced to colonize. They have traveled here in a very primitive military type rocket from only a few light-years away. They are a very savage people. They, however, die off after only 60 to 70 years on Earth. Their descendants remain to found the Myan civilization.
At one period while living among the hordes of Eurasian, The Engineer teaches some nomads to capture and ride horses. They are the first Chap-Ben-Dar. (26) He teaches

them to play a game on horseback called Bush-Cas-he and they quickly learn to conquer and rule the hordes of Asians because of their great advantage over foot soldiers when mounted horseback.

The Professor helps the natives of England to understand astronomy and assist in building Stonehenge. It is used for telling the coming of the seasons, the eclipses of the sun and days of the year. Later, he becomes known as Merlin of King Arthur's court and helps establish the city of Camelot, which later becomes London.

The Commander becomes an assistant to Leonardo DiVinci and helps him understand concepts like the air screw and flight which are reflected in his writings. Athena is a friend and associate of Ludig von Beethoven and inspires him to compose many of his great symphonies.

In 1850 in European Prussia (on a peaceful rolling countryside) there is a company of foot soldiers spread out and moving forward as though attacking. As they come closer, they are charged by mounted Dargous who ride into the soldiers and a bloody battle ensues.
On a nearby hillside is an open carriage, in it are seated three men and a coach driver. The Professor suggests to The Engineer that if he had not been fooling around teaching those nomads how to ride horses so they could play that damn game Bush-Cas-he, then possibly this type of thing would not have come about. He replies that who is to say what we have taught them and what they would have learned for themselves.

In 1900 in Dayton, Ohio, The Engineer meets two mechanics who run a bicycle repair shop. They explain to him their interest in building a flying machine and he shows them some simple principles. (27) Using the two brothers, he has them walk through examples. He has one lean on a wall and see how difficult it is to move along the wall; then he has them both run a race starting from the same point, but with one taking a straight route and one running a curved route. See, he says, now you understand. They did not understand but they figure it out later. When the first un-powered flight leaves from a hillside in Ohio, our four space-travelers are standing nearby observing. At a university in the U.S., prior to WW II, The Commander is visiting with Dr. Einstein. Before leaving, he walks to the blackboard and changes some equations, reducing them to $E = mc2$.

As The Commander leaves the university building, he is met by The Professor who has been waiting for him. They agree that although the work which they will be starting at Pennumundy in Germany, will be in danger by the Americans developing the atomic bomb, that it must be done. They have lost faith in Hitler's ability to rebuild the Roman Empire. Besides, The Professor says, I believe we can continue our space research here in America once this war is ended.

It is now 1978 on Earth. A small missile is launched from Cape Kennedy. In the NASA launch control center we find the three space travelers. They work here now and it is quitting time. They leave sharing a ride in a large limousine. This is very similar to the beginning of our story, except that it is indeed Earth, 1978. The missile just launched was a routine communications satellite firing.

The three pull up to a large mansion in a isolated and very exclusive rural neighborhood. Also just pulling in the drive is Athena in a Jaguar roadster. She remarks that she had always preferred her 1939 model, but that it had finally worn-out. The four enter the house together. A servant meets them at the door, Charles and, and is greeted by name. The inside of the home is both posh antique and ultramodern combined.

Servants greet them saying dinner will be ready shortly. They have dinner served to them at a large dining table. After dinner, they have coffee in a impressive room which opens onto a terrace and garden area. In the garden are large hybrid B-Anana plants which Athena still raises as a hobby. Athena is talking with Charles about something that had occurred during World War I. However, Charles is no more than 40 years old. As Charles leaves the room, The Professor remarks that he was proud of Athena for her work with Charles. Charles had been cloned from a servant whom had been with them for over a hundred years. They were very fond of him and therefore hated to lose him. It is their first totally successful attempt at cloning. It was considered so because Charles had retained his full memory. He had been told only that a youth experiment had been conducted on him which had been successful.

The party of four now retire to another area of the house which is the center for much of their research. The Commander has been searching the stars for another Earth-like planet. He has found several suns that look rather promising. Among them he has also found two planets that are suitable except for their absence of blue-green algae which is a necessary basic building block to life forms.

The third planet, located in Andromeda seems to meet the requirements for supporting humanoid life.
It is decided the Andromeda E-5 will be the next planet which they journey to. They have been looking for a new planet which they can journey to because it has been discovered a few weeks ago that some possible aging is now occurring. Until now they have not aged; they theorize that because the normal aging process has began again, that the real-time since they had entered hyper-light has now elapsed. In other words, the journey that took a week at hyper-light speed would have taken them thousands of years to date to complete at the speed-of-light and even longer at sub-light speeds.

The two planets which have no algae, it is decided, will have missiles containing DNA fired toward them aboard a hyper-light nose cone which will be mounted aboard one of the routine communications satellites launching soon. This will prepare these planets for colonization in the event there needed at a later time.

The Professor reveals that NASA now has the technological capability to build a hyper-light craft and that he will start to work immediately on project STARCHILD II (two). The Engineer suggests that it is now time to take their private Lear Jet to Egypt, to the oldest pyramid, and to recover their two companions who had been stored there. They agree and depart that night. They arrive at a small desert airstrip near the ancient pyramids along the Nile. They load the portable cloning equipment onto a truck and proceed to the original pyramid. Knowing the secret to its entry, they enter the pyramids hidden passageway. The equipment is set up and their two companions are cloned in an 18 hour process.

The two are as they were before, there last memory is of the day each was injured originally. They greet their friends and are filled in on what all has happened since each of their accidents. The six now return to the waiting jet and depart. The Commander and one of the revived Technicians pilot the jet. The Technician is amused at the primitive craft as he is checked out on how to fly it. The topic of discussion during the trip home is about how the people of the Earth can be made to understand that they must not destroy their environment.

A plan is devised, based on the fact that music is a universal language, (28) to form a Rock Music Group. After all, had they not taught David to play the harp and helped Beethoven write some of his better symphonies On stage at rock concerts, the group performs in costumes and makeup that hides their true identities. They become the number one music group in the world.

A five month concert tour is ended in London at an outdoor concert where 200,000 people attend. The concert is being televised and broadcast by satellite throughout the world. The performance is stopped. The leader of the group steps to the microphone. He makes an urgent appeal for the people of Earth to save their planet's environment while they still can. Silence falls over the crowd. The group of six walk through the crowd protected by police. On the back of a semi-trailer truck is the spacecraft STARCHILD II, (29) draped in canvas. The cover is removed and the six board the craft. Radio and TV commentators are explaining what is happening. The craft lifts off, hovers for a moment, then speeds out of sight. (30)

Aboard the craft, the six original space-travelers insert the STARCHILD II into hyper-light. They wonder if the children of Earth, their children, will heed their warning and save the planet Earth while there is still time. What new worlds lay ahead? Will they be able to do better or worse on this new planet? But even more shocking to them is the sudden realization that they may be the seed from which all life throughout the universe will spring. Traveling from planet to planet, aging only a few months through thousands of years, they will populate the universe.   *STARCHILD, copyright 1978*

FOOTNOTES:
(1) This is basically the description of the Apollo 17 launch.
(2) Einstein's law of relativity states that the speed-of-light is the ultimate speed and his special law states that the speed-of-light can be exceeded due to time warping. Hyper-light speeds are conceivable, but the explanations are too lengthy to discuss in this writing.
(3) The fact that Terra is not Earth in the 1990's, but another planet entirely, will not become known until later in the story.
(4) Cloning - the biological hypothesis in which one cell of a living body can be used to grow an identical while body.
(5) Decaying orbits of warhead satellites is a real problem. As recent as January 1978, a Russian atomic satellite disintegrated over Canada.
(6) The 'A" strain plant has been dropped for a hardier 'B" strain which will be called the B-anana. Some writers theorize that the Banana tree is not native to this planet.
(7) Using a Marine Corps Harrier jump-jet VTOL aircraft which is modified to simulate the spacecraft.
(8) Using the actual film of the earth as viewed from a moon voyage, adding special effects.
(9) A theory in geology, that this area known as the Mediterranean Sea was once a fertile river valley, a garden of Eden and the cradle of civilization. Later, the oceans poured through the Straits of Gibraltar, covering the valley.
(10) They have not gone backwards or forwards in time. Real time in the universe cannot be changed, only our position in distance relative to the universe. The earth is exactly in the era it is when they land. Terra was indeed destroyed several weeks ago. Therefore, Terra was thousands of years advanced over the earth in the development of civilization and technology.
(11) A Ryan Aircraft Rocket Back-Pack currently operational today, is used for this. Except that the jet blast sound is omitted and it is flown in a dust free area to give the effect it is other than jet powered.
(12) The humanoids, which are found on earth at this time, are of two types. The homoneanderthalensis was more primitive and was believed to be a long time

native of earth. The other called Cro-Magnon was a tall large brained man and did not appear on earth until aproximately 25,000 to 10,000 years B.C. Neolithic man appeared about 10,000 to 5,000 years B.C.

(13) Chapter 6:4 Genesis of the Bible.

(14) This may account for the legendary gods of mythology and their strange powers. These gods of old were recorded in every culture throughout history.

(15) Chapter 6:1 and 2 Genesis.

(16) Chapter 5:1 thru 8 Genesis.

(17) A procedure is used often in animal breeding and creating new breeds.

(18) Cross-breeding refers to mating with the native humanoids. In-breeding refers to mating with distant relatives.

(19) Chapter 6:3 Genesis.

(20) BoDa looks very much like today's statues of Buddha.

(21) In Africa today, there is a cult which has known of the twin Star Sirius (in the constellation Canis) for many generations prior to modern astronomy being able to detect it. Canis means dog. It is interesting that the Egyptians often painted men with dog's faces.

(22) Examples of current flow in the Atlantic Ocean and how easy it was to cross the oceans. Without sails in 1969, Tom McClean, in a twenty foot boat, crossed from Newfoundland to Ireland in seventy days. In 1970, Sydney Genders averaged thirty-seven miles a day crossing from England to Florida in a nineteen foot boat.

(23) Some people theorize today that there is something deep in ocean floor near Bermuda Triangle which throws navigational instruments off and disorients travelers in this area.

(24) The islands of Crete and Peloponnesus were the foothills to the Mediterranean Valley before the great flood. The inhabitants of the valley migrated to this area. The rest went south into Mesopotamia.

(25) The Olmac look is like the carvings on ancient Maya stones, having large broad facial features.

(26) Chapbender; Houseman. The game polo probably evolved from Buschashe.

(27) These are two ways of explaining Benallie's principle - 'As velocity increases, pressure decreases.

(28) Music is mathematical and has been suggested as a means of communication in other popular science fiction stories.

(29) Here again, we use the modified USMC/VTOL Harrier jump jet. The jet blast sound is omitted to give the effect of silence and a clean paved area is used for takeoff to minimize the dust, etc. stirred up by the jet blast.

(30) Like a UFO, it glows as its departing speed increases.

***

Chapter 22   STARCHILD II - Screenplay Treatment

Based on a 1978 screenplay concept,
ihis is a rewrite of the original storyline,
developing a simpler and updated plot.
WGA 601262 08/07/95 and 07/19/00

In the darkness, the faint outline of a large missile on its launch pad is faintly visible. The sounds of the night are a cricket chirping and a faint slapping of the water against the shoreline (Title and major credits.) As the rocket gantry begins to glow with the launch, music is combined with the chest pounding sound of the blast off. The giant rocket lifts ever so slowly from the launch pad and disappears into the night

In the bright morning sunlight, a patrol helicopter follows a lone automobile speeding along a white sandy beach. The car pulls into the missile launch control center and the driver, the Professor (a rocket scientist) leaves the car and enters the building. The car is of a futuristic design.

Inside the mission control center, all are discussing the early morning launch. As the Professor enters the control room, he is greeted by the director of the space center. Brief congratulations are exchanged and the two men walk towards a private conference room.

Entering the conference room, there are two men and one woman seated at the conference table. Others are present in the room. Introductions are made. The first man is an experienced astronaut, the second an astrophysicist and a longtime friend of the Professor. The woman is a biologist who is known for her research on the effects of space travel on plants and animals. The woman is also a personal friend of the Professor.

Several in the room offer congratulations to the Professor. The Director opens a discussion on the significance of the recent test. On top of the missile just launched was a nose cone which housed the first test of a hyper-light insertion device. The Professor begins by briefly reviews the theory of relativity for those in the room. Space travel (velocity) is limited by the Mass factor in the E=MC2 theory.

It has been confirmed by recent space flights approaching the Speed-of light, that aging slows in relation to those left behind. For example, a twenty-five year old man traveling at half the speed-of-light for thirty years would return from his trip only twenty-eight years old. While his wife, children and friends, he left behind, would be thirty years older.

It will never be possible to go back in time. Backward time travel is pure fiction. Who or what ever designed this universe saw to it that history cannot be changed. As the poet put it, "You can't go home again". Amazingly, however, one can go into the future.

The test just conducted confirms that the M-factor (mass) can be overcome and an object can be accelerated beyond the speed-of-light.
This is referred to as hyper-light insertion. Science fiction writers have for a long time predicted that things like "star gates" and "warp drives" could exist, but until now it was only a fantasy.

As the meeting continues, the people in the room are being viewed on a monitor screen from an unknown office some distance away. The people watching the monitor from this unknown office are themselves being watched through a window in the office building (a space needle). Another monitor screen, viewing those in the office building is onboard a space station. The people watching the monitor on the space station are viewed through the window of the space station from a point in space. Others are watching. (triple pull back).

As the meeting proceeds, the Professor explains how hyper-light insertion works. Actually, the answer was very simple. It was only a matter of applying technology already available to the problem. Like the first caveman that figured out how to use a wheel, the answer was right there in front of us all the time.

An object is taken into polar orbit. As it passes either pole, negative or positive, a magnetic oscillator is used to set the objects polarity the same as the pole being crossed. Opposites attract, like objects repel. For just an instant the smaller object, a spacecraft for example, becomes weightless. More specifically, the object is without mass. Any power applied to the object at this instant, even its own forward motion, will send the object careening of into space in excess of the speed-of-light.

As a result of this morning's test, it is now known that a few minutes at hyper-light speeds will produce a time differential of thousands of years. This was born out by the clocks onboard the craft launched this morning. The craft was inserted into hyper-light for only one second, and it took several hours for it to return. In fact, it appears that the acceleration is exponential. The longer it stays in hyper-light, the faster it goes.

"How do you stop the damn thing?" asks the Astronaut. "Simple," replies the Professor, "shut down the magnetic field by turning off the oscillator." The Astronaut asks, "How do you guide the craft?" "Well," replies the Professor, "we haven't quite figured that one out yet. It kind of goes in the direction it's pointed. Seriously though, it seems to move in the direction of the magnetic flow being crossed.

The Astronaut says "Tell me something, in all of the exploring we have done to date, have we found any sign of other intelligent life?" The Physicist answers, "None that I know of, but then it's more of a timing problem. Relative to the age of the universe, any given civilization only lasts for a very short period of time. You see, when they exist, we do not and vice versa."

"What can one expect to experience when traveling at hyper-light speeds?" asks the Scientist. The Biologist responds, "Unlike approaching the speed-of-light where your body weight would exceed the mass of this planet, weight is not a factor." She continues, "At hyper-light speeds you experience a red-blue color spectrum shift inside the cabin. This may cause disorientation until you learn to adjust to it. Outside, you will only see a field of black in the direction you are moving, but you should be able to see those things behind you. Objects on either side will appear curved or distorted." The Astronaut laughingly quips, "Like flying blind, right?"

It is becoming apparent from little clues, like clothing styles, signs on the walls, uniforms, and the general design of objects that the location is not in the United States and is not under the control of something like NASA. It is further apparent that the time period is not the present and possibly it is not even the planet earth, although the similarities are great. In fact, it is the planet Terra, a planet which has evolved similar to Earth, both in physical and scientific development. Terra is a planet only slightly more technologically advanced than present day Earth.

As the parties to the meeting leave the launch control center, the
Professor invites them to his house for drinks that evening to celebrate the recent rocket test. Seven of the persons at the meeting get into waiting vehicles which drive off towards a large aircraft hangar.

The Director, the Professor and five others enter the heavily guarded hangar. In the center of the large hangar floor is a single fighter aircraft with an oversized pressurized cockpit. As the group of seven walk around the nose of the aircraft, the name on the side reads STARCHILD. They are told that this aircraft is capable of inserting itself into hyper-light due to a massive magnetron built into its fuselage.

During hyper-light entry, the configuration of the craft is not important, a square box could be inserted into hyper-light. This particular aircraft, an atmospheric type airplane, was selected because it can enter the high altitude regions around the magnetic poles. It is also a VTOL jump jet, which will facilitate takeoffs and landings. The hull of the craft is made of a composite material that will dissipate the thousands of degrees of heat which will be encountered during re-entry into the atmosphere. The cockpit has been modified to carry six persons.

At the Professor's home that evening, a small group of scientists, politicians and military personnel have gathered (the military uniforms are Russian style). In the course of the evening, the discussion turns to the current political turmoil and the impending problems related to doomsday devices which were placed in orbit some years ago as a deterrent to all-out nuclear war between major nations.

A small group of nine remains after the party is over. The Director opens a conversation regarding the rumor that one of the doomsday device's orbit was beginning to decay.

The Physicist confirms that it is not just a rumor that he has been watching from the university's observatory and that it will re-enter Terra's atmosphere within the next forty-eight hours. The result will most likely be a high altitude atomic blast which will cause a long nuclear winter. During this period, most life on Terra as it is now known will cease to exist. It could take a million years before the atmosphere clears and life evolves back to its normal state. It is possible that life might continue on Terra, but only in a very primitive form.

The Professor brings up the fact that the yet untested Starchild hyper-light craft, with a life support system for up to six persons, has been developed and is presently in a guarded hangar at the air base nearby. The group in the room, decide that three men and three women should board the Starchild and insert themselves into hyper-light so as to return to Terra at a later point in time. It would be the only guarantee they have of preserving the present level of scientific knowledge if the catastrophe occurred. It might also be the only chance for their species survival.

In the early morning hours of the following day the Professor, the Astronaut, the Biologist and the Physicist meet at the hangar where the Starchild stands ready. Two support personnel, the Scientist and the Technician, are also present. Over coffee, they watch the morning news on television. Just announced is that the doomsday satellite's orbit is now rapidly decaying and will enter the atmosphere.

A newswoman is explaining that people are advised to remain in their homes in the event of nuclear flash. However, continues the news broadcast, there is no apparent danger to life or property at this time. "Bullshit," says the Physicist "when that baby hits the atmosphere, it will set off a nuclear burn which will react with the upper atmospheric ion particles."

"Well are we going or not?" asks the Astronaut. The Professor replies "Yes, but you all understand that if this is a false alarm, all of our careers are ruined. In fact, we will most likely go to prison if we fail. Hell, we might all be killed in that untested contraption setting out there (all in the ready room sit quietly). Okay, get the two women on the phone and get them down here, we lift off in one hour." The Astronaut's girlfriend is involved in a car crash on the way to the air base. The Physicist's wife refuses, at the last minute, to come as she will not leave her two small children behind.

Time is running out for a launch prior to the collision of the satellite with Terra's atmosphere. The Scientist and the Technician, who were there only to aid in pirating the Starchild, volunteer to go and take the two vacant seats. Six souls, five men and one woman, board the Starchild.

The hangar doors fly open. The guards, unable to stop the craft, run for cover. The Starchild taxis out of the hangar, blowing dust and debris with its jet blast (A Harrier jump jet with a modified cockpit.). Lifting off vertically, the craft noses forward and climbs high into the atmosphere headed north.

As they pass through 120,000 feet, the Astronaut, at the controls, advises that they are approaching the north polar region of Terra. The Physicist thinks that he has devised a method of celestial navigation that can set them on a reasonably correct course in space. "Here goes nothing," says the Professor as he engages Starchild's magnetic oscillator. The Starchild craft disappears into a black star field.

On board the craft, the crew members experience the red-blue light shifts which distorts their vision as they look around the cabin. They make a great effort to overcome the disorientation. They are uncertain as to where they are headed, but are amazed that they are even alive and apparently traveling faster than the speed-of-light. Entire solar systems pass in the distance behind them.

The Physicist is attempting to plot some type of an inter-staler course, and says that his best guess is to drop out of hyper-light after about three hours have passed. He feels that by that time, they will be in a region of the Galaxy rich in stars about the size of Terra's sun. This should give them the best chance at finding a life supporting planet.

The magnetic oscillator is disengaged and the Starchild pass near the small blue planet Earth. Weather it is luck, fate or a reasonably good scientific guess. It appears that the planet just ahead might be able to support life similar to that on Terra. The gravitational pull of the planet allows them to descend into the upper atmosphere. Skipping like a hot rock over a pond, the Starchild descends into the heaver air and the standard flight controls can now steer the craft.

The Physicist quickly takes readings from the instruments on the oscillator's control panel in order to obtain a fix of their position in space. They have traveled much further in space and time than they had intended.

Flying over the planet Earth, the group is astonished to find that Earth is presently in the late Jurassic period. Passing low over the planet's terrain, they view giant animals and prehistoric forests. It is a hostile and foreboding planet. The evolutionary development of this planet is millions of years behind that of Terra.

After some discussion, the decision is made to return to Terra. Several millennia have now passed and it is possible that Terra's atmosphere has rejuvenated itself. It is even possible that the catastrophe they expected did not occur when they departed the planet. If so, the civilization on Terra would now be advanced beyond anything they might imagine, and they would only be part of its forgotten past.

The Starchild enters Earth's polar region and is inserted into hyper-light. The Physicist estimates that based on his calculations, they should be able to return to Terra. Three hours later, returning to their point of departure in space, the Starchild drops out of hyper-light. Terra is seen as a dull gray, dark and foreboding planet with little hope of life existing on its surface. Their worst fears have been realized.

The hyper-light disorientation is taking its toll on the six crewmembers and they are depressed over what they have just seen. The Physicist is sure that he can return to the point in space where Earth was located. Without further discussion, the Starchild is placed on a heading for a return to Earth. The three hour journey to Earth will transverse several million Earth years; arriving on Earth at an unknown point in time (about 2,500 BC).

A second approach to Earth is made. The Starchild descends over a large desert area south of Mesopotamia. The craft is landed and parked near a palm grove. The crew members exit the craft with the intention of remaining at this location, at least for a while. They move toward a tent encampment of nomads. The people they have just encountered are Jordanians, early ancestors of the Israelites. They are greeted suspiciously by the elders of the tribe, but are eventually accepted by the group.

This tribe of several thousand Jordanians had been fighting for their survival against several local Semite tribes. Another battle with one of the neighboring tribes is imminent. Two feuding factions within the tribe must now unite behind one leader in order to defeat the Semites. The symbol carried on the pole by each warrior leader is a triangle. The Professor persuades them to join together. He takes each of the two triangles from their poles and throws them together on the ground. They cross to form a six pointed star. "This," says the Professor, "is the new symbol all of your legions will fight under".

The Terrains find themselves fighting alongside the Jordanian warriors when they are surprised and attacked by the Semites. The Scientist, one of the Terrains, is killed in the ensuing battle. He dies in the arms of the Professor who promises him that somehow he will take him home to Terra.

Later around an evening campfire the Jordanians sing and dance (music: ES) in celebration of the days victory over the Semites. They tell the Terrains about their belief in one God. A child is born the next morning to this tribe who is named Abraham.

The Terrains now understand that everyone and everything they ever knew no longer exist. They vow to return home to Terra someday.

During their stay with the Jordanians, the Astronaut meets and falls in love with a young Jordanian girl. When the Terrains prepare to leave, she wants on go with him. It is explained that if she leaves she will never see her people again. She insists on going anyway and leaves with the group in the Starchild.

The Terrains fly the Starchild (regular jet flight) to ancient Egypt where their deceased companion is preserved in a cocoon (mistaken for a mummy by the locals). Cocooning is an age old method of preserving a body on Terra. They steal the king's mummy, from the Pyramid now under construction, and bury his mummy it in the sand (comedy relief). The Astronaut marks the cocoon with a six pointed star in order to be able to identify it later. The cocoon of the Terrain is put in the king's sarcophagus and closed.

The pyramid is due to be sealed the next day. As they are leaving they discover a stash of gold medallions and jewelry stolen by the worker and hidden to be retrieved later. Presently of no value to the Terrains, the Technician thinks the gold might be good metal for making replacement electrical contacts for the Starchild's magnetic oscillator system. They take what they can carry with them.

The Starchild is very low on fuel and some of the electronic circuitry is beginning to fail. They estimate that they need to be about 4,000 to 5,000 years further into the future of this planet's technological development. The technology needed to repair the Starchild should be available by that time.

Six board the Starchild, four men and two women. Having made several hyper-light jumps, they now feel that they can more closely control the time lapse. A short hyper-light flight, remaining in Earth orbit, is made into the future. Descending on New England, the Terrains land the Starchild on a small grass airstrip (music: Jazz).

They arrive in opulent upstate New York in the latter part of the roaring 20's. The Terrains are without any currency with which to purchase everyday necessities. The Technician takes the gold medallions and jewelry he acquired in Egypt and sells them to a dealer for enough money to assimilate the group into the local society. A wooden hangar is rented on the small grass air field to store the Starchild. A down payment is made on a country manor where the Professor and the Biologist take up residence. The others remain as house guests on the estate. They are accepted as Europeans because of their thick accents and broken English, but quickly learn speak American English.

After moving into the manor house, neighbors arrive and they welcome them on horseback, dressed in fox hunting attire. They dismount and introduce themselves. The Biologist introduces herself as an exiled Countess from a European royal family and the Professor as her husband. When the guests depart, the Professor quips, "What does that make me, some kind of a Duke?"

The Professor takes a position lecturing at a nearby university. While teaching a physics class on electrodynamic bodies in motion, one of his student asks if the speed-of-light in truly the ultimate speed in the universe. The Professor replies that it was an interesting question and that he understands that the German born Albert Einstein, who developed the Principle of Relativity, had also been working on what Einstein called the Special Law of Relativity. Someday in the future, the answer may be known for sure.

One night the Professor and the Biologist are lying in bed in the manor house's stately master bedroom. The Professor asks the Biologist, "Do you love me?" She answers, "What do you mean, do I love you?" He asks again, "Do you?" She replies, "I have worked beside you for twenty years, I have been your mistress for almost that long, I follow you half way across a universe, and you ask me if I love you?" He asks again, "Well, do you?" She answers, "I'll think about it, go to sleep."

 The Biologist really gets into the spirit of the times. She volunteers at a local hospital, helping them set up a new research center that is named after her. She purchases a Duesenberg roadster and later admits that it was the only thing she hated to leave behind. "I loved that car!" she said (comedy relief).

 Large garden parties (Great Gatsby style) are given at the country manor hosted by the Jordanian girl (who is now married to the Astronaut). She likes to dress up in costumes which are variations on her own tribal dress. Her attire is a cross between flapper and a Middle Eastern dancing girl. Her dress styles are copied by other ladies in the area, trying to keep up with the latest fads

 The Astronaut manages the air field (grass strip) where they had landed. This allows him to keep watch on the Starchild which is parked in the old wooden hangar. He gives flying lessons in a WWI biplane. One day while teaching a young student pilot, they run off the end of the runway and crash nose down. Another of the Starchild crew members may have just been killed! Not so, as a small crowd runs towards the crash, the student and the Astronaut emerge unscathed. "Laughing'" the Astronaut says, "Don't worry about it kid, I always say any landing you can walk away from is a good one. Besides, I've been wanting a new plane anyway". The next day his new Waco biplane is delivered.

The Physicist and the Technician start an electrical engineering company which produces technological advanced components for radios. The company begins to show a profit. The corporation is named SCA for Starchild Corporation of America.

Over the next year, the electrical system on the Starchild is repaired patchwork and it might now be used for a short hyper-light flight. However, it is not likely that in its present condition it could be used for an extended period. The Physicist makes jet fuel from kerosene which is readily available.

The Professor, knowing that one additional short jump into the future is going to be required, meets with a stockbroker to arrange to invest in some securities which he thinks might be promising. His hope is that upon returning in sixty or seventy years, the investments will be worth a considerable amount of money. Thus, giving them the financial resources they will need to build a second Starchild craft.

Several in the group become very involved in a local Christian movement. The Technician and the Biologist are instrumental in sponsoring an old time Christian gospel revivals which takes place on the estate in a large tent (music: gospel). The Technician meets a young Christian girl and decides to marry her. Influenced by her strong beliefs, he becomes a Christian.

Almost a year has passed and the time has come for the Starchild to make its short jump into the near future. The Technician remains behind with his wife. This is as far as he intends to go, although he will always long for his home on Terra.

Five board the Starchild, three men and two women. The Starchild is inserted into hyper-light for only a minute or two (music: folk). Upon descending into the modern day San Francisco Bay area, the Astronaut sets the aircraft down at a busy international airport. They are met by an FAA representative who is bawling them out for landing an experimental aircraft at a busy airport and failing to obtain proper radio clearance for landing (comedy relief). The group talks their way out of the problem and arrange to park the Starchild at a nearby electronic facility. The large sign above the hangar reads SCA.

The Starchild's onboard systems have now been damaged beyond repair. The temporary repairs made prior to the last flight have all failed. The electronic facility where they parked the Starchild turns out to be part of the electronic corporation founded in 1928 by the Physicist and Technician. They find out that the Technician is alive and lives in San Francisco. They contact him. He and his wife come to the facility immediately to greet them. They arrive by chauffeur driven limousine. He is now an old man in failing health, but very glad to see them. He explains that the company has made millions in profit, but there is still not enough funds to finish developing another Starchild.

The Professor goes to the phone to find how well his stock investments have done. He finds that during the crash of 1929, every stock that he purchased had failed and many he had decided against would have made millions. He fumbles in his pocket and pulls out a shiny new Indian head nickel, goes to a nearby coke machine which reads, "Deposit sixty cents" (comedy relief).

A twofold plan is devised. First, the electronic company will market a new type of integrated computer chip based on those used in the Starchild's systems. Now that the Starchild is here, a sample chip will be removed and sent to the factory for duplication. This new chip will blow the competition away. The ad campaign in all the computer magazines reads, "Don't be a Pentium Puppy, join the Starchild generation."

Secondly, one of the holdings of the electronic company is a major recording company (kind of like Motown). Stock had been issued to SCA for equipment the company installed and the recording studio couldn't pay for. Four of the Terrains form a rock group. They recreate a sound based on a synthesized instrument that had been a big hit on Terra. Their first two albums go platinum on release and go to number one on the charts (music: heavy metal). In order to hide their identity, they dress in rock costumes and use full face makeup for all live performances which are now being demanded by the fans.

They use their private helicopter, an Astar, to get to their concert performances without having to move through the crowds. They need faster private transportation for long distance trips, so the Astronaut and his wife go to a used aircraft dealership and purchase a Lear Jet. They remark that it's not their old Waco, but guess it will have to do. The Astronaut loves flying the Lear and is trying to teach his lady to fly it (comedy relief).

After several successful live concerts, the Starchild rock group has managed to amass enough money to pay for the final development of the new hyper-light spacecraft, the Starchild II.

The original Starchild lays in pieces on the hangar floor beside the new Starchild being built. Music on a tiny sounding radio station is playing in the hangar where the men are working (music: JT). The Starchild II is nearing completion and the time is drawing close for the return to Terra.

The group is called to the bedside of the Technician who is dieing of old age. His wife, who was only seventeen when they married, has always known his secret and informs the group that she wants to return to Terra with them. There is one empty seat and she will take it. She also wants her husband to be returned to Terra.

Several of the group board the Lear Jet and fly to Cairo, Egypt. The pyramid has been excavated by some archaeologists and the sarcophagus containing the Terrain cocoon has been placed in a museum. In the still of night, they break into the museum. A sign beside the cocoon reads, "This very unique example of an early mummified king bears an unexplained mark resembling a Star of David." The cocoon holding the Scientist is loaded aboard the Lear jet.

Upon returning to San Francisco, two cocoons (the Scientist and the Technician) are loaded into the baggage compartment of the completed and waiting Starchild II.

As the final concert ends, the Starchild rock group boards
the helicopter and departs, amid search lights and
fireworks, over the throngs of rock fans. During the flight
the Professor explains that he sold the Lear Jet and given
the money to the hospital center that was named for the
Biologist. The Technician had already signed over the
electronic corporation to a trust fund prior to his death.
"When they find out what those new computer chips were
really designed to do, I don't know what they will do with
all the profits," remarks the Technician's widow.

The helicopter approaches the airport where the Starchild
II is hangared, and is given clearance to land. Only a gas
boy is on duty. "Aren't you the kid I saw taking flying
lessons?" asks the Astronaut as he exits the parked Astar
(rotor still spinning down). The kid nodes his head yes.
The Astronaut throws him the keys to the Astar and says,
"What's your name?" The boy replies, "Billy." The
Astronaut says, "No, I mean your full name." "William
Johnson, sir," replies the boy. Writing his name on the title
of the helicopter, the Astronaut hands it to him saying,
"When you finish learning to fly this one, sell it and go to
college."

Six persons enter the hangar and board the Starchild II,
three men and three women. In the darkness, the Starchild
II rolls from the hangar, noses forward and lifts off on its
journey, the return to Terra. The Starchild II quickly
accelerates to Mach-two and heads due north for the pole.
An air traffic controller from the tower says, "What the
hell was that!" A radar operator replies, "Beats me, it's off
my scope already."

The Starchild II drops out of hyper-light and descends into the beautiful blue atmosphere of Terra. The Starchild II comes in low over a pastoral valley near a small village. A lone shepherd, dressed in a kilt and sheepskin is tending his flock. He looks up and watches the Starchild II passes overhead. The craft circles and lands in an open field (music: BTMV). The scene looks as though it had been taken right out of eighteenth century Ireland. The six occupants exit the cockpit looking around in amazement at the beautiful valley where they have just landed. They are near a dirt road that leads to the small village in the distance.

The shepherd, an old man with a white beard, greets four of the crew members walking towards him. They recognize an ancient Terrain dialect when he speaks. In the background the workers from the field approach the Starchild II. One of the workers reaches out to touch the side of the craft as if to question what it was, but no questions are asked. "It is a ship that sails on the sky like a ship that sails on water," the Astronaut tells them. "Oh," replies the worker, "I think I understand." Two of the crew members begin to unload the two cocoons stored in the Starchild II baggage compartment. The workers from the field help them.

Two graves are dug on a nearby hillside and closed. On one of the two
graves is placed a Star of David and on the other grave is placed the
Cross of Christ both made of wooden sticks. Returning the two Terrains was a promise kept.

As the group walks down the dirt road towards the village more
Villagers come to meet them. There are children in this group. The Astronaut has stayed behind. No one needs to tell him what must be done. In the distance, the Starchild II is set aflame and is quickly engulfed. None of the crew members look back at the burning craft.

The shepherd asks, "What were the symbols which you placed on the two graves?" The Professor replies, "They represent people we met on our journey. I will tell your people about them someday."

As the small group walks toward the village, the rays of the setting sun shoot into the evening sky. The Physicist puts his arm around the Professor as they walk and says, "Well old friend, who says you can't go home again?"

(fade to black)

(music: variation on an old Gallic melody)

(written) "There were giants in those days, when the sons of God came unto the daughters of men, and they bore them children, these were the mighty men of old, the men of renown and legend. Genesis 6:4"

(roll minor credits)

Author's Note: Most space traveler stories jump around the universe hundreds of years in the future, never bothering to explain how this is accomplished. The fact is that based on what we now know about astrophysics, it would take a life time just to travel to the nearest star. This story is based on present scientific knowledge. It explains in detail how it might be possible to travel faster than the speed-of-light and the effects of doing so. It uses the Principle of Relativity, as stated by Albert Einstein, for its bases. Only the hypotheses of a magnetic hyper-light device and the possibility of parallel human life on another planet is fiction, at least at this writing. Music expressing the modes of the period is important to the story. The story is rich in action, comedy and adventure, but is also a serious and emotional story. A story of space and time travel based Einstein's theory of relativity and Thomas Wolfe's "you can't go home again.

Miscellaneous Notes: This is the story of an aircraft named the Starchild. Actually, the Starchild was little more than an airplane which was pretty much a standard fighter reconnaissance aircraft of its era. It had, however, been modified to carry a scientific experiment used in aerospace research. The aircraft was manned by a minimum crew of six, the pilot, co-pilot, navigator, armaments officer, radar operator and electronics countermeasure operator. This is the story of the Starchild and the travelers who would venture forth in the unique one of a kind aircraft. The time is not the future and the time is not the past. The time is now. The place is the planet Terra.

CHARACTER DESCRIPTIONS MAJOR ROLLS:

Professor - Terrain male, age fifties, the unofficial leader of the
 group, intelligent, very responsible and kind towards others.
Biologist - Terrain female, age late forties, intelligent and vibrant,
 companion to the Professor. Very much her own person.
Physicist - Terrain male, an expert in astrophysics, dignified, long
 time associate of the Professor. Comes up with workable solutions.
Astronaut - Terrain male, a young hot rock jet pilot type, can fly
 anything and will try anything at least once. Good sense of humor.
Technician - Terrain male, age late twenties, electronic wiz,
computer
 nerd, eccentric, but likable, way out with his ideas.
Scientist - Terrain male, middle aged, involved in analyzing and
 researching theories, shy and withdrawn, dies early in story.
Jordanian - Earthling female from 2500 BC, young brunette,
attractive,
 sings and dances, always willing to try new things.
Christian - Earthling female from 1928, young blonde, highly
 sophisticated and attractive, ages over 70 years.

CHARACTER DESCRIPTIONS MINOR ROLLS:

Patrol Helicopter Pilot   Mission Control Personnel (10-15)
*Director of Space Center   Other in Conference Room (5-8)
Persons in Office Bldg. (2-3)   Persons in Space Station (3-4)
Drivers (2)   Guards (3-5)
*Military Officer   Cocktail Party Guests (10-15)
*Physicist's Wife   *Astronaut's Girlfriend
*Newswoman on TV   Jordanian Tribe Members (50-100)
*Jordanian Elder   *Jordanian Warrior Chiefs (2)
Semite Warriors (50-100)   *Jordanian Campfire Dancers (6)
Egyptian Pyramid Workers (12)   New England Neighbors (5)
*New England Neighbor   *Student at University
Students in Class & Campus (15)   Crowd at Revival (50-100)
*Evangelist   *Gospel Singers (12-30)
Patients & Staff at Hospital   Guests at Garden Party (40-60)
*Student Pilot   People at Airstrip (3-8)
Workers in Electronic Lab (6)   *Stockbroker
Ground Crew Int'l Airport (3)   *FAA Representative
*Electronic Corp Manager   Limousine Chauffeur
Technicians on Starchild II (6)   *Recording Studio Director

Staff at Recording Studies (4)   *Aircraft Salesman
Backup Musicians (5-8)   Rock Concert Fans (1,000 plus)
*Gas Boy at Airport   *Shepherd on Terra
*Worker on Terra   Workers in Field on Terra (5)
Villages on Terra (10-15)   (*) SPEAKING ROLLS

***

SPACE TIME JUMPS: Jump 1: A low level pass over the planet Earth which appears to be presently in the Jurassic period (6 persons on board, 5 men and 1woman). Decision to search further and reinsert into hyperspace.

Jump 2: Return to Earth after several weeks in hyperspace. Time period is about 40,000 BC. A landing in the Mediterranean Valley. Establishment of a settlement on the island of Atlantis. Two visits; one to China and one to South America. After several years, decision is made to return to Terra in the hope that environmental disaster has passed. One crewman elects to stay behind. (5 persons on board, 4 men and 1 woman).

Jump 3: Low pass near the planet Terra shows a disastrously destroyed planet. The ship is reinserted into hyperspace and returns to Earth during a period of the early pharaohs of Egypt. The Mediterranean Valley had disappeared due to a break in the Gibraltar Straits and the Island of Atlantis had sunk with no trace. The landing is made in the desert near Israelis tribesmen. Our travelers become involved in a battle and help the Israelis defeat the enemy. A celebration with music is held after the battle. One of the travelers is mortally wounded in the battle. His body is transported to very early Egypt and preserved there in a cocoon. (6 persons on board, 4 men and 2 women.)

Jump 4: It is decided based on the natural evolution of this planet that they need to be about 2500 years into the future. They can now control their jump times a little more accurately and decide to insert into hyperspace one more time. An Egyptian girl goes with them. Returning to Earth in 1926, the Starchild makes a final approach to a small New England airport and is struck by lightning during landing. Much of the electronics is seriously damaged. The craft will still fly, but will not insert into hyperspace. The travelers merge into the local society, buying a country estate and living quietly for several years. Investments are made in various companies, cars and electronics are experimented with. The desire to return to Terra is still their goal. The Starchild will fly sub-light and as a jump of only 70 years is needed. The travelers decide to do this sub-light.

Jump 5: Starchild returns to Earth in present day period. Their investments have not gone that well as they cannot see into the future. The technology they need is now available and they must devise a means by which to make enough money to obtain the necessary devices to rebuild the Starchild. They decide on the music business and establish themselves as rock stars. Finale is group leaving concert in helicopter to go to where Starchild II has been built and departing. The government is on to them and trying to catch them and shut them down in order to obtain their advanced technology.

Jump 6: Starchild returns to Terra and makes a low pass over a pastoral planet. Beneath them lie shepherds watching their flocks in peaceful valleys as the Starchild II descends overhead. The travelers exit the Starchild and the Starchild is destroyed. "Who says you can't go home."

***

Chapter 23   STARCHILD III - Screenplay Treatment

Subtitle: "The Long Way Home"
Screenplay treatment and outline
WGA #798712 ©1998

On a planet that orbits a distant star from Earth, there is a world similar to modern day Earth. It is the planet Terra. Things are similar to what Earth might be like in a few decades. Terra is only slightly advanced over Earth's present technology. The cars are modern, but not readily identifiable as to make or model.

Signs and directions are familiar, but read more like they are in a foreign language. All the people look very normal, but their dress is slightly modern. At the beginning of the story, it is not stated the this is Earth.

The scientific community is dealing with several problems at their space program center (their equivalent of Earth's NASA). A satellite, containing a nuclear power plant, has been sent to gather information about Terra's sun. Its orbit was not intended to return to Terra, but due to an error in telemetry, it is now headed back towards Terra.

The scientists working on this project now believe that the satellite will soon impact the upper atmosphere of Terra. Normally, this would not be a problem as satellites burn up on re-entry, but the nuclear reactor on board the satellite will reach critical mass as it collides at its angle and speed. When it hits, it will start a nuclear burn in Terra's upper atmospheric gasses. The end result of this impact will be to create a winter so long that most of life on Terra will not be able to survive.

The story begins as a test rocket (similar to a Titan) is launched into space. On board is a device to be tested once the rocket is in space. The test will prove the workability of a new magnetic propulsion device developed by the Professor, who works for the Terra space agency in the research and development center.

The device called the Fluxtron may be the answer to hyper-light speed travel. The opening scene is a slow motion close-up of the rocket being fired from the launch pad. The rocket climbs out of sight and quiet returns to the swamps around the launch pad. The sound of birds are heard and a caption on the screen reads "Spring Morning 2020".

The action then follows, via a view from a patrol helicopter of a car leaving the launch bunker and arriving at the space center headquarters. A press conference is being held at the space center to announce the first successful launching of a space craft exceeding the speed-of-light.

After the press conference, a closed door meeting is held where the sun orbital satellite and its consequences are discussed. The Professor takes this opportunity to present the recent findings on the rocket propulsion test on the Fluxtron and its implication for future deep space travel. In doing so, he explains the Theory of Relativity in simple understandable terms.

At this same time, a new vertical take-off air/space craft has been developed. This craft is capable of transition into an extremely high altitude flight and lower planetary orbit. The craft is called the Starchild and was manufactured by the Starchild Aircraft Company which has been building aircraft on Terra for the last seventy years.

Its founder, Clyde Starchild, died several years before the development of the new Starchild craft. It has been named in his honor and has been designated the S-1. The craft has been delivered to a hangar on the air base at the space center and is being readied for flight testing. The craft was not designed to be equipped with the new Fluxtron, but this will change.

One of the Professor's associates at the research center is a woman Scientist who is also a close friend. Other close friends of the Professors are an Astronaut and the chief Engineer at the space center. After today's successful rocket launch, a cocktail party is given at the lavish home of the space center's Director.

The Professor and his friends are gathered together in a corner of the room and are quietly discussing the inevitable disaster that will occur to the atmosphere caused by the nuclear chain reaction from the out of control satellite. The Wife of the Astronaut is with them, but when she sees the familiar face of a female Staff officer, leaves the group to join her. The Astronaut is unaware that the Staff officer is his wife's lesbian lover.

The Engineer's son enters the room and approaches his father. He has been drinking and embarrasses the Engineer by proclaiming that his father is to blame for his mother's early death. A friend tries to steady the son, but he stumbles backwards and crashes over a coffee table.

The party pauses. The son leaves and his father starts to follow, but is told by his friends to let his son go and he will cool off. Also in attendance are several high ranking military men. One such military Officer has had many run-ins with this group of close knit scientists and has questions their loyalty. He feels the group is keeping secrets from the military and is jealous of the influence that they have in the space agency.

Among the military officers he is conversing with, he remarks that this small group of space agency employees bear watching.

After many meetings over the next several days, the decision is made that the Professor, the Astronaut, the Astronaut's wife, the Scientist, the Engineer, the Engineer's son will attempt to leave Terra in the Starchild. The group now makes plans to equip the Starchild with the Fluxtron technology believing that is their only chance of escaping the pending doom of their planet.

The Engineer's Son has spent all night drinking and is killed in a spectacular car crash on the way to the air base. At the last minute, the Astronaut is called to the phone in the hangar. His wife tells him on the phone that she has been assured by her father, the Director, and her close friend the Staff officer, that there is no danger from the falling satellite. She is not going with them.

It is time to depart. The Scientist remarks that she hates to leave her red sports car behind, but other than that she has no regrets. A Technician, who has worked on the Starchild is just finishing up as the group is boarding the craft. He asks the Engineer if he can have one of the empty seats and it is agreed. A Mechanic, who has also worked on the Starchild is present and is asked if he would like the remaining seat. He declines as he is going home to be with his family. A last minute attempt is made by the Staff officer to send someone to stop them. The tower refuses to authorize takeoff, but the Starchild departs.

The group of five which we will now call the Travelers, take off in the Starchild and climb into lower planetary orbit. As the Starchild is inserted into hyper-light speed (much faster than the speed-of-light), the out of control satellite returns in the direction of Terra and strikes the atmosphere.

A slow and ever increasing burn (the planet does not explode) envelopes Terra. On board the Starchild, the celestial navigation autopilot is set to navigate to a star (Earth's Sun) that shows signs of wobbling, this wobbling effect has been proven by astronomers to generally indicates a planetary system around a sun. The Travelers conclude this is the most logical destination and the Fluxtron is engaged.

The acceleration of the craft is a constant one G-force, but the acceleration doubles ever fraction of a second. On board the Starchild, the Travelers experience the sensation of traveling through the light speed-of-light. Those sensations being the red-blue light spectrum shift the curvature of light and the distortion of time. The past, present and future of the moment are experienced simultaneously.

After a predetermined period of time, which has been set into the celestial navigation system's autopilot, the Fluxtron is disengaged. The craft is now coasting in space, but steadily decelerating. The effect of the gravitational fields of distant stars and the few widely space molecules in free space are geometrically slowing the craft. If needed, the Fluxtron can be engaged behind the craft's direction of flight or left and right of the direction of flight to steer the craft.

After the Starchild is dropped out of hyper-light speed and slows, it is positioned in a high orbit around Earth. Descending into the Earth's atmosphere, the jet engines are started, enabling the Starchild to fly like an aircraft. They descend to a few hundred feet above the terrain and fly over beautiful spreading prairies and tropical forests.

They discover that they have arrived on Earth during the Paleozoic Age (about 65 million BC, Earth time). Dinosaurs are grazing on the vast plains (computer graphics are used to simulate these) as the Starchild flies over the Earth at a low altitude surveying the terrain. The Travelers consider themselves fortunate that they have discovered a planet capable of sustaining plant and animal life and hopefully, human life.

The Starchild's database has recorded the flight since leaving Terra, but relative to having traveled millions of light years in just a few hours, all of the stars positions have now shifted. Also, millions of years have passed back on Terra. If by some miracle, any living thing, be it plant, animal or human, had survived the atmospheric collapse, everything that had been known to the Travelers would have been gone millenniums ago. Traveling at a hundred multiples of the speed-of-light, the Travelers have reached Earth millions of years into the future and arrived at a planet that is presently entering the Paleozoic Age.

By applying the Laws of Relativity, which allows that one can travel forward in time, but not backwards in time, the Travelers decide once again to insert the Starchild into hyper-light speed, but into a solar orbit (a flight path similar to that of a comet). This should have the effect of moving them forward in time in relation to the time on the surface of the planet, but not cause them to stray too far from what is now known to be an inhabitable planet (Earth). When the Starchild is once again dropped out of the hyper-light speed after only a few minutes, the Travelers find themselves in orbit above Earth in about 3000 BC.

The Engineer relates that there is only a limited amount of conventional fuel remaining on board the Starchild, just enough for one more flight. They know that if they engage the Fluxtron inside a planet's atmosphere, it would fry the craft and all on board. The decision is made to land the craft immediately. The Astronaut lands the craft on the flat surface of a desert which appears on the horizon. During the decent, the Travelers observe people working on a construction site of a huge stone structure.

After landing, the Travelers leave the craft and walk toward the construction site, mingling in with some of the workers. At first, language is a problem, but through hand gestures and learning some of the local phrases, they are soon able to communicate.

The Travelers find that they have landed in Giza in ancient Egypt and are witnessing early construction on the Sphinx. The Travelers are taken in by a small group of friendly workers and live among them. The Technician must make minor repairs to some of the burnt wiring on the Fluxtron.

This will take at least a week or more. On the tenth night of their stay, a young Egyptian girl decides to dance before the group after the evening meal. She has become fascinated with the Engineer and dances provocatively in front of him.

The Engineer is mesmerized with her beauty and dancing and finds her later and takes her to bed. A young warrior, who is betrothed to the dancer finds out about the incident and kills the Engineer in a fit of jealous rage. The young girl becomes pregnant with the Engineer's child.

The Travelers decide they must leave Egypt. The Technician must now take over the copilot's navigation duties. The Professor calculates that they have one more chance to move forward in time to a more modern technological era.

This next flight will require only a fraction of a second at hyper-light speed, but they will have expended all of their conventional fuel. The four prepare to leave. During the Travelers brief stay in ancient Egypt, the Technician has befriended a young orphaned Girl. The Girl was the daughter of a minor ruler in the area who lost a border war. He and his wife, the Girl's parents, were executed in front of her when she was six years old. One of the elders working on the Sphinx took her into his household. She is now age fourteen. She is treated little better than a servant girl among the elder's other children.

She understands that the travelers are not gods and equates them to other royalty that she knew as a child. She asks permission to go with them on their next journey. The Travelers and the elder agree. They say their good-byes to the small band of workers and disappear into the desert and board the hidden Starchild and depart.

The Starchild is once again drops out of the hyper-light speed and the Travelers find themselves in orbit above1950s Earth ready to enter the atmosphere; descending somewhere over the eastern United State of America. The craft glides easily, while the Astronaut searches for a remote area to land. He is flying the Starchild like a space shuttle, passing through the sound barrier creating a sonic boom occurs. The sonic boom is heard by many across the New England countryside.

At this particular time on Earth, many people were reporting sightings of flying saucers, so the boom and the sighting of a unique metal object were attributed to this phenomenon. The Astronaut is on a committed final approach when he sights a small grass strip outside a New England village. The Starchild is damaged on landing as it runs into trees at the end of the runway. The Travelers find themselves unharmed and pull the Starchild into an old empty hangar on the run down airport.

As the Travelers journey toward the village, from a distance they notice an old county estate and see a woman real estate Agent placing a For Sale sign on the property. The Travelers tell the Agent they are a group of foreigners who have arrived in this country to work in the scientific community.

The Agent tells them the property is owned by an old WW I Flyer who lives alone and is anxious to sell as he wants to move to the Florida Keys and deep sea fish every day. The estate includes an abandoned air strip with an old hangar on it (where they hid the Starchild). They relate to her they would like to purchase the property.

When the Scientist opens the doors of the old garage and finds an old, dust covered, Duesenberg Phaeton. Fondly remembering her sexy red sports car, she decides wants this classic automobile. She is told that the Duesenberg goes with the estate. The Scientist fully restores the old Duesenberg and drives it everywhere she goes (Dusty rides again).

The Travelers settle in the estate and each has their own room and are pursuing separate interests. Before the old Flyer retires, he stays for a while with the Travelers. He and the Astronaut become good friends and the Flyer teaches the Astronaut how to fly his old biplane. The Professor and the Scientist occupy the master bedroom. One morning, she asks him when he intends to make an honest woman out of her and he replies, maybe when we go home. This is the first that she realizes the Professor is seriously considering returning to Terra. Everyone and everything they had ever know on Terra has vanished millenniums ago and it is very likely that the environment has not fully recovered.

Realizing that in order to survive, they need the currency used during this time period. The Technician uses a laser device out of the Starchild to make a set of printing plates and proceeds to make counterfeit money. After a period of time, two government Investigators come to the small nearby town to talk to the Sheriff about the counterfeit bills that seem to be originating from the area. The problem, the investigators explain, is that the bill are not poor quality, but are better than those produced at the Treasury. When the Professor gets wind of this from the sheriff, he has the Technician stop counterfeiting the money and destroy the printing plates.

The Girl is fascinated with all the new things like the electric stove and television and takes care of the household. The Technician tinkers at the airport hangar with parts from the Starchild and is building an electronic music synthesizer in his spare time. The Scientist goes to work at a small medical clinic and does gene research in her spare time. The Professor takes a lecture position at a nearby university where he mentors an astronomy Student who is his teaching assistant. Next year, when the Student graduates, he will take a position at the Arecibo Radio Observatory.

There has been a continual investigation into UFO sightings in the area for the past two years. Persons an unnamed government agency (men in black types) starts to investigate the reports that were generated from the Starchild's decent.

The Astronaut encounters a young Lady attorney who works for the government agency. He is now operating the airport, selling gas, giving flight instructions and sight-seeing rides in an old Steersman biplane. He became briefly involved with the Lady agent and takes her flying in the biplane.

The next morning, after they have spent the night together, she leaves before he wakes, leaving him a good-bye note. Due to the fact that she works for a clandestine agency, he is unable to find her again. She reports back to her supervisors that the suspicions of UFO activities in the airport area are a hoax. She believes that the reports were a hoax, in spite of the fact that the Starchild was in the hangar only forty feet from where she had been standing the day before.

The decision is made to abandon the New England lifestyle and move the small band (five) of Travelers to Dallas, Texas where the cover of a big city and corporate security will be a safer haven for them. The Professor has received offers to become involved in guiding several leading edge technology research and development projects.

The Professor acquires major holdings in the Sytel Corporation in Fort Worth and Anaconda Electronic Research Company in Austin. An aircraft overhaul operation on Love Field also becomes one of their holdings. The Astronaut arranges to take delivery on one of the pre-production Learjet aircraft being developed in Wichita, Kansas. He intends to bring to their corporate hangar on Love Field. The plan is to fit the Learjet with the Fluxtron and equipment similar to that used on the original Starchild.

The Fluxtron is not dependent on any kind on an aircraft or spacecraft to operate. It could be installed on a dumpster and it would fly at hyper-light speeds. A high altitude aircraft is used for two reasons, first to get out of the dense atmosphere to prevent the craft's structure from overheating; secondly to provide an environment for those onboard.

The Lady attorney is working with two other government Agents that have now arrived in Dallas and are involved in a revived investigation of the Travelers. She once again becomes involved with the Astronaut when they meet at a well-known restaurant and bar. They end up together again for the night. The Lady agent is sophisticated and elegant acting until she gets around the Astronaut, at which times she seems to turn into a babbling schoolgirl. The next morning, the Astronaut is up first. She asks him why it is that every time they meet, they wind up in bed together. He rousts her out of bed saying they need to get going that they have a lot of ground to cover today. He drags her out the door still pulling on her clothes and trying to straighten her hair. At the Love Field hangar, they take a Cessna 310 and fly to Wichita.

At the Lear factory, a prearranged meeting is held in the CEO's plush office which overlooks the aircraft ramp. In the discussion, the Astronaut explains that he cannot wait for certification of the new jet as he needs to take possession now. He hands the CEO a certified check for three million dollars.

The CEO accepts the check and shakes hands, but tells the Astronaut that he still cannot release the aircraft as it has not been flight tested. The Astronaut, dragging the Lady behind, walks onto the tarmac where the Learjet is being readied for flight testing.

A Man in a white lab jacket, with a clipboard in his hand, is standing by the airstair. As the two approach, he asks them who they are. The Astronaut takes the clipboard from his hand, telling him that he is the newly hired flight test pilot. He scribbles a signature on the clipboard and hands it back to the Man. The Man is talking to someone on his two-way radio as the jet is firing up.

The answer over the radio, from the CEO, is to suggest that the Man return to the factory and go to lunch. The Man, now standing by the Cessna 310 they left behind, is still stammering over the radio as the jet rolls down the runway. The Man, a trusted employee for many years, goes to the CEO's office. The CEO tell him of a dream that he had when he was first working on designing the jet. The Man is told that he would probably never see that particular jet again. It is suggested that in a few months, the aircraft be written off as our static test model.

Enroute to Florida, the Astronaut sees how high he can get the jet. At 40,000 feet, it won't climb anymore. It has to do better than this, maybe some booster rockets under the wings the Astronaut remarks. The Lady, although tagging along, is still in the dark about what is taking place. She hasn't reported to her office in two days and is quite sure she is probably in trouble for it.

It is a nice day for flying the Astronaut reminds the Lady of the time they had gone flying in to old biplane back in New England. The jet lands at an airport in Key West where they are greeted by the old Flyer. He has a seaplane, an old PBY, waiting for them. The other four Travelers are there to meet them. All board the seaplane and taxi into the water. The old Flyer is piloting the plane. The Astronaut, seated in the copilot seat, reminds the Flyer to stay low over the water, under the continental air defense radar (ADAZ) as they are not filing a flight plan.

The sun is setting over the water to the west of the island as the seaplane materializes on the horizon and lands on the water near the beach. As the plane taxis on the beach, a bullet passes through the cockpit window, narrowly missing both pilots. The Astronaut and the Technician jump from the plane and run into the bushes while bullets are kicking up the sand at their feet.

They have no idea who is shooting at them. Except for the Astronomer, who will meet them in the morning at a prearranged place up the road, no one should know that they are here. The Lady attorney swears she has told no one. The Astronaut and the Technician circle around behind were the rifle fire is coming from. They jump two grungy looking men in dirty khakis. The men are rum Runners waiting on a boat. They smuggle duty free, boot leg rum in knock-off Bacardi bottles to customers in the States. It is a case of mistaken identity. The rum Runners thought that the Travelers were either the Feds or a competitor coming to raid them.

Things settle down and the Travelers join the two rum Runners at their campfire that evening for dinner and pineapple juice with rum. The two black men helpers entertain with some Reggae style music until the early morning hours when everyone passes out and falls asleep. The morning sunlight coming through the palm trees awakens them.

A van up the road is honking. It is the Astronomer who has come to pick them up. The old Flyer says he will stay with the seaplane that is parked on the beach. The six Travelers make their way through the tropical bushes and to a clearing beside the road where the Astronomer is waiting. Greeting exchanged and they get in the van.

They drive up the mountains to the Arecibo Radio Observatory where they park the van and enter the facility (an opportunity for aerial shot to music like Alpine Drive). At the Observatory, no one pays much attention to them as there are several groups of tourists visiting the site. The Professor and the Astronomer walk out to the center cone of the large array as only the weight of two people are allowed out there at a time. They are out there to realign the cone as the Earth is about to pass through the portion of the sky where Terra's solar system is located.

The other five Travelers go to a recording center under the antenna to take the required readings. These new and more accurate readings will be run through a computer to determine the precise future location of Terra's sun.

The Travelers return to Love Field, Dallas. The Lady attorney, who has been privy to all that has gone on, still has no more of a clue of who these people are and what this group is working on than she did when she started. She only knows that now she is sure that they are not of any danger to anyone or society in general. She also knows that she would probably trust the Astronaut with her life. The new Learjet will be reconfigured into the Starchild II. It is pushed into the corporate hangar where work will begin on the necessary modifications. The first requirement will be to install an environmental system that is independent of the jet engine as well as to strengthen some of the bulkheads. The next modification that will be required is the addition of a solid propellant rocket under each wing. Finally, the airframe field coil and the Fluxtron which is being built at the Anaconda research center's laboratory.

The Professor and Scientist go to the Anaconda corporate offices in San Antonio to take delivery on the second generation Fluxtron. The prototype will be taken to Dallas Love Field for installation in the Starchild II. At a luncheon between the Travelers and the Anaconda corporate executives, there is discussion about new electronic devices which the Professor has designed and his plans to turn over to Anaconda.

Hovering above the San Antonio Hemisphere Needle is a helicopter with a telephoto lens which is transmitting the video and the audio of the meeting back to the government agency's headquarters where the meeting is being watched on a television monitor. The audio is being furnished by a Mole in the group of executives.

Upon their return to Dallas, the Travelers begin making preparations for their departure to Terra. The Starchild II is being fitted with everything except the Fluxtron which is coming from Anaconda. So as not to arouse suspicion, the

Fluxtron has been shipped FedEx routinely. The following evening, the Professor is speaking at SMU and lecturing to a group of young scientists and students.

The Technician, who has completed all the work except installing the Fluxtron, is at a rock concert where he has promoted his way into performing with the rock group. When the FedEx truck arrives at Love Field hangar, the Astronaut puts out a call to the Professor and the Technician on their mobile phones. The message is that the package has arrived.

The Professor is signaled by the Scientist who is in the audience to wrap it up and come on. The Professor is leaving the meeting as he is approached by a young scientist with several questions. Reaching into his briefcase, the Professor pulls out a large handful of notes. Handing them to the young scientist, the Professor says that it's all right there if you can figure it out. They jump in the Duesenberg and race through the North Dallas streets.

The Scientist who is driving goes sliding onto the tarmac in front of the hangar. At the same time, a limo, with the Technician and the Girl, arrive. The Girl is now pregnant. The Technician still has his rock star outfit on and both run for the hangar. The Scientist takes one last look at her Duesenberg as she is approached by the gas boy who admires the car. Pitching the keys to the boy, she tells him that it is his, take good care of it.

The government Agents are closing in on the Travelers. The Lady attorney arrives just ahead of the other two government Agents as the Starchild II is towed out of the hangar. Night is falling and a slow drizzling rain is starting. She runs across the ramp, losing her shoes as the

Travelers board the Starchild II. The aircraft starts to taxi and the airstair door is shutting. She is yelling for them to open the door.

The airstair door opens, but the craft does not stop taxiing as she jumps aboard. She has decided to go with them at the last minute. She doesn't know where they are going, but has decided she is going to go with The Astronaut wherever that might be. The government Agents arrive too late to stop them from departing. As the Starchild II is cleared for takeoff. It climbs like a BOH and one of the control tower operators remarks to the other, what was that taking off. The other operator replies, oh I think it's one of those things that they work on out at Hangar 51.

The six Travelers travel through space and time, returning to the planet Terra. Millions of years have elapsed since their departure from the planet. The civilization which they left behind has long since died off. The planet is at a point of development roughly equivalent to 16th century Ireland, a rural agrarian society. This poses the question of whether or not any civilization will ultimately destroy itself with technology and if it did, will it have a second chance.

Thomas Wolfe said that "you can't go home again." In scientific fact, you can never go backwards in time, only forward. When the Travelers land near a peaceful village on the planet Terra, there is a chance for a new life. Four of the group go on ahead toward the village. As the Astronaut and the Professor finish unloading some personal items from the Starchild II, they also start to walk toward the village.

As they stroll up the dirt road in the beautiful blue sky valley in which they have landed, the Astronaut raises his right hand. In the palm of his right hand is a small remote control and he pushes the button on the control. In a gigantic mushroom cloud, the Starchild II and all its technology is destroyed. The last words are of the Professor who turns to the Astronaut and remarks, who was that guy who said, "You can't go home again."

***

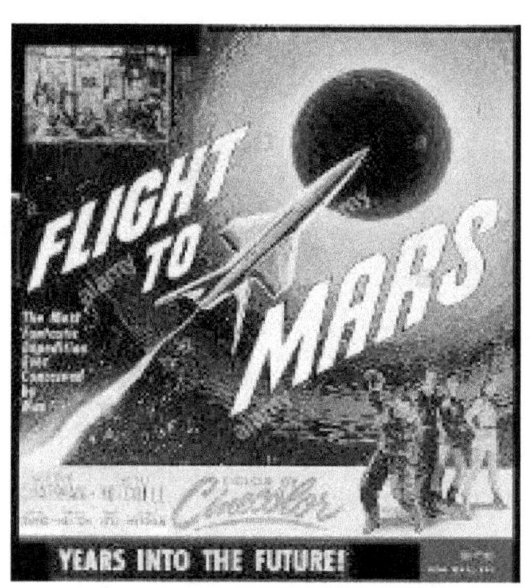

Sci-Fi Movie Poster

Chapter 24   STARCHILD III - Scene By Scene

Subtitle: "The Long Way Home"
STORYBOARD INDEX CARDS

SETUP - ACT ONE, THE BEGINNING:

Location: The Planet Terra. The Planet Terra looks like earth in many respects, including the people, except certain tell tail indications like the make of cars, sign etc. will appear to be unidentifiable and presently not recognizable (more like a foreign country). The style of dress is only slightly different, a little futuristic and there are a few people in Natiz like uniforms. The Terra space program is very much like Earth's NASA program. This could be an alternate history on Earth or it might be Earth in the not too distant further. Actually, it is the planet Terra which orbits around a sun a few thousand light years for Earth. This is not explained.

Scenes series #100s

101. Ext. Slow motion shot, very close up of large rocket launch. Russian or French launch with the markings computer enhanced so as not to be identified aa NASA. Film title and credit are superimposed. Thundering sound with ("2001" type) symphony orchestra music in background.

102. Ext. Long distance, pull back shot as the rocket climbs and disappears into the distant shy. All is now quiet except a few bird calls and natural sound of the meadow. Sub-title on the screen "Spring morning, year 2020"

103. Int. Cut to looking out of patrol helicopter window over the shoulder of black uniformed pilot we follows speeding sedan. Telephoto Shot: follows sedan down beach coastal road of complex (like Cape Canaveral).

104. Ext. Airmail shot follows the sedan to launch center headquarters where in pulls into a reserved parking space.

105. Ext. Crane shot of the Professor exits his car and enters building greeted with congratulations of workers at the center. The cars are Citron, DeLorean and Bricklin look alike.

106. Int. Shot follows the Professor down hallway. People gathering in large conference room. There are civilian and uniformed people entering a conference room.

107. Int. Wide angle shot of the conference room the Director announces that this was the first successful launch of a spacecraft equipped with the new top secret Fluxtron device on board.

108. Int. Close up shot of professor in discussion. The spacecraft actually vanished for only a fraction of a micro-second. When it's beacon signal was finally located, it was a billion miles from the point it had disappeared. The tracking center personal assumed that it had desineragrated because it took so long for the tracking beacon signal to get back.

109. Int. Slow zoom in on those seated at the table on an elevated stage, the Professor is introduced by the director from the podium. The press are permitted photo ops and a few questions before the conference begins.

110. Int. Close up shot of a woman reporter who is asking questions about the satellite which has been rumored to be re-entering the atmosphere.

111. Int. Zoom Shot: close up of another space program Manager who rises to his feet to explains that it was not a satellite that it was actually a probe that was sent to orbit the sun and that it was intended to fall off into outer space. Unfortunately, it was headed back towards earth and might enter the earth's atmosphere and burn up. There was no danger, he explained.

112. Int. Cut to a women and a TV cameraman, the reporter asked if they not attempted to send a shuttlecraft to intercept the satellite.

113. Int. Cut to the project Manager who replies that their technology was such that an orbital shuttle or planetary rocket would not be able to rendezvous and intercept the probe due to its tremendous speed.

114. Int. Shot of several reporters who continues to query saying that reports had been circulating that the satellite was nuclear powered and that at the right entry angle and speed, a chain reaction could be set off.

115. Int. Wide angle and pan shot of the room. This is denied several from the podium and the press is ushered out of the conference room.

116. Int. Close ups and pull backs shots from several angles as the Professor begins a long explanation of the theory of relativity and how this craft had been able to jump (or appear to jump) to another point in space by the

aid of the Flux generator (the Fluxtron). The test rocket had exceed the speed-of-light.

117. Int. Close up shot of persons who interrupt the Professor several times to ask questions.

118. Int. The meeting is adjourned with an invitation from the Director to a cocktail party at his home to celebrate the occasion.

119. Int. That evening, at the exclusive estate home of the space program's Director, a cocktail party is being held to celebrate the success of the test launch. Uniformed and civilian officials are in attendance.

120. Int. Close up shot of the Corneal who has been sent from military headquarters (like Pentagon) to oversee the results of the resent tests and there possible military applications.

121. Int. Cut back and forth to person speaking, the Professor, an Astronaut, an Engineer, a Scientist (female) and the astronaut's Wife are huddled in a discussion about the decay of a nuclear satellite's orbit. If the decent hits a critical velocity on re-entry, it could ignite a upper atmosphere chain reaction endangering all life on the planet.

122. Int. The Wife gets to greet a guest, a female Staff officer in a black uniform. It is actually her lesbian lover.

123. Int. The Engineer is approached and embraced by his drunken son and has a brief argument ensues; the gist of the argument being to the effect that the son's mother would be alive today if it wasn't for his father.

124. Int. The Engineer stand to steady his drunken son who pushes him away. His son stumbles backwards over a coffee table, crashing through drinks and food.

125. Int. The conversations stop as everyone watches the son gets up and stumbles towards the door to leave. The Engineer starts to go after him, then drops his hand in discuss. The Astronaut takes him by the arm to the couch and bus of the cocktail party begins again.

126. Ext. The following morning at the hangar building where the new Starchild SVTOL jet is being developed and flight tested.

127. Int. Inside the hangar, in the pilot ready room, there is a discussion between the Professor, the Astronaut, the Engineer and a Technician who works for the Engineer. The discussion is about the possibilities of installing the Fluxtron device on an aircraft's airframe like maybe the Starchild's. In theory, at least it should work. The Technician says it's no problem. The Engineer tells him to start looking into the possibility, but keep it to himself. The Technician walks away and the conversation turns to the latest news about the satellite that is scheduled to reenter the atmosphere the next day.

127a Int. Early satellites had been solar power plant, but this one was the first of a new nuclear powered series. The onboard commands were damaged when it past too close to the magnetic field of Terra's sun and it cannot be controlled during its descent when and if it strikes Terra's atmosphere. They is a is a possibility that an atomic chain reaction might occur. When the moisture in the upper atmosphere is electrically charged and the hydrogen begins to separate the core of the satellite would start a nucular reaction. The major factor is the speed and angle of the re-entry. The Professor says that this information will be available late tomorrow night or early in the following morning.

128. Int. Series of quick close up shots of work on Starchild as the Engineer, the Technician and the Mechanic work nonstop to install the required field coils in the Starchild's airframe. (All is being done without the knowledge of the program magnet. Their jobs are on the line, but more likely their lives are.)

124. Int. Early the next morning, the Professor, the Scientist and the Astronaut arrive at the hangar ready room. Each one enters quietly and pours a cup of coffee. They are watching a television broadcast. A news anchorman is saying that the nuclear satellite decay is inevitable, but there is no danger repeat no danger, to the general public.

125. Int. The Engineer enters the room and asks well Professor what's the verdict. He reply the worst, will that thing fly? The decision is made to try and escape the certain doom of Terra in the Starchild. Everything is ready except for plugging in the Fluxtron.

126. Int. The Fluxtron device is still at the lab where the Professor works and it must be smuggled out that night and taken to the Starchild's hangar. Professor and Scientist discuss how they are going to steal it.

127. Ext. That night the Scientist who also has an office at the lab. The Professor is already there under the pretext of working late.

128. Int. The Scientist distracts the security guards with a contrived story while the Professor struggles to smuggle the 40 pound Fluxtron out to his waiting car. (Comedy relief)

129. Int. The Starchild shown in a darkened corner of the flight test hangar, it has not yet shown up close or fully lighted. (the aircraft looks like a small six place version of the Valcuree or an SST. The six people whom it is planed will be occupying the six seats are: the Astronaut in the front left pilots seat; the Engineer who will navigate from the front right co-pilots seat; the Professor in the left passengers seat behind the pilot; the Scientist in the right passengers seat behind the co-pilot; the son's seat which is taken by the Technician behind the Scientist; and the last seat by the door where it is planed that the astronaut's Wife will set.)

130. Ext. Cut to a bright blue skied afternoon with large puffy clouds looking at the partly opened hangar doors; a red roadster pulls into the hangar. (The Travelers are preparing to leave.)

131. Int. Shot follows the Technician and an older aircraft mechanic as they unload the Fluxtron from the trunk of the Professors car and carry it to the Starchild still partly shrouded in the hangar shadows.

132. Int. Looking into the Starchild's cabin center isle through the boarding door, the Technician is bolting the Fluxtron to the aircraft's floor and running the control cables down the aisle to a cockpit console which is mounted between the pilot and co-pilot seats.

133. Int. The Astronaut is called to the phone in the hangar office. It is his Wife who explains that she is not going to go with them. She will take her chances here on the home planet. Her father, the Director, has assured her that the descending satellite will cause no harm as this is what he has been told. The Staff officer, her lisbian lover, has also told her the same thing. She assures her husband that she has told no one of their plans. This is not true because the Staff officer informs the authorities, but too late to stop the Travelers departure.

134. Int. The Astronaut exits the office and tell the others that they are ready to depart. As he walks by a nearby pillar, he pushes the power button that starts the large hangar doors opening. The now only four walk silently and slowly through the darkened hangar that is now being flooded with bright daylight by the slowly opening doors. They Travelers approach the Starchild prepared to board. This is the first time we see the Starchild in all its splendor. Soft orchestra music begins to builds: (Jimmy Buffet's "Only Time Will Tell" would work here, maybe he could score the whole film)

135. Int. At the boarding door of the Starchild the Engineer, last to board, turns to shake hand with the Technician and thanks him for everything. He doesn't offer his hand in return, but asks who's going to use those two empty seats? The Engineer replies, why you want one? The Technicon says, well I got to pack first, steps over to his rollaway tool box grabs a hand full of tools and troughs them into a bag. Placing his foot on the rollaway tool box, he pushes it so hard that it goes careening across the hangar floor and crashes into a pile of sheet metal parts.

He turns back the Engineer who is smiling and says that it was fine with hem. They both board the Starchild.

136. Int. The Technician stops at the top of the airstair and turns back to Jose a say there's one more seat left and asks if Jose wanted it.

137. Int. Shot of Jose backing away an waving he is saying that he has too many kids and he hasn't seem his wife in three days, he's going home.

138. Int. Cut to the Technician. The whine of the engine starters starting to come on line. He yells, Hay Jose is this baby gonna fly and Jose yells back from a distance, you can bet your ass. The Technicon mutters, I guess that's what I'm doing, come to think of it.

139. Int/Ext. The hangar doors are now fully open. The engine are fired off and thing laying around in the hangar are blown in every direction. The Starchild taxis into the bright sunlight and onto the and across the tarmac. (Normally an aircraft like this would be towed out of the hangar with a tug and a toe bar. The pilot, the Astronaut could not take the chance of being tethered to a tow bar in case someone decided to stop their takeoff.

140. Int. Inside the cabin as they are taxing the Professor is fumbling with his seat belt, trying to buckle it. The Engineer turns to him a remarks that he should worry with it because if this baby don't fly there won't be enough of our atoms left for someone to identify.

141. Ext. Like a Harrier jump-jet the Starchild lifts about up off of the tarmac to about twenty feet in the air and rotates hormonally about ninety.

142. Int. Cockpit interior shot as sounds are being heard over the radio. The Astronaut is running through a pre-takeoff check list with the Engineer. The tower is asking who is flying the Starchild. The Astronaut picks up the mic and replies Captain Jack. The tower operator asks who authorized this flight. The Astronaut replies, Almighty God, I hope. The tower supervisor is now on the radio demanding that the Starchild return to the hangar ramp. The Astronaut reaches over and turns the radio off as pushes forward on the throttles.

143. Ext. The Starchild starts it's takeoff roll down the long runway and thunders into the sky at a high angle of attack.

145. Ext. Long distance shot of the Starchild as it climbs into the distant clouds higher and faster than any aircraft has before it. This is the prototype of a generation of aircraft that can obtain planetary orbit as well as operate in the atmosphere.

(PLOT POINT ONE)

CONFRONTATION - ACT TWO, THE MIDDLE:

Location: On board the Starchild. Terra date is modern and Earth is in the Paleozoic Earth period.

Scene series #200

201. Int/Ext. On board the Starchild, the Astronaut is in the left front seat and the Engineer is in the co-pilot seat. Seated in the two seats behind the cockpit are the Professor

on the left side and the Scientist on the right side. The last seat is empty on the left and the Technician is sitting on the right.

202. Int. Emphases on empty seat were Astronaut's wife would have sat.

203. Ext. The aircraft is climbing higher into the upper atmosphere and the sky begins to turn black. This aircraft is capable of lower orbital flight around Terra. The Engineer is calculating time and distances. Recent studies had shown that a star in the nearby star cluster had shown signs of wobbling due to the possibility of planets similar to those around Terra's sun existed. It is these calculations that are being figured and discussed between the Engineer and the Professor.

204. Int. Behind the Technician's seat is the small devise about the size of a five galleon can, the Flextron, bolted to the floor with cables laying on the isle floor running up to a set of controls in the cockpit.

205. Int. The Technician gets out of his seat fooling with on the Fluxtron.

206. Ext. Looking out the window, the Scientist sees the beginning of the decaying orbital satellite strike the upper atmosphere. A nuclear burn begins to make its way around the planet, as though the sky was on fire.

207. Ext. The Starchild is inserted into hyper-light. The red/blue shift begins to occur (as it actually does near the speed-of-light) red if you look in one direction and blue when looking in the opposite direction. (The craft does not

fly into a starburst blur as in popular science fiction light speed insertions.)

208. Int. Time is distorted. This is referred to as a God like view of time. The past, present and further can all be seen at once.

209. Ext. After a brief period of time, the Fluxtron is disengaged and the Starchild is in orbit around an earth-like planet. Relativity has moved them billions of miles from their home planet arriving at planet in Paleozoic age.

210. Ext. Descending from orbit, the craft makes a slow pass over the jungle-like terrain. Dinosaurs are grazing in the open fields.

211. Int. Some of the wiring around the Flextron are overheating and are smoking. Some repairs are going to be required.

212. Int. The Fluxtron can be used to advance in time as well as travel across space. After a lengthy discussion, the Engineer calculates the insertion time required to pass several millions of years into the future. Much of this is guess work because of the large numbers involved. Based on the fact that as velocity increases, time decreases. Thus, a space traveler traveling at the speed-of-light for only a few years, will return home and find that his family has aged many years.

213. Ext. Coming out of the second insertion, they once again descend in the Starchild to the earth's surface to discover that they have landed at a time approximately 3000 BC A relatively good guess for the factors involved.

Location: Ancient Egypt shortly after the building of the Sphinx and predates the Pyramids by thousands of years as some archeologists believe. Time span is only a few weeks.

Scene series #300

301. Ext. The Starchild circles the Sphinx looking for a landing spot in the Gaza desert.

302. Int. Smoke in the cabin is coming from wiring on the Fluxtron cables.

303. Ext. The Starchild lands and comes to a stop in a cloud of dust.

304. Ext. Several Travelers walk toward a small tent village of locals who are the workers at the construction of the Sphinx.

305. Ext. They are greeted by some local tribes people. Through a series of hand jesters and picking up some of the native phrases, they explain that they are travelers just passing through.

306. Ext. The Starchild is parked some distance away, hidden from the local peoples sight. The five Travelers stay for two night with the locals observing the construction on the Sphinx.

307. Int. Some of the wiring on the Fluxtron has been burned and the Technician begins making patchwork repairs. He is visited often by a young girl who brings him food and water as he works. The girl is an orphaned. The daughter of local tribal leader she lives with her family.

308. Int. At a dinner in a large tent, on the third evening, the Engineer has had too much wine and ends up in bed with one local woman dancers.

309. Int. hat night four of the Travelers are asleep together, except the Engineer who is sleeping in the Dancers tents.

310. Int/Ext. The Engineer hears a noise in the middle of the night and gets up to investigate. It is the woman's jealous lover who steps out of the darkness and stabs the Engineer in the stomach with a knife.

311. Int/Ext. Engineer's body is mummified and preserved one of early tombs which predate the pyramids. Plan is to return for him with advanced bio-technology and restore his body to life.

312. Int. After lengthy discussion, Travelers decide to make one more jump in time (always forward, relativity does not permit backward travel in time) to see if they can arrive at a period of time where more modern technology is being developed. (Hopefully, in earth's 21st century)

308. Ext. During preparation for departure, young Girl who has befriended by Travelers announces she is going with them and boards the Starchild upon departure.

Location: Aboard the Starchild between 3000 BC and 1959 AD orbiting earth. The Engineer is left behind, the Technician takes the co-pilot's seat and the Girl takes the empty sixth seat.

Scene series #400

401. Int. The Technician (now the co-pilot, navigator) estimates the time that they will have to insert themselves into orbit using the Fluxtron. It is a best guess for the time duration.

402. Ext. There is only a moment or two of time that passes and the Astronaut is at the controls of the Starchild as it breaks out of time and space into orbit above earth. The aircraft wings are overheating and the dissent angle is greater than needed. Several systems fail during descent.

403. Ext. The east coast of the U.S. looms on the horizon.

404. Int. The glide angle is set for what would turn out to be the countryside near a small New England town and there appears to be a small airstrip nestled among a wooded area.

405. Ext. As the Starchild touches down, it has too much speed and runs off the end of the runway into the trees. Aircraft is damaged, but no one on board is injured as it comes to a stop. There is now only the stillness of the countryside with birds chirping.

406. Ext. They exit the aircraft and walk back toward an old metal hangar, There are several bi-planes parked around the grass strip airport.

(MID PLOT POINT)

Location: The New England community where Travelers establish a local identify. The Professor becomes involved at a local university, the Scientist eventually goes on staff at the hospital, the Astronaut eventually takes over the small airport and the Technician becomes involved with music. The problem that current technology does not allow for the development of the type of systems needed for the Starchild repairs. This is as close to modern times as their best guess a relativity navigation is able to bring them to. These guesses being based on calculations in micro-seconds. To attempt to jump again, even though the Starchild might be able to be repaired at some future date, could cause them to miss a future date by thousands of years rather than a few decades. This bad of a miss could bring them into a planetary environment having just undergone a nuclear holocaust or a poisoned environment. If that happened, their chances of moving forward (cannot go back) and finding a suitable environment would be much less practical than taking their chances on survival where they are now.

Scene series #500

501. Ext/Int. The Starchild is stored in one of the old metal hangars under lock and key. It is damaged beyond repair based on current technology.

502. Ext. After learning to fly the old biplanes, the Astronaut takes his fellow Travelers for rides.

503. Int. The Professor devises a plan for developing micro-circuitry which can be sold via a cover corporation that he has created.

504. Ext/Int. The Travelers have now leased a large home on an estate where they reside as a group. The house is a turn-of-the century mansion.

505. Int. In the Starchild hangar, the Technician is working on the Professors ideas for the latest advanced technology. He is also building a music synthizor, as music is his hobby and her want to be a rock star.

506. Int. The Scientist has found an old Duesenburg which she has restored and drives to work every day at the clinic where she works. She delights in taking it out on the backroads of the countryside.

507. Int. The Professor and the Scientist have developed the beginnings of a relationship an she want him to marry her. He tells her, his reason for waiting and kids her about it.

508. Int. A relationship is developing between the Technician and the Girl (who is eighteen now) has always idolized him.

509. Int/Ext. Several years pass and technology is on the threshold of breaking through to the advances needed by the Travelers in order to rebuild the Starchild. The Travelers attempt to stay uninvolved, but now several government agencies have begun to investigate foreigners and thinks the Travelers may be communist sympathizers.

510. Int. At the small airport, the Astronaut is preparing to go flying in a restored Stearman biplane.

511. Ext. He encounters the Lady government agent investigator who has snooping around the airport and investigation who the Travelers are.

512. Ext. The Astronaut invites her to go flying in the biplane. There is an attraction here, but it is not pursued.

513. Ext. She leaves convinced that the Travelers are not suspicious, but with some lingering doubts.

514. Int. The Professor makes the decision to abandon their quiet country life and set up a major corporation in Dallas with a subsidiary in Austin. The mansion is sold and the airport shutdown. The Scientist insists on keeping her Duesenburg roadster and has it shipped where they are going.

Location: Dallas, Texas in the 1950s. The Astronaut is working very closely with William P. Lear following the development of his new Learjet. Both the Astronaut, Professor and Technician are working as consultants and serving on the board of directors of several electronic companies. One of which will develop advanced computer chip technology.

Scene series #600

601. Ext. In the early days in Dallas, the Professor and Technician go to work at Texas Gauge developing new electronic systems.

602. Int. The Professor helps the company design and develop miniaturized solid state devices. The Technician joking privately with the Professor reaches in his pocket and opens a small of what appear to be grains of sand (parts from the Starchild), placing his finger in the box several adhere. He remarks, he wonders what the company would say if they knew the circuitry in one of these. The Professor acknowledges this with a smile.

603. Int. The Scientist is working with a bio research company developing gene technology. She hope to make

advances into cloning, a project she had been working on in Terra. She hopes, at some future date, that they might be able to recover the Engineer's remains from ancient Egypt and clone him. She and the Astronaut discuss the possibility of returning to ancient Egypt where they left the Engineer in 3000 BC

604. Ext. The Astronaut is flight testing the prototype of the new Learjet and a trip to ancient Egypt is planned.

605. Ext. Four of the Travelers, the Astronaut, the Technician, the Scientist and the Girl all return to an abandoned desert location which they had marked with celestial navigation coordinates; or maybe not. The spot is covered with sand and the tomb appears not to exist. Working through a local archeologist, the Travelers convince him to provide the local labor to excavate what they believe to be an ancient artifact. When the tomb is reached, it is found to be totally destroyed and nothing that they can remember, including the remains of the Engineer , is identifiable. The Travelers give up and return to Dallas. The Girl cannot believe that only a few years ago in her lifetime, all she ever knew and remember had existed on that barren spot. A civilization lost in time.

606. Int/Ext. The Astronaut and the Lady fly to Wichita to get the new jet which as yet has not been flight tested.

607. Ext. The travelers and the Lady meet the old Flyer in the keys and fly to Arecibo, Porta Rico.

608. Ext. They meet and befriend some smugglers; spend night with them.

609. Int/Ext. They visit the radio observatory and meet with a student of the Professor's. New charts of the sky are made and taken with them.

610. A Dallas Love Field hangar is leased and under heavy security guard. The first delivery of a commercial air jet placed in the hangar. Wrecked remains of original Starchild is recovered from the old airport hangar in and trucked secretly by night to the new Love Field hangar. Project is funded by stocks from Professor's investments electronics companies.

Location: Professor lecturing at university on astrophysics and travelers extensively to Austin and San Antonio from the Dallas area where he, the Astronaut and the Scientist serve as consultants and members of the board of directors. Once again, their actions have aroused the suspicions of several government agencies and they are now being actively pursued. The Lady that had encountered the Astronaut earlier is once again part of the investigation. The Technician has become part of a rock group that is performing concerts; plus a flight to Arecibo.

Scene series #700

701. Ext. The scene here is a triple pull-back first from a meeting of the Travelers and some major corporation interests in a room atop the San Antonio space needle. Out of the window, to the helicopter with a camera.

702. Int. Looking at a television monitor, the camera from the helicopter and the sound from the wired mole is being watched by unknown persons.

703. It is decided that more accurate data for star positions needs to be recovered, so the Astronaut plans to take a seaplane to Aerocebo and visit an astronomer acquaintance who is working there. Hopefully, during this visit, they can record some of the data that is needed to more accurately recalculate the time and distances for a return to Terra should the Travelers be successful in eventually reproducing the original Fluxtron technology.

704. That night at a local restaurant/bar, the Astronaut recognizes the Lady who is a government investigator on his trail. He invites her to have dinner with him as she is obviously following him anyway.

705. Int. The Astronauts apartment bedroom, the Astronaut and the Lady had spent the night together. As the Lady wakes and asks, how commit is that we always seem to end up in bed with each other.

706. Int. The Astronaut is in the bathroom shaving and he tells her to get up and get ready that he is going to take her somewhere. He drags her off still as she is trying to get her clothes and makeup on.

707. Ext. They arrive at the airport where they fly depart in a Cessna 310 for Wichita, Kansas.

708. Ext. Arriving at Wichita Municipal Airport, they meet with the CEO of the aircraft factory in plush offices with windows overlooking the ramp.

709. Int. In Mr. Lear's office, they discuss the work that the Professor has been providing them for the development for new electronic technology; 8-track stereo tape and solid state inverters. The Astronaut hands Mr. Lear a cashier's

check for payment in full and takes delivery on one of the first Lear Jets built. The FAA has not yet certified the aircraft.

710. Ext. The Astronaut goes to the ramp where the jet is parked and begins to preflight it. The Lady is tagging along behind him. The chief flight test engineer is standing near the airplane with a clipboard. He tells the Astronaut he cannot fly the plane as it is only being used for test flights. Taking the clipboard out of the engineer's hand, the Astronaut signs it as test pilot. He and the Lady board the aircraft and crank the engine.

711. Ext. The Astronaut flies to the Caribbean and lands at a small airport near Miami, Florida. There is an old Catalina flying boat parked on the beach nearby. The Professor and the Technician and the Girl have arrived in a chartered aircraft to meet them.

712. Ext. They board the flying boat and takeoff and fly under the ADAZ of radar to a small coaster town in Puerto Rico. At Aerocebo, where the radar observatory is located, they proceed up the mountains to meet with an Astronomer who is an acquaintance of the Professors.

713. Int. As work progresses on the Starchild in the Dallas Love Field hangar, a meeting between the Travelers is held to discuss more accurate celestial navigation if they were to attempt a return to Terra. It is estimated that millions of years have passed since they had left the planet and that there is a possibility that a total ecological recovery of the planet could have taken place.

714. Int. he Lady meets with her subordinates in the government agency and it is decided that while the motives

of the Travelers are unknown that they should be hauled in for extensive questioning. The Lady is now beginning to ask lots of questions, some of which will soon be answered. There is a change of allegiance that is similar in the heroine in the "Thomas Crown Affair."

Location is Dallas Love Field, corporate offices in San Antonio, the University of Texas at Austin and a music concert at the Cotton Bowl.

Scene series #800

801. Int. The Starchild II is nearing completion and Travelers meet to discuss their departure from earth in hopefully successful return to Terra. There is a lengthy discussion about what the Travelers are to expect when they get home to Terra. Group goes into the hangar where Starchild II is.

802. Int. The next evening, the Professor is lecturing at a nearby university and the Scientist is attending with him.

803. Ext. The Technician and girl are at a rock concert. This scene basically involves the Technician performing at a rock concert in the StarPlex, Far Park Dallas. Performers wear makeup and customs like Kiss.

804. Int. The Astronaut is working in the hangar when the Lady arrives trying to argue her way past one of the security guards. The Astronaut hear the commotion and goes to lets her in the hangar. She explains government agents are planning a raid on the hangar to discover its contents in middle of the night. The Astronaut contacts on beeper (not used at this time).

805. Int. The Professor, leaving the lecture is followed by a young student who asks for a further explanation on some points in his lecture. Opening his briefcase, the Professor extracts a fistful of notes, handing them to the student. He says that some of the calculations may not be correct, but all of what you ask about is here.

806. Ext. The Professor and the Scientist run for her Duesenburg in the parking lot and race through Highland Park to Love Field.

807. Ext. It is late evening now and a slow drizzling rain had started. On the north side of Love Field, at the civil aircraft ramp, the Technician arrives in a limo with the Girl just as the Professor and Scientist rounds the corner and skids onto the tarmac. The four run for the open hangar door. Sirens in the background indicate that the men in black, with help, are on their way.

808. Ext. The Lady Government Agent is standing on the tarmac talking on her hand-held radio as the engines on the Learjet are fired up by the Astronaut. Starchild II starts to taxi toward the four that are running for the aircraft. The airstair door is down as the four board the aircraft, the airstair is being pulled up by the Technician.

809. Ext. The Lady is standing in the rain watching the jet taxi by. He hesitates then runs waving to the Astronaut. She has decided to go with them and run to get on board. The jet does not stop rolling, but the airstair come down and she jumps on board.

810. Int. She announces that she doesn't know where they are going, but she intends to go with them.

811. Ext. The airstair door is shut as the jet taxi onto the runway and the tower gives clearance for takeoff.

(PLOT POINT TWO)

812. Ext. The Learjet rolls down the runway and lifts off into the darkness with its beacon light flashing climbing skyward.

813. Int. In the ATC an operator is looking at a radar screen. He remarks to his co-worker, what the hell was that taking off. The other controller replies, oh, probably one of those things the government is experimenting with out there at Dry Lake, some people refer to it as Aera-51.

RESOLUTION - ACT THREE, THE END:

Location is aboard the Starchild and the return to the planet Terra. Landing on the planet Terra they discover that it now has a beautiful evolved environment with no industrial pollution whatsoever. What has taken place on Terra is that the satellite did not actually destroy the entire planet as the Travelers had first believed. The environment was seriously damaged and there was much suffering and starvation. As the planet began to recover, there was another major leap in technology. Unfortunately, there were two major powers which evolved to control the planet's countries. These two powers met in an all-out nuclear war a few hundred years after the Travelers had left and for all practical purposes most of civilization was lost. The survivors became prehistoric cave men and had never reached any significant level of technology. All of this is of little importance to our story because millions of years after the Travelers had originally departed. Everything they ever knew had been lost in antiquity.

Scene series #900

901. Ext. The Fluxtron is engaged by the Technician who is seated in the co-pilot's seat as they reach the highest obtainable altitude of earth. The Starchild is transitioning into light speed with the six Travelers on board.

902. Int. Aboard the Starchild, the crew is experiencing the effects of light-speed they are desperately trying to calculate the time and distance back to Terra as accurately as possible.

903. Int. The Lady who has gone with them is very excited about what she is experiencing and expresses unbelievable amazement. The Fluxtron is disengaged and all wait anxiously to see where they have arrived in space.

904. Ext. The Starchild is coasting just inside the orbit of Terra's largest of two moons with the earth-like plant in the distance. It is obviously different than earth because although it is the same blue and white planet, the continents are shaped different than the known world of Earth.

905. Int/Ext. As the Starchild enters atmosphere, the airframe is overheating and it is questionable as to whether or not the aircraft will hold together during the descent. As soon as some atmosphere is encountered, the Astronaut (pilot) engages the jet engines to decrease the descent angle.

906. The Starchild circles over a rolling hillside and turns to make a final approach in an open meadow not too far from the village. The spot they will land at resembles a

small village in southern Ireland with thatched roofed houses and stone fences.

907. Ext. In the distance, there are people who look up to watch the Starchild land and a small crowd of a dozen gather near the village.

908. Int./Ext. The Starchild comes to rest with some dust flying in the wind and the airstair door opens and the Travelers depart.

909. Int./Ext. The Astronaut and the Technician are unloading equipment from the aircraft; personal items and sourviers from Earth. Without explanation, the Technician appears to be monkeying a device wired to the Fluxtron. He hands what looks like a small handheld remote control to the Astronaut and walk up the dirt road towards the village people.

910. Ext. The Lady and the Girl are dancing in a circle for joy, if for no other reason than that they are still alive.

911. Ext. Several of the Travelers throw packs over their shoulders. All of the group walks on ahead toward the village except for the Astronaut and the Professor. Both are smiling.

912. Ext. As they continue to walk, the Astronaut has a small backpack over his left shoulder. He raises his right hand containing the small remote control when they are about two hundred yards from the Starchild which is behind them in the background and pushes the button.

913. Ext. The Starchild explodes in a gigantic mushroom ball of fire filmed in slow motion. Pieces are falling to the ground like feathers from the sky.

914. Ext. Neither man looks back, only ahead at the villages who are now greeting the Travelers who went on ahead. The Astronaut says, "Who says you can't go home again."

915. Ext. Crane shot of two men walking to village, aril pull away circling higher and higher, Celtic music, fade to black and roll credits.

***

Chapter 25 STARCHILD III - CHARACTERS

Professor - (male: Alexander Covoliski, called Alex, age mid 50s)
Home planet Terra. Alex is a university professor with a Ph.D. in Astrophysics and an expert on the Theory of Relativity. He is well known for his work in the field of theoretical physics. As a child, he was considered to be a nerd, not a good student and was bored with his classes. His high school physics teacher saw in him the potential scientist and took an interest in him, encouraging him in his studies and his interest in astronomy and photography. After college, he had difficulty holding a job as he was more interested in developing his own ideas and inventions than he was working for others. Alex was a handsome man, but always seemed to have trouble with women until he met his wife, Tudy, whom he married when he was in his middle twenties. After he married, he became serious about furthering his education. He received his Ph.D. in astrophysics and taught at a university. In her late thirties, Tudy died in child birth, along with the baby and he never forgave himself for what had happened. After her death, he left the university for a position in the space program and threw himself into his work. He never remarried. As our story begins, the Professor is the lead project person on the new Fluxtron development project at the Terra Space Center. His experience in dealing with scientific development programs is vast, as for many years, he worked as a consultant on many secret space projects and served on various boards of directors.

He is soft spoken and kind. He solves the most complex of problems with short and exacting solutions. His father had passed away several years ago and his mother, whom he loves very much, has been in a rest home for several years. On his last visit to see her, she no longer recognized him. When life gets really heavy for him, he seeks the comfort of Dusty, a colleague, who he can confide in. He is the highly respected leader of the group of Travelers who depart Terra, travel to Earth for thirteen years and then returns to Terra. The press has always hounded him as he is known to be one of the top physicists in the known world, but he dislikes the fame. (Starchild seat #3)

Scientist - (female: Desdemona Aramora, called Dusty, mid 40s) Home planet Terra. An expert in the fields of human biology, anatomy and space psychology. Also, a medical doctor. She married a young medical student in her late teens and worked as a waitress to put him through school. Doctor Jerk (as Dusty now refers to her ex-husband) became involved with his bookkeeper and financial adviser after he went into practice and divorced Dusty. Dusty went back to school after the divorcee and worked her way through college, obtaining a grant and some loans to go to graduate and medical school. She is good natured, sarcastic and is a hard kidder. She is still paying off some of her college loans and makes a game out of jacking her bill collectors around. She is a poor money manager and an impulsive shopper. She is not tight, but would just rather spend her salary on things that catch her eye. Recently purchased a real expensive hot little red roadster which she drives like a bat out of hell. Most of her friends, including the Professor hate to ride with her and make up excuses not to have to. Dusty, short for Desdemona, unwittingly helped to make her nick name stick by coming to work late and sliding into a parking space at her office dirt surface parking lot. She has widely varied interests of which the most recent is restoring antique machinery in her spare time. She and the Professor are friends and from time to time, he goes to her house for dinner and stays over. They become closer in 1950 Earth. (Starchild seat #4)

Astronaut - (male: Jackson Pollard, called Jack, age late 30s)
Home planet Terra. Currently the chief test pilot in Terra's space flight research programs. The best of the right stuff, he was an Eagle Scout, president of his senior class and star athlete. Always does the right thing. Has a likable and outgoing personality. His father was an alcoholic and died win Jack was away at the academy. His mother has just recently passed away. He married daughter of the Director of the Terra space program in a high profile ceremony at the Terra Space Academy after graduating top of his class. A former jet aircraft test pilot at the Terra flight research center, he became famous when he successfully ejected from an out of control lunar lander a fraction of a second it exploded during testing. He has rose rapidly through the military ranks before applying to enter the astronaut program and presently holds a reserve commission as captain. He has been selected to go on Terra's next deep space mission. Due to his position at the space center, he is aware of the development on the new Fluxtron device. His assignment to the Starchild project and will most likely make him the first pilot to fight test the new aircraft. He and his wife have no children. His wife may be having an affair with another woman and their marriage is on the rocks. His job brings him in contact with the Professor, they become friends. (Starchild seat #1)

Engineer - (male: Samilio Kizermen, called Sam, age late 40s)

Home planet Terra. Chief engineer for the space program. Works for the Director of Terra's space program, but does not respect his judgment nor like his political leanings. His dad was one of the pioneer engineers in the development of early electronics during the world war. He and his dad designed and built a motorcycle when he was fourteen. His interest in mechanics lead to building up several hot rods during his teenage years. The summer after high school he married his high school girlfriend. They were divorced after only a short time, but she had a son. She moved away refusing to allow Sam to see the boy. Her death when the boy was in his early teens and the boy came to live with his father. The son is now in his early 30s, drinks too much and blames his father for all his mother's failings. Sam joined the Marines when he was nineteen and was a chopper pilot in the Mongrel Wars which were fought on another continent on Terra. He was shot down and wounded in action, but escaped back to his own lines. Sam put himself through college at Terra's prestigious Institute of Technology. In his early years at the Institute, he was a drinker and a womanizer, but began to get his life together when he went for his master's degree in mechanical engineering. He developed a special talent for electronics and computers those years and designed and built the first celestial navigation devices used in the Terra space program. He is a bachelor, but maintains a home for his deadbeat son. Sam lives with different women from time to time. He and the Professor met and became associates years ago when the Professor was on staff at the Institute. During the first Earth landing he, becomes involved with a native women, a member of an ancient Egyptian tribe whom he leaves. He dies during an encounter with a local tribe member. His remains are mummified and left behind where the Sphinx is being carved out of a stone outcrop. (Starchild seat #2 until killed.)

Technician - (male: Theodore Vetech, called Ted, age late 20s)
Home planet Terra. One of the audio-visual set in grade school. Into rock music and computer games by high school. A brief tour in the military assigned to the electronic warfare group. Has become a whiz kid in rigging electronic and computer devices. Some comic relief in his nature, he imitates characters like Monty Python and the South Park kids when make fun of his superiors behind their back. Is a very talented musician and would like to be a rock star. His hobbies are electronically synthesized music and hacking into computer systems where he never does any damage, but just likes to see if he can get in. He work in the hangar where the Starchild aircraft is being prepared for testing. Because he is kind of a rebel, the chief Engineer has taken Ted under his wing and has Ted report directly to him. The Engineer know that he can count of Ted to rig almost anything. He has become somewhat of the Engineer's protégée. Ted is more like a son to the Engineer than his own son. The Engineer is about the only one that Ted has enough respect for to not make fun of behind his back. One of the seats was to be for the Son, but at the last minute Ted takes it. On Earth he rises to the occasion and takes the Engineer's crew position after the Engineer is killed. On Earth, he eventually marries the Egyptian girl when she about age 20. The Girl has idolized him since they first met and follows him everywhere. For a brief period just before leaving Earth, Ted fulfills his dream of

becoming a rock star. (Starchild seat #5 on first flight and then seat #2 after Engineer is killed.)
Girl - (female: Effertities called Effie, age seventeen when first met)
Home planet Earth. A young very pretty, dark completed, brunet. An orphan girl of the Egyptian tribe in ancient Gaza. Her father was a ruler in one of the rival tribes and he and his wife where both beheaded after losing a battle in a territorial dispute. Effie, at age six, was made to watch the execution. She was adopted by the tribal leader, an elder called Horace who is married to his wife of many years. He and his wife have several grown children who treat Effie little better than a servant. She befriends Ted as he is working on the aircraft and makes up her mind to follow him wherever he goes. Some of the tribal people view the Travelers as gods, but Effie understands that they are only people from a more advanced culture. In her mind she relates there past to the past that she can remember as a young princess. She joins the Travelers when they jump forward in Earth time and learns to adapt to modern day Earth with the Travelers. Before their return to Terra, she Ted are married and she is with child when they leave Earth for the last time. (Starchild seat #5 after first flight)

Lady - (age mid 30s) Home planet Earth. Was a gangly and awkward child. Born to elderly parents she was somewhat sheltered as a child. She attended college and law school on a trust fund administered by her uncle, a retired government agent. She is now a very attractive and elegant looking woman. She went to work for an unnamed government intelligence agency (men in black types) right out of law school on the recommendation of her uncle. She is highly intelligent and has a lot of class. Her first encounter with the Travelers is in the 1950s New England

Earth when she meets the Astronaut at the small airport during an investigation. Generally, very mature and reserved, she seems to become a babbling school girl anytime she is around the Astronaut. He takes her flying in an old Stearman biplane and ends up in bed with her. She leaves him a note which he finds the next morning. They do not meet again until several years later in Dallas when they become more involved. In a visit with the Scientist, a blood sample reveals that she has several genes which are unique to Terraians. The only answer is that her many-times-grandfather had been the Engineer. She returns with the Travelers to Terra. (Starchild Seat #6 return to Terra)

Left On Terra:

Director - (male) Is the director of Terra's space program. Father of

Astronaut's wife, host of celebration cocktail party at his home. Present at the conference after the test launch.

Wife - Married to Astronaut. Daughter of Director of the Terra space program, age late 20s. Young slender light complicated Arian looking blonde. Scheduled to escape the planet Terra on the Starchild with her husband. She backs out and elects to stay behind on Terra. She has been having an affair with a lesbian staff officer. (Her seat on the Starchild is empty on first flight.)

Manager - The project manager at the space center who was in charge of the nuclear satellite solar orbit fiasco

Son - The son of the Astronaut; hot-head, drinker, age early 20's. Does not get along with his father whom he came to live with after his mother's death. There is a seat on the Starchild for him, but he is drunk and is killed in a spectacular car crash scene on the way to the space center hangar.

Mechanic - Harold is an older gentleman, gray hair with a black mustache. An aircraft airframe and power plant maintenance man that work at the flight test hangar with the Technician. He served in the Marines during the Mongrel wars with the Engineer.

Military Officer - (male) Staff officer in the elite Terra high command. Sinister, Nazi like in a black uniform. Watches the Terra space program and reports directly back to the Triad-head, ruling government. Present at cocktail party.

Staff Officer - (female) Staff assistant also member elite command, hard case. Black uniformed dike. Gains the confidence of the Astronauts Wife, convinces her not to leave with the Travelers and reports the plot to leave in the Starchild.

Actress - Daughter of the deceased Clyde Starchild, the founder of the Starchild Aircraft Company, the manufacturer of a long line of military and commercial aircraft on Terra. The new S-1 was named her in her father's honor. (i.e. Fairchild, Vought, Douglas, Cessna)

Others - patrol helicopter **pilots**; crew and workers at space center; television newswoman and cameraman; attendees and press people at the news conference; after conference attendees where the Fluxtron is discussed behind closed doors, a mix of civilian and military guests at the cocktail party.

Paleozoic Era Earth:
Computer generated prehistoric animals grazing in the fields like in "Jurassic Park". Graphic - fly by of the Starchild across the primitive landscape as several dinosaurs look up at the aircraft passing overhead.

Ancient Egypt:
Note: Effie enters story here.
Elder - Tribal leader, Horace, wise, elderly, gray bearded man.

Befriends the Travelers and takes them in while their craft is being repaired. **Effie** is a member of his household.

Dancer - A tribal women, a dancer and a real beauty, attaches herself to the Engineer and is impregnated by him. After the Traveler's leave, she gives birth to the 200x grandparent of Cara Jones. She is betrothed to the man who kills the Engineer.

Killer - The tribal warrior whom the Dancer is betrothed. Motivated by blind jealousy, he stabs the Engineer to death in the middle of the night when the Engineer goes outside his tent to investigate a noise.

Elder's wife and family members; workers on the Sphinx; tribe members; dinner guests.

Old Flyer - A WW I fighter pilot by the name Gus Malcomb. The old fellow who operates the grass strip airport where the Starchild crash lands. He sells the airport to the Astronaut and retires to Florida. Is back again when the Travelers fly to San Juan.

Astronomer - At the radio observatory in Arecibo, Puerto Rico. An acquaintance of the Professors whom he met when on staff at the New England University.

Others - staff at the clinic; students and faculty at the university nearby; merchants and townspeople; project Blue Book investigators; Treasury agents; local town constable re-enters the story here. Flyer and the Astronomer re-enter briefly.
Wichita Kansas Lear Jet – Jack and female (Elizabeth) FBI agent become involved
Executives - Head of a Dallas based Electronics Company similar to Texas Instruments person like Eric Jonson (Textron Instruments).
General - Head of Dallas based electronics corporation, retired military and former head of military intelligence (Anaconda Electronics).
Admiral - Head of Austin based research company similar to the one headed up by Admiral Inman. (Sytel Corporation).
CEO - Stereo-typed after William P. Lear, electronics inventor and the designer of the Lear jet (Ling Aircraft).
Agent1 - Head investigator following the Travelers. They are from an unnamed (men in black type) government agency. He is
Cara's boss since she was transferred to Dallas.
Agent2 - Works under the head investigator. He is a screw-up type that is always messing up something. Cara covers for him a lot so they become friends. Agent1 is upset with him most of the time.

Man - Flight test specialist in white lab coat at the Lear jet factory. Checks out the new jet to the Astronaut

Ricardo and Rios - Two rum runners who are encountered by accident in Puerto Rico when they mistakenly fire on the Travelers when they land their seaplane nearby. The Travelers spend the night with them.

Others - corporate board members; engineers and designers; fixed base operation workers; tower operators; rum runner's helpers.

Return to New Terra:

Travelers return to be greeted by others people from the small village near where the Starchild lands.

***

<u>**Character Appearances**</u>

<u>On Tropia</u>
Director Space Cntr Alfred (Al) Dietrich
Sam's Wife Janet Conner (stays behind)
Astronaut's son Jack, Jr. (dies car crash)
Reichs Guard VIP - General Hinkle
RG Officer - Commander Von Dormer
RG General's Aide Lt. Marilyn (bimbo)
Stays Behind - Harold engine mechanic

<u>Depart Tropia (7-seat Starchild I)</u>
Scientist Noah (Professor) Langston
Biologist Desdemona (Dusty) Aramora
Physicist - Sam Conner – researcher
Astronaut - Captain Jack Harkins - pilot
Astronomer - Tom Bradley
Extra seat1 - Leica Braun – female Tech
Extra seat2 - Hans Dieter - male Tech

<u>Return to Tropia (8-seat Starchild II)</u>
Scientist and PhD – Noah
          (The Professor) Langston
Biologist and MD – Desdemona
          (Dusty) Aramora
Physicist PhD - Sam Conner
Astronaut - Captain Jack Harkins
Technician - Leica Braun
Technician - Hans Dieter
Egyptian Girl (ancient earth) Efra
Tom Bradley (Efra and her new baby)
FBI agent (from earth) Liz Abrams

<u>Beginning TROPIA</u>
News people at press conference
Space Center Guests
Space Center Office Workers
Helicopter Crew (2)
Guests at Cocktail Party (40-60)
Starchild Hangar Workers
Misc Guards & Security Personal
Tower Operators

<u>PREHISTORIC EARTH (1ˢᵗ Jump)</u>
Dinosaurs

<u>EGYPT 2,500BC (2ed Jump)</u>
Navigator Tom Bradley stab in Egypt)
Egyptian Girl Efra (2ed-jumps a seat)
Tribe Members Pyramid Workers
Tribe Elders & Warrior Chief
Tribal Campfire Dancers (6)

<u>Modern Earth 3ʳᵈ Jump</u>
Dallas (White Rock) Neighbors
Dallas County Sheriff
Old Flyer Theodore (stays on Earth)
Students at University
Students in Class & Campus
Patients & Staff at Hospital

<u>Move to Metroplex</u>
Workers in Electronic Labs
Lawyers and Stockbroker
FBI Agnt Liz Abrams (goes to Tropia)
FBI Agents (several)
Ground Crew Airport (3)
Electronic Corp Manager
FAA Representatives
Aircraft Factory Salesman, Wichita
Rum Runners, Porto Rico
Limousine Chauffeur
Technicians on Starchild II
Rock band Smack members
Recording Studio Director
Staff at Recording Studies
Backup Musicians
Rock Concert Fans (thousands)
Gas Boy at Airport gives 310 to
<u>Future Tropia (Starchild II) 4ᵗʰ Jump</u>
Shepherd on Tropia
Workers in Field on Tropia (5)

<u>Notes on character changes</u>
In Egypt and Efra comes on board
Hans pairs up with Leica
Noah and Dusty stay together
Sam and an earthling pair up
Jack pairs with agent Lisa Abrams
<u>Substitute names</u>
Tropia – home planet (was Terra)
Vialacta – galaxy, Milky Way
Solar Star – sun
Zea – the small closer moon
Zeo – the large more distant moon
DioGurr – planet similar to Mars
Cyclatron –Fluxgate, Fluxtron, WarpDr
Stasis Field – fictional state of existence
Paradigm Shift - revolutionary change

Chapter 26   STARCHILD III - THE BACK STORY

Subtitle: "The Long Way Home"
Screenplay: WGA #798712

TERRA: Most Sci-Fi stories are based on a made-up technology that the reader or movie-goer must accept in order to make the story work. As unbelievable as this story might be, it is based on hard science that is known today. The exception to this being that there is currently no evidence that there is or ever were any life forms similar to humans on Earth or known to exist in the universe.

CATCH 22: The major catch to finding life in other parts of our galaxy, one might believe, is of the great distances that exist. Well, not really. The catch or the culprit in the equation is time. The brief period of modern man's knowledge has only been a micro-second in the billions of years that cosmic space has been around. Thus, in the times before and after our presence here in the universe, giga-billions of civilizations could have evolved and died off. There may not presently be any civilizations in our local neighborhood of stars during the same micro-seconds of time that we are here and searching for them.

THEORY: Einstein's theory of relativity (E=MC2) stated Energy is equal to Mass (or density and size. On Earth, it would be weight times the Constant (or a stated velocity, assumed presently to be the speed-of-light) squared. To over simplify, it states that any object with a mass will weigh an infinite amount of pounds as it is accelerated to the speed-of-light. Thus, a traveling object becomes so heavy that it cannot exceed the speed-of-light. Time is a veritable in this equation. Time remains normal in the object that is accelerating, but relative to its point of departure, a greater length of time elapses. Therefore, time slows or may even stop relative to the traveling object. This has been proven with atomic clocks and space missions. Astronauts are actually a few seconds younger when they return from space than when they left Earth. Of course, they do not come anywhere close to approaching the speed-of-light in modern space flights.

TIME: Based on applying the theory of relativity, backward time travel is not possible, but forward time travel is possible.

SPEED: At the present time, no one knows what effect traveling at the speed-of-light would have on the human body or even if the human body could survive at speeds halfway to the speed-of-light. However, as time might remain normal within the traveling object, there may be no effect. The Earth itself is hurling through space at a great speed. Thus, putting humans into hibernation for space travel would only be required at speeds well below the speed-of-light.

RELATIVE: If a fighter aircraft is flying at 600 mph and fires a missal from the aircraft that flies at 800 mph, is the missal traveling at 800 mph or 1,400 mph? The answer is "relative to what?" Relative to the fighter that fired the missile or relative to the ground or relative to the object being fired forward. What if a spacecraft already traveling at or near the speed-of-light (remember that relative to itself, the spacecraft is sitting still) could the spacecraft now launch a missile (or itself) at the speed-of-light? If so, then the object launched would be traveling at twice the speed-of-light, at least relative to where the spacecraft started.

FLUX: How can we travel really fast? Well, have you ever put a nail close to a strong magnet? It jumps over to the magnet so fast that you can't see it move. Without other forces like air, gravity and friction working on the nail, it could move even faster. The answer to adequate power to launch a spacecraft at ultra-high speeds is not more powerful rockets. It is probably a propulsion device like a graviton, magnetron, flux gate or anti-gravity field generating device, similar to the nail and the magnet.

JUMP: How is the light speed scenario handled by the Sci-Fi writer? Well, they makeup something like hyper-light-insertion or jump-to-light-speed. The star field blurs and everything turns into black space. How this is accomplished is not ever really explained. Nor is how they keep from running into the occasional sun, planet or asteroid explained. Some writers use the warp-drive concept which folds flat space into an accordion like piece of paper and have the spacecraft punch through it like a pencil through the folds of the paper. Still other writers find holes in space, natural short cuts through space. All of them seem to walk around inside the spaceship in some form of artificial gravity occasionally hitting bumps in the space road that throws them out of their chairs instead of splattering them up against the bulkhead like a bug on a windshield.

MASS: Popular scientific belief holds that our universe is a mass which is expanding outward from a central point (the big bang). Other less scientific theories hold that the universe is circular. If you started at one point and flew for an eternity, you would end up back where you started from. This author's personal theory is that the universe might be shaped in the form of a Mobius loop. No one really knows for sure, but it's a really big place.

DEVICE: Staying with simple physics, we know that a magnetic field will work in space. The device we will use (let's call it a Fluxtron, for lack of a better name) will create an artificial magnetic field just ahead of the spacecraft. In our story, the spacecraft (the Starchild) is a vertical take-off, super-sonic, high altitude, six seated aircraft. The craft will be fitted with the newly developed Fluxtron device which is about the size of a five gallon can. This device could be installed on a trash dumpster and it would still work.

CRAFT: We need to provide an environment, landing capability and some comfort for our human passengers so we will use a high altitude aircraft. In addition to the Fluxtron, which is crudely mounted to the floor in the aft of the aircraft, there are coils that must be installed around the object (in this case the airframe). This is to polarize the object similar to what is used on nuclear submarines to neutralize the magnetic field of their anomaly signature. When the Fluxtron is turned on it will create a magnetic field ahead (or any direction) of the craft. Thus, the spacecraft would always be trying to move (be attracted to) into the attracting field just ahead of it.like a carrot on a stick that it can never be obtained. In theory at least, nothing would stop the craft from going faster.

SPACE: How do we keep from flying through solid objects? Every object in space has a magnetic field around it. Suns (stars) have large ones, planets have smaller one and even asteroids have a small one. An autopilot that can detect these magnetic fields would adjust the position (heading) of the artificial field just ahead of the craft and stead a course away from the object. Space is not really very crowded. There is a lot of open space to explore out there.

FORCES: How does a human being (or more specifically, the anatomy of a person) react to traveling at speeds close to the speed-of-light? When the railroad train was first developed, it was questioned as to the ability of the human body to transition from horse carriage speeds to speeds of thirty and forty mile per hour. This skepticism continued even through the speeds required to break the sound barrier with the Bell X-1. Based on our rudimentary rocket knowledge to date, it seems to be that the human body only responds to relative acceleration and deceleration forces. Thus, the human body, at any speed, appears to function normally.

DOPPLER: What would a person expect to experience when approaching the speed-of-light? From theory and rudimentary experiments, light appears to curve. This was proven during an eclipse based on an early prediction that Einstein had made. In other words, you can begin to see around corners before you get there. Secondly, there is a light wave shift which is the same as the Doppler effect is to sound. It is known as the red-blue light spectrum shift. Therefore, a person traveling at or near the speed-of-light would experience distorted vision. They would also see red discoloration looking in one direction and blue discoloration when looking the opposite direction. Would the human body get infinitely heavier? The answer is simply, unknown. It appears that because their anatomy is relative to their speed (and if the velocity is not changed rapidly) that relative to their present position, mass would remain unchanged. What about that old clinker "time"? What may begin to occur, some theorize, is a God-like view of time. Both the past, present and future would all be seen at the same time.

WHERE: Let us briefly discuss traveling to another planet or culture. Survival in a strange place dictates that a living being of any kind must adapt to that specific environment. For example, we could take you out of your present environment and drop you in the middle of the Amazon forest. You may know how to drive a car, you may even be able to repair one, but until you or someone builds roads and an automobile, this knowledge is not of much value to you. You may know how to cook on an electric stove, you may even know how an electric stove works, but until you or someone mines and melts the iron and builds an electric power plant and runs the wires to you, you better start building a campfire. Such is the plight of the Travelers in our story. They must survive on a similar, but never the less alien planet until technology can catch up with their needs.

TECHNOLOGY: Unlike your typical Sci-Fi characters, the Travelers in our story are not able to take an old radio receiver and build some kind of space transporter device. All technology rides on the backs of the technology before it. First, you make a stone ax to cut wood, then you build fires. Next you identify iron, then you forge steel and so on. Much later, you can make a computer chip.

LANGUAGE: It is very likely that humanoids, much like us, could evolve on a planet like Earth. In fact the more similar the planet is to our Earth (size and distance from its sun, etc.) the more likely it would be that evolution would follow a similar path. However, it is not likely that customs and languages would be the same. Simple proof of this are the many differences right here on Earth. For the sake of our screenplay, we will have the characters speak English on their home planet. When they encounter a new culture, they will at first seem to speak a language similar to a Slovak tongue. They will also use hand gestures. Their language will change to English again. Actually, this is not too unrealistic. This author has traveled in several foreign countries and after a very short time, one is using and understanding many local phrases. We don't have to deal with the problem of Germans speaking English with a German accent.

SCENARIO: Finally, we must consider technological development. As a civilization advances towards higher and higher forms of technology, the ability to destroy one another and their environment increases geometrically. The question is whether or not a highly advanced civilization will destroy itself at some future point in their development or do they overcome and master technology in order to survive and go on to develop an even more advanced civilization. The story will end with what is only this author's best guess scenario.

After the story ends, in reflection, one might ask… was Terra, Earth or was Earth, Terra.

Writer's Notes:

WW I flyer, Josh Malcomb, was found in his fishing boat by two smugglers. His ice cooler was still half full of beer.

He had obviously died peacefully in his sleep while taking a nap. When the two smugglers were arrested by customs agents, they told this story and that they had buried the old man in an unmarked grave on a small island off the coast of Islamorada.

The two smugglers, Ricardo and Rios, posted bond, but never appeared at their hearing. They presently live on a sugar cane ranch near Orange Walk City in Belize. Rios's son married Ricardo's daughter and the two of them now operate their own coconut rum distillery under their own brand name, R&R.

The CIA personnel records of Ms. Cara Jones were recently released under the Freedom of Information Act. The last notation in her file is. "Agent is missing in the line of duty and presumed deceased".

A famous General, a retired military intelligence officer, retired again after leaving the research and development company, whom he consulted for. He was sitting in his study in Highland Park home, a Dallas suburb, when an assassins bullet narrowly missed its mark. The perpetrator was never apprehended. A few years later the General died of natural causes.

Eric Johnson, one of the founding fathers of Texas Instruments became mayor of the city of Dallas. He was highly loved and respected by all that knew him. He is now deceased.

Jimmy Ling started with a fledgling electrical contracting business in Dallas and built it into a major industry absorbing Tempco and Vought aircraft companies. Ling also lived in Highland Park, but died a pauper after his empire collapsed.

Admiral Inman, retired Naval Intelligence Officer, headed his own company in Austin, Texas, primarily doing pioneering research. He was nominated for the position of Secretary of Defense under

President Carter, but declined for personal reasons. His views on UFO's are well known. The electronics industry utilized vacuum tubes for fifty years when the transistor diode was invented giving us the infamous transistor radios and digital clocks. Coincidentally, this all occurred a couple of years after the Roswell incident. All electronics took a giant leap forward after that. The US technology became so advanced that it was copied by the Japanese and Russians.

Smart weapons, like those used in the Gulf War and the Balkans, utilized some of the most advanced electronic technology ever known to man. They have enabled the United States to become the only world's super power. In the development of the space shuttle, only solid propellant rockets were found to be cheap and efficient enough to boost the spacecraft. Additionally, it was well understood before the first flight that a spacecraft could coast back into the atmosphere. Where did these ideas come from?

Did a small band of galactic travelers have anything to do with these quantum leaps in technology during the 1950s and 60s? Probably not. Are there people walking around on the planet earth today who are just a little smarter or a little more advanced than the average homo saphians? Is it possible that these persons have some rather unique genes from an alien life form? Probably not, but we will never really know, will we?

There are enough nuclear weapons in the world's arsenal to destroy the planet Earth's environment ten times over and daily we continue to increase the atmospheric pollution. At what point in technology do we say enough is enough?

****

SCRIPT FORMAT - 1st DRAFT
WGA #798712 ©1998

LOCATION: THE PLANET TERRA

The planet Terra looks like earth in many respects, except for certain telltale indicators like make of cars, signs and style of dress. Things are familiar, but unidentifiable as they might be if filmed in a foreign country. The Terra space program is much like earth's NASA program. The setting is such that it could be earth a few years in the future. Actually, it is the planet Terra, which orbits a sun thousands of light years from earth. This is not explained.

EXT. LAUNCH PAD - EARLY MORNING

A Saturn rocket on launch pad (NASA file footage with computer modified identification) blasts off. Film title and credits with thundering sound in background.

Rocket climbs high into the sky and disappears. All is quiet except for natural sounds like birds in a meadow. Sub-title on screen: "Spring Morning, Year 2012"

INT. HELICOPTER COCKPIT - BRIGHT SUNNY DAY

Looking over the pilot's shoulder to the launch pad below, the helicopter follows a speeding sedan down the coastal road where it pulls into the parking lot of the control center.

EXT. CONTROL CENTER - DAY

A man, the PROFESSOR exits the car and walks into the entrance of the control center administration building.

Professor rushes through hallway being greeted by assistants, peers and military personnel on their way to conference room for the announcement of the results of the launch.

INT. CONTROL CENTER CONFERENCE ROOM -
AFTERNOON

Conference room with all of the participants gathered to hear the
results of the experiment launched on board the rocket. The Space
Center DIRECTOR steps to the podium.

DIRECTOR

As you all know, we have just fired a missile containing the
controversial Fluxtron device. The preliminary results are
amazing. I'd like to introduce Professor Alex Covoliski who
will fill you in on the details.

PROFESSOR
(Professor steps to podium.)

Thank you. The unit we tested today was engaged for only
ten microseconds and we estimate that it covered the distance
of over one hundred light years in that amount of time.
Technically, it disappeared from our time frame, but for the
one-thousandth of a microsecond we were able to maintain
the track, it proved that the device works as predicted. We
now have the capability to travel faster than the speed-of-
light, phenomenally faster.

INT. CONTROL CENTER CONFERENCE ROOM -
AFTERNOON

Reporters and television crews, who have been invited, are yelling
out questions.

FEMALE REPORTER
Professor. Professor! Is it true that the nuclear powered space
station presently orbiting the earth is about to crash back into
our atmosphere?

Professor ignores the question.

PROFESSOR

We're here today to discuss the Fluxtron project. I'll take
questions regarding today's test?
Voice from across room.

MALE REPORTER

Professor, we understand that the nuclear system on the
decaying space station will react with the atmosphere causing
a nuclear chain reaction, is this true?

Professor looks back at the Director who steps forward. There is
confusion and mayhem in the conference room.

DIRECTOR

This will conclude today's press conference. Will the guards
please usher the press out of the building.

INT. DOOR WAY TO ROOM ADJOINING CONFERENCE
ROOM - LATER

The Professor, SCIENTIST (female), ENGINEER and
ASTRONAUT walk with the Director to a small room adjoining
where the conference was held. They are discussing the resent test
among themselves. The Director shuts the door behind him.

DIRECTOR

We'll have a detailed review of all that has transpired at
tomorrow afternoon's meeting. Until then, your presence is
requested at a cocktail party, my house on the estate at 6 p.m.
See you then.

INT. DIRECTOR'S HOME COCKTAIL PARTY - EVENING

Ladies are in stylish dresses and gentlemen in evening attire. Several uniformed officers (male and female) intermingle. Uniforms are Nazi-like in style, but with unidentifiable insignias. There is a celebrating atmosphere in the room.

Professor is standing talking with the Scientist, Astronaut and Engineer as a high ranking military officer and his female aid walk up to congratulate them.

MILITARY OFFICER

I would like to personally commend you and your group for your scientific breakthrough in Fluxtron research.
Turning to the Astronaut. I understand the experimental aircraft, the one code named Starchild, is about ready to be integrated into your Fluxtron program.

ASTRONAUT

Yes, I believe that's correct.

Military officer leaves, Starchild project Engineer walks up.

ENGINEER

What was that all about?

PROFESSOR

The usual political brown nosing, but I think it was a subtle 44hint that the military is going to back our requests for full funding of the Starchild.

ASTRONAUT

That's the way I read it too.

Turning to the Professor and the Scientist.
I noticed that neither of you offered to answer the questions
about the space station's decaying orbit at the press
conference. What is your opinion? The pundits seem equally
divided whether it is a doom's day scenario or a hoax.

SCIENTIST

My calculations say that if you've got any unfinished
business you want to finish before you meet your Maker,
now would be a good time to get it done.

ENGINEER

Yes, I agree. I went to the databanks on the computer system
and reviewed the mass and velocity myself. It'll be a miracle
if the entire atmosphere of our planet doesn't flash on re-
entry.

PROFESSOR

I understand the military is trying now to adapt some of the
shuttles to try and pull the station into a higher orbit. It's all
being kept hush-hush, but if that fails, I believe you are
correct. The three of you meet me at the flight test
development hangar in the morning.

EXT. FLIGHT TEST DEVELOPMENT HANGAR - MORNING

The hangar is a heavily guarded dark structure. In the vehicle that
approaches the gate is the Astronaut. He is saluted and passed
through the gate by the guard.

INT. HANGAR – MORNING

In the darken hangar is a large aircraft, a cross between a Learjet and a Harrier. It has room for two pilots and four passengers. The craft will not be shown fully until later.

Astronaut comes through doorway where the Professor, Scientist, Engineer and a young Technician are sitting having coffee. The Astronaut goes to the coffeepot and pours himself a cup as the other four greets him.

PROFESSOR

I've asked Ted here to join us. He is the technician whom I have asked to be assigned to the project and is an expert in Fluxtron electronics. It has not yet been approved, but I'm going to take it upon myself to transport the experimental Fluxtron device over from the lab and have Ted begin installing it in the Starchild.

ASTRONAUT

If I read you correctly, this has something to do with the orbital decay we were discussed last night.

SCIENTIST

It's no longer supposition on our part. The government is now estimating that two-thirds of the population will not survive. But, if you're not with us, keep your mouth shut or it's our necks. I guess it's our necks no matter which way it goes. Come on, Jack, join us and play Bet Your Life on E=MC2, but remember the writer who said "You Can't Go Home."

© SCRIPT PROTECTED BY COPYRIGHT

***

Chapter 28 – A Short Story

Starchild X-2

Both of Terra's moons were below the horizon and this always made for a very dark night. Across a small inlet of water sat a giant rocket on the launch pad. The gantry was well lighted and shone brightly in the darkness.

All was quiet except for the ripple of the water against the shoreline and the noise from insects and birds off in the distance.

Suddenly, the gantry came alive with flames from the rocket engines and engulfed the spacecraft. Like a Phoenix rising from the midst of an inferno, the missile lifted into the night sky. The chest pounding noise of the rocket engines broke the silence of the still night air.

The sky glowed a bright yellow-gray, then slowly faded back to black. The missile became only a speck of light among the vast star field. Then it seemed even darker than before and the soft sounds of night returned.

***

Inside a brightly lit launch control center, several dozen launch specialists went through their normal post-launch procedures.

Standing back from the midst of the action were three men and one woman. The Professor, a tall slender middle-aged caucasian man, stood beside a woman Scientist, his longtime lady friend who also worked at the Space Center. The other two were the guidance control Engineer, a brilliant young oriental fellow and the tracking command officer, a handsome dark skinned fellow who was a former Astronaut.

The four watched as the giant monitors that circled the wall came to life with telemetry and a loud cheer went up in the room as the workers began congratulating one another.

The launch supervisor approached the Professor.

"Congratulations, Sir. Your theory worked exactly as predicted," he said as he shook the Professor's hand.

The Professor headed the special research project on hyper-light space travel. He was there to observe the launch. The code name for the project was Starchild X-1.

Mounted atop the spacecraft was a special nose cone containing a Flextron; a small device had proved capable of exceeding the known constant, the speed-of-light.

The Professor said to his trusted colleagues, "Meet me at the Geek Works later this afternoon," as he left the control center. Geek Works was the nickname given to the hangar used to house the top-secret development projects.

The Professor walked across the parking lot to his car. The cars in the lot were conventional, but futuristic. As he drove away, the surroundings he passed by were more modern than 21st Century Earth. The environmental conditions, however, were very poor and the sky hazy. Many things were different from Earth; people's attire, road signs and architecture.

This was not the planet Earth in some future time, but a similar planet many light years away. This was the planet Terra, which at this point in time, was only slightly more advanced than present day Earth. Terra, as Earth may become, was suffering from impending technological destruction of its atmosphere.

***

A patrol helicopter followed the Professor's car as he drove to a large, isolated hangar some distance away. The well-guarded hangar entry sign read Restricted Area. The security guard recognized the approaching Professor and passed him through.

Inside the very large, dimly lit hangar, a sleek, very modern craft about the size of a medium jet bomber sat alone in the center of the darken hangar.

The Professor walked slowly around the craft engrossed in deep thought. The name on the side of the craft read Starchild X-2. The six passenger, plus crew of two, spacecraft had been built to test the hyper-light theory; phase two of the project. Phase one of the project was the unmanned nose cone atop the missile launched earlier that day.

Footsteps across the hangar floor caused the Professor to look up. A darkened figure approached and he recognized the Director of the Space Center.

"The nose cone exceeded the light-speed for only three micro seconds, but may be as far as a full light year away. No trace of it has been found as of yet, but I feel that even with our sophisticated tracking equipment, it might take years to find and recover the nose cone at sub-light speeds!"

The Professor recognized the Director's voice and turns to greet him, "As I suspected, "You don't read my progress reports I send to you, do you?"

"I do when I get time," the Director replied.

"Well, if you had read my latest report, you would know that we put a mod on this unit that will cause it to hold its destination location for twenty-four hours, get a star fix, and return to its place of origin," explained the Professor, "By tomorrow afternoon it should be in high orbit above Terra. All you have to do is send someone up to get the damn thing."

"Oh really," the Director said and then asked, "You seem pre-occupied is anything wrong?"

"It's just that I don't understand how science can accomplish something as complicated as developing a hyper-light spacecraft and then stand idly by and let nations and corporations destroy the world's environment," the Professor raged.

The Professor realized that it wasn't the Director's fault, but the entire world's fault and he apologized.

The Director accepted the apology from his most gifted scientist and took his leave.

***

The Professor again stood alone in the darkened hangar staring at the shiny new Starchild X-2 deep in thought as he waited for his other two colleagues to arrive.

The Scientist had arrived earlier and was waiting in the hangar office. The Engineer and the Astronaut soon arrived accompanied by their wives. The Professor had asked them earlier to bring their wives.

The group of six seated themselves around a table that the hangar mechanics used to play cards at during the day. The discussion centered around what would happen if a carbon nuclear bomb were setoff in the present unstable carbon monoxide atmosphere on Terra.

The Professor commented, "I would not want to be around to test that theory."

The Engineer looked very concerned as he explained, "A foreign power placed several carbon-nuclear warhead satellites into orbit years ago. I was involved in tracking these satellites and we discovered that one of the satellites is in very low orbit which is decaying rapidly."

The Astronaut added, "I am also aware of this. If one of these satellites were to enter the atmosphere a nuclear chain reaction would likely occur. I suggested that the satellite be shot down by a missile and was told that it is already too close to our atmosphere."

The Professor then revealed, "This is, of course, why I asked you to meet with me this evening. You see the untested spacecraft, the Starchild X-2 out in the hangar, is ready for flight. The craft is capable of carrying unlimited weight, but there are only life support systems on board for six souls."

The discussion went on a little longer, but it was mostly agreed between the Astronaut and Engineer and their wives that they should leave the planet immediately.

The Scientist smiled pleasantly, paused for a moment and then she said to the Professor simply, "I'm with you!"

***

The Starchild was readied for the flight in the hangar and rolled out just before first-light.

With only minutes to spare, all were on board the Starchild and the craft lifted off into the dark starlit sky.

"We must remain sub-light until we are well clear of the atmosphere," the Astronaut, who was piloting the craft, explained as they reached the threshold of space.

The six space travelers looked back at their world. The atmosphere of Terra began to glow red at one small point and then the red glow engulfed their familiar blue-white planet.

The nuclear chain reaction was no longer a theory. There was sadness among the six amateur space travelers. The world as they had known it, no longer existed.

The Professor assisted the Astronaut in operating the Fluxtron device and inserted the Starchild into hyper-light.

Terra became only a point of light in a vast star field behind them.

***

They had been traveling at hyper-light speeds for some time when the Engineer, an amateur astronomer and celestial navigation expert, said, "I have calculated that we should be nearing a sun approximately the same size as our old sun and it has shown signs of a wobble indicating an orbiting planet. We need to drop out of hyper-light and search for a habitable planet."

As the Starchild slowed and the starlit sky ceased to blur, looming ahead was the planet Earth. It was so much like Terra that they were suspect of what they saw.

Entering Earth orbit, the Scientist made a spectra-analysis of the planet's atmosphere and she exclaimed, "The air is pure. This is almost too good to be true!"

The Astronaut searched for an area with smooth terrain to set the Starchild down. Finally, they made a safe landing in a fertile valley nestled between two large rivers.

For many years, the small band of travelers and their offspring lived in the valley between the two rivers, which they named the Tigris and the Euphrates. Except for some friendly animals and wild game, they were all alone on the planet.

***

Decades passed and the three family groups had grown very large. The three elders met and decided that their best chance of continued survival on this planet would be for them to disburse. They left the beautiful valley that had been their home.

However, no one chose to travel east. They knew of the large continents across the great waters because of stories their ancestors had told them having seen them many years ago from the sky. That was, of course, back when men could fly and Flying Carpets really did exist.

The main reason no one choose to travel to the far continents was mostly due to the peril. All who set out to journey there never returned.

The Professor took his clan, now called House Europa and journeyed north seeking a cooler climate.

The tribe of the Astronaut, now called House Serengeti, traveled south to settle in what would become known as Africa.

The Engineer, Chin, House China, journeyed east to a land at the foot of the great mountains.

Thus, the origin of the three great races of man on the planet Earth began.

"There were giants in those days, when the sons of God came unto the daughters of men and they bore them children. These were the mighty men of old, the men of renown and legend."

Genesis 6:4

***

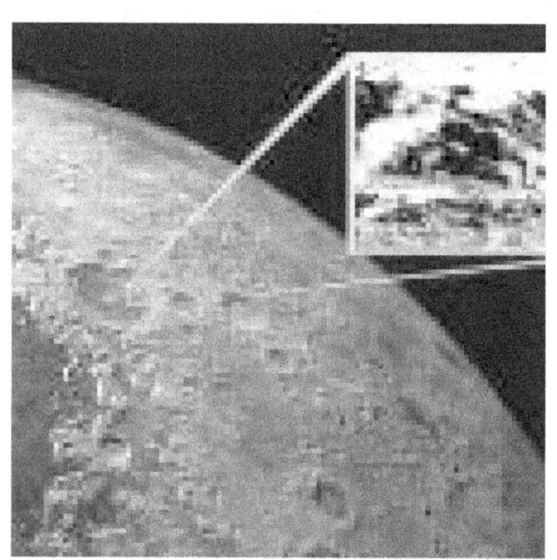

Alien Moon Base

Chapter 29   January 17th - A short story

January Seventeenth

The enemy had invaded John's country in December. John was nineteen and his girlfriend, Mary, was eighteen. They had planned to be married in June, but John, like thousands of other patriotic young men, volunteered to join the military service and defend his country.

On January Seventeenth, John told Mary that his unit was shipping out. Mary promised to wait for him and to write every day. She could never love any other man except him.

A year went by. Mary had written faithfully as she had promised. She had received dozens of letters from John, but then they stopped coming. John's letters started being returned to her. It was on January Seventeenth, that Mary received the news. John was missing in action and presumed dead.

Mary cried every day. It was months before she could make it through a day without crying at least once. Mary made the decision to devote the rest of her life to God. She took her vows and became a nun. In a couple of years, Mary was assigned to the old cathedral downtown across from the large city park.

- - -

Five years later, on January Seventeenth, Mary entered the sanctuary for her daily prayers. There was a tall, frail, middle aged man waiting in the darkened hallway. It was John. The war was over and he had been found in a prisoner-of-war camp nearly half dead.

Mary ran to him and held onto him for the longest time. John told her what he had been through in the years they were apart. He wanted her to marry him now, if she only would.

Mary told him, "You own my heart and you always will. I will never love anyone the way I love you, but I cannot, I will not, break my vows to the Lord."

- - -

Over time, John came to accept Mary's wishes. He took a job at a local factory. In a couple of years, he met a woman and they were married. A year later, on January Seventeenth, a little girl was born. John named her Lisa after his grandmother. John's marriage to Lisa's mother was not a good marriage. She was a lazy and unhappy woman.

On Saturday afternoons, John would take Lisa to visit Mary at the church. Lisa called her Sister Mary. On an afternoon when Lisa was six years old, John came home from work and found Lisa alone.

"Daddy," Lisa said, "Mommy left a note in an envelope on the table for you. She said for me to be sure to tell you."

John went to the table and read the note 'I am leaving you. Please don't try to find me. Take good care of our daughter, I know you will.'

John was sure that she had run away with another man. He had suspected she might for some time.

On the following Friday afternoon, John left work at the factory early. It was January Seventeenth and it had been storming all day. He did not want Lisa to have to walk home in the freezing rain. When school let out, he was there waiting for her.

When Lisa got in the car she asked, "Can we go see Sister Mary today?"

"Sure, why not." John replied.

The rainstorm was getting worse and John was trying to drive carefully. A car passing him swerved to miss an oncoming truck. It forced John off the road and his car crashed into a tree.

"Are you alright, Lisa?"

"Yes, Daddy I'm fine."

John got out to have a look at the damage. His old car was not going anywhere.

"The rain has let up now. Come on, Lisa, we'll need to walk to the church from here. It's not far."

"It's okay, Daddy, I'm not cold at all."

Lisa held her father's hand as they walked.

Lisa looked back at the car, "Look Daddy, there are some people gathering around our car."

John glanced back and joked, "I guess they just wanted to have a better look at a beat up old car."

- - -

When they entered the church, Lisa said, "Oh, look Daddy, there's Mrs. Wilson from the grocery store."

"Yes, Lisa, but don't bother her now she's going to prayer.

In the hallway, they passed a priest. Lisa spoke to him, "Hello, Father Murphy."

The priest walked on past them without speaking.

"It's okay Lisa, Father Murphy was just in deep thought. He probably just had his mind on his liturgy for this coming Sunday morning's service."

Lisa asked her dad, "Where do you think Sister Mary might be?"

"She's most likely over in the west tower. You've been up there with her before. She likes to go there because it's quiet. She often goes there to meditate and pray.

John and Lisa entered the tower and Mary is so very happy to see them.

Lisa ran to hug Mary, "There are some coloring books over there and I've gotten you some paper dolls to cut out."

Mary turns to John and smiles, "I just thought you two might be coming by to see me today."

John takes Lisa's coat off and lays it over a chair with his.

Lisa goes over to see the things Mary had laid out for her.

The storm passed and the lightening stopped.

The sky outside ceared and bright light flooded the room and filled it with warmth.

- - -

It was summer, two years later, in the park across the street from the cathedral. An old man was seated on a park bench reading a newspaper.

A young couple walked by and the old man spoke to them. "Good morning."

"Yes, good morning to you, sir," the young man said, "Say, maybe you wouldn't mind answering a question for me?"

"Sure, son, will if I can."

"I used to play in this park when I was a young boy. The church across the street, well, it looks different now."

"Yes, it does. They did an excellent job of repairing it. A couple of years ago we had a bad storm. Didn't let up for days. Lightning struck the west tower and it collapsed. Happened January Seventeenth, as I recall."

THE END

Epilogue – Forty Years Later

The notes on this page are from a screenplay treatment and have not been written into the unfinished novel yet. The story will change considerably.

Before There Was A Starchild, The original three screen plays, 30 year ago there was no Computers, cell phones.

Entertainment business, the Peggy Taylor Agency, Aviator, Design Engineer.

Thomas Clayton Wolfe, (born Oct. 3, 1900, Asheville, N.C., U.S.—died Sept. 15, 1938,Look Homeward, Angel (1929) and You Can't Go Home Again (1934) Baltimore, Md.), American writer best known for his first book

Thomas Kennerly Wolfe Jr. (March 2, 1930 – May 14, 2018) was an American author.

Jan 17th some where to put it, Titanium rotor hub, Things have changed, 2001 Stanley Kubrick the star baby

T-shirts and rock band, Internet much more about Starchild, Things have changed

Three most obvious changes Terra to Tropia, Fluxtron to Cyclatron and Vialacta to Zoatropia for the Milky Way

BRONCO AUDITORIUM

By chance, I heard that Lamar Hunt was trying to revive the old Bronco Auditorium in Oak Cliff he had owned for years. So I made an appointment with Hunt to pitch my idea for booking concerts into the auditorium.

Hunt also owned the Kansas City Chiefs. As it turned out, he was a rather unassuming fellow. He listened and told me to go ahead and try out my idea. I booked everyone from Moe Bandy and Kitty Wells to a Mexican band to play on Cinco de Mayo into the Bronco.

One reason Bronco was less than successful was because it was located in a dry precinct and no alcoholic beverages could be sold on the premises. I imported Near Beer from a brewery in Arkansas and was able to pick up a few hundred extra bucks at each concert by operating the concession stand.

My sister-in-law, Nancy, worked the concession stand for me on Cinco de Mayo one night when my help didn't show up.

An old Mexican gentleman staggered up to the counter and said to her, "I've drank six of these beers and I'm not feeling anything yet."

Nancy didn't have the heart to tell the fellow that there was less than one percent alcohol in a can of Near Beer. Nancy still sends me a Cinco de Mayo card every year in remembrance of the night she worked her tail off at Bronco.

On Saturday nights when a big name performer was not booked into the auditorium, I promoted it as the Bronco Jamboree. I used local entertainers to makeup a C&W house band. They started calling themselves the Bronco Band. Taking turns as the lead singer the band members did the warm-up acts and worked for the exposure. Several went on to successful careers.

One of the male leads was a VW service mechanic on his regular day job, but he could sing *Jingle Bells* and make it sound like a country song. A tall fellow by the name of Kenneth played piano in the band. He was more of a Van Cliburn than a C&W star, but he'd put on a ten gallon Stetson and get a real kick out of the gig. Kenneth could play anything and follow anybody.

I haven't a musical bone in my body, but I often had to MC the show so I'd play with the band too. I'd stand out there and strum a C-cord on my Bona Venture guitar and mouth the words.

I've told people many times, "I'm a professional singer. I've been paid to stop several times."

Saturday night's work wasn't over till we struck our set and set up the stage for Sunday morning church services. A tall, distinguished looking evangelist leased the auditorium for church services. His long wavy, gray pompadour hair reminded me of Andrew Jackson.

The stage was set with a giant dove of peace on a red and gold velvet backdrop. The evangelist preached and his orchestra played praise music. It was not unusual to see diamond rings and hundred dollar bills thrown on stage.

The auditorium seated about 3,000. I was never able to fill the place except for Cinco de Mayo, but the church services were standing room only. The evangelist hated Rock-n-Roll. I saw him one Saturday night in the balcony and spoke to him. He told me he was praying for the failure of the rock group on stage. As I recall, that particular group didn't really need a lot of assistance from him.

I tried my best to revive Bronco to its glory days, but it was not to be! With the exception of a couple of failed concerts I had promoted in and around Dallas, Bronco was a close second.

COUNTRY MAGAZINE

A freebie music events magazine in Dallas called *Buddy,* named for Buddy Holly was a monthly magazine catering to rock music fans and survived financially on paid advertising. There wasn't a good venue for promoting C&W entertainers in the area, so I started a similar publication and called it *Country* magazine. The record companies and saloons also needed a place to advertise and beginning with the first issue, *Country* magazine made a profit.

National Geographic magazine published an article on Willie Nelson that included a color photo of Willie doing a show in Dallas. On stage, he is wearing a red *Country* magazine T-shirt.

Working with the local C&W radio stations, I was given free press passes to all the best concerts. Suzie and I met and visited with Dolly Parton, Crystal Gale and at length with William Shatner. I got to know Buck Owens and worked with Lorne Green in a movie.

After publishing *Country* for about a year, a photographer, who worked for me part time and who hung out down at Whiskey River with the Willie Nelson and David Alan Cole crowd, offered to buy the magazine. I agreed, because I was one of the sorriest music promoters to ever come down the pike.

The *Country* magazine photographer's brother worked Saturdays at the Bronco Auditorium helping me with the sound and lighting. After our last scheduled performance, we were tearing down to set up for the church services the next morning and we started talking about what we did for regular day jobs. I told him I was a between jobs design engineer and had done a lot of contract work and I wasn't exactly sure how I had gotten into this business.

"How about that," he said, "I'm a rep for a job shop engineering company."

As it turned out, he was a manager for one of the job shop companies I had worked for years before. One thing led to another and he explained that he really needed someone to fill a job out at the Aerospatiale Helicopter Corporation located in Grand Prairie.

I told him, "No sweat, I could handle it," and that's how it happened I went to work at Aerospatiale. I went to do a three month job and stayed ten years, funny how life takes its twists and turns

***

OTHER BOOKS BY MARVIN ARNOLD

FLYING STORES - How I Came To Be A Pilot
And What Happened After That   out of print
1st Ed - Author House, Hardcover and Paperback
FLYING STORES - How I Came To Be A Pilot
And Engineer And What Happened After That
2nd Ed - 1st Books & Create Space, Paperback
3rd Ed - Amazon & Create Space, out of print
FLYING STORES II -How I Came To Be A Pilot
And Engineer And What Happened After That
1st Ed - Create Space, paperback, current edition
2nd Ed - Create Space, paperback, due out 2019

FLIGHT OF THE SETTING SUN - The Life And
Adventures Of Captain Jake Martin (novel)
1st Ed - Author House, Hardcover and Paperback
2st Ed - Create Space, paperback, current edition

LINCOLN AND CONTINENTAL - Classic Motorcars
The Early Years (illustrated, nonfiction history)
1st Ed - Deluxe Hardcover edition by Taylor Fine Books
2st Ed - Create Space, B&W paperback, current edition
3nd Ed - Create Space, B&W paperback, due out 2019

CLASSIC MOTORCARS - Lincoln And Continental
The Early Years (illustrated, nonfiction history)
1st Ed - Create Space, B&W paperback, current edition
2nd Ed - Create Space, B&W paperback, due out 2019

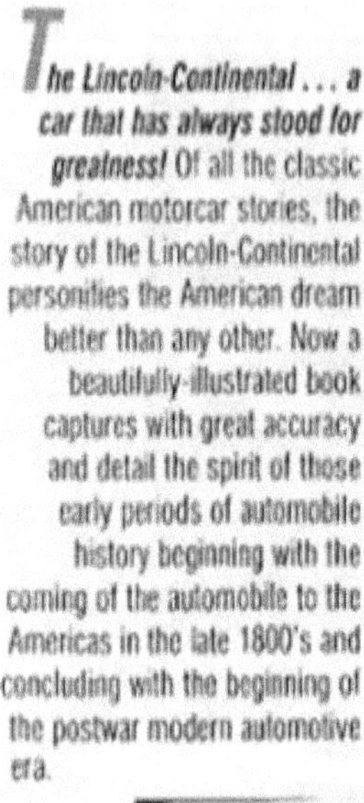

The Lincoln-Continental ... a car that has always stood for greatness! Of all the classic American motorcar stories, the story of the Lincoln-Continental personifies the American dream better than any other. Now a beautifully-illustrated book captures with great accuracy and detail the spirit of those early periods of automobile history beginning with the coming of the automobile to the Americas in the late 1800's and concluding with the beginning of the postwar modern automotive era.

A 256-page book, 9" x 12" limited edition richly illustrated with advertising art

Author Marvin Arnold has combined the exciting story of the marque with the technical and developmental aspects of the automobile itself packing this beautiful volume with information you just won't find anywhere else. His longtime interest in this classic car began in 1952 with the purchase of a used 1939 Zephyr Coupe. Over the years Arnold has owned more than 100 makes and models of automobiles — many of them Lincolns and Continentals — and has personally restored several dozen of them.

Lincoln and Continental Classic Motorcars — The Early Years.
by Marvin Arnold

Over 1000 illustrations and 32 pages of full color depict the story that parallels the evolution of the automobile industry!

Collector's Edition of the original print run Hardcover with dust jacket, large coffee table edition (32 pages in full color) by Taylor Fine Books Division.

Samco Publishing - *www. Storydomain .com*